ALPHA'S CLAIM

AMELIA HUTCHINS

Copyright ©April 2021 Amelia Hutchins

This book is a work of fiction. Names, characters, places, and incidents are either the product of the author's imagination or are used fictitiously. Any resemblance to actual persons, living or dead, or to actual events or locales is entirely coincidental.

This book in its entirety and in portions is the sole property of Amelia Hutchins.

Alpha's Claim Copyright©2021 by Amelia Hutchins. All rights reserved, including the right to reproduce this book, or portions thereof, in any form. No part of this text may be reproduced, transmitted, downloaded, decompiled, reverse engineered, or stored in or introduced into any information storage and retrieval system, in any form or by any means, whether electronic, paperback or mechanical without the express written permission of the author. The scanning, uploading and distribution of this book via the internet or via any other means without the permission of the publisher is illegal and punishable by law. Please purchase only authorized electronic editions and do not participate in or encourage electronic piracy of copyrighted materials.

This eBook/Paperback is licensed for your personal enjoyment only. This book may not be re-sold or given away to other people. If you would like to share this book with another person, please purchase an additional copy for each recipient. If you're reading this book and did not purchase it, or it was not purchased for your use only, then please return to the place of purchase and buy your own copy. Thank you for respecting the hard work of this author.

The unauthorized reproduction or distribution of this copyrighted work is illegal. Criminal copyright infringement, including infringement without monetary gain, is investigated by the FBI and is punishable by up to 5 years in federal prison and a fine of $250,000.

Authored By: Amelia Hutchins

Cover Art Design:

Copy edited by: Melissa Burg

Edited by: Melissa Burg

Published by: Amelia Hutchins

Published in (United States of America)

10 9 8 7 6 5 4 3 2 1

Warning

This book is dark. It's sexy, hot, and intense. The author is human, as are you. Is the book perfect? It's as perfect as I could make it. Are there mistakes? Probably, then again, even New York Times top published books have minimal errors because, like me, they have human editors. There are words in this book that are not in the standard dictionary because they were created to set the stage for a paranormal-urban fantasy world. Words in this novel are common in paranormal books and give better descriptions of the story's action than other words found in standard dictionaries. They are intentional and not mistakes.

About the hero: chances are you may not fall instantly in love with him, that's because I don't write men you instantly love; you grow to love them. I don't believe in instant love. I write flawed, raw, caveman-like assholes that eventually let you see their redeeming qualities. They are aggressive assholes, one step above a caveman when we meet them. You may not even like him by the time you finish this book, but I promise you will love him by the end of this series.

About the heroine: There is a chance you might think she's a bit naïve or weak, but then again, who starts out as a badass? Badass women are a product of growth, and I am going to put her through hell, and you get to watch her come up swinging every time I knock her on her ass. That's just how I do things. How she reacts to the set of circumstances she is put through may not be how you, as the reader, or I, as the author, would respond to that same situation. Everyone reacts differently to circumstances, and how she responds to her challenges is how I see her as a character and as a person.

I don't write love stories: I write fast-paced, knock you on your ass, make you sit on the edge of your seat, wondering what is going to happen next in the books. If you're looking for cookie-cutter romance, this isn't for you. If you can't handle the ride, unbuckle your seatbelt and get out of the roller-coaster car now. If not, you've been warned. If nothing outlined above bothers you, carry on and enjoy the ride!

FYI, this is not a romance novel. These characters are going to kick the shit out of each other, and if they end up together, well, that's their choice. If you are going into this blind, and you complain about abuse between two creatures that are NOT human, well, that's on you. I have done my job and have given you a warning.

Dedication

This one is for the tribe and my girls. You know who you are. Without you cheering me on, I'd be lost. For Asher, who only got 12 days on earth and is missed. You are loved. For my darling aunt, may you sing in heaven and smile and laugh as you did here on earth. And to those who hate me but will read this book anyway and then complain about something. I hope you get all the karma this world loves to give people like you. For Texas, who worked through COVID, kicking its ass while managing to finish the edits, you're a badass.

Books by Amelia Hutchins along with reading order for series

Legacy of the Nine Realms

Flames of Chaos

Ashes of Chaos

Ruins of Chaos

Crown of Chaos - 2021

The Fae Chronicles

Fighting Destiny

Taunting Destiny

Escaping Destiny

Seducing Destiny

Unraveling Destiny

Embracing Destiny

Crowning Destiny

Finished Series

The Elite Guards

A Demon's Dark Embrace
Claiming the Dragon King
The Winter Court
A Demon's Plaything

A Guardian's Diary

Darkest Before Dawn
Death before Dawn
Midnight Rising -TBA

Playing with Monsters series

Playing with Monsters
Sleeping with Monsters
Becoming his Monster
Revealing the Monster 2021

Wicked Knights

Oh, Holy Knight
If She's Wicked
Book Three -TBA

Midnight Coven Books

Forever Immortal
Immortal Hexes
Midnight Coven
Finished Serial Series

Kingdom of Wolves: A world where Alphas rule.

KINGDOM OF WOLVES

Enter the Kingdom of Wolves, a shared universe created by a set of fantastic authors that feature psychotic and possessive wolf alphas, intoxicating relationships, fated mates, and strong, badass heroines. Kingdom of Wolves will keep you up all night, addicted for more.

Make sure to leave your manners at the door. These wolves don't play nice when it comes to the women they want.

These stories are all set in the same world and can be read in any order. Some books are standalones, and some are the start of a series.

This shared-world will bring you books by the following authors:

Wild Moon by C.R. Jane & Mila Young

Lost by M. Sinclair

Torn to Bits by Katie May

Crossed Fates by Lexi C. Foss & Elle Christensen

Shift of Morals by K Webster

Rabid by Ivy Asher & Raven Kennedy

Alpha's Claim by Amelia Hutchins

Lunacy by Lanie Olson

Check out all the books in the Kingdom of Wolves collection!

If you're following the series for the Fae Chronicles, Elite Guards, and Monsters, reading order is as follows.

Fighting Destiny

Taunting Destiny

Escaping Destiny

Seducing Destiny

A Demon's Dark Embrace

Playing with Monsters

Unraveling Destiny

Sleeping with Monsters

Claiming the Dragon King

Oh, Holy Knight

Becoming his Monster

A Demon's Plaything

The Winter Court

If She's Wicked

Embracing Destiny

Crowning Destiny

ALPHA'S CLAIM

AMELIA HUTCHINS

Chapter One

People from different regions and packs gathered in our territory tonight, at the very top of our mountain, to celebrate and witness a mating. The Harold Haralson pack was uniting with the Carlson Jorgensen pack through my arranged mating, procured by my father. Carlson was known to be a cruel alpha, but that hadn't stopped my father from gifting me to him like a prized pig. Tonight, I was supposed to walk out of this room, lie down, and let the brutish prick mount me in a pergola in front of our packs and guests.

I could think of a thousand other things I'd rather do, one of which was to swallow razor blades and shit them out. If everything unfolded correctly, by this time tomorrow, Carlson and my father would both be dead. They deserved what was coming to them. My concern was that I hadn't been allowed outside of the room in the last twenty-four hours and could not ensure everything was happening according to plan.

My gaze slid to Toralei's, meeting it briefly in the mirror where I sat preparing for the mating. The dress Carlson gave me to wear was flimsy with sheer material, allowing all the guests to see what would belong to Carlson tonight. The only comfort I had was the lace bralette he allowed me to wear, which, thankfully, covered both breasts. My panties had enough material barely to cover my rump, but at least my sex was shielded.

The mating ritual was an ancient rite that allowed those who had traveled to witness the mating couple, ensuring they had honored the age-old tradition between packs. I'd begged my father to prevent the public spectacle from occurring, but those pleas had fallen on deaf ears. I'd known he wouldn't stop it, but it had been worth a shot.

"It's time," one of Carlson's betas who had been left in charge of my care, informed.

I stood from the stool, stealing one last glance at myself in the mirror. My eyes were covered in smoky eyeshadow and dark eyeliner meant to make my soft blue eyes pop, yet it couldn't make them sparkle. My lips were slathered in a deep red lipstick that I wouldn't have ever chosen to wear on my own, and I fought the urge to wipe it from my mouth. It was more makeup than I preferred, but Carlson's harem was charged with preparing me for their alpha and appeared to take pleasure in my distress.

Tonight wasn't a celebration. It was a tragedy. I already had a mate, one I'd pushed away and rejected to keep safe from my father and my demons. Saint Kingsley had been a shock to my senses and the last person I'd ever predicted the wolf god, Fenrir, to choose for my soul mate. The one summer we'd had together had been the first time I'd ever felt alive.

Saint was rough around the edges and older than me. His group of misfits had driven me crazy with their antics to fit in and become part of the pack, which my father had unfortunately noticed. Saint was an orphan, and I was considered untouchable since my father was our pack's alpha. Saint was the bad boy from the wrong side of the tracks, yet I'd wanted him with every single part of my soul. Saint brought me to life, and in the same breath, he'd made me crave things I'd never wanted or even thought possible.

It was amazing, right until my father found us spending time together and threatened Saint's life. The deal? Make Saint believe I hated him and force him to leave the pack or watch him die by my father's hand. There had been no world where that boy didn't exist, not for me. So I betrayed Saint in the worst way possible to save his life.

I'd stood in front of the entire pack and accused him of forcing me to believe that what we had was a true mating call instead of merely the lust between two teenagers. I'd rejected him, and that was the one thing you never did to your soul mate. After all, true soul mates were rare, and if you were lucky to have found one, it only happened once in a lifetime, and I had just banished mine from our pack.

A scream tore from beyond the door, forcing my mind back to the present. Everyone inside of the room went still, staring at the door as if it would burst open. My slipper-covered feet padded silently across the floor, a sinister smile playing on my lips as the idea of my coup starting earlier than planned entered my thoughts.

When I opened the door, the power went out, and whispers filled the room as Tora moved into position behind me. Her hand touched my shoulder, assuming it was likely our allies within the pack starting the coup, filling us both with relief and hope.

My sight adjusted, allowing me to see in the dark as we floated down the hallway. There was no way in hell I was missing out on the fighting that was undoubtedly unfolding. The scent of blood made my nostrils flare, and my chest tightened with the reality that everything was on the line for my pack and me. A body came into view, and my feet faltered as air refused to leave my lungs.

"Lars?" I whispered, kneeling beside him.

"Run, Braelyn," he replied, blood trailing from his lips. "It isn't us. Someone else is attacking. Run!" he choked out as veins of silver moved up his face.

I lifted my eyes toward the darkened room that lay ahead of us. My heart clenched while my mind spun at the thought of the silver rushing through Lars. Toralei grabbed my hand from him, knowing that silver would poison me, even from touch. Standing, I turned, watching Carlson's betas rush toward the shadow-filled room we'd just left.

"Hunters?" I asked no one in particular as I turned and rose. "No, this can't be happening. Not now. They've probably closed off all the mountain passes, preventing my crews and reinforcements from reaching us," I muttered, moving toward where the sounds of fighting grew louder.

I paused before the enormous doors that led into the lodge, throwing them open to stand in the large courtyard. My eyes slid over the hunters fighting against the pack, and air escaped my lungs on a cry of disbelief as I watched men slaughtering the guards. Five more steps into the mayhem, and it was undeniable that my pack hadn't begun the coup against my father and Carlson.

Hunters fought against mine and Carlson's packs using guns and silver blades. Women were crouching on the ground, crying over dead men or trying to escape being trampled. My stomach churned, searching the crowd for anyone familiar. Tora's hand yanked on my arm, but I couldn't look away from the pandemonium unfolding.

Gunshots and blades hitting one another drowned out the screaming and cries of death filling the air. My attention slowly moved over my people as I noted the tang of blood painting the dead and flowing through the large courtyard.

I paused upon seeing the largest male with the hunters, covered in blood and tattoos, swinging his swords effortlessly. He fought in pants, with nothing else covering his flesh to prevent damage. I drank in the sight of him, watching the way he fought off three men at once with dual blades, easily taking down anyone stupid enough to cross his path.

He turned, and the air escaped my lungs as the world went silent. Greenish-blue eyes held mine prisoner, causing an array of emotions to slam into my chest. I whimpered, ignoring the burning tears that escaped as I stared into the last pair of eyes I'd ever thought to see again. His scent floated to me, washing away the copper of the blood, replaced by soothing sage and bergamot.

"Saint," I whispered breathlessly.

The look in his eyes turned murderous, even as he started toward me. Men closed in around him, and reality came crushing back into me with the force of gale winds. The last words Saint had shouted at me ten years ago replayed through my mind.

"I will come back here, Braelyn Haralson. I will return, destroying you and everything you love," he'd whispered, silent tears pooling in his eyes, but he'd never let them fall. Saint hadn't shown weakness at any point during my rejection of his mating claim. Only pure hatred had burned in his stare, and the scent that once soothed like a balm had become a curse that turned bitter.

"Fuck! Run!" I shrieked, watching as more faces from my past became visible.

Saint hadn't returned alone. He'd brought his pack of misfits with him, and the scent of these alphas inside the yard was smothering. Tora still held my arm, even as both of us rushed back inside, closing the door and placing a bar across it. My heart thundered against my ribs, and breathing past the pain from seeing my true soul mate again was difficult, forcing short pants of air to escape my lungs.

"Holy shit! They're back!" Tora exclaimed.

"They brought hunters and monsters with them!" I seethed.

In the short time I'd been able to look out onto the battlefield, I'd not only spotted hunters, but I'd also seen demons and a variety of wolves forming a makeshift pack. Saint hadn't come back to be accepted. No, he'd returned to do what he'd promised when he and his misfits were banished. Saint had returned to destroy us all. The door cracked, and I yelped, turning to watch as an ax cut through the wood.

"Hide," I demanded, and Tora shook her head. "Tora, get the children out of here. Saint will follow me, and his men will follow him because he's their leader. You must get the children out. Tell me you will do it. Find Chaos, and get him the fuck out of here, now!"

"Not without you, Brae," she started, but the ax slammed into the door once more, making us both jump.

"Get my child out of here, now," I ordered, starting toward a dark hallway that led to a dead-end.

My eyes slid to Toralei, watching as she rushed off to the playroom where the pack omegas were entertaining the children. I exhaled past my fear as the ax continued tearing into the thick wood of the door, moving deeper into the mansion that Saint and his misfits had once considered home.

In the hallway I paused as their voices echoed in the main room. Turning my head, I peered at the doorway that led to the outcrop building, and I rushed toward it. I didn't think I would escape Saint and his men, not when I knew how they tracked and their ability to do so. I was merely buying Tora time to run with the children, hoping they wouldn't end up as collateral damage.

"Come on, Brat. Don't play hard to get," Saint's deep baritone voice filled my ears, sending a wave of unease into my belly.

"She always enjoyed when you chased that ass," Eryx injected, which caused the hair on my nape to rise with awareness.

Laughter echoed around me as I slid behind a large shelf inside the newly renovated library. My heartbeat was erratic, and the scent of my fear was smothering to my senses. I projected it, allowing them to catch it before I shed my robe, shoving it onto a shelf and rushing to the other side of the room.

"Mmm, she always smelled like trouble, too. A little fear, a little woman, and a whole lot of promise for the sexy little bitch she'd become. Come on, Princess. We want to play with you," Sian chuckled, his laughter wicked and dark like the soul he held within him.

Another voice entered the one-sided conversation. "Her lips are to die for, but then they're as poisonous as the bitch that owns them," Phenrys grunted. "I always wondered if they'd feel as good around my cock, but then little Miss Prim wouldn't ever give up the goods. Would you, Brae?"

I almost snorted, listening while they moved through the library's large, elaborate layout as one unit. It was how they did everything. They had hunted me once, which had terrified and excited me. It ended with Saint discovering me and our link igniting in this very room since the library was where I'd spent most of my time.

"Come on, woman. Don't keep us hanging. Let us see you. You know you want to play with us. This brings back memories, doesn't it? Us hunting you down, and you finding out your mate was one of us, only to fuck him over in the cruelest way? I didn't take you for a sentimental bitch, Princess." Zayne's tone held amusement, causing a shiver to rush down my spine.

I heard them pounce where I'd discarded my robe, and grunts of laughter escaped to fill the room. I lifted my eyes to the window that led into the courtyard, beyond where the pack had gathered. My body trembled as I dashed forward, hearing their cries of discovery as I left my hiding place, rushing toward the window.

I launched my body into the air and yelped as something solid collided against me. I bounced, landing on the floor with a bone-jarring thud. Flipping onto my ass, I stared up as Saint looked down at me. His men formed a V behind him, all foreboding in their attire.

They'd grown up. Saint was the largest and roughest around the edges. Phenrys was smaller than the others, but he was Saint's beta and always had been. Eryx was sex incarnate in his impeccable suit. Tattoos peeked from beneath his rolled-up sleeves and the collar of the crisp white shirt, running up his jawline to vanish in his hair. Cassian, aka Sian, was covered in blood with too much flesh showing. A deep V-line led into his jeans, whispering promises of sin, tattooed in the lines leading to his cock. Zayne, the nerd of the pack, wore red suspenders with a bright blood-red bowtie, also covered in blood that had splattered his glasses. Not that Zayne needed the glasses, but he still wore the things because he thought they made him look smart. And Bowen, the brute of the group, known to make women scream for hours on end, even before he'd become an adult.

"Miss me, Brat?" Saint asked, causing the surrounding men to chuckle.

His stare slid over my scantily clothed body with hunger and a glint of something sinister and cold in his eyes that terrified me. My chest rose and fell with my labored breathing as they all watched me, hoping I fought against them. Saint's generous mouth curved into a wicked grin as he strode closer, lowering to his haunches and grabbing my thighs painfully.

"I asked you a fucking question, Braelyn."

"Why the hell did you come back here? You were free. All of you were free of this place. You could have gone anywhere and done anything you wanted with your lives. Yet you came back here?"

"I promised to destroy you. Don't you remember? I've always kept my promises, haven't I? Unlike you, Princess. I should have known you were just like your father. Guess I won't make that mistake again. Right, boys?" Their sinister laughter filled the library, sending a tremor of fear rushing down my spine. "Get up, now."

Saint stood, watching as I struggled to get to my feet. The moment I succeeded, I kicked my foot out, gasping as he dodged it, grabbing my arm to yank my body against his. The nearness caused my wolf to peer out, itching to get to his. My body heated from his touch, burning for what we'd failed to do the last time we were together.

Saint's eyes glazed over, turning crimson as his wolf peered into my gaze. Our bond wasn't something either of us could ignore, but apparently, he intended to fix that issue. The scent he oozed caused my lips to part as a soft moan escaped my throat. He walked me backward until my spine slammed against the wall, and his hand slid up and around my throat. He didn't apply enough pressure to cut the air off to my lungs, but it was enough to feel the dominance he held over me.

"Fight it all you like, Brae. In fact, I hope you fucking do fight me. This thing between us—it's happening. After I've claimed you, you can do whatever the fuck you want as long as I approve of it. You're about to know how the bitches beneath you feel when they're nothing but a fucking breeder. That was your worst fear, wasn't it? Being nothing more than a pretty womb that some alpha used to breed his pups?"

I didn't answer him. Instead, I studied the changes in his face. He'd grown into a primal male that exuded alpha pheromones. He'd surpassed all my expectations. Sea-green eyes that changed with his mood held mine, and the midnight hair that dusted his forehead and shoulders held a blue tint beneath the moon's illuminating light.

His eyes drifted over the changes in my face, no longer the teenage girl he'd fallen in love. My body had blossomed in his absence, and my breasts had gone from an average B-cup to a D. My hips had filled out, accentuated by a slight bubble butt that gave it a healthy bounce. I'd also shot up, reaching six feet in height, which still made me seem fragile and delicate to his nearly seven-foot frame.

"You grew up, Brat. You grew up good, didn't you?" Saint mused with a thickness in his tone that caused my nipples to harden from an eagerness to feel his heated breath against them. His thumb moved, rubbing over my full lips before he snorted. "Red isn't your color. What's the matter? Can't speak without your daddy present to hear your words?"

"I don't need my father to tell me how fucked I am right now, Saint. I can do the math on that one myself." He lowered his mouth to my ear and nipped my earlobe. He tugged it with his teeth, releasing it as a growl escaped his chest with a deep vibration that slithered over my body.

"You have no idea how fucked you really are, but you will figure it out soon enough. Now be a good girl and show me to your bedroom. I can't have you watching me slaughter your daddy while you're still wearing your fucking mating gown; now can we, boys?" Saint smiled cruelly as they laughed. "Move, or I'll remind you why pissing me off isn't a good idea."

Chapter Two

Saint and his men walked me through the hallways that were now crawling with strangers. Unfortunately, in true fashion, they blocked anyone from seeing my skimpily clothed body while keeping me from seeing anyone else. The scents of human hunters, demons, and wolves inside the lodge set off warning bells in my head. Those three types of creatures never went together. No matter how hard they tried to be allies, it always ended in a bloodbath.

At the door to my room, Eryx reached past me, opening it only to groan as they discovered it was filled with women. His startling green eyes moved back to meet mine, and then a deep, loud growl rumbled from his chest, sending the betas and omegas in my room into a frenzy. My body pulsed, and Saint chuckled, yanking me back as his arm slung around my middle, pulling my body against his.

The women slinked out of the room, some of them

crawling on their knees in fear. I had to fight the urge to kick Eryx for creating their panic, but I was certain I'd pay for any slight against them. Saint's thumb rubbed my nipple, the action done on purpose to let me know he smelled the arousal that was oozing from my body.

Once the room was emptied and the men had checked it for weapons, Saint shoved me inside without warning. I tripped, catching myself before I could face-plant onto the floor. Turning, I watched as he entered behind me, closing the door. He silently moved his eyes over my scarcely filled room, picking up a chair that he placed at the end of my bed, sitting on it to watch me.

"Strip," he growled, sitting back in a relaxed pose with his hands on the armrests of the chair.

"No," I snorted, crossing my arms over my chest to hide the tremor in my hands from his raspy tone. Saint's lips twisted into a sardonic smile as his eyes sparkled with mirth while he let his gaze slide down my lithe frame.

"Take off the fucking mating gown, Braelyn. I won't ask you again," he warned huskily.

"I told you no, Saint." He stood abruptly and moved toward me without warning.

I back-peddled, and a soft cry escaped my lips when my rear connected with the dresser. Saint's hands landed on either side of me, caging my body against the wood. The amusement in his expression sent a ripple of warning through me. His mouth lowered, brushing against mine, hovering there without touching my lips. I knew he felt my body tremble from his nearness, smelling the anxiousness his proximity created.

"It wasn't a request, Brat. I wasn't asking you to take it off. I was telling you to remove the gown you intended to fuck Carlson in, now," he murmured softly, sending confusion through me.

He stood back, watching me as his hands trailed over my shoulders, sliding to the front of the gown before he tore it wide open.

My chest rose and fell with labored breathing. Saint held my stare captive, never dropping his gaze to my breasts. The gown slithered to the floor, pooling around my feet before something cold pressed against my stomach. My entire body shuddered at feeling a blade against my naked belly. My attention remained on his face, uncaring that it would probably be the last thing I ever saw before he murdered me.

Lips trembling, I gasped as the cold blade moved over my heated skin. His lips curled into a sinful smile before he lowered his attention to my bralette, sliding the knife blade beneath it to cut through the lace, revealing my left breast. He did the same with the other, leisurely moving the blade higher to cut the straps and then the middle fabric that hugged my ribs.

"Did you fuck him?" he asked softly, running the dull edge of the blade against my erect nipple.

"No," I replied honestly.

"Did you want to?" Saint stared at my chest as I shook my head in reply. "Use your words, Princess. I'm playing with your nipple, and I'd hate to slip."

"No, I didn't," I whimpered, gasping as the blade cut into my breast. Saint lowered his heated mouth, trailing his tongue over the small cut he'd made. His saliva healed the wound, but the bite of pain remained as he stood back, studying me.

Snorting at my answer, he slid his eyes behind me before he reached over, leaning against my body to light the candles that sat on the dresser. When he was done, he turned me around to face the dresser. His hands grabbed mine, placing them onto the wooden top before he pushed my thighs apart with his foot.

"Are you afraid of me or excited? Your body is responding to mine, but you reek of fear, Princess," Saint chuckled, his tone thick and husky.

"Both," I admitted, hating that he could smell the state of my body.

Warm lips moved over my shoulder, sending a violent tremor rushing through me down to my toes. My stomach clenched with need while fear tugged at my mind.

Saint laughed against my skin, sending heat pooling to my core as he stepped back to take in my ass, arching for him. I was twisted, but who wouldn't be with a mate like this asshole? My nipples pebbled into hard peaks, begging for his mouth to pleasure them. My scent released, and no matter how much I fought the wolf within me, she refused to behave with her true soul mate this close.

The dull side of his blade lowered from the base of my neck, slowly trailing to the curve of my ass. I dropped my head forward, fighting the moan that built in my throat. Saint used the blade to cut the soft material that was my only defense from him. His heavy stare burned against my skin, and I didn't need to see his eyes to know he was taking in the curve of my spine, bowed in submission.

A deep, rumbling growl built in his chest until he finally unleashed it on me. It quaked against my skin, causing small bumps of awareness to continue until his tone bordered on demonic. The air left my lungs in a whoosh, and arousal coated my sex from the deep, demanding growl he released. My spine lifted and arched up invitingly, begging him to take what I offered. It wasn't just need rushing through me; it was a visceral ache that tore at the genetics embedded in my soul.

"Holy shit," I murmured, hating that my body wanted to gyrate and spread for Saint to fuck me hard and fast before burying his fangs into my body, leaving me marked deeper than ever before. It shouldn't be that easy to get me, yet everything within me was screaming for him.

This mate crap was for the birds, not wolves.

Saint slipped his hand around my waist, lifting until his palm touched against my throat. His other hand was slowly sliding down to my sex that clenched and begged him to fill it with his essence. The savage wolf within me didn't understand or even care that he intended to hurt us and leave us in a heap of destroyed ruins. Saint jerked my body back, chuckling as a moan bubbled up, escaping my lips.

"Tell me this isn't for me," he urged, his fingers sliding through the arousal he'd created by allowing his wolf to speak to mine. "You're so fucking wet right now. You'd let me fuck you, wouldn't you? Your wolf wouldn't let you fight it right now. Tell me I'm wrong,

Brae. How is it she responds to me so easily if you're not mine?"

"She has a split personality disorder on her best days," I whispered huskily, rubbing my pussy against his fingers.

"She knows she's mine by right." He pushed a single finger into my body, and it tightened, holding him within. Everything went haywire inside of me. My stomach coiled, a deep ache throbbed where he slowly worked his finger into my opening. He withdrew, lifting his finger until the sound of him sucking it clean entered my hearing. I gasped, shuddering against his heated body.

"You're not marked," he pointed out, slowly releasing my throat to step back. The heat I'd felt diminished, and left me cold. "How is it you intended to mate that prick tonight, yet his mark doesn't grace your flawless skin?" he demanded, but his voice had come from across the room.

I peered over my shoulder, taking him in as he lounged in the chair. I spun around slowly to face him, hating the need still coursing through me. The look in his eyes made my body tighten and burn with desire. Saint lifted his hand, and his finger motioned for me to come toward him. Instead, I leaned against the dresser, knowing that if I obeyed, I wasn't leaving this room a virgin.

"Come here," he rumbled, his voice a mixture of lust and anger that made my nipples harden with anticipation. "Don't make me come get you. You won't like what happens."

Swallowing past the tightening in my throat, I walked to where he sat reclining in the chair. I remained out of his reach, but he sat forward abruptly, grabbing my hips to pull me forward. My body toppled against his, catching his shoulders as he sat back, forcing me to straddle his body or remain lying on him at an awkward angle.

Saint's tongue swiped out, tasting the rosebud that taunted him. I gasped at the feel of his heated mouth against my nipple, whimpering as he nipped it playfully. His fingers bit into my hips, holding me down against his hard arousal.

"Did you miss me? I missed you. I missed the taste of your lips and the way your eyes sparkled when you were thinking inappropriate thoughts. The way heat painted your cheeks like they are right now. Mostly, I thought about ways to punish you for what you did to me, to us. Tell me I'm not your mate. Tell me you don't feel me as deeply as I feel you right now."

I shook my head softly, peering down at him while he watched. His attention moved from my face to drag slowly down my body. Saint sat up abruptly, forcing my chest to press against his. Finger's trailed up my spine to clasp at the back of my neck before he brought his mouth against mine.

A hungry growl slipped from my lungs, and my body rocked against his. His tongue slid along my lips, pushing past them to tangle with mine. Raw, intense need rocked into my core, and I unleashed what little control I held. I lifted my hands from his shoulders, pushing through his thick hair to hold him against my mouth. The scent of my need freed, filling the room to duel with his as he dominated me harder, using just his kiss.

Saint lifted me, forcing my legs to wrap around his waist as he moved us to the bed. Following me down, he lifted his head, peering between our bodies where my arousal was coating my needy sex. He placed his forehead against mine, slowly backing up to look between my thighs.

"You are exactly what your father told me you were, Braelyn. A needy, willing whore that would fuck anyone, even your enemies, if they came to pillage and plunder your cunt," Saint snorted derisively. "Cover yourself, and act like you're not some easy pussy that fucks anyone willing to touch it."

His words left me speechless as tears pricked my eyes. My body shook with rage and confusion. Pulling the sheet up around me, I moved to my dresser, grabbing panties, a tank top, and shorts that hugged my thick curves. His words stung since I hadn't ever been willing to fuck anyone.

"I suggest you don't fight me when we exit this room. If you do, I will ensure you're tied to a bed and left there until I finish using you. I'm going to murder your father, and then if you beg me enough, I may let your intended escape here unscathed. He was, after all, lured here by the promise of your pussy. Wasn't he?"

"Kill him," I uttered thickly, dropping the sheet to step into the black panties and shorts. Tugging the top on, I turned to stare at the man I'd once loved more than my own life.

I'd needed a reminder that he wasn't the same

person I'd fallen in love with all those years ago. It had been ten years after all, and while he may smell the same and seem the same, he wasn't. Saint was a stranger now, covered in tattoos with something dark and sinister burning within him. We'd grown up, both of us changing while separated. I couldn't expect him to be the same boy. This wasn't the Saint I'd fallen madly in love with in the summer we'd spent together. This was a man that had been banished because of me, and as a result, had become a monster. He wasn't back to reclaim our love.

He'd come back for one purpose and one alone—to destroy me and everything I loved.

Chapter Three

Outside, the debris and bodies that previously littered the courtyard had been cleared. People were gathered there now, watching what was happening near the middle of the square. Saint and his men walked me through the crowd, and the surrounding voices hushed as we got closer. I didn't need to see what everyone was staring at because I could smell the blood filling the air and scent the male to which it belonged.

Saint's men parted, revealing my father seated on the ground, on his knees. My eyes slid over him, and my heart thundered against my chest the moment his cruel eyes lifted, locking with mine. Madness peered up at me, his hatred of me shining in his multi-colored depths, condemning me.

"You've been judged and found guilty, Harold Haralson," Saint's voice boomed, causing me to jump. His green-blue eyes lifted to mine, a cocky grin spreading over his lips.

"You don't have the right to judge me, boy!" my father snarled as spittle ejected from his bloodied lips. "Braelyn will never take you back. And even if she did, she's nothing but a broken little beta now, with nothing to offer a true alpha."

"Yeah? How about I breed your pretty little bitch where you can see me fucking her?"

My father laughed, his eyes still locked with mine. "Did you tell her what I did to you, boy?" he snarled, spitting out the word boy like a curse. "No, you didn't tell Braelyn what her rejection did to you because then she'd know the truth."

"She'll know it soon enough. I intend to show her exactly what you allowed to happen to us. I'm going to destroy your pretty daughter, Harold. I'm going to breed her like a bitch, listening to her scream against my ear. You promised me I'd never be good enough for her, yet I have her now. You may have poisoned her mind, but I don't want that from her. I just need her womb to finish the bloodline her mother started. We don't need you alive for that, though, do we, boys?" Saint asked as his fist sailed toward my father's face, sending him reeling to the side.

"No, we don't need his evil ass alive to take everything from him. Right, Bowen?" Sian asked, snorting as he grabbed me, holding me tightly. My heart thundered against my ribs as he inhaled my scent, cupping my breasts tightly. "I think we'll all enjoy fucking your perfect little Princess on your grave, Harold," he chuckled. "What do you think, Bowen, you want to fuck Braelyn's tight body on her father's grave?" Sian shoved me toward Bowen while Saint watched, his eyes noting the way my body trembled with actual fear instead of lust this time.

"Fuck, yes. I want to hear her scream as I rail the bitch. I bet she likes it hard, don't you, Princess?" he growled against my ear, wrapping his hand around my throat until the air failed to escape past my lips. "Zayne, you down to fuck her ass while I rail her pussy?" he asked, and before I could push away from Bowen, Zayne was against my chest.

"Mmm, my pleasure. You take her ass, and I'll start on this side," Zayne crooned, lifting my chin to hover his lips against mine. "What do you say, pretty pussy cat? You want me to rail your cunt so hard you don't know anything else but the feel of me stretching it full?"

"She's got lips, gentlemen, and I require them around my cock," Phenrys announced, sliding in front of Zayne, then pushing his thumb into my lips while I slowly blinked past the stars, blotching my sight. "Suck me off, Princess? I always wondered how your soft lips would feel wrapped around my cock. I know you kiss clumsily, but a guy can hope you figured out how to use your mouth for something worthwhile in the last ten years, right?"

My legs started to buckle, and Bowen released his grip around my throat slightly to let me gasp air in past Phen's thumb. It was instinct, closing and opening my mouth as I sucked air into my starving lungs. Phen chuckled, watching me as someone's hand slipped between my thighs, stroking my sex roughly.

"What do you say, Princess? Do you want to play with us? All of us? We intend to play with you. We can let your daddy watch since you always did everything

ALPHA'S CLAIM

he asked of you. I bet you make some sweet noises when you're packed full of cock and choking one down your throat. I bet Saint will even let us take a shot at breeding your needy cunt," Sian chuckled, watching as I struggled in the arms of the others.

Something wet splashed against my face, and I blinked, scenting the coppery tang of blood. Eryx, who smirked at me with his dark onyx eyes, turned my head forcibly. The look that burned in them terrified me more than the hands roughly exploring my body.

"I think we should all take turns making her come. Once that pussy is swollen, I say we fuck it raw until she only knows pain. I've always wanted to fuck you, but you knew that before you ever belonged to your mate. Didn't you? You used to hide from me and run if I even got close to you." Eryx's grip tightened until I screamed, then he stepped out of the way to show me what was happening.

Saint was pounding my father's face into the ground before he ripped him to his feet. My father's face was little more than a bloodied pulp, but that wasn't enough. Saint's hand shoved through my father's back, punching through his chest with his beating heart held in his palm. The crowd cheering him on as he'd pulverized my father went silent. Saint pulled my father's heart back through his chest with one hand. Using a blade in the other, he severed his head from his body, sending more blood to splatter over his men and me, watching it unfolding.

"Your daddy told us all about you, Braelyn. He even brought me pictures of my mate being fucked. I say we tie her up and use her until she's nothing more than what she craved to be for her daddy. His precious little whore he passed around to his friends, using her pussy to lure his enemies into slaughter. How many children did you lure in for him? Hundreds? Thousands?" Saint moved to stare down at me as his men still held me. His words echoed in my head, but I couldn't make sense of them.

Saint's crew parted, allowing him to slide in front of me. He lifted his bloodied hand, curling his fingers tightly around my jaw before shoving my father's heart against my lips.

"Fucking eat it, bitch," he seethed, watching me through crimson eyes. I opened my mouth, and my canines descended, taking a bite from the rough muscle organ. Blood dripped from my lips, running down my throat as he watched me. I ripped it off, holding the tears at bay as I chewed the gritty meat. Saint held the organ to his lips, ripping off a sizeable chunk before passing it around to his men. My body buzzed with the wrongness of having this many males close to me, but my eyes didn't leave Saint's crimson alpha gaze while I swallowed the meat. His lips curved into a sinister smile before he leaned closer. "How does daddy taste?"

"Salty," I whispered, causing the men to laugh.

Saint's eyes returned to normal before he leaned closer, brushing his bloodied lips against mine. He lifted his hand, pushing fingers through my hair before wrenching my head back, slamming his lips against mine while Bowen held me in place. His kiss wasn't gentle, fueled with the rage and lust that death created in our breed. He devoured me as if I was next on the menu.

"The interesting thing about your rejection, Princess, is that Saint doesn't crave you as much as you crave him. That means he won't be disappointed when he finds out you like my cock more than his," Eryx laughed, watching my head roll back as Saint lifted his, staring down at me.

"I get her first, boys. After all, she fucked me the hardest," Saint snorted, glaring at me as he stepped back. "Bring out my mate's chosen alpha that she intended to fuck tonight. I find myself wanting to murder him too. After all, he dared to touch what rightfully belongs to me. Afterward, we'll get to know each other better, mate."

Saint's men didn't release me, even as Carlson was pulled from where he'd been watching everything unfold. Unlike my father, he fought off the men who grabbed him. Saint snorted, lowering his head while the struggling alpha was brought closer against his will.

"Did you touch her?" Saint asked, and Carlson's glare searched me out.

"No, I didn't. I should have. She wanted it well enough," Carlson spat, glaring at me as if this was my fault.

I snorted, sliding my unimpressed gaze down his body. Carlson growled, but my body didn't respond as it grew in sound. Saint examined me as I turned my lip up at Carlson's weak attempt to make me react. Saint growled from deep in his chest, and I lifted my ass, whimpering as my legs threatened to give out. Eryx smirked, canting his head as his nostrils flared.

"And so the ice princess melted, and her pussy

wept to be filled." Eryx smiled with darkness peeking out from within him that terrified me. Out of all Saint's friends, Eryx was the most twisted and insane. The fucker had worn a suit to battle, merely rolling up his sleeves as if he'd worried about getting them dirty.

"Fucking whore," Carlson snapped, spitting on the ground in a show of disrespect.

"Just not whore enough to trip and land on your dick, though, right?" I taunted, watching the anger pulse through him.

"I ought to wreck your fucking vagina, bitch."

"Let's be honest here, Carlson. The only vagina you've ever wrecked was your mother's when you came out of it. From the stories I've heard from your betas, you're rather—lacking down there," I laughed, watching the anger reach a boil as his eyes turned crimson.

The men holding me snorted and chuckled as Carlson lunged toward me. Saint's fist landed against Carlson's face, slamming him back without warning. Carlson sailed backward, turning his attention on the larger threat present. The pack went crazy, howling and cheering as they watched two evenly matched alphas face off together. Fucking savages.

Even I enjoyed watching Saint beating the fuck out of the other alpha. Carlson threw a punch, and Saint dodged it, his body, a rippling mass of sinewy muscles, glistening in the torchlights. Saint was toned in all the right places, and the tattoos he'd chosen to adorn his skin fit him perfectly, contouring against his muscles. Saint's anger fueled the crowd as his skilled moves fed them energy.

Saint fighting was a sight to behold. He dodged every attack easily, landing several hard punches in the process. His body pulsed and tensed, moving fluidly like a dance. My body hummed with lust, undeniably so. His scent filled the air, forcing my wolf to the front of my mind. My nipples hardened, and when Bowen noticed, he strummed his thumb over the tank top that covered them while grunting in my ear.

"He fucks like he fights, Princess. Hard, fast, and with no fucking mercy against those who betray him or touches what belongs to him. Saint is going to enjoy your pretty screams," Bowen growled. Eryx turned toward me, his mouth slanting up into a wicked smile that made his maddening, dark eyes sparkle.

Saint howled, forcing our attention back to him. He stood in the middle of the courtyard, holding Carlson's severed head, announcing himself the new alpha of the pack. It was a loud, mighty howl that forced the pack to their knees. Even I tried to drop, but the arms holding me prevented my body from doing what it demanded I do. Submit.

Green-blue eyes slid to mine before Saint tossed Carlson's head toward me. He rolled his neck, and before I could react, Saint used his power to slam against me, forcing me to the ground. My body thudded against it, and when he lowered to me, I immediately wrapped my legs around Saint's waist as his teeth pushed into my shoulder, claiming me.

Pleasure and pain fought against one another. My eyes stared up sightlessly, seeing nothing past the red-haze of lust his mouth against my flesh created. Saint pushed his cock against my apex, slowly licking over the mating mark he'd placed on my shoulder, declaring me off-limits to everyone else—everyone except the men, who watched us with molten lust burning in their stares. He slammed his fist into the ground beside my head, studying me as I gasped at the need he'd created.

"Now, you're mine, Brat. Eryx, have the women set up the mating bed. Bowen, get the whiskey and alcohol flowing. The rest of you, murder those Carlson brought with him and give the women a choice to join us or die with their alpha. Phen, ensure everything is ready for me to mate my little bitch the moment that moon rises tonight. I'm not chancing her escaping me again." Saint pulled me up, forcing me to walk forward toward the lodge. "Move, you need to bathe before the mating, Brat."

I started forward, sliding my eyes to the pack where Toralei stood. Panic ripped through me, knowing that if she was here, so were the children. My stomach churned, and Saint grabbed my arm, dragging me past her as I dug my feet in, staring at her.

"Walk, or I'll carry you, Braelyn. You still need to learn the terms of your surrender. Unless, of course, you prefer we all come to your bedroom, and you entertain us?"

I swallowed past the lump in my throat, walking with Saint out of the courtyard. I could hear the pack already descending on the bodies of dead alphas, which would be consumed as a show of disrespect. It was one reason I'd been able to keep my shit together. Saint's men had taunted me about fucking me on my father's grave, but honorless alphas weren't buried; they were consumed and shat out as a statement of how the pack truly felt about them.

The lodge's broken doors came into view. Saint's people were already repairing the ax holes, or, more to the point, patching them from the enormous holes he'd made to remove the board that had barred it. Inside, Saint refused to release my wrist as he dragged me behind him. My pride was hurt, but I wasn't upset about his return. The timing had been shit, but what would he have done if he'd shown up after the coup had happened? Too bad I'd never know.

Chapter Four

In my bedroom, Saint closed the door behind him, sealing out the world. My body shivered violently, battling the combination of lust and bloodlust, which to our kind, was harder to do when both were present. We were savages derived from Viking bloodlines.

"Strip," Saint ordered, forcing my head to whip in his direction.

"You want me to sit at your feet too? You best be offering me some treats if you expect me to do tricks." His eyes sparkled as he moved toward me, his body pulsing, still bathed in the blood of my father and Carlson. I was covered in it, too, my mouth caked in the blood from my father's heart.

Saint didn't take the bait. Instead, he leaned against my dresser, studying me like cornered prey. I stood awkwardly, noting every single contour of his chest on display. He hadn't been this brazen before I'd banished him. He'd hardly ever gone shirtless, and if this was a new habit, I could get behind it.

Looking at Saint, I noticed the same darkness in his eyes that his men now had. It made me curious to know where they'd been, what they'd done while I'd been stuck on this mountain, picking up the slack from my deadbeat father. He'd never lifted a finger to help the pack, forcing me to do it through members of the pack loyal to me. I pretended to be a dutiful daughter, but I secretly ran the pack since before my tits had even blossomed.

My entire life went to shit when my father murdered my mother for birthing only female offspring. On her second pregnancy, the midwife announced she carried yet another female. My father caught her off guard, murdering her while I'd stood in the room, watching. The problem for him was that I held the pack through my ancient, powerful bloodline, traced back to the first wolves created by our god, Fenrir.

If it hadn't been for Fenrir's blood running through my veins, I had no disillusion that my father would have murdered me on that floor right beside my loving mother. I hadn't made a single noise when he killed her, bashing her head into nothing more than an unrecognizable mess. She'd taught me to hide my fear and to protect and control how I reacted to it. It was just an emotion, after all. A useless one that enemies would exploit the moment they scented it.

"I don't think you're grasping the situation here, Braelyn. Your status has been reduced to nothing unless I decide otherwise. If I want you to sit at my feet, you will. I just murdered your father and spared your life. You were supposed to die alongside him, but I decided

I didn't want you dead. I want you to suffer as we did. You allowed your father to hurt us for fun, and now it's your turn."

"Excuse me?" I asked, backing up the moment he stepped forward.

Saint prowled closer, and I darted away before he could pin me in. His hand shot out, slamming me back against the wall before his body hit mine. My teeth clashed together, causing me to bite my tongue. Blood pooled in my mouth as he smirked, glaring at me through darkening eyes.

I shifted, lifting my hands to push his massive body away so that coherent thoughts would enter my brain, but the motion didn't end well. His large hand grabbed my wrists, wrapping around both easily before he slammed them against the wall above my head.

Those eyes I once wished to drown within turned cold, and before I could guess his thoughts, he released my hands and ripped my shirt open. A startled scream tore from my throat, echoing through the room as he reached down, shredding my shorts. My body shuddered, and then my hands darted forward, trailing my nails down his massive chest as anger shot through me.

Rage-filled eyes peered down at me; pure, white-hot rage studied me through round, darkened depths. One minute I was doing something insanely stupid, like pissing Saint off, and the next, he'd flung my body to the floor. The air exploded from my lungs violently, and I crawled on my elbows, moving toward the drawer that held my gun. Hands grabbed my ankles, turning me over as he peered down at me, smiling cruelly.

Blood dripped from his chest, marring the utter perfection of it in the wake of my nails. Anger pulsed from within Saint, filling the room with his presence. My room was large before he'd entered it, but now it was filled with the sheer magnitude of him and his overwhelming presence. My body trembled, and the moment Saint released my ankles to get closer, I kicked out, taking his legs out from beneath him.

Instead of landing on the floor, Saint launched his body onto mine, grabbing my arms painfully to hold them above my head. I bucked wildly beneath him, screaming in frustration. His blood coated my breasts and my lip, seeping down my chin.

"Fuck you!" I snarled, fighting against Saint as he glared at me with a sinister expression burning in his gaze.

"I'm about to fuck you, Brat," he chuckled, rocking his massive erection against my exposed core.

My body reacted, and I fucking hated it. My core clenched, and my wolf howled her need within me. Desire flared in Saint's eyes, and his nostrils moved as he inhaled my arousal. Fucking savage asshole. I twisted my arms and my hips, forcefully trying to unseat him where he lay, holding me prisoner with his weight. The asshole weighed half a ton at a minimum.

He wasn't even moving, just watching me realize how helpless I was. I tried twisting my wrists from his grasp, but he slammed them down against the hard floorboards. I whimpered, bucking against him to get free. His mouth lowered, and he bit softly into my lip, forcing a scream to bubble up from my throat as he held it between his teeth, threateningly.

His other hand slipped between our bodies, pushing against the bundle of nerves between my thighs. I moaned, slowly lifting to his touch. My hard nipples throbbed at the contact, and he released my lip, smiling into my gaze before pushing his fingers into my body, stretching me.

"Good girl," he whispered. His nose rubbed against my cheek as he released his scent, filling the air with his enticing aroma.

The fight fled my mind, replaced by pleasure. Saint continued to hold my body against the floor while he slowly stroked the fire within me. His fingers parted inside my pussy, causing a soft cry to escape my throat. The moment he released my hands, I attacked anew.

Saint grabbed me up, shoving me forward against the wall before he slammed my hands behind my back, holding them at the base of my spine. His deep growl filled the room, and his scent exploded as if he'd been holding back.

As alpha, Saint could soothe an entire pack with his scent, but it rendered me helpless but to submit to the dominance in it, no matter how much I hated doing so. His other hand pushed through my hair, twisting it as he rubbed his body against my ass, forcing me to grind my need against it.

"You want to fight or fuck, Brae? I can't tell which one you crave more right now. I can do both," he chuckled, freeing my hair before his cock was against my ass.

I pushed my forehead against the wall, arching my ass for him to run his cock through the arousal between my legs. The deep rumble that escaped his throat created more, and my whole body pulsed with need. I could feel the thick tip he rubbed along my opening. He was using my arousal to coat his dick, intending to fuck me.

The tip had barely pushed into my body when the door burst open, and something slammed into Saint, causing him to curse as I remained against the wall, spread out. Voices entered the room as multiple scents assaulted my mind. Something crashed against the floor, and more curses sounded as I whimpered, rocking my hips, oblivious to what was happening behind me.

"Gods damn, that's fucking hot," Bowen's voice met my ears, forcing air to get stuck in my throat.

"Don't fucking touch her, asshole," Saint growled in warning.

"She wouldn't even know it wasn't you, Saint," Eryx's voice sounded behind me, his hand slowly lowering to the dimples at my spine. "Who the fuck you got there?" he asked, and my mind fought to return through the lust driving it into the mating frenzy.

Fucking savage.

Saint had used his scent to drive me to the edge, and it was taking everything I had and more to fight against it. I growled loudly, pushing away from the wall, only to drop to my knees at their feet. My eyes slid to crimson, exposing the fact that I wasn't a beta at all. Only three people knew that truth, and now these assholes knew it too.

"That's unexpected, Princess. Didn't see that one coming," Eryx chuckled, lowering his body to push the hair away from my face.

Saint held Chaos in his arms, pushing him against the bed where he'd exposed himself to help me. Tears burned my eyes while Saint studied my face, noting the red eyes that teetered more toward purple from the intensity of their normal blue coloring.

"Leave him alone," I hissed past the tensing of my jaw.

"You made babies, Brae?" Eryx asked, turning to take in the sea-green eyes of the child Saint held.

"He did," I growled, pointing my finger at Saint.

The room went silent at my words, and Saint's stare dropped to the son he'd left behind. Of course, he hadn't known Chaos even existed. He'd gotten Cherry, his ex-girlfriend, pregnant before our link was cemented. She'd said nothing, choosing to abandon Saint's son to the omegas. Right after that, she'd vanished.

"I didn't fuck you," Saint snorted, yet his eyes didn't leave the matching ones that glared up at him.

"He's not mine," I ground out. "Fucking release me!"

"Not alpha enough to top me, huh?" Saint snorted, but he released the scent that unclenched my muscles, freeing me to sag to the floor. "Take the boy and get out. Don't let him out of your sight," he told Eryx.

When they were out of the room, I pushed off the

ALPHA'S CLAIM

floor to stand. Saint studied me, anger pulsing violently in the air between us. His jaw ticked, but he didn't move toward me. Instead, he went to the chair once more, tilting his head toward the bed.

"Sit, now," he ordered.

I did so, but only because my legs were a little more solid than pudding. Saint's eyes examined me, and a smirk played on his mouth as I sat, pulling the sheet over my body to hide it from his prying eyes.

"Explain to me how you're an alpha when I know you were a beta, Braelyn. After that, tell me how the fuck I have a son that you kept hidden from me."

"I didn't keep him hidden, Saint. You left, and I found him in the nursery. That's not on me or my fault. You fucked Cherry and made Chaos."

"You named him what we had intended to name our son?" he asked, dragging his attention over my bloodied face.

"It seemed fitting since I never intended to have a child," I admitted. "I was born alpha, but it was latent. It occurred after you'd left."

"You're going to get into the bath and wash your body. After that, we're going to walk out of this room together with you at my side. I'm going to fuck you in the mating tent in the courtyard and finish the claim to seal our mating rite, Braelyn."

"I don't think so, Saint. You see, I am protected from being forced into a mating."

"That only works if you're a virgin, and we both know you're not. Your father made damn sure I knew what my sweet, docile mate was doing during my absence. He even brought me pictures to show me you'd not only betrayed me, but you'd become the pack's whore. That was something I didn't think possible. It goes to show how much I fucking knew the little bitch I'd been stuck with by the fickle gods."

I laughed, glaring at Saint as I rolled my eyes. My fists clenched into the sheets, deflecting the look of loathing burning in his expression. The problem with my protection was that it would work against everyone except my mate, which means it wouldn't protect me from Saint. There was no denying the gods had created him for me, and I for him. It had kept me from being raped or bred by my father, who craved a son, intending to use my womb to achieve his goal of a male heir to the pack.

"I'm not mating with you, asshole. You came here to hurt me. So fucking do it, and get it over with already," I challenged.

"Oh, it's not that simple. I came back to take your pack from you. I returned to claim my rightful place at your side, even if I have to muzzle you to do so. You have connections I need and intend to use. Your punishment is a life dictated by me, never knowing when I'll strike out and hurt you the most, just like you did to me. I fucking loved you. I let you see inside of me deeper than anyone else ever had. You were my fucking heart, and you ripped it out like it was nothing.

"You will walk out of this room and pretend you're happy with this mating. Because if you don't, Braelyn, I'll unleash the boys on the pack," he growled coldly, rising from the chair to kneel between my knees. "I'll unleash the ones waiting in the woods, holding those men you were waiting to come save you. I'll burn this place to the fucking ground, and then when you've lost everything, I'll make sure you're left in the fucking coals of this worthless fucking home you loved so much."

Peering into his dark gaze, I knew he wasn't playing. Saint had returned with a cold, calculated persona he hadn't had before. The others, his crew, were the same now. They'd enjoyed the bloodshed, craving the kills as much as Saint had when he'd murdered my father and Carlson. Saint lifted his hands, placing them on my thighs as a victorious smile played on his full mouth.

"Smart girl. Go bathe because I'm impatient to fuck my mate. We have ten years to make up for."

Chapter Five

I sat in my room, inhaling some herbs to calm my anxiety. Eryx watched me from where he leaned against the wall, his dark gaze sliding over the dress I now wore. It wasn't sheer like a traditional mating gown, but then I hadn't even owned one until yesterday. My mind whirled with how Saint and his men had infiltrated the compound, slipping past the other packs without detection. Either someone here had helped them, or they'd turned some packs around the mountain against us.

"Are you planning to hide out there until he returns for you?" Eryx asked, his voice coming from right behind me. I spun on my heel, stepping back against the railing of the balcony as he smiled coldly. He reached for my hand, pulling the herb stick away from me before holding it to his nose. "Does this shit help?"

"It calms my nerves and helps to hide what I was from my father."

"A treacherous bitch?" he snorted, pulling a drag from it then slowly exhaling it.

I turned my attention back to the pack which had already started celebrating. In the middle of the vast, sprawling courtyard sat the mating tent. Unlike the last one that Saint had ripped apart during the fight, this one had black gauze that would offer a layer of privacy. Inside, candles were lit, and sage was burning.

A shiver rushed down my arm the moment Eryx touched his hand against my skin. I jerked away, staring at him before realizing he was handing me back the smoke. Accepting it, I peered at it silently.

"I don't have fucking rabies, and if I did, you'd have them as soon as he shares you with us."

"You're so sure he will?" I asked cautiously.

"A lot has changed since you had us banished," he snorted, watching as I lifted the smoke to my lips. "You should die for what you and your father did to us."

I shivered, refusing to meet his stare. I could feel the hatred in the air. His eyes slid over my profile, and then he grabbed the smoke from my hand, inhaling deeply. Peeking at him, I watched the glowing end slowly move closer to his lips. He flicked it, withdrawing a tin from his pocket to produce another smoke.

"Did daddy know his princess was smoking herbs?" he asked, lighting it before handing it to me. I took a drag, coughing violently when it turned out to be marijuana instead of the soothing herbs I was expecting it to be. Eryx snorted, shaking his head. "Saint is going to hurt you. After he's bored with you, Brae, you will be ours to play with when we want. Do try to let loose a little. No one likes a stuck-up bitch that thinks she's better than everyone else. That will only make us play with you harder, and no one likes broken toys."

Eryx's words made my heart clench, but I didn't think Saint would do that. He hated me, sure, but he'd always respected women. He loved his mother at one time. She'd raised him until she'd been unable to continue doing so, abandoning him here, vanishing into the night without telling him goodbye. She'd left Saint an orphan, and that had forced the pack to place him into the care of the omegas, where he'd met his crew.

"You shouldn't have fucked Saint over. He let you in, and you broke him."

"My father gave me two options—make him hate me or watch him die. My world didn't exist without Saint in it, Eryx. If my father had told me to rip my heart from my chest or watch Saint die, I wouldn't have hesitated. I'd have reached into my chest and pulled it out, still beating. You can think the worst of me and make me the villain, but glass houses hide the ugliest monsters. Careful throwing rocks because once you know the truth, you can't ever go back from knowing it."

"And what would a pampered princess of the pack know about monsters?" Saint's voice caused me to jump.

I didn't turn, choosing to grab the joint from Eryx, ignoring the asshole behind me. What would a spoiled princess know? I wouldn't know that answer. I hadn't felt love since my father killed my mother, not until I'd found out Saint was my mate. I'd worked endlessly

ALPHA'S CLAIM

to hide what my father had done to me, to hide what happened in the dark, to keep the pack fed. I'd been a child providing for a pack, assisted by many loyal followers who offered the details and suggestions for our daily living to my father as their ideas.

I'd known nothing other than the struggle to provide food, shelter, and everything else a pack needed to live on a mountain range that was impassable for months during winter. This left us rushing through most months, preparing for the roads to close and for us to live off the land. In another month, the snow would hit us, and we'd be stuck on the mountain until the spring thaw came. It was a blessing and a curse. The hunters couldn't reach us, but we couldn't escape the cold.

I felt both pairs of eyes on me as I exhaled slowly. Saint snorted, leaning on my other side to reach over, grabbing the joint from me. Peering over at him, I paused as he held it between his teeth, drawing the smoke into his mouth as it wafted around his face.

"You ready to party, Brat? You seem to have started without me," Saint smirked, lifting his eyes over my head to stare at Eryx.

"Don't blame me. Brae was out here smoking some weak-ass shit."

"It wasn't weak. It just wasn't pot, asshole. It was herbs, which suppresses my anxiety and stops the alpha tendencies from being uncontrollable. It's formulated, and we distribute it ourselves. Three people knew I was an alpha until you assholes came back here."

Both men went silent at my words, and then Saint grabbed my waist. He held me over the edge as he sat me down. Eryx watched with a sinister look in his eyes, excited at the idea of Saint tossing me over the edge. I gripped Saint's shoulders, but he quickly shrugged me off. His eyes were angry, and the tic was back hammering in his jaw.

"What else have you and your daddy grown up here?" Saint demanded, his eyes condemning me. "I asked you a fucking question," he snapped, pushing me further over the edge to teeter precariously.

"Nothing!" I cried, turning to look at the drop which would kill even an immortal. "Nothing, Saint! My father didn't know we grew it. My mother's people brought the herbs with them from Norway, planting them all over the mountain to increase the alpha's calmness. It simply suppressed his need to kill everything and the rage that drove it!" I tore my eyes from the ground, looking back at his angry face.

"Why do they always look down? It only increases the fear they feel at dangling over such height," Eryx asked, pulling off the joint while he enjoyed the show.

Saint jerked me over the railing and shoved me against the wall. His hand pushed against my throat before he turned to Eryx, grabbing the joint to inhale it deeply. Saint grinned and pressed his lips against mine, forcing the smoke into my lungs. He lifted his hand, holding it against my nose and mouth as my lungs burned.

When he finally released me, a deep cough clapped out of my throat, and I tapped my hand against my chest. He turned, nodding his chin to Eryx. "Let's go. There's whiskey calling our name, and my sweet, willing mate needs to show the pack she's eager to be mounted like the whore she is."

"You're going to feel like such an asshole," I muttered, watching as he turned to gaze at me over his shoulder. I smiled inwardly, slowly trailing after them.

Outside, the pack was already drinking, being rowdy, but still cautious for some reason. I lifted my nose, catching the scent of hunters and dark, wicked desire that screamed of demons. Saint grabbed me by the waist, walking me toward a group that stood away from the pack. His crew was there as well, observing as the pack drank and stared back at the hunters.

This was a catastrophe in the making. Hunters lived by strict codes, most of which included hunting down our kind. They didn't care if we remained away from humans because they thought they were the superior race. Humans didn't enjoy the fact that they weren't at the top of the food chain, because more often than not, they were tasty with some added herbs.

Saint pulled me into his body the moment we were in front of his crew and the outsiders. They all looked at me, slowly taking in my features while I remained as still and stiff as a statue. No one spoke, making an awkward silence. I had to bite my tongue to keep from blabbing anything that would fill it since I didn't do well with strangers or pretty much people in general.

"Have a drink, Braelyn," Bowen announced, smiling as he pushed a bottle of tequila in front of me.

"Yeah, Princess. Drink with us," Sian chuckled, grabbing the bottle to pour shots.

My eyes slid to the lone female in the group, taking in her warrior braids while she returned the stare. Her eyes were blue and vibrant with intelligence shining while her mouth twisted in amusement. Judging by the way she watched me, she had already decided I'd look better six feet underground.

"It's a beautiful place you have here, Braelyn," a man in his thirties stated.

"Had," the female inserted, watching me.

"My mother's people settled here one hundred years ago," I replied, grabbing the bottle and tossing it back, ignoring the seriously hot demon that observed me silently. I polished off the fifth, setting it down before turning toward Bowen, whose rounded eyes peered over my head. "Come on, Bowen. Don't let a little pampered bitch out-drink you. Next bottle? I really don't want to remember tonight, ever."

Blue eyes speckled with dark flecks locked with mine across the makeshift table. The male's hair shone in the fire's light, and the way he watched me felt as if he was accessing every dark sin I'd ever committed. This male didn't just look at you; he gazed into your soul, slowly picking it apart while you stood there, helpless to look away. His mouth curved into a soft smile, and his gaze released mine as if he hadn't just fucking dissected me like some wild animal.

"This is Xavier. Xariana is his daughter," Saint stated, nodding toward the woman and the older gentlemen. "This is Enzo and Ezekiel. They're…" he paused, turning to look at me with a smile playing on his mouth.

"Hunters and demons, and the one behind him is fae. Which type, I'm uncertain. There are fifty-three hunters, seventeen demons, three witches, and one fae within pack territory. Five hunters are looking at the wolves across from us, wondering which will shift and cause a problem, allowing them to be killed. The answer is simple; none will change because we're not shifters, unlike the wolf standing at their back. The demons are incubuses. The smell of sex rolling off them gives it away. One is something else, but he has no scent other than the darkness that envelopes him in secrets, but he wants it that way. There are over sixty shifters, each wanting to get their itches scratched, and they really don't care how they do it. Three totem wolves and five Lycans are within the wolves, hiding their scent among them. In short, you brought a shit-show to the mountain. Am I missing anyone?" My eyes held Saint's, watching as they narrowed on me in surprise. "I may have grown up in the mountains, but I am not stupid in the ways of shit that can kill us."

"I think you covered it very well, Braelyn," Enzo said, tilting his dark head and smiling at me as if he knew something I didn't.

A bottle was put in front of me, and I reached for it, but Saint's hand landed over mine, removing the bottle from my grasp. He poured drinks into the cups on the table and placed one in front of me as he brushed his heated lips against my ear.

"You will not be able to forget tonight, mate," he murmured, sending a shiver racing down my spine.

"A girl can dream, Saint. Sometimes, dreams are all that's left when everything is burned to ash."

"Finish your drink, and we will retire to the mating tent, Braelyn."

"I'd rather swallow razor blades and deal with that aftermath," I muttered, seeing Enzo's smile widen.

"They'd probably be gentler than I plan to be with you tonight," he continued, sending a blush rushing to my cheeks. "Drink so that I can fuck you."

I tipped my glass back, finishing it, then wiping my mouth with the back of my hand. Someone said something to Saint, forcing him to turn toward the voice. My eyes slid up, which normally didn't happen at my height. I stared into Nordic-blue eyes that slid over me before shifting back to Saint.

"Blessings and may the gods be kind and fill your womb tonight, Braelyn Haralson. It is rare to find your true soul mate, and I am curious. Why did you reject him?" the male asked. He wasn't just any male—he was Lycan. A savage breed, they were.

"I was a young girl, trying to protect Saint from my father. He gave me two impossible choices. I chose badly, apparently."

"You may find happiness yet, brother."

"Braelyn, you know of Leif Knight, right?" Saint asked, watching the blood drain from my face. "Don't worry. He isn't here to murder your pack. He came with me."

"Velsignet er ulven og hans blodlinje, kong Leif."

"She speaks Norwegian," Leif stated, bowing his head. "Blessed is the bride of the wolf who carries his bloodline within her womb, Princess."

"I'm not actually a princess. They just enjoy calling me that to taunt me."

"Your mother was a princess, and a very beautiful one at that," Leif returned softly.

"This world holds no titles, and neither do we anymore," I whispered, moving away from them to hide the shame of being blackballed wolves. Leif's family had hunted mine down, driving us out of Norway. It was how we'd ended up here.

"That was rude, Brat."

"You brought enemies to our doors, and you want to speak about being rude? You realize Leif hunted my family down and murdered most of them, right? Simply because he was a Lycan, and we weren't."

"You will respect my guests, Braelyn. You've lived a sheltered, privileged life here. That group consists of survivors who make it their business to hunt down monsters. The only reason you're not on their kill list is that I promised to tame you and make you pay for your trespasses against all creatures."

"And pray tell, how have I trespassed against these creatures?" I demanded, pausing just outside the tent.

Saint's eyes burned with anger as drunken women grabbed me, whisking me into the tent. I yelped, surprised, as they began stripping me. Tora's eyes met mine as she pretended to be drunk, plopping whiskey down beside the furs they had forced me onto after being stripped naked. This shit tradition really needed never to be used, ever again.

"Are you okay?" Tora whispered, her eyes lifted to the front of the tent where Saint had entered with his men, all of them staring at us.

"I'm fine. Everything is fine. I'll be okay," I promised, uncertain if I was telling the truth.

"She'll be fine, Toralei. She's my mate, not yours. Get out and stand guard with the others who will protect us for the duration of the night," Saint hissed. My best friend and the worst beta ever because, like me, she wasn't actually a beta at all, slipped through the flap to do as Saint instructed.

Saint's eyes slid over my marked shoulder and then lowered to where I clenched the furs to my naked chest. His crew didn't help him shed his clothes, but they didn't leave right away either. Instead, they all stood inside the tent, crowding it while I sat awkwardly watching them.

"Make her scream for us, yeah?" Eryx snorted, patting Saint on the back.

"She'll scream for me," Saint promised, holding my gaze locked to his.

The men chuckled, exiting the tent, leaving me alone to face Saint. He pushed down his pants, exposing his cock to my heated gaze. I turned away from the sight of him as nervousness plagued my mind. He was hugely endowed, and that shit wasn't fitting into any tight spaces without an intense amount of pain.

He tugged at the furs, causing my wide eyes to swing back to where he stood, studying me. My grip tightened as a soft smile played on his mouth. His attention slid to my white-knuckled grip and narrowed before he exhaled, walking to the side of the fur pallet, crudely made for our mating. Blood rushed to my cheeks as I closed my eyes against the sleek build of his body. I could survive this, right? No matter how brutal he intended to be, I would survive this, too. I had to. My pack counted on me for their survival. I could handle one dick because, well, there wasn't any other choice.

Chapter Six

Saint sat beside me, his leg brushing against mine, sending a flurry of butterflies erupting into flight inside my belly. His hand lowered, and once more, he tugged on the blankets before expelling air from his lungs. He didn't rip them out of my hands, choosing to lean over me to retrieve the cup and wine.

He poured the wine into the pewter goblet as my body trembled, knowing that I wasn't escaping tonight. It wasn't that I feared sex with Saint; it was that he'd discover the truth and turn something that should be beautiful, ugly.

He offered me the wine, and I reached to grab the cup as he pulled the covers away from my body, smiling in victory. My lips touched the goblet, and his eyes slid down my naked body with a hunger that consumed my thoughts.

I'd wanted him, and this. He'd been the only lover I'd ever wanted. When I'd denied him as my true soul mate to save him, I'd settled into a life of subpar reality. Sipping the wine, I licked my lips before offering him my cup.

It was tradition to drink the vile-tasting bitter wine that lacked the kick of whiskey. Saint took a small sip, turning up his lips at the taste before offering it back to me. Shaking my head, I slowly lay back, uncertain of how to start the entire catastrophe happening.

Saint slid his hand down my belly, and I swallowed the moan that rolled to my tongue. Lowering his heated mouth, he licked my nipple before nipping at it with his teeth. Heat curled in my belly, with how his fingers trailed over my stomach, drawing the runes for fertility. I understood why he did it, considering he was here to destroy me, and he promised to breed me for his heirs.

Saint shifted, causing me to tense, forcing his eyes to lift to mine. Something passed over his face briefly, but before I could figure out what it was, it had vanished behind the mask he wore.

"You're skittish, Brat. Afraid I'm going to hurt you?" he asked, his eyes holding mine prisoner.

"Yes," I replied honestly, watching as he pushed my knees apart.

He laughed, choosing to leave me guessing about his intentions. His mouth lowered to my sex, and my knees dropped open, exposing myself to him. I inhaled deeply in anticipation before his lips turned, kissing the inside of my thigh, repeating the action on the other. He growled, staring at my apex while a whimper rushed from my lungs.

When his tongue found my clit, I hissed as pleasure

rolled through me. I lifted my hands, grabbing his hair to hold his heated breath where it was. He curled his arms beneath my thighs, forcing my spine to arch as he slid his tongue through the arousal of my core. A small cry of pleasure escaped my throat as my hands dug into his soft hair.

Saint laughed against my sex, lapping at it hungrily, watching me rock against his heated kiss. A ball of need grew within my belly, but a moment before it would have unleashed, Saint lifted his head, studying my face. He climbed up my body, slowly dragging his fingers through my sex.

"I'll worry about foreplay later," he grunted, something dark passing over his face.

I didn't speak because what the hell would I even say to that? Settling between my thighs, I gasped as he pushed his thick cock against my opening. Panic shot through me, and his eyes narrowed on my pinched features. He snorted, thrusting into my body. A scream ripped from my lungs, and he went still, pushing his arms up to stare down at me.

"What the fuck, Braelyn?" he growled.

I looked away from him as his men turned, inhaling the unmistakable scent. Virgin blood smelled different from regular blood, which was once considered a prize given to only a true soul mate.

"I told you that you were going to feel like an asshole," I whispered, fighting against the pain of his entrance and the uncomfortable sensation it created.

It burned and ached as my body clenched, trying to dispel him from within me. I rocked my hips, unwilling to meet his damning stare. Saint lowered his body, and he turned my head, forcing me to look at him.

"I saw fucking pictures," he hissed, uncaring that his men were listening.

"I'm sure you did, thinking the worst of me without ever speaking to me about it or hearing my side." I peered into his eyes challengingly. He snorted, leaning back to look at where we joined.

There was no pleasure, only pain as Saint slowly withdrew to the tip. He hissed and swore violently, rubbing his hand over his face as he took in the blood covering his cock. I could smell it, which meant everyone around us could as well. Slowly, he pushed back inside of me, and this time there was less of an ache, but it wasn't comfortable either.

Sex wasn't sexy like the novels promised. It fucking hurt. Saint was entirely too large to be pleasurable. His thumb slid to my clit, rubbing small circles over it, his eyes never leaving mine. His deep chuckle made tears prick my eyes as shame tightened my chest. I sucked my lip between my teeth, pinching it as he exhaled, leaning over to enter my body fully.

"There's no way to make this painless. You're way too fucking tight, which will limit the amount of pleasure you feel. Brae, fucking look at me," Saint hissed, cupping my cheek. "Jesus fuck," he swore when tears slid from my eyes, trickling down my cheeks.

He flipped us, and I gasped, crying out as I stared down at him, impaled on his cock! I lifted, trying to escape him, but his hands captured my hips, using them to guide me. He examined my expression as I lowered my hands to his chest, needing to flee the pain.

"Touch yourself," he instructed. "Let me control your body, and you touch your pussy. Make it sing for me, Braelyn."

"It can't sing because it fucking aches," I snapped, frustrated that everything hurt. Smirking, Saint lifted his head to clasp my nipple between his teeth. His tongue rolled over the hardened peak, and I gasped.

I could hear his men breathing outside the tent and knew they craved what was happening inside. It wasn't helping the mood. My body was tense and locked tightly around his. Saint sat up, releasing his scent, and I shivered from the intensity of it. His mouth crushed against mine, and he went even deeper into my core, causing me to gasp and cry out as he swallowed the noises.

I wrapped my hands around his shoulders for balance, slowly rocking against him to adjust to his size and ease the growing tension. It felt like he was tearing me apart from within, and a coil was unfurling. I relaxed my body, chasing the taste of pleasure as he devoured me. Saint started moving his hips once I'd settled, kissing me deeper, devouring my mouth like he was starving for oxygen, and I was his supply. He cupped my breast, moving his thumb over my nipple as he released my mouth to kiss my throat.

I dropped my head back, giving him more access as I began sliding my body faster on his cock. My legs wrapped around his waist, and he pulled back, watching me ride him methodically. The heat in my belly was rolling toward my apex, growing hotter while I continually moved against him. I dug my nails into his flesh as my orgasm slowly unleashed.

I cried out, opening my eyes to lock with Saint's, and everything collided into a violent storm. Light filled my vision, blotching it with small, dark dots as he took control. He used my hips to grind me against him, thrusting harder. I whispered his name, lost in the pleasure he was giving me. The moment the orgasm began to fade, Saint shoved me onto the soft furs, pushing into my body, and I arched, allowing him further access.

Saint's chest was covered in sweat, even though our breath was sending soft clouds of steam into the air from the chill of autumn. He increased his speed, staring into my eyes with an intense look of possessiveness. Grunting, he exhaled, gazing down at me, and a soft smile played on his mouth before he moved to the side, pulling me against him.

"If I had known you were a virgin, I'd have spent a lot more time preparing your body for me," he admitted.

"If I had told you I was, you wouldn't have believed it," I whispered.

Resting my head on the crook of his arm, I closed my eyes as exhaustion took hold. The day had started like crap and then hit shit-show status when entirely too much big dick energy showed up. Saint adjusted me, placing my head against his chest, forcing my heart to sync with his. My eyelashes fluttered against my cheeks, and heaviness filled my mind.

I could feel the mating link settling in, the need to be close to him. It left us lost within ourselves; our bodies flush against one another while his crew was outside, protecting us. Once the link started, it was like a drug that forced you together, and yet I had no sudden urge to climb back on his cock, because fuck, that thing hurt.

Chapter Seven

Groaning loudly, I burrowed deeper into the heated body beside me. Lifting my head, I stared into blue-green eyes that smiled at me as I slowly woke up. I pulled away from Saint, but he pounced, landing on top of me as his hand covered my mouth. Lowering his lips against my ear, he rumbled low in a raspy voice.

"Don't make a sound, Brat," he growled, pushing into my body.

I trembled around him, groaning at the ache he'd left between my thighs. My body screamed at his abrupt entrance, which was already sore and achy from the three times he'd taken me throughout the night. I lifted my spine and wrapped my legs around his waist to adjust to his size. He growled, creating more arousal to ease his slow thrust as he studied me.

His scent was heady, causing my stomach to clench as he methodically worked my body toward the precipice of release. Saint smiled, lowering his mouth against my ear as he grunted, rocking into my body's welcoming heat.

"If you make any noise, I will turn you over and fuck you until the entire pack knows exactly how you sound finding your pleasure, Princess," he warned, removing his hand from my mouth to place it against the fur-covered ground.

Saint thrust his body faster as I buried my lips into his throat, kissing it while he worked his shaft deeper into my sex. I parted my lips, kissing his shoulder, and my teeth started to descend, preparing to mark him. Sensing what I was about to do, he lifted his hand and slammed my face into the pillow, holding it down. His thrusts turned angry, slamming into my body without care for the pain he created.

Tears burned my eyes as his denial of my claim shot through me. His grunts sounded against my ear as I bit my lip to keep the moans and cries buried in my throat. When Saint shoved my face down as he continued pushing it into the pillow, he dispelled any illusions of this mating being anything other than him marking his claim by scent. His body jerked as a loud grunt echoed in my ear, hot fluid slipping from my body as he withdrew and rolled away from me.

"Get dressed, Braelyn. I'm finished with your cunt for today," he snorted, uncaring that I hadn't finished with him.

I retrieved the panties and dress I'd worn last night. I didn't wait for permission to slip out of the tent, ignoring his order as I emerged. People were already moving around the courtyard. Some appeared still to be drunk and celebrating, while others slept out in the open, near where Saint and I had mated. Had they heard my cries throughout the night? Had they heard him being cruel this morning?

"Braelyn," Saint snapped from behind me, his voice cold and unfeeling while I continued to ignore him.

My hair was a mess, and I needed a hot, steaming shower to remove him from my core where he was dripping down my thigh. People stopped to watch as he dug his fingers into my shoulder, spinning me around to face him.

"I didn't give you permission to leave the tent," he barked angrily.

I snorted, shaking my head. "I didn't ask."

"From now on, you will ask for my approval to do anything. You're a prisoner, and you have no rights."

His men were gathering around us, blocking our argument from the pack that was watching. My chest rose and fell, breathing through anger as my body ached. My sex was swollen and covered in the multiple releases he'd taken through the night. Not to mention, I could smell the blood from our first mating still crusted against my sex.

"I'm going to go wash you and your obnoxious scent from my vagina. I don't need your fucking permission to shower, Saint. If I don't wash away the scent of my blood, it will empower other males to take me for a chance to mate. Unless, of course, you want to watch them rape me. I guess that would be something that you'd enjoy, correct?" I challenged, watching the anger burn in his translucent cyan-colored eyes.

"Eryx, go with my mate and don't let her out of your sight. Not even when she showers," Saint grinned with amusement.

"Come, Eryx. Maybe you can get me off since Saint didn't have what it took to make it happen this morning. After all, I am a whore. Right? Don't let my pesky virginity fool you. I fucked anything and anyone willing. Isn't that the story they fed you?" I laughed soundlessly at the way Saint's eyes narrowed on my mouth.

"Just because they hadn't fucked your cunt doesn't mean you didn't allow other things to happen," Saint returned, cruelly. "You're dismissed, Princess."

I smiled coldly, laughing inwardly while walking to the hallway that led to the living quarters. Saint was acting cold and indifferent. Well, I could play that game, too. I didn't even acknowledge Eryx as I entered my room, going into the closet to grab clean clothes.

Inside the bathroom, Eryx leaned against the counter as I tossed the clothes beside him. Stripping down to my skin, I heard him growling low in his throat before I stepped into the shower, ignoring his existence.

Resting my head against the tiled wall, I groaned as every ache and pain in my body made itself known. Eryx's scent drifted into the shower, the steam making it thicker with his foreboding presence. Dismissing it and doing my best to ignore how potent it was, I grabbed the peony-scented shampoo, lathering it into my hair before rinsing it. I followed up with conditioner, using soap to remove Saint's scent as best I could before slipping from the shower.

Eryx's midnight stare slid down my body with something terrifying burning in his gaze. I reached for the towel, only for him to grab it before I could touch it. My eyes rounded as he crept closer, boxing my body against the wall.

A tremor of unease moved through me, sending every instinct I had on high-alert. Eryx's nostrils flared as he lowered his lips to my throat, placing a soft kiss against my thundering pulse. His hand moved, skimming his fingers over the curve of my hipbone. Deep, wicked laughter escaped him before he lifted his mouth to press it against mine. I turned away, keeping my lips at a distance from his.

"Come on, give me some sugar, Brae. You and I could have ended up together if you'd stopped running away from me ten years ago," he urged, but there was a catch in his voice.

"You and I have nothing in common, let alone a connection."

"You have a pussy, and I have a cock. What other connection do we need?" he mused, stepping back to drag his heady stare down my body.

"If you think that is all that is needed to breed with a mate, you're fucked, Eryx."

"No one said shit about breeding. Sometimes it isn't about connecting, Princess. It's about unleashing anger on your partner. You'd enjoy being manhandled and fucked so hard that you'd forget your name by the time I released you. Do you want that? That leg-shaking, bone-breaking, soul-crushing sex that destroys you until you're nothing but a single orgasm that doesn't stop until I'm finished fucking you?" Eryx leaned back against the counter, smiling with sexual carnage, leaving me curious as to what he meant.

Eryx was trying to fuck with me, and I'd had enough shit happen in the last twenty-four hours. I slowly stepped forward, mirroring his pose by placing my hands on either side of the counter behind him. Lowering my lips to his pulse, I nipped at it before letting a sultry growl escape my chest. I lifted my hands, turning his mouth toward mine until we shared breath.

"Fuck, the fucking hell off, Eryx. If I'd wanted to fuck you, you'd have been fucked. I fell in love with Saint. It went beyond a basic we have matching parts connection. You're trying to scare me or get me to react, and the thing is, fuck you." I grabbed my clothes, exiting the room to find Saint leaning against the wall, glaring at me. "And fuck you, too," I snorted, going into my closet to change.

I shimmied into panties, pants, and a white tank top. Grabbing a flannel, I took it with me into the bathroom. Once inside, I tried to close the door, but Saint pushed his way into my space. He immediately started stripping, giving me a view of where his name, Kingsley, was tattooed over his shoulders, with skulls and black ink dominating his skin.

Ignoring him, I grabbed the brush and started two braids on either side of my head, then a larger one on the top. It was a Viking style worn by the Fenrir wolves and one I'd just begun using. It was an easy style to maintain since we spent most of our time doing chores, preparing to be stuck on top of the mountain until spring came, and the roads were passable.

Steam billowed from the shower, and I smirked wickedly. Eryx was leaning against the doorframe as I reached over, turning on the water in the sink. Opening the drawer, I withdrew my toothbrush and paste and began slowly brushing my teeth as Saint screamed from the shower, stepping out of it a shade redder than when he'd entered.

His eyes held mine before moving to my mouth, where the frothy paste was covering my lips. I cleaned my tongue, turning to look at him with a lifted eyebrow.

"Problem?" I asked, muffled by the paste and brush between my lips.

"You're pushing me," he warned.

"What are you going to do to me? Fuck me crudely and treat me like a whore? Oh, wait, you just did that. Spank me? You might not get the result you want. I might be into that shit, Saint." Grinning, I pointed to his head with my toothbrush, "You have soap in your hair. You will need to get your own. Unless, of course, you don't mind smelling like me all day long." I deadpanned him so hard he felt it. "The shampoo is enhanced with my scent and nullifying herbs that make my heat-cycle remain hidden and muted to the males. I'm uncertain if it works for someone with a cock instead of a vagina. Let me know if it does so I can market it for unisex production."

Turning around, I spit out the paste before grabbing the mouthwash and swishing it while I held his angry glare in the mirror.

"Oh, do you mind that I am brushing my teeth

without permission? I forgot to ask if that was allowed. Should I ask permission before I piss, too? You're going to need to write down the rules, as I have always been shit at following them. It tends to make my pussy wet when I disobey the rules and indulge in being a rebel. You remember, don't you? When you told me I couldn't touch myself, and I did it anyway, making you listen as I came for you? Oh, that's right. You didn't mind it at all."

His eyes sparkled at my words as if he was enjoying my mouth running. He didn't get back into the shower where the scalding water still ran. He just stood there, letting the bathroom filled with steam, which did nothing to hide the fact that he was stark ass naked.

"I'm leaving to do chores," I announced, exiting the room before he could cage me in against the counter or make my brain turn to a sediment one stage less than mush.

"What the fuck do you think you're doing?" he demanded.

"I'm going to do princess duties," I snorted, sliding on my flannel as his attention lowered to my hard nipples straining against the tank top that exposed my midriff.

"You're not to leave this room."

I began tapping my foot while I glared at him. "I'm sorry, what? Because it sounded like you just tried to ground me to this room. I have shit to get done today. Just because you come in swinging that big dick energy with your crew doesn't change the season. If things don't get done around here, we will freeze and starve to death when the mountain becomes unpassable."

"I'll handle it. It's not like the pack needs some bossy little alpha bitch telling them what to do," Saint snapped, forcing my anger to rise.

"Is that so? And tell me, Saint, what do you think needs to be done to prepare this pack for winter?" I challenged as the tic in his jaw hammered at the taunt. "You wouldn't know what is needed because you haven't been back here in ten years. This is my pack, even if you're the alpha now. So, I'm going to make sure shit is handled properly, and you can swing your dick around all you fucking want. It still doesn't change facts, and facts don't lie. Have a good day doing whatever it is you plan to do. After the meal, I'll be back here to play a good little bitch and do what you need of me inside the bedroom. Outside of this room, though, keep the fuck away from me."

I spun on my heel, escaping the bedroom before Saint could get a word in or stop me. My home and territory were crawling with unfamiliar faces. It only catapulted my anger once I reached the main hall, finding strangers lounging everywhere, with trash scattered. I didn't pause, not even when Xariana and her father thought to approach me. My eyes slid over Leif's powerful physique as his gaze glided over my braids. Exiting the lodge, I flagged down Lucas, a member of my pack, nodding toward the side of the building.

"Get the pack over here. We have shit to get done before winter comes," I mused, watching his eyes slid over my body.

"Are you okay?" he asked, then grinned at the wicked smile that played over my lips.

"No, but there's a woodpile screaming my name, and I have an ax to grind on it. That should relieve the anger and stress that Saint's sudden appearance has caused me."

Lucas chuckled, pushing his fingers between his lips before an ear-piercing whistle cut through the air. I didn't wait to see if my pack responded because I fully intended to do what I'd said by taking my anger out on the woodpile.

Chapter Eight

Sweat beaded on my brow, and my arms burned as I brought the ax down hard onto the round log. The pile in front of me was higher than I could see over, while the men beside me continued complaining that I was putting them to shame. I'd done this every day since my father had banished Saint. Splitting wood seemed to relieve pain, stress, and anger all in one satisfying loud bang as the ax bit into the log, sending it over the edge of the stump I used as a chopping block.

We'd been at it for hours while the children and betas emptied the piles. They stacked the wood in large sheds used to keep it from exposure to the elements. All around us, people worked. Hunting parties brought in deer to gut and clean, hanging it to be butchered into small enough pieces to fit into the walk-in freezer where perishables were stored.

I watched as Lucas laughed with Garrett, both men covered in blood as they carried a deer into the courtyard on poles that rested on their shoulders. Women picked the last of the vegetables to store in the underground cellars, and the children assisted the omegas, preparing material to be cut and used for blankets and clothing.

Lifting my ax, I started to swing, only for someone to grab it. Turning, I found Saint sliding his eyes down my dirty frame. My brow rose in a silent question as he wrenched the ax from my calloused hands.

"Get your own ax, Saint," I growled, noting the way he glared at me through heated eyes. He stepped closer, forcing me to back up and notice that his men, Leif, and the other uninvited guests all sat behind us, observing the pack work.

Assholes.

Saint removed his shirt, allowing my gaze to slide down his muscular torso. Rolling my eyes at falling into his stupid male trap, I looked back over the pack at the children moving about. The ax slammed against the wood, sending it crashing into my thigh. I gasped, stepping back to glare at Saint as if he'd done it on purpose.

"Try aiming for the middle, so you don't hit everyone else with the wood," I growled, stepping away from him, heading toward the semi-truck pulling into the area to unload goods.

Away from the woodpile, I looked back as the others converged around Saint. His men slowly relieved the others, who, of course, began packing the wood into the shed with the betas and kids. My hungry gaze locked onto Eryx and Enzo, who were both anything but woodcutters.

Enzo slipped his shirt off, smiling at me as he tilted his head, lifting his brow. It was almost like he read my mind because the look in his eyes was most definitely a challenge. His sides held tattoos in dark ink that drifted down into his suit pants. The muscles on his abdomen bunched together as his thick arms lifted the ax, sending it smashing into the log, effortlessly slicing through it. He didn't cut the next piece immediately, choosing to crook his finger at me, and a frown tugged on my lips. I spun on my heel, ignoring Leif, who was also shirtless, wearing jeans that allowed the deep, chiseled V-line to show.

Tattoos and men. Sex and sin. Fucking great. It was everything we didn't need here. I'd been fine without them!

My attention slid toward laughter, finding Zayne in his suspenders, with his sleeves rolled to his elbow, smashing his ax through the wood. His bright eyes lifted, meeting mine as a smile played on his full mouth. He turned his head, and my gaze swung to Sian, who was also shirtless and had at least washed the blood off of himself. Eryx had rolled up his sleeves, leaving his olive-colored forearms exposed, showing off his colorful tattoos.

Tearing my eyes from the men, I noticed the truck was backing up entirely too fast to stop. A toddler was standing behind it, her wide, blue eyes following an orange butterfly in front of her. I glanced back at the truck, and a scream ripped from my lungs as I took off. Clearing the space between us, I tossed the toddler out of the truck's path, leaving myself in harm's way.

The truck smashed into my head, and I reached for the tailgate, pulling myself up just as Lucas got the driver's attention, screaming over the music playing from inside the truck. The startled driver slammed on the breaks, and I dropped to the ground, grabbing my forehead where blood was dripping down my face. Rounding the back of the truck, I ran to the driver's door, opening it to rip him out of the vehicle.

"What the fuck?" he demanded, growling at me with his fangs exposed. "Stupid bitch, I'm the only motherfucker willing to make the drive up this mountain!" he snarled, sending anger rolling through me.

"You almost ran over a child!" I shot back, and he lifted his shoulders, dropping them in a shrug.

"One less fucking mouth to worry about feeding then, bitch," he snorted.

I jumped without warning, hooking my feet beneath his armpits and my hands around his waist. Using the momentum, I flipped him into the air, grabbing the back of his head as he fell toward the ground, slamming his face into the dirt. Hard. Bone crunched, and I walked around his large frame, oblivious to the crowd watching.

The truck driver, a shifter, came up quickly, forcing me to roundhouse kick him in the face and lowering my body to the ground, removing his feet from beneath him. Before he'd hit the dirt, I used a spurt of speed to drive my fist into his face, smiling as I felt his teeth snapping off beneath the gums.

The moment he came back up, I was ready for

him. However, I wasn't prepared for the ax that swung through the air or for the driver's head to go sailing across the courtyard, painting my face in blood. My eyes followed the body to the ground, slowly lifting to hold Saint's angry stare.

"What the fuck did you do that for?" I demanded.

Saint snorted, staring at my forehead where blood still dripped from the gash made by the truck hitting me. "You're my mate, and only I get to talk to you like that, Braelyn."

I huffed as I walked toward the large semi, crawled into the driver's seat, and backed it into the delivery dock. Putting the truck in park, I jumped out and strolled back to the mess Saint had made, whistling loudly.

"James, toss the prick's body into the pen with the hogs. Caiden, grab your bike and an overnight bag."

I lifted the truck's hood and hefted myself onto the front of the truck. Pushing my hand past the scorching engine block, I grabbed the GPS tracker and tossing it to Caiden, who caught it and held it up.

"Ballard is going to notice this shit," he grunted, lowering his hand and folding his arms over his chest.

"He will, which is why you're going to take the tracker and drive your bike to the nearest truck stop in Billings, Montana. By the time Ballard figures out he's missing, the snow will have started. He won't come looking until spring, and by then, this truck will be in a million pieces, and that asshole can eat shit. He won't be able to prove his driver died here. Drive twenty miles an hour down the mountain and slower on the corners. Don't go over sixty and slow your ass down on the passes like an 18-wheeler would drive with an empty trailer. When you get to the truck stop, find a truck with out-of-state plates and plant the tracker somewhere on its trailer. Get this bitch unloaded and then get her buried on the side of the mountain until spring. Move, we're wasting daylight," I growled, lifting my hand to signal the truck carrying the herbs from the field to back up.

Once the truck was in place, I went to the shed to retrieve my gloves before heading back to unload the cargo. Saint watched me silently, as if he was waiting for me to thank him for interfering. He'd only created more work for everyone by murdering the one crazy son-of-a-bitch who would drive up the mountain to deliver the canned foods.

Jumping onto the trailer, I grabbed a bale of wet herbs and tossed it onto the ground, immediately getting back to work. If I were lucky, I'd be so exhausted tonight and stink from sweat that Saint would seek rest elsewhere. Or maybe he already intended to do that? He'd claimed rights to me with his bite while leaving himself free of mine.

That had stung, and it made my wolf furious that he'd rejected her mark. Not that either of us should care, but if I were honest, it did sting. He was the perfect male for me, picked by the wolf god, Fenrir, and Saint had rejected me.

Lucas jumped onto the trailer, grabbing my shoulder when Larson stepped up, checking my forehead. He smiled, knowing I was going to send his ass away. I'd heal quickly enough and didn't need him to fuck with my wound.

"That's a nasty gash," Larson complained, holding up the suture kit. "Let me fix it, Brae."

I stepped back, tilting my head as a soft smile played on my lips. He growled loudly, producing the stapler, which I yanked from his hand and slammed against the wound four times before handing it back. Larson groaned, staring at the fresh blood caused by the staples. I felt eyes on me, turning to look at Saint, who stared at us. His arms were crossed over his chest, and he pursed his lips.

Lucas handed me a water bottle, which I used to wash off the blood before handing it back, and started working again. The trailer bounced, and I peered over my shoulder as I lifted a bale. Holding it up, I waited for Saint to move aside. Instead, he stood there, looking at the wound then stepping out of the way so I could throw it to the men waiting to take it to the shed for storage.

"You could have been hurt worse than you were, Brat," Saint grumbled, lifting a bale to toss to the ground.

"The child could have been killed, and I would have only been wounded. One of those things is permanent, and the other isn't. It was an easy choice to make. Now, either throw the bales over the side or get out of the way. We have five more trucks coming in today. More deer are expected, which need processing, and the hay for the horses has to be stocked, so pick a chore."

Saint smirked, grabbing two bales and tossing them

over the back of the trailer. "Your shirt is wet, and I can see your nipples, Braelyn."

"Then stop looking," I replied icily.

We worked side-by-side until country music started playing from inside the courtyard. Colt Ford's Workin' On echoed through the speakers, and I was guessing it wasn't something Saint and his men jammed out to very often. I sang along with those around me, continuing to work until sweat trickled into the gash on my forehead. The music changed, and a rendition of My Mother Told Me started, and the entire courtyard paused, singing the song loudly as the children danced around.

A smile played on my lips as I noticed Saint peering at the men, women, and children who belted the song. So we'd watched Vikings a lot, but up here, it was Blu-Rays and recorded shit through the winter, and we didn't bother staying inside any more than necessary during spring and summer.

Saint's eyes met mine, then narrowed before dipping to my lips. Memories of our summer spent working together and escaping to find somewhere to make out filled my mind. He shook his head, and I shoved the memories to the back of my mind, into the box where I kept them, refusing to let them back out.

Once the truck was empty, I jumped down, removing the gloves to accept a bottle of water as You are the Reason started, sung by Calum Scott and Leona Lewis. My stomach clenched, and my eyes slid to the stereo where Toralei stood, her arms folded over her chest. I wanted to strangle her, knowing it was my song for Saint. That song and Unsteady by X Ambassadors made me need him close, and now that he was here, I wanted him to leave before he ruined every part of me that still loved him.

Exhaling, I stared up at the sun to determine the time, then lowered my eyes to assist the oversized trailer into the yard. By the time we finished working, it was time to go to the kitchen to help the staff prepare food for the extra people Saint had brought with him.

"Where the hell are you off to?" he asked. I spun on my heel and narrowed my gaze on his muscular frame.

"I help the kitchen staff after assisting the outside workers. I normally work from dawn to sundown and then fall into bed stinking like a stuck pig, three days after being hung up to dry for the smoker."

"Not today, Brat," Saint snorted, dragging his eyes over my dirty attire. "Tonight, you eat beside me. Go freshen up. There are things you and I need to discuss."

I swallowed hard, glaring at him before I swung my attention to where the kitchen staff waited. Clearing my throat, I explained what was happening while Saint and his men waited behind me, listening. At their groans and cross looks at Saint, I assured them that even if they served the pigs who had invaded slop, I'd still love them.

We approached the hall, and Saint grabbed my arm, staring at me. "You do this shit every day?" At my confused look and sharp nod, he snorted. "You cut wood and throw bales of hay and herbs, all day, every day?"

"No, just when they arrive. Tomorrow we'll be getting the second shipments and fixing the outcrop buildings. The day after that, we'll be building an add-on for the people who come up the mountain before the freeze starts. Some live below in sparse buildings that won't protect them against the cold. And after that, we'll continue doing whatever the hell needs to be done to feed the pack and protect them from the elements until the snow thaws." I wrenched my arm out of his hold, walking away while he stared after me.

"That there is a Viking woman, Saint. If you don't want her, I sure the hell do," Leif snorted. "It's a rare breed that will work from dawn until sundown, protecting her people. Fenrir blessed you, even if you can't see it, daft bastard."

"She rejected me and banished my crew, allowing her father to torture us. She may be the most gorgeous creature I've ever seen or wanted, but she's as cold-hearted and evil as her father." I swallowed, overhearing Saint's words, frowning as I replayed what he'd said. I didn't slow down or even acknowledge the men as I entered my room, flinging off my clothes before jumping into the shower and pulling out the staples from the healed skin with my claws.

I hated the new Saint while still craving the old one that whispered into my ear, brushing his knuckles against mine in the courtyard when no one was watching. He had been the one thing driving me to keep moving forward, and now that he was back, he was screwing up everything.

I leaned back against the shower stall and closed my eyes. His scent hit me, and I opened my eyes, jumping as I found him leaning over me, staring down at my naked body.

"We're moving to a larger room tomorrow. Yours is too small, and we need a larger bathroom."

"I like my room. You can move," I muttered, staring at his mouth.

Saint's lips tipped into a wolfish smile as he turned, grabbing my shampoo and pouring entirely too much into his palm. Still, I didn't complain or rail against him using it while my eyes slid down his sinewy body, noting he was hard and ready to go. He turned to face me, his mouth opening to expose his canines.

"You'll be handling that problem soon enough. Wash the dirt off your body. We have more guests showing up."

"You can use your hand for whatever pleasure you had planned for yourself. How are these new guests getting here?" I asked, wondering how they could sneak up the mountain without setting off any of the alarms.

"I won't need my hand. I'll use you, and the other matter is none of your fucking business, Brat. Wash up. I don't want my guests meeting the mother of my children in filth from her working all day."

My heart clenched at his words and got stuck on the mother of my children. I glared at Saint, hating him more for calling me that. He knew I wanted babies, and I had a feeling he intended to change his mind on that, too.

Chapter Nine

Saint

I sat in a chair in Braelyn's room, waiting for her to leave the shower. Memories of our time together played through my mind, craving to go back to those moments. The problem was, we couldn't ever go back to how it was prior to my being banished. I wasn't the same person I'd been when she'd thrown me to the pack. She hadn't given me mercy, and I couldn't offer her any now, even if I wanted to.

Braelyn had rejected me in the worst possible way a mate could. I'd bared my soul to her, showing her everything I was, promising her the world. It hadn't been enough for the pampered little bitch. Yet, I still craved her. I wanted to believe that she hadn't been a part of what I'd endured, that she didn't know about the evil her father had planned for me, but there were hints that made me believe Braelyn had known, and she had still banished me.

Eryx had shared in my fate, having been sold to the same unfeeling, murderous bitch that had purchased me. Together, we'd been ripped apart and sewn up afterward. Harold sold his people, members of other packs, and humans into slavery to be endlessly tortured or murdered on camera as entertainment for the cruel and evil creatures living amongst us. You didn't escape that type of thing unscathed. Death was always the end goal.

An entire year of endless torment and pain had passed before Leif and the Gemini twins, Enzo and Ezekiel, had found our location and freed us. They'd given us an option: heal and hunt down other sites used to torture immortals and humans or return to our pack. The choice had been easy.

Eryx and I bonded with them, meeting hunters and others who all shared one cause—end the trafficking of anyone unfortunate enough to be sold on the black market. Our first focus was to find the rest of my crew that had been banished with me, bringing them out of their endless torment one by one. When we'd finally been reunited, we aimed our sights at coming here and bringing down the head of the operation.

I had warned everyone that Braelyn was my true soul mate, even if she'd rejected me. I didn't necessarily want to hurt her, but I did want to break her down to bare-bones and see if she was worth saving. If I discovered that she'd been a part of her father's operation, I'd agreed to release her, giving her a chance to run before we hunted her down. This was the fate given to the others who had knowingly helped torture and murder innocent people. None of them escaped our hunt alive.

The problem was that I couldn't prove one way or the other if Braelyn was involved. I wanted to save her, and there was a slim possibility that she hadn't been part of this mess if what Brae said was true, and she thought she was saving me from her father instead of delivering me into his hands. But the Brae I had known would do whatever she'd been told, jumping to fall in line when her father commanded her.

I'd asked her once to leave here with me, to just slip into the sunset and leave this place. She'd scoffed it off, and within days, she'd rejected me and humiliated me in front of the pack. I could still hear her words, filled with hatred and loathing like I was the fucking villain in her story.

"You lied to me. This isn't love or anything to do with mating. It's just lust that you made me feel. I hate you," she'd paused, her entire body trembling while nothing escaped the grip she held on herself. I couldn't smell or sense her emotions over the anxiousness that swelled from me and the pain she was causing. "I never want to see you again."

"Don't do this, Brat. You don't mean what you're saying. You're my fucking air, Braelyn. You are my soul. I can't breathe without you. Come on, Brat, it's me. I let you in so you could see the parts of me that no one else has. Please don't do this to me, to us. I love you. I love you more than I ever thought possible to love another person. Brae, look at me. This is us. This isn't you, because you love me, too. I know you do. I feel you as deeply as you feel me."

"I never want to see you again. You need to leave

and get as far away from here as you can. Do you hear me? Leave and don't come back. I never loved you. I never wanted you. I couldn't love you, ever."

Anger had pulsed through me as her father snorted, watching as his pretty daughter tore out my soul and shredded it while the entire pack watched.

"I will come back here, and when I do, I will destroy you and everything you love. Last chance, Princess. Change your mind."

"I can't ever change it. I have decided. Leave!"

Harold dragged me and the others away from her. He told me to run, to leave before he released the alphas on my friends and me. I thought that was the end until I saw the alphas waiting for us at the bottom of the mountain. Harold never intended for us to escape, and I suspected Braelyn hadn't either. It had been a ruse, one that was orchestrated in advance to make the pack think we'd left in banishment.

Braelyn slipped from the bathroom, her wide, blue eyes slowly meeting mine from across the room. She was the most beautifully crafted woman I'd ever encountered. Her hair was a mess of colors, which might look awkward on other women, but it worked for Brae. Her auburn curls were mixed with caramel strands that hung in sinful waves down her back and over her shoulders. Nordic blue eyes, the color of freshly frozen lakes, watched me, knowing I fully intended to fuck her again.

Her tiny button nose flared, and those pearly white teeth pinched her bottom lip between them. I could scent the arousal of her tight pussy, see the way her eyes widened while peering between me and the closet. She was planning to run from me or to fight.

"Come here." She lowered her head as her eyes slanted into an untrusting glare. "I'm not asking, Braelyn."

She didn't move, her body sliding against the wall toward the closet with her hands gripping the towel. Panic entered her pretty eyes, and I smirked at the scent of fear that filled the room, mixing with arousal. She may hate that I'm her mate, but she craved me as much as I craved her traitorous ass.

"Do you prefer I force you to do everything? I won't ask again. I will make you come to me, either by scent or as your alpha, Brat. Choose how you wish this to play out."

Braelyn pushed off the wall, dragging her pretty feet the entire way until she stood before me. Leaning up, I snatched the towel she was using to shield her body from me. She'd grown up in the ten years I'd been gone. No longer the girl with a hint of the woman she'd become, Braelyn was all sexy curves and ample breasts that begged to be suckled, and I noted the small, caramel-colored patch of hair that covered her sex was neatly manicured.

Braelyn had never been short, not even as a child. She wasn't as a woman either, and I enjoyed I didn't have to crouch to touch or reach her. Lifting my hand, I gripped her hips and sat up further. Moving one foot to the chair, I stared between her legs at her healed sex. Inhaling, I growled at finding my scent gone from her body.

"You washed my scent away, Brat? That wasn't smart," I growled, leaning closer to drag my tongue through her pretty, pink flesh. Her hand landed on my shoulders and tightened as I tasted her arousal.

Finding out that Braelyn was a virgin during our mating ceremony had floored me. It left me stunned after being told repeatedly about all the men that Brae had entertained, using them to get anything her father wanted. She'd whored herself out to the highest bidder, just like she'd planned with Carlson. I'd been told the stories in graphic details a million times because my tormentor had discovered that I could ignore the pain, but I couldn't shut off my reaction to hearing about and imaging my mate being touched by strange men. Had the stories all been a lie, or had they killed the men she'd seduced once her father had gotten his payment? How she'd maintained being untouched in the most basic way, as a highly sexual wolf, was beyond me.

Braelyn's soft moan filled the room, and I chuckled at how responsive her body was to me. She fucking hated that it caved to the baser needs of sex. Braelyn despised she was as defenseless as I was for the shit happening between us. This was the reason I'd pushed her away.

If I let her claim me, I'd go to war to protect her. Shit, chances were I still would. I'd let her see my flaws and the part of me that no one else ever had or would. I'd let her into my heart, deeper than anyone ever had been except my mother, and then she'd ripped it out.

I lifted without warning, grabbing Braelyn's body to move her to the bed. She didn't fight me, but I sensed it was coming. I could smell the alpha within her needing to test me. It was basic fucking wolf genetics. Alpha mates ripped one another down to the most primitive form to see which one would be more dominant in the relationship.

Once Brae was sprawled out on the bed, I let my hungry gaze slide over her form. Fuck, she was the most gorgeous woman I'd ever seen in my life. We'd never gotten to this stage of our mating, and now I was rushing through it. I'd marked her, setting claim to her soul, and she was mine now. That knowledge left me reeling with how to handle her.

"Lift your knees, and touch yourself," I demanded, watching as her forehead creased and a white line marred her mouth. "I wasn't asking."

Braelyn obeyed, but just barely. I doubted anyone other than her father had ever forced the princess to do anything. That sadistic prick had cherished his only child, and it hadn't been in a healthy way, either. He'd been almost obsessed with her, and it had forced us to create our own language to escape his notice.

I watched Brae's clumsy fingers moving to her core, slowly sliding her fingertips through the mess I'd made by simply tasting her. Settling between her thighs, I watched her working them through the folds, and yet she never once touched her clit. Pushing my pants down my hips, I began stroking my cock, which pulsed with the need to be buried in her tight cunt.

Brae lowered her eyes, watching my hand slide along my shaft as her own moved faster, finally working the bundle of nerves that ached for release. Her breathing grew labored as if watching me turned her on. Her hand paused, realizing she'd done what I wanted, and her eyes burned with anger. I knew it was coming, bracing for it as her foot lifted and slammed into my chest, sending my body several feet away from hers.

I steadied myself then smashed into her, pulling her legs apart to glide my cock against her needy pussy. A strangled cry ripped from her throat, and I could smell her need to fight and fuck, marking her as an alpha to her fucking core.

"Come on, Brat. Show me what you got," I laughed, watching as she turned, bucking against my body. "That's it. Come on, Brae. Show me those pretty red eyes."

I craved the battle, the need to slam her down and fuck that fight burning within her out. She knew it too, which was why she fought her wolf and me. A deep, ominous growl rolled from her lungs, and I matched it, knowing my men were outside the door, craving to join us. Every male within a fifty-mile radius would smell her body struggling to be the dominant wolf. They'd all relish the fight, but my scent would prevent them from reacting.

Reaching down, I spread her thighs apart and shoved into the heat of her tight pussy. Her growl exploded into the room, and I didn't need to see her eyes to know they were the color of freshly spilled blood. Instead of fighting me, she slammed her need to the base of my cock, forcing my body to shudder as she clenched hungrily against my cock.

"Fuck," I moaned, watching her fuck me as if I was a war she waged without needing to be told to rise to the battle.

Braelyn fucked like she was wounded, unhinged. Like she was one of us, a tortured soul, so fucking twisted and mutilated that it was already stripped down to bare-bones. I didn't move, didn't need to. She continued slamming against my cock with a violence that shook me to my core. It was ten years of need unraveling within her soul, matching mine. When she slowed, I leaned over her, grabbing her leg to hold it up, going deeper into her body until she whimpered.

Her fingers found my thigh, pushing her nails into my flesh while giving me as good as I was giving her. I increased the speed of my hips as her face dropped to the bed, and she started thrusting back onto my cock again. I had only bitten her once, and she'd allowed me to take her needy cunt like she knew it was mine. I released her leg, moving to her hair as I threaded it through my fingers, wrapping it around my fist before I yanked her back.

Braelyn's eyes rolled back in pleasure, making my balls grow heavy with the need to spill my seed within her achingly tight pussy. I could feel the walls of her channel clamping down on my dick, knowing it ached to be fucked as hard as I was taking her. She didn't complain or beg me to stop. Instead, Braelyn fucking howled, gasping as her entire body tightened and her breathing turned to ragged breaths before she whimpered my name, whispering it against the bedding as I rode her harder. Fucking hell, she'd come from the violence and wasn't even stopping me.

Turning her body over, I pulled out. I leaned over her heaving chest and stared into her pretty, Nordic gaze. Ice-blue eyes held mine captive and widened as I pushed back into her body. Fucking hell, she was exquisite. She lifted her feet, wrapping around my hips as I slowly moved against her pussy. It clenched, tightening with every thrust into her welcoming heat.

I'd expected a fight, but she wasn't fighting me at all. She was submitting, which was confusing and pleasing at the same time. If she didn't want me for a mate, why wasn't she fighting it?

"I fucking hate you, bitch," I hissed.

"I hate you too, asshole," she whimpered, rocking against me.

If she hated me, why was she fucking me as if I mattered? Why did her eyes stare into my soul like she recognized it as a part of her own? Nothing Brae did ever made sense. It was as if she feared letting me see the darker parts of her soul, yet she was taking me like I was hers by right.

"I'm going to fuck you so hard that every time you move tomorrow, you'll feel me fucking this pussy."

"Then do it already because I like you much better when you don't speak." She slammed her ass up, seating my cock so fucking deep into her body that we both gasped, trembling from the pleasure.

I unleashed my anger and pent-up rage on her, slamming her body against the bed and pushing her thighs up to her shoulders. She cried out, gasping as I repeatedly smashed into her pussy until we were both growling and panting with the need to come. Neither of us looked away from the challenge burning in our silent gazes. We knew our wolves were watching their mates find pleasure while asserting dominance. Braelyn exploded, her eyes widening as her lips parted with my name sliding off her tongue. It was all I needed to bury my face against her shoulder, biting into her flesh, sending me over the edge with her.

The taste of her blood was heaven, causing my wolf to howl with his need for her to mark us back. It wasn't fucking happening, but the idea made my balls ache to fuck her again, and I hadn't even finished draining them into her pulsing cunt, still clamping against my cock while sucking it dry.

I collapsed on top of her, fighting to control my breathing as she did the same. Brae's scent hit me, and I shuddered against her warmth, slowly forcing myself to shield my emotions on how she made me feel. Pushing up to my knuckles while boxing her against the mattress, I sneered.

"You're weak. Are you sure you're not a beta? You fuck like one. No alpha pussy here," I announced, watching her features smooth out so as not to reveal how my words made her feel. She shut down like it was a mask she wore, pushing me away from her as she sat up. "Go clean up and make sure you look presentable. I won't have you running around like some mountain bitch when you're to be the womb that carries my children."

Her eyes slid to where I sat on the bed, and before I could guess her move, she'd slammed her foot into my face, sending me across the room. My anger radiated inside the room, but Braelyn didn't react. She just stared at me with her features cooled, and not a whiff of her emotions carried in the air between us. She'd struck hard and fast, and if I hadn't seen it was her, I'd have thought someone else had attacked me. Silently, she watched me get to my feet, and I glared at her as anger pulsated through me.

"Fuck you, asshole. Find someone else to carry your offspring," Braelyn snorted, standing to move into the bathroom. "Wrong bitch, Saint. You can find someone else to use and carry your babes. You've successfully done it before. I won't be that girl—ever, dick," she fumed, and yet there was nothing to alert me to her anger. Wolves scented emotions, but Brae's were—missing.

I stood there, shocked that she'd moved as fast as she had. I'd met three other creatures that could move that fast, and two were standing inside this room. I tilted my head, hearing the sink turn on as she cleaned up, leaving my scent on her sore pussy. She didn't climb back into the shower as most women would, which meant she didn't care who knew she was mine.

"If you ever try to wash my scent off from you again, as you did earlier, I will chain you to the bed and fuck you until I am so deeply embedded into your womb that you won't be able to eradicate my fucking scent. I won't let you leave it until you're dripping me out of your sore, bruised cunt, Brat." Lifting my nose, I waited for the smell of her anger, but all I found was her scent that drove me crazy.

Braelyn's scent had always called to me, even before I'd known we were mates. She smelled of peonies and vanilla orchids, which weren't strong as other women's odors. I'd enjoyed Brae's aroma because there was a sexy undertone that spoke to the woman she would become. Everything about her had been perfectly balanced and gorgeous.

She exited the bathroom, stared me dead in the eye with a smile curving her lips. "You could try, but I doubt you'd get what you want from me in that aspect. Clean up, asshole. I won't have the pack thinking you're some weak-ass city boy who can't handle being alpha to a mountain pack. Put something on that tells them you're not as weak as you fuck."

"I think you like being fucked hard. Don't you?" I challenged, watching her eyes sparkle with amusement. She fucked me with her eyes harder than either of our bodies could ever do. Braelyn looked at me, her pretty mouth curving into a smile that made my balls ache. "Come on, Brat. Admit it. You like being fucked like a dirty girl. You like being bruised and taken hard. Last night when I was gentle, you hated it. Why is that?" I questioned, already knowing the answer. It didn't change me wanting to hear it from her mouth.

"You don't care how I want it, Saint. You like to hurt me, and maybe I've come to accept the fact that I was made to be abused by those who are supposed to love and cherish me. You didn't want it slow and nice, either. You wanted to hear me moan as you fucked me hard and fast. You wanted the entire pack to hear me screaming for you. I'm not an idiot, and I don't need it spelled out for me. If I'd have been quiet, you'd have done whatever it took to make me scream. Plus, I was into it, too. It reminded me that you returned simply to punish me. I know where we stand. I'm just the bitch you want to break, and you're just the man I used to love."

"Love? You don't get to speak to me about love

anymore, Brae. You had mine, and you threw it away."

"I protected you from my demons. You think I lived a posh life being pampered and spoiled. I know what I did was wrong, but I had no other alternative. And don't stand there like you're innocent—careful throwing rocks at glass houses. You may not like what you find." Her eyes held mine briefly before dropping her gaze to the floor. I saw the pain in her aura that made me want to explore it, but I wouldn't.

I had expected her to fight me, but she hadn't. She was an alpha, which I could see in her stare when she didn't lower her gaze from mine. I'd expected her to be weak and easy to break. The old Braelyn was meek and sweet. This one wasn't. Mating between alpha pairs was usually violent, yet she'd barely struggled. Instead, she'd given me back my anger, unleashing her pent-up need on my cock, and she hadn't tried to mark me.

"I think I like your mouth better when it's working my cock," I snorted, watching her tongue jut out to lick around her lips while she held my stare. Fuck if my cock didn't jerk and take notice.

"I bet you do. Too bad I don't really care what you like, Saint. Help me out here. Do I get on my knees like some brainless whore, or do I get dressed? I'm uncertain of what you're expecting of me now. I can get dressed, making sure that I don't look like some uncouth mountain bitch, or I can stand here while you fucking insult me some more, but I can't do both."

I stared at her, trying to keep my mouth from gaping at the balls on this bitch. She wasn't what I had expected her to be, and it left me reeling with how to treat her. I'd hoped to come back to the woman that had banished me. I'd returned to a different woman altogether.

I'd been shocked at her work ethic today. As the daughter of the pack alpha, she didn't have to work. Her pack members had moaned and groaned because it was apparent she did it often. Instead of getting the hint and taking a break when I'd relieved her of the ax, she'd moved to another task without hesitation. She paused only to let her wanton stare slide over the men, then back to me with lust. She'd examined my men with curiosity, but she ogled my body like she wanted to ride it vigorously, and that had turned my dick hard. Hell, watching her do anything made me hard with the need to make up for the time we'd lost.

I'd watched Braelyn with respect burning within me that had pissed me off. The pack had acted like it wasn't a huge deal for the pack alpha's daughter to pitch in and carry her weight. When she'd said she was going to do pampered princess shit, I'd assumed she meant a massage, not manual labor that was shit full-grown men did within the pack. We'd all watched from where we'd exited the lodge as Braelyn worked the ax like she was taking out her aggression and anger on the wood—just like men fucking did.

She'd placed her own life in danger to save a toddler and then fought a shifter without hesitation. It felt like I'd stepped into a dream, watching the woman who'd once been weak and feeble lead the pack by example. Shit, most alphas didn't do that sort of thing.

I'd left here when Braelyn was on the brink of becoming a woman, or at least by wolf standards. She'd seemed small and frail against my body. Yeah, she held herself at arm's length, but she was the alpha's daughter, and there had been a ton of pressure on her. Never in my wildest dreams had I expected to return to a warrior who didn't pass off the most challenging jobs to the men or other members of her pack, choosing to do them herself.

"Tell me about Chaos, and how you found him," I asked, listening to Braelyn rummaging around inside the closet as I pulled on my pants.

I'd spoken to my son, and he'd bragged about having the alpha's protection. I'd felt scorn at thinking Harold had raised my son, but Chaos laughed it off and said Braelyn had raised him. That had sparked a multitude of questions because he acted like she was the pack alpha. I want to know why she had raised my offspring. Chaos told me she'd plucked him from the omegas at a very young age and raised him herself. That wasn't what females did when faced with the offspring of their mate from some other woman. Most mates would have scorned Chaos or denounced him immediately. Braelyn hadn't, though.

According to my son, Brae had raised him in a manner that never made him feel anything less than wanted and loved. She'd told him about me, explaining that I hadn't left by my choice. She'd told him about rejecting our mating and that I'd been banished as a result. Yeah, she'd skipped telling him the part where she sent me off to be tortured, but then again, he was only ten. And, of course, admitting to Chaos that she'd allowed his father to be continuously tormented for the sick entertainment of others wouldn't have gone over well with any child.

"What about him, Saint?" she asked from inside the closet.

I moved toward her, leaning against the door as she bent over, rolling on a sexy-as-fuck stocking and connecting it to her garter. Her panties were plain and black, covering most of her luscious ass, and shouldn't have been as sexy as they were. She turned, looking at me with the same blank look in her eyes as she had the day she sent me away. My eyes slid over her flat stomach, and I squashed the urge to see it swollen with our child. That had to wait until I knew if she was part of what had been happening here.

The idea of Braelyn carrying my child sent warmth rushing through me. We'd often spoken about how many children we'd have, and she told me she'd give me as many as we could have because she'd wanted to carry my children. I could still see Braelyn's sparkling eyes, filled with tears, her pretty lips curling into a blinding smile as she'd whispered her love, promising to protect our babies from monsters.

"Why'd you raise my son, Braelyn?" I asked, somehow managing to hide the emotion those words caused. "What is he like?" I swallowed the urge to smile as her eyes sparkled in amusement.

"He won't talk to you, huh?" A shit-eating grin curved her full lips before she smoothed it out and shrugged. "Chaos is so smart, Saint. He's stubborn as hell and so prideful that he ends up in a ton of fights. He wins, of course, because he is strong, even though he's smaller than the other boys his age. Chaos is wild and adventurous, and nothing scares him. If you asked me, I would say that he took after his father a lot more than his mother." I hung on to her every word, watching her smile beaming at my son and his stubbornness. "I raised Chaos because I couldn't find you. I looked, you know, but the first year you were just gone. It was like you and the boys had all vanished. I had assumed it would be easier to find a crew of wolves out causing mayhem, but you guys must have stayed hidden for a while. Then, I fell in love with him, and even though he doesn't carry my blood, I treated Chaos as if he were my own, and I've loved him just the same." Braelyn turned, giving me her back as I narrowed my stare on her spine.

"It would have been impossible to find us considering what you and your father did to us. You sort of hid us yourself, didn't you?" I snapped, watching her attention shift back to me with her dress held in her hand.

"Excuse me?" Her scent filled the air with fear and something else I couldn't discern. "What did you just say?"

"Is that fear I smell?" I crept closer to her and grabbed the garment from her hand. Holding it up, I looked at the slinky black dress and placed it back onto the hanger, withdrawing the crimson dress instead. "Or guilt?"

"Both," she admitted in a breathy tone, watching me drag my stare over her naked tits, which hardened beneath my gaze.

"Why would you feel guilty?" I helped her into the dress, and she remained still, staring at me as anger rippled from me, unchecked.

"Because I lied in front of the pack," she whispered, dropping her gaze. "Because you are my mate, and we both knew it. The pack knew the truth, Saint. I was trying to protect you from my father."

Her words caused anger and pain to slice through me. Admitting she lied and that she'd still done what she had didn't help soothe my resentment. Her rejection had been the worst day of my life and ended in a year of unimaginable pain. Every night I slept, I dreamed of her finding us and freeing us from the unending pain we endured.

Braelyn's scent soothed me when it shouldn't have. I would still catch it inside my dreams and would awake, wondering if she'd been in my cell while I'd been sleeping. But she wasn't because she hadn't cared that her father sold us to the highest bidder. Braelyn had only cared about herself, and I needed to hold her at arm's length.

"You were protecting yourself, you selfish bitch. You were always good at protecting yourself from everyone, weren't you? You pretend to be so selfless, and the moment you fear repercussion, you go into self-preservation mode. It's what you've always done. You are your father's daughter, Braelyn. I just failed to see that truth when I let you past my shields and showed you who I was. The first moment you got a deeper look into the fucking mess that was me, you ran. When you saw inside my soul and glimpsed my pain, you abandoned me because you are nothing more than a self-serving bitch." Braelyn's eyes widened, and I pressed on, needing to strike her down. I hated that I'd opened up my soul to her, and instead of wanting to look deeper, she'd rejected me.

"You were always running from anything that made you choose between your father and us. You and me—we were written on a dying star that was burning out before we'd ever etched our names onto it. Now get fucking dressed and stay the fuck away from my son. I won't let you ruin him as you did me. Do not embarrass me tonight. Try to pretend you're a lady and not some spoiled bitch who knows nothing else but this fucking mountain you love so much. You're nothing more than a silly girl raised in a bubble," I sneered as I waved my hand around in the air, signifying her territory. "You wouldn't know one thing about the world beyond these walls and past this mountain."

I hated that I loved the fact that she didn't care what the outside world thought about the packs. Braelyn was a breath of fresh air, yet she was also poison ivy that looked innocent enough until you rolled around in it.

Braelyn's face dropped, and her scent turned to rejection and pain for a brief moment before it vanished altogether. Her mask slid into place, and she turned away from me, grabbing her heels while I took in her curves. I hated that I wanted to take the words back and remove the pain I'd glimpsed, but I also knew I wouldn't do it. I needed to push her away. I needed to remind myself of who she was and why we were all here.

Braelyn drove me insane. She pretended she wasn't aware of where my crew and I had been all this time. Fuck her. I could play stupid, too. It was probably a good thing she'd reminded me of the fake bitch she really was because for a moment, my guard had lowered, and I couldn't afford to let that happen again. Especially since I was so close to figuring out where the children were being held for transport on this mountain. Several children had recently been taken from the surrounding packs and were traced to a server on this mountain that had uploaded their images to the web.

I'd find the children, and then I'd figure out how to deal with Braelyn. I'd had people scouring the mountain for days, searching for the missing children and for clues as to where they could have been hidden. Braelyn's people were slowly being told what was happening and what had transpired under Harold's orders. Eventually, her people would turn against her if it was discovered that Braelyn had anything to do with Harold's actions. Pack rules were simple, and if broken, they'd turn against even those in which they were most loyal.

Some of her pack had already begun to switch loyalties, and Braelyn hadn't noticed it yet. Lucas, one of her closest friends, was shocked by the news. He'd listened to our story, his anger building at the idea of what had happened right under his nose. In denial, he had defended Brae's innocence, but I'd caught the hesitation burning in his eyes when I'd told him where Eryx and I were taken after Braelyn's rejection.

Lucas's mind had spun, and he'd hesitated when answering my questions, his turmoil palpable. Like us, he wasn't able to prove Braelyn was innocent, and while it upset him, he'd still defended her. I'd listened as he'd told me how closed-off she'd become as if hiding part of herself from the pack. Harold had done the same thing, easily concealing his dark activities, appearing to be innocent of his crimes. It left us assuming Braelyn was as guilty as her father because she was hiding her emotions. Lucas admitted there were weeks where Braelyn would vanish, only to return with no proof of where she'd been or why she'd been gone.

That information alone left me sick, turning the facts over inside my head. Was she in on it and helping Harold with his human trafficking when she vanished? It explained her disappearance, which also coincided with shipments of those Harold had sold. Lucas confirmed she'd gone missing last May for three weeks, and I knew there'd been a large shipment of children at the same time. Lucas remembered this time well because he said Braelyn returned a little worse for wear and seemed troubled. But she was Brae, he'd said, and Braelyn always bounced back and went about business as usual, even if twisted shit was happening here.

Chapter Ten

Saint

I studied how Xariana and one of her fellow hunters sprayed luminol around the apartment in which we stood. The apartment was a series of small rooms with tables inside of each. I'd seen the setup before, knew it intimately. It was the perfect place to create snuff films that could stream their content out into the dark web, made to accrue revenue from the pain others endured.

My phone went off, and I peered down at the screen, watching the image of Braelyn flipping Phenrys off as she moved around her room back at the compound. It made my stomach churn. Pushing the phone back into my pocket, I watched as Eryx walked the alphas into the apartment.

I didn't bother to ease their fear since I planned to watch and study their reaction to what they were about to see. The TV screens mounted on the wall were all showing static. But in the next few minutes, the alphas would learn the truth of what was happening on their pack's land.

Xavier nodded, indicating the feeds would be up momentarily. My chest tightened with worry for Braelyn. In a matter of moments, I'd be condemning her in the eyes of her peers. I'd come back here to end this shit, and while it created hell for my mate, it had affected others in worse ways.

Xariana pushed her warrior braids away from her heart-shaped face, and Carleigh walked toward me, brushing against my side. I'd known Carleigh for ten years, working beside her in the hunt to end the trafficking ring that had exploited both of us to make money.

Carleigh had been a light at the end of a dark tunnel. She understood the pain I'd endured and hadn't judged me because of it. We'd fucked, but there had never been emotions involved, at least on my part. Not like Brae, not like what had just gone down inside her bedroom. With Carleigh, it was just mindless sex to ease the ache and unleash my anger. But with Brae, shit was twisted as emotions unfurled and unleashed from within us.

"I miss you in my bed," Carleigh whispered, her fingers rubbing circles on my palm.

"Do you now?" I didn't get the rush of heat or need to slip away with her that usually happened when Carleigh was close at hand.

"Is your mate everything you hoped she would be?" she asked, causing my stomach to tighten at her words.

Was Braelyn everything I hoped she would be? More. Braelyn had floored me inside her room, fucking me hard, unleashing her pent-up anger. But that wasn't something I wanted to admit to out loud, and not to someone I'd fucked merely for release.

"She's Braelyn," I announced, turning as the alphas began sitting on the far side of the room, where they'd have a front-row seat to the multitude of monitors Zayne had set up. "She was untouched," I admitted, and Carleigh's green eyes slid toward mine.

"But she isn't now?" she asked, and I smirked. "You took her to your bed even after suspecting she is involved in her father's operation?" Carleigh's lips jerked into a smirk as her fingers slipped through mine, tightening around my hand. "You deserve better, and you know it, asshole. She's not worthy of you."

"And you are?" I countered, wondering why my body wasn't reacting to her touch.

"I didn't say I wanted you, now did I? I simply stated the truth. Braelyn threw you away, and we both know you deserve better than that. I'm available later, in case you were wondering. I could use some mindless orgasms."

"I bet you could," I teased, nodding to Xari, who moved toward the light switch. "I won't be available, though. I have a mate to punish for her wicked ways. I quite enjoy my role as her mate and tormentor at the moment."

"You intend to keep her?" Carleigh asked, her eyes sliding over Ezekiel and Enzo before briefly returning to mine. "She's poison, Saint. You told me that yourself. Plus, if Braelyn is part of her father's endeavors, she's dead. Can you knowingly fuck her and slit her throat if she is guilty? Because that is the cost for selling people, Saint. We've all agreed, and the compact only works if we all keep the promise we made to punish those who've profited from the trafficking. If she's at fault, I will be the first in line to call for Braelyn's blood, just so you're aware."

"If Braelyn is guilty, I will end her life myself. I am aware of the agreement since I was the first to stipulate the rules with Xavier. Don't mistake me wanting to fuck my mate for feelings of love. She lost that from me when she refused to stand up against her father. Braelyn is mine to put down if she's guilty."

"You called me here for a reason. What would that reason be?" Carleigh countered, her tone sharp and filled with pain.

Smiling, I grabbed her hand, bringing it to my lips to brush them over her knuckles. "You're one of a kind, Car, you are. You were there for me when I was lost and couldn't find my way out of the dark hole they'd put me in. You will always have a part of me that no one else will. I can't change that Braelyn's my mate, though, and you know it as well as I do. Braelyn broke my trust and destroyed me. We both know that even if she isn't part of this operation, and that's a big if, it will never be the same between Braelyn and me. I don't know if I can ever forgive her for her part in what happened to me and the others, but she's mine either way. Either to put down or to see if I can salvage what little there is between us. You, you're the best fucking tracker I know. I brought you here, Carleigh, because there are children someplace on this mountain, and we have to find them before winter sinks its claws into this place. They won't survive until spring thaw comes, and you're here to help us find them."

"Can you honestly say you'll be able to rip out Braelyn's heart if she willingly sold you and the others into slavery?" she asked, watching me closely.

My cheek pulsed with the reality that I wouldn't be able to do it. However, Eryx would put her down in a humane way, and I could live with that. I hated the idea of Braelyn knowing what had happened to my crew and me. But the chances of her not being involved in her father's business were slim at best. My heart clenched with the reality that I'd returned to find her untouched and everything I'd ever wanted, only to end up murdering the woman custom made for me by the wolf god, Fenrir.

Eryx stepped up, smirking at Carleigh with amusement sparkling in his eyes. "Carleigh, come to make Saint's mate jealous?" Eryx folded his heavily tattooed arms over his chest. "Or did you come to ride us both again? I did enjoy our last night together before we started back to this shithole we called home."

"That depends," she purred, tracing a blood-red fingernail over my arm.

"On?" Eryx asked, narrowing his stare on her finger.

Carleigh laughed, her eyes growing hooded with memories of us double-teaming her on our last night together. "If you can convince Saint to play with us, or not," she said in a husky tone. "You know I want him, but he's hung up on his silly little mate. Convince him, and I'll take you both on again."

Eryx snorted, shaking his head. "They're ready for us, Saint."

I smirked, starting toward the alphas and Lucas. "Gentlemen, you're aware that we asked you here today to discuss pack matters," I started as Lucas held up his hand.

"Why isn't Braelyn here? If this is about pack business, she should be here." His blue eyes scanned my face carefully.

"What we're about to show you is related to our previous conversation about Braelyn. You're here to help me determine if she was involved in her father's business or not." I held his stare until he nodded his head and dropped his gaze. "Harold was into some shady shit, and I need to know if you or anyone else was a part of his trafficking ring."

"Trafficking?" one of the older alphas asked.

"Yes. Harold trafficked wolves, humans, and creatures that he or his people could easily subdue and sell into slavery," Eryx stated, watching the alphas for any sign of guilt.

"What the fuck are you talking about?" one demanded, his eyes sliding over the other men and women inside the room slowly with new interest.

"Harold was selling creatures for monetary gain. He sold me and others into slavery, where they used us for shit that would make torture look fun." I hated the tic that started in my jaw as my throat tightened with the admission of being used and helpless.

"Fuck off," the alpha snapped, standing up as the lights turned off and the luminol started glowing, revealing blood splatter all over the walls, tables, and floors. "What the fuck?" The alpha sat down slowly, as if in shock.

"As I was saying, Harold was into some shady shit. You're about to watch videos that we obtained from his library. Harold worked with Carlson and other area alphas to sell orphans, misfits, and anyone else who wouldn't be missed. He fucked up, though, when he started selling humans, which caught the hunters' eye. That began their search for those taken, and it was how they found my crew and me at one of the many places Harold owned. He was profiting from porn, snuff films, and the more sinister ones that featured children raped and murdered." I stepped back, leaning against the wall, close enough to be able to scent their guilt if they so much as released a whiff of it.

Sian and Zayne started the monitors up as Carleigh leaned against the wall beside me, but her presence didn't offer comfort. Nausea pushed against the back of my throat, burning it as my gaze moved to the Jane Doe on the monitors, as Harold sliced away her skin in small patches.

Of all the victims Harold had, he enjoyed Jane Doe's pain the most. The look in his eyes was pure evil as he removed more of her skin, dragging the knife blade over the bloodied muscle beneath it. I knew that pain intimately since he'd done the same to me on multiple occasions. I'd escaped, though. There were nearly a hundred videos of Jane Doe, and one was already cued up in the feed. She was his favorite, having tortured her from the time she was a child. That's why I believed Jane Doe was still out there, and I wanted to save her.

My gaze met Xavier's, and a pained look filled his eyes while his hands shook with rage. He'd been trying to find and free Jane Doe since he'd started this gig, ending the trafficking of creatures. Sure, Xavier was a hunter who policed the otherworld creatures, but Jane Doe had been his focus for the last few years, and the trail had gone cold a year ago. He feared Harold had grown tired of his pet and that she'd been murdered or sold to someone who wasn't into sharing their victims.

Slowly, my attention shifted back to the monitors showing children and women tortured and mutilated by their tormentors. The entire wall was covered in monitors, showing off Harold, in all his glory, as he raped and tortured his latest victims. There was no denying it was him since he hadn't even bothered to hide his face from the camera. He'd barely left the mountain to be recognized, and when he had, he stuck to the darker territories where those of his ill-likeness welcomed him with open arms.

I nodded to Xari, and she flicked the light on so that I could take in the alpha's expressions. Each one looked horrified as pain filling their eyes. Swallowing down relief, I jutted my chin for Zayne to kill the feeds to the monitors.

"This is what the alpha did to feed his people. He streamed some of the sessions live, and then the subject was auctioned off if they survived the torture. Others were filmed and then sold for purchase on the dark web. When Braelyn rejected my mating rite, Harold sold me to Bella Donna, a woman who enjoyed hurting men." Pointing my fingers to the monitors, I lowered my voice, "That is why I returned, not to claim Braelyn as my mate properly. I returned to find out how deep this shit goes. There's also a secondary place somewhere on this mountain that Harold held his victims. This feed," I nodded to Zayne, who brought up the image of children held in chains within a dimly lit room, "is a live stream of those he has available for purchase, and the numbers on their chests are current bids for their lives. They're here, on this mountain, but we haven't been able to locate them."

"You think Braelyn is a part of this?" one of the alphas asked, and Carleigh nodded, her eyes smiling as she caught mine. "Braelyn wouldn't do this. She's not like that."

"Or she's good at hiding it," Carleigh offered, and my anger rose at her need to charge Braelyn with the crime.

"We don't know if she is or not. I know for Harold to do this on the level he has, it would be hard for his daughter not to have been involved. We've found no proof of guilt yet, but we also haven't found any to suggest she is innocent." I gave Carleigh a look of warning to back off.

"No way," Lucas stated. "No fucking way would she do this? Braelyn works her ass off with us. She takes care of the pack, and she's earned our respect because of it. She would sooner cut off her own hands than hurt our people."

"And yet she threw away her mate? She lied to the pack about Saint, and she allowed her father to sell him and his friends. Braelyn committed the worst crime she could by lying to her pack about her true soul mate," Carleigh injected, her anger rising at what had been done to me and the others. "Did you know she knowingly denied her mate?"

"Yes," Lucas stated, causing my eyes to narrow on him. "I knew she had a mate and that it was you, Saint. Braelyn didn't deny it to me when I asked. She said if you love something, you protect it, even if you have to protect it from yourself and the monsters within your glass house."

"Which leads me to believe she knew exactly what was happening in her home and on her mountain," Xariana injected smoothly. "Others have told me the same thing. Why would she say that unless she was aware of what her father was doing and that he was a monster?"

Lucas sat down, his face scrunching up at Xari's words. His dark head shook, but he couldn't argue it; no one could. My stomach tightened, and a vice clenched around my heart. We'd been questioning the pack about Brae, and everyone said the same thing. Brae never argued that her father was a monster, backing that opinion up with her own words.

"We believe there's another lodge somewhere on this mountain. We don't have very long before winter comes, and it goes without saying the children won't survive without food until spring. We must find them soon before the snow comes," I stated, changing the subject from Braelyn.

"I can send my sons out, but I can confirm already that there's no hidden lodge on the mountain." A silver-haired alpha stated, his light blue eyes holding mine briefly. "We've patrolled the area for many years. There's no secondary lodge, at least not above ground."

I turned his words over in my head before exhaling slowly. Moving my attention to the monitors showing the children huddled in groups, I studied the area around them. We were missing something, and time was running out. Sliding my gaze over the walls behind them, I paused.

"It could be underground. Maybe that's why we can't locate them. We've been looking for a lodge, not considering they could be beneath the surface. It would explain not being able to smell or catch their scents. They're fucking underground, which means they're freezing, and we're losing our window to save them," I exhaled, glancing at the monitors and studying the way the women clustered around the children, using their body heat to keep them from freezing.

We'd assumed they were their mothers, but looking at them now, it was doubtful; they seemed too young to have children of their own. Tragedy and fear created bonds between the victims, just as it had my crew, Carleigh, and me. Pushing my fingers through my hair, I schooled my expression to cover the fact that we were losing the fight because time wasn't something we had.

"What we discussed here tonight doesn't leave this room. That's an order as your alpha," I announced.

"That's a shit order. If Brae is in on this, we deserve to know," one of the alphas growled, his red eyes meeting and holding mine. "If she is involved, we've been working side-by-side with someone who has betrayed us. I will not respect a woman who sells her people, let alone bow to the bitch."

"Agreed," another stated, forcing my gaze to slide over the men seated against the wall.

"We don't know the level of her involvement yet. Until we know for sure, Braelyn is considered innocent," I warned. "She is my mate, and if she is found guilty, I will take her life. That is my vow to you. Her punishment is mine to give. As her mate, it is my right to handle her how I see fit. Until I say otherwise, she isn't to know that we're aware of what was happening here. I don't want to give her the chance to cover her tracks or hide anything from me. It could be that she's unaware of what her father did, as you all were."

"Or it could be that she was a knowing participant. After all, she sent you into slavery to star in several porn and snuff films," Carleigh sneered, her lips tilting into a cocky smirk. "I'm biased, though, since I've tasted her mate and crave him for myself."

I studied Carleigh for a moment before dismissing her to excuse the alphas from the room. Ezekiel and Enzo approached slowly, staring at the monitors that showed the room filled with children of varying ages.

"There are ways to get answers out of your mate quickly. Let us play with her, and she'll tell us everything you want to know," Enzo stated, his lips curving into a deadly grin.

I snorted, studying the Gemini twins. They were incubus demons, who fed off sex, and they ran a club that was known for granting people their deepest, darkest fantasies. I'd often heard the rumors of how they seduced their prey, and once they had them in their thrall, both would feed on the same victim. They always asked for consent and were never denied.

We'd actually encountered the twins on a hunt where they'd been tracking down a child that was stolen from one of their hives. Cocky, arrogant, evil pricks they were, but they had heart, and we shared the same goals to stop the trafficking. Or at least when it suited them and fit within their terms. Witches were their hard limit, hating them with a vengeance due to a curse in which they weren't eager to share the details.

"I'm going to pass on letting you fuckers get close to Braelyn. No offense, but if she isn't guilty, I don't want her craving you twisted assholes once you've finished corrupting her."

"We'd play nice with her," Ezekiel promised with a grin.

"No, we really wouldn't. My brother is lying. Your mate would be ours forever because you'd never satisfy her once we'd given her our love," Enzo bragged.

"Yo! Ying and Yang, fuck off. Braelyn is Saint's mate; not a plaything," Eryx snapped, his gaze on Carleigh, who stood beside me, anger oozing from her pores as she glared at me. "You too, sweetheart," he laughed. "You can play with me, though, Car. I will enjoy giving you what you crave. Let me hurt you, and you can act like you don't like it rough for me. What do you say?"

"Fuck off, Eryx. You know I only play hard to get

for Saint," she snorted.

"He isn't interested in playing with you anymore. He has Braelyn, and their bond—it's absolute. You're not even on his radar as long as she lives."

"As long as she lives, which at the moment, doesn't seem likely," Carleigh smarted off, turning to look at me. "I'm hoping she's found guilty sooner rather than later. I miss being yours, Saint." Carleigh pushed her hair over her shoulder before starting toward the door and slipping out of the room.

My stare slid to Eryx, who smirked the moment he noted the anger burning in my eyes. "What the fuck are you doing?"

"Killing two birds with one stone," he snorted. "Piss off the hound, and she may nip at the heels of the wolf. You're the one who fucked a hellhound and then invited me to play with her. Carleigh came here for you, and you know it. She's going to be gunning for Brae, and wanting her to be guilty, Saint. You invited a jealous bitch onto your playground, and Brae doesn't even know she's here yet."

"Maybe I should be using Carleigh to get Braelyn to unleash her anger? Women often let their words go when they're upset or jealous," I mused as Xari lifted a blonde eyebrow at my suggestion.

"Or they kill you in their anger. As someone who has experience with cheating pricks, might I suggest you not go that route? I'd hate to have to put your guts back into your stomach, and sew them up again, asshole. Once was enough for me." Xari rolled her pretty eyes and crossed her arms over her corset-covered chest.

Xari was a little badass, fae halfling, with a skill set most immortals didn't have in their arsenal of tricks. But that's not surprising since she's Xavier's daughter. He's the man that started the hunter organization, and he had overseen her training. Xari has been hunting since puberty, and her old man trained her to kill without hesitation. I'd met her with my entrails hanging out, and she hadn't balked as she shoved them back into my stomach, sewing them up, then complained that I was whining like a bitch the entire time.

"Have you asked Braelyn how much she knows about what her father was doing?" Xavier asked with a worried expression. "I hate to say it, but I don't think you're going to be able to kill her if she is guilty, Saint."

"If he won't, we will," Ezekiel stated, running his thumb over a blade as shadows wafted around him.

"I'll be the one to kill her if it comes to that," Eryx folded his arms and glared at Ezekiel and Enzo. "Braelyn is pack, and that makes her our responsibility. No one else is to hurt her. If Saint says the word, I'll put her down as gently as possible. She's his mate, and no matter what has happened, he needs to know that she will be released from this life humanely for him to get out of this with his fucking soul in one piece." Eryx picked invisible lint from this sleeve before meeting my gaze. The pain in his expression was momentarily visible before he shut it down and replaced his mask of civility.

"Dinner should be fun," I ground out, exhaling, and everyone gave a soft chuckle at my expense. "Shove it, assholes. After dinner, you're with me, Eryx. We'll question Brae about what she knows regarding Harold's business. The rest of you, start looking for underground caves or storage containers. I saw shipping containers outside of the compound. Harold could have had some buried and is using them to hide his shipments. He would have had them close to the compound because he was a lazy prick who thought he couldn't be caught in the act. Not to mention, the video feeds in this shithole leave the back entrance dark. It's that way for a reason."

"Harold didn't want anyone seeing him hauling out bodies; I take it?" Xavier frowned, peering around the room.

"That's what I'm guessing, and he didn't want to be seen bringing his victims in either," I grunted, running the newest facts through my mind.

My gaze slid back to where Zayne pushed pause on an image of Jane Doe. Her face was always facing away from the screen and covered by what looked to be a pillowcase, concealing her features.

"What if Jane Doe is a Fenrir wolf? It would explain her never being raped since the wolf god would have protected her. She'd have to be a willing participant to get past Fenrir's protection. And this," I said, pointing to the monitor, "does not appear consensual." I turned to look at Xavier, and he nodded.

"Could be, or it could just be that wasn't what he wanted from her. She's Harold's first victim, that much I know. I'm still combing through the tapes, and there are a lot of them. He enjoyed her the most. You can see it in his eyes. They don't sparkle with the same excitement when he's with the other women or children. There's a madness he unleashes on Jane Doe that is sickening." Xavier lowered his tone, his eyes locking onto the faceless body. "Harold never shows her face, and there's no sound recorded when he's with her, so we can't tell if she's begging him to stop or if she can speak at all. He's gone to great lengths to hide her identity from those paying to watch these sessions. I hate thinking that we're too fucking late to save her. I fear he tired of Jane Doe or went too far one last time."

"Wish we could resurrect Harold and kill the prick again." My attention moved back to the woman bound to the bed, with her legs and arms splayed wide apart, her face hidden behind the black cloth. My eyes slid down to her stomach, skinned down to the muscular tissue, and huge, gaping chunks of her arm and leg muscles that were missing. "I shouldn't have killed him, but I had to gain control of the pack…"

"You did what was needed," Xavier stated.

"Monsters like Harold wouldn't have told you anything. They enjoy holding that power over you," Enzo said, his darkening eyes holding mine. "We know because we are like that, too. Knowledge is power, and when you hold someone's life with that power, it is addictive."

"You know you're scary as fuck most days, but you're pushing that limit today," I snorted, watching the evil grin that tugged at the corners of Enzo's mouth.

"You should see us when we're really angry." Ezekiel laughed, but the look in his dark gaze was anything but friendly. "You sure we can't play with your mate a little? We can unveil her darkest fantasies and desires with merely a kiss."

"I think I can handle my mate, but if she proves to be too hard to crack, I'll consider your offer." The twin's eyes turn a wicked shade of blue before the color swallowed their eyes, and black swirls slid over their arms and hands. "Kill the demon vibes, assholes. You're making Xari uncomfortable, and she gets stabby when she's uncomfortable."

"Noted," Enzo smirked as he tilted his head, eyeing Xari with a darkened expression. "I like stabby women."

"Cool the shit," Xavier demanded, laughing Enzo and Ezekiel off. "She's not into demons or twins that share their toys. She's my fucking daughter, assholes. Get your minds on the fact that there are children here, starving, and tonight the temperature's dropping to forty degrees."

"We do dinner, and then you guys head out and cover the ground in a grid pattern. Just like we did on Mount Rainier last summer." I swallowed down the fact that I was about to have dinner with a jealous hellhound and my mate, and the fireworks that were bound to happen would be entertaining for everyone except me.

Chapter Eleven

Braelyn

I walked into the dining hall with my heart in my throat. Phenrys hadn't spoken a single word to me the entire time I fixed my hair and makeup. Instead, he'd chosen to glare at me as if I were a rodent he wanted to exterminate. It was unnerving to be the only one talking while the other person examined you like something he wanted to hurt.

The moment the dining room came into view, I paused as the pack rose to their feet. The alpha's table was empty, causing my hackles to rise. Usually, I sat with them to avoid my father's table. I searched the room, only to be nudged forward by Phenrys.

"Move it," he ordered, causing me to start forward without finding the alphas.

The pack remained on their feet as I moved between the rows of the tables, heading for the one at the hall entrance. I hadn't sat there since I was a child, trying my best to escape my father's attention. Now I was being forced to sit there again, and my body wanted to turn my ass around involuntarily, hightailing it back to my bedroom and the safety it offered me.

I stalled at the sight of the blonde woman sitting beside Saint, her big green eyes on him with a look of possessiveness that made my stomach churn. Closing off my emotions, I stepped up to the chair, dragging it out to sit where Phen had directed me. Across from Saint, instead of beside him, where he'd purposely placed the blonde. It was my spot, and it wouldn't go unnoticed by the pack.

My eyes slid over the female who returned the slow examination before turning up her nose at me. Her hand slipped through Saint's elbow, pulling him closer as she whispered into his ear, causing his eyes to meet and lock with mine. They sparkled as if she was telling him a secret.

Dismissing them both outright, I glanced down the length of the table, filled with hunters, demons, and the wolves of varying breeds Saint had brought with him. There wasn't a single person seated at the table that I recognized from my pack, and none of the alphas were here.

"You look beautiful, Braelyn. You're the spitting image of your mother," Leif announced, causing my gaze to swing to his in shock.

"Thank you," I said softly, if not a little hesitantly.

"The pack respects you," he continued as if everyone else wasn't listening to his every word.

"They do, but then unlike my father, I work beside them."

"Indeed, you do. Your ability to keep up with your pack today impressed me. You remind me of home. I longed for the fjords for the first time in a very long time, Braelyn. Had your pack not been so weak and feeble all those years ago, I may not have slaughtered them so easily. You would have stayed my hand had you been born when I set siege to your line."

I blinked, trying to figure out what the hell one said to the maniac who chased our pack from the shores of Norway eons ago. This man slaughtered my grandparents, murdering them for being different. Holding his stare, Leif smiled, fully aware that he'd left me without recourse to say something.

"Do you not work beside your pack?" I asked, watching his lips jerk at my question. Lycans usually don't live in packs, but it was rumored in certain circles that Leif was indeed working to integrate a large number of Lycan wolves into a pack. "Or, are we supposed to pretend that you're not trying to build a pack?"

Leif smiled before nodding his head. "You do remind me of your mother. She had a fire in her eyes and soul. It saddened me to hear that she passed. Having a babe, wasn't it? It was stillborn, and she could not deliver, right?"

"My mother didn't die giving birth or because of pregnancy complications," I stated, slowly turning to find Saint and the others hanging on my every word. "My father discovered my mother carried another daughter. Displeased, he took an ax to her as she tended to the fire in our apartment. He then removed her heart, leaving her and his child to die on the floor."

"And you did nothing to prevent it? Fenrir women are warriors from birth." Leif's accusation stung as his words hung in the air.

"I was five when he murdered my mother. She'd told me never to allow my father to see my emotions. I was terrified of him, and he knew it. He wanted an heir that could hold the pack by the blood in their veins."

"Fenrir packs are normally led by their women, born as natural alphas to their packs," he stated, pouring bourbon into a glass before pushing one across the table toward me. "Harold wasn't aware that you were his alpha heir, was he?"

"No, and since I had beta tendencies, it was easily kept hidden. I wasn't aware that I was an alpha until nine years ago. I suppressed it after that, but my father noticed. It's why he'd agreed to allow Carlson to take me as his mate. My father wanted me away from the pack so that I couldn't take it from him."

"Because you would have by right," Leif laughed, shaking his head while holding my stare.

His eyes sparkled with the laughter, reminding me of the pictures my mother had shown me of the Nordic seas and fjords. Leif wasn't pretty; he was gorgeous. He had a rugged look of masculinity and sin combined into a perfect package. His hair was inky black and adorned in warrior braids that would have looked silly on anyone else but fit him perfectly. The flannel shirt he wore was opened in the front, revealing his heavily tattooed chest that was a feast for my eyes.

"To your mother," Leif held up his glass while waiting for me to do the same. "May the gods bless her soul and cherish her during her eternal rest." The sound of glasses clinking together echoed through the hall as I tipped mine back, downing the bourbon, burning its way down my throat. "And she drinks like a Viking," he announced, refilling the glasses.

"So she does," Saint grunted, his eyes slipping between Leif and me with something similar to jealousy burning within them.

"Braelyn, isn't it?" the woman beside Saint asked, her venom-laced tone grating over my nerves. "I'm Carleigh. Saint and I spent a lot of time together over the past ten years."

I blinked while waiting for her to continue, but she reached for Saint's hand, threading their fingers while studying me. The entire room went silent, and the tension at the table was growing until Leif laughed, pushing the glass back toward me.

"How long have you led the pack under your father's nose?" Leif asked, dispelling the tension.

"Since I was eight," I admitted, finding it surprisingly easy to talk to the Lycan. "Harold didn't care for the pack, and he failed to understand the gravity of being stuck on the top of a mountain peak during winter. The other alphas helped me, of course. I would instruct them on what needed to be done, and they would bring it up at the meetings as if it were their ideas. I had to maintain the relationship with the alphas, encouraging them to assist me in running the pack. I was a child, after all. Even as the daughter of the alpha, to them and everyone else, I was a beta female, secretly helping the pack survive."

"And they didn't try to mate you to their sons?" Leif turned as Carleigh whispered into Saint's ear, causing him to snort loudly at whatever she'd said. I did my best to ignore the pathetic attempt to make me jealous.

"They did, but Harold wasn't interested in making a match with our people. My match with Saint came as a shock to both of us since, originally, we couldn't stand one another. Saint had his crew, and I was the spoiled little bitch they enjoyed tormenting."

"I will agree with that remark," Eryx chuckled, leaning back where he sat beside me. I could feel their eyes heating my face while they listened to the conversation. "Braelyn was a pampered princess who was off-limits to the pack, according to her daddy. But she discovered her mate in Saint. And we all know what happened from there, don't we?"

My attention slid to Saint, who watched me as his jaw ticked rapidly. Carleigh was running her fingers over his forearm while gawking at me. My heart clenched with the memories of the summer we'd spent together, hiding and learning each other. It hadn't been sexual, but we'd spoken of our desires and exposed every little detail of ourselves to one another.

"I'm guessing your father didn't approve of Saint as your mate?" Leif asked, his tone neutral without the condemnation the others held in their stares.

"My father wanted to breed me because, through me, he thought he could get an heir to his line. He wouldn't have approved of anyone," I admitted, downing the cup as those at the table went silent. "Luckily, Fenrir protects females from being raped or forced to breed with anyone who isn't their true soul mate. He would have done so if he'd been able to, but I remained untouched to prevent it from happening."

Leif stared at me with wide, horrified eyes. His mouth opened and closed, and then he slowly blew air out before nodding with understanding.

"He wanted a purebred Fenrir wolf heir, and he already had one under his nose the entire time. Your mother would have rolled over in her grave."

"My mother never loved nor cared for Harold. They weren't true mates," I disclosed, running my finger over the rim of the glass.

"And yet she allowed him to mate with her, creating you, Princess," Leif stated.

"So she did, paying for it with her life. I am not a princess, though. That's just something these pricks call me to get a rise out of me."

"You are a princess, Braelyn. Had I not murdered your grandparents, you'd have been the Queen Alpha of the Norway packs. Your mother was a princess. I know because I fully intended to claim her as my mate, forcing her to give me sons to piss off her father." My eyes locked with Leif's as Saint snorted, leaning closer to Carleigh's ear to whisper something into it. "Had you not discovered you were soul-mated to my friend here, I'd be taking you away with me."

"A Fenrir wolf must remain on the mountain, or the blessing of the land will fail," I returned, ignoring his comment about Saint.

"Your mother was buried on this mountain, eternally blessing the land with her presence. The gods are rather fickle with their terms, leaving them open and misinterpreted more often than not." Leif smiled before he sat back, allowing the servers to place his meal in front of him.

I ate in silence while those around me talked pleasantly with one another, proving their camaraderie extended beyond this mountain. Saint held a conversation with Carleigh, who laughed and boasted loudly about their time together for my benefit. Eryx snorted at something she said, forcing my attention to the blonde, annoying woman who was drinking and shoving food into her mouth without care.

I felt alone, watching as they all talked about old times, reminiscing about things they'd done together. My people surrounded me, yet Saint had secluded me by forcing me to sit away from them. Listening to my pack speak, I craved to be a part of their conversation, which hadn't ever been something I'd desired.

Saint joked, flirting openly with Carleigh while ignoring me. She laughed, and he'd echoed it while the others cut in, talking about something that had happened. It had never occurred to me that Saint had a life away from the mountain while I'd been forced to stay here, surviving while he'd lived and gone places I'd never dreamed of going.

I drummed my fingers on the table, absently considering what life would have been like if I'd been strong enough to stand up to my father. Would Saint and I have had children by now? Or would he have ended up on the table beside me, being dissected while

I'd be forced to watch?

No one spoke to me or about me—not until Carleigh purposely laughed loud enough that it caught my attention, allowing her to make eye contact. She slid her eyes over me and smirked as if she found me pathetic and lacking. Her eyes sparkled with delight, holding mine before she leaned closer to Saint, whispering in his ear again as he grinned at me. Rolling my eyes, I turned to take in my pack as they consumed their meal.

They didn't seem upset that we had a new alpha. Nor had the other alphas joined the meal, which still bugged me. It wasn't alarming for them to miss a meal, having their packs scattered throughout the mountain. But with a new alpha taking Harold's place, they should have been present to learn what was happening. So where were they?

A scream ripped through the room, and my attention moved to Cora, a member of my pack. She was holding her pregnant stomach, howling in pain. I rose from my seat, going to her as she bent over, and another scream ripped from her lungs.

Cora dropped to the floor on her back, and I saw that her water had broken. Lifting the skirt of her dress, I rubbed her leg slightly. "It's okay, Cora. I just need to take a look." Dropping her legs open, Cora screamed again, just as I saw the head of the babe crowning, escaping her body. The babe slid free from its mother's womb, and I captured it in my hands. Standing, I lifted the babe to my body, smiling until I caught the vacant stare in Cora's eyes. She reached down and ripped the placenta free as foam and saliva dripped from her open lips. Patches of red broke through her hazel gaze, and before I could prevent her from moving, she lunged at me.

Toralei appeared from nowhere, shoving Cora back as I fumbled with the slippery newborn in my arms. Handing it off to another woman, I turned and saw Tora shove Cora away. A tremble of unease rushed through me at the reality of the situation. Cora had lost her mate, Fang, in the fighting last night. Fang was my father's beta, and if Saint's people hadn't killed the bastard, I would have.

Fang was sick and twisted and got off on creating pain in others. He was one of the many men my father allowed to torture me. Unluckily, Cora had been soul-mated to the murderous prick.

"Find Lucas, and tell him to come," I growled, watching Cora, who snarled and shifted toward Toralei with a feral gleam in her eyes.

When one loses a soul mate, we didn't shift to ease the pain. We couldn't just vanish into the woods like shifters. There was no escaping the pain when we lost the other half of our soul, so the wolf within us becomes feral, and that was dangerous. The human half went silent, leaving only the predator to control the shell. If left alive, Cora would escape or murder anyone she could, needing to cause the same pain she felt at losing her mate. It was a death sentence. Exposure to a feral Fenrir wolf wasn't something that could be allowed, so her life would be have to be forfeited.

Cora attacked, and I slipped out of her path, and she lunged at her child. I grabbed Cora, hearing the people around us gasp as my arms wrapped around hers, holding her as Toralei bound her wrists. She bucked against me, slamming her face into mine, sending pain ripping through my nose. The scent of blood filled the air, pooling into my mouth.

"We can't find him," someone shouted, and I closed my eyes.

Cora was Lucas's sister, the only living family he had left. My nails extended, and my heart clenched as I lost my hold on the woman fueled with extra strength from her wolf. She spun around, breaking free of Tora's hold, shoving her hand into my chest as I did the same. I withdrew her heart as pain tore through me. Peering down at my chest, I inhaled as Toralei grabbed the hand that tore through my chest, prying the fingers from around my heart before Cora's body dropped to the floor.

I stood there gasping for air, pain shuddering through me. Blood dripped from my nose and chest as Toralei stood in front of me, blocking my weakness from the pack. I stepped back as a commotion stirred at the front of the room, and Lucas entered, noting the crumpled form on the ground at my feet.

Blue eyes lifted to mine, filled with accusation. Lucas crept closer, his eyes holding mine as anger fizzled through him, smothering me. He paused in front of me, staring at me with a look I'd never seen in his expressive gaze before.

"She turned feral," I explained through the chattering of my teeth.

"You fucking bitch," he whispered with hatred. "They were right about you."

ALPHA'S CLAIM

"What?" I whispered, using everything I had to remain upright on my feet. "Who was right?"

"I should fucking challenge you right now, Braelyn," he snarled, but something over my shoulder made him pause.

"She was feral, Lucas," Toralei snapped, shoving him back away from me. "Your sister turned because her mate died. That isn't on Braelyn. She fucking hesitated because of you since Cora was your fucking sister. It could have cost her greatly, and you want to be an asshole about it? Feral wolves don't get a pass, no matter who they are."

"I thought they lied, but you're a murderous whore just like your fucking father," Lucas accused, staring at me. "I thought I knew you, Braelyn. It turns out none of us do. You're a monster."

I didn't speak, turning to find Saint and his men standing behind me, silently watching the chaos unfold. Saint's eyes slid to mine as understanding slithered through me. My heart clenched, and my attention moved back to Lucas, who glared murderously at me.

"Your sister was feral, and that is a death sentence. You have a nephew that needs you now," I replied icily. "You're dismissed, Alpha Lucas. Toralei, please remove Cora's name from the pack roster and replace it with whatever Lucas names his nephew. If you'll excuse me," I stated, letting my proverbial mask slid over my features to hide the pain his accusation caused.

Lucas had been my strength when I'd lost Saint. There hadn't ever been anything sexual between us, but he'd held me up when everything else had gone adrift in rough waters. Lucas was my friend or had been until now. His chest rose and fell with his anger. But Saint standing behind me, stayed the hand Lucas would have used to end my life. It would have been a simple thing for Lucas to do in my weakened state.

Stepping back, I turned to move toward the chef's table, where steaks were still being seared. I grabbed the pan from the red hot burner and held it against the gaping hole in my chest. I gasped, whimpering softly as my flesh sizzled, sealing the wound. Taking a moment to catch my breath, I straightened and slowly walked back to my seat, sitting silently.

Everyone watched me, taking in the blood that poured from my nose and the exposed flesh that Cora had revealed when she ripped through my dress to reach my heart. Saint sat in his chair, his gaze widening as it slid to the bottom of my exposed breasts.

"What the fuck," Eryx grabbed me, causing me to gasp in surprise.

"Why aren't you screaming?" Saint asked, as if at a loss for words. "What the hell is wrong with you?"

"I should go clean up," I stated calmly, standing, showing no pain in my expression as everyone at the table studied me. "If you'll excuse me, I'll return shortly."

Chapter Twelve

I slipped out of the dining hall, smothering the tears that threatened to fall at any moment. I'd long since learned to hide my pain from the pack. It didn't mean I was immune to it or that it hurt any less. I'd almost fucking died, and that was terrifying all on its own. This was the first time I had hesitated to act, and because of it, I'd lost my friend.

Saint was turning the alphas against me; that much was clear now. Lucas said he hadn't believed their accusations, but in his grief for his sister, he'd changed his mind. What had they told him I'd done? My legs faltered, and I reached for the wall to steady myself. Strong arms wrapped around me, lifting me from the ground.

"Put me down. I can walk," I growled, and Saint snorted against my ear.

Eryx settled in beside us as we moved through the empty halls toward the living quarters. Nausea churned through me, and I hated the weakness of my body from my near-death experience. It wasn't even the first time I'd felt fingers skim over my heart, threatening to remove it. It was, however, the only time I'd needed my beta to intervene.

"Why the fuck would you kill her?" Eryx asked harshly, his eyes on the bloody mess on the front of my dress. "Feral wolves can come back."

"Not mated wolves that have lost their mate. You killed her mate, and she'd have murdered anyone who slighted her. That would be the worst-case scenario if she remained here on the mountain. If she'd escaped the mountain, she'd have likely exposed us to the humans and brought hunters here to harm the pack. Soul-mated wolves are together for life. When one of them dies, so does the human half, leaving only an emotionally wounded wolf behind."

"Why aren't you screaming in pain?" Saint asked, allowing Eryx to open my bedroom door. "Your chest was punctured, and you sealed it with a fucking pan, Braelyn."

"So I did," I replied. "Put me down so that I can wash up and change, please."

"Dinner is over. I doubt anyone is eating after watching that shit unfold," Saint snapped, sitting me on the bed and ripping my dress down the middle. The material tore where it had melted to my skin when I sealed the wound with a scalding hot pan. I gasped, inhaling through my nose, exhaling slowly through my mouth. His angry stare burned my naked breasts as he glared at the spot that was raw and blistered.

"Call in the healer," he instructed.

"Do not call the healer. It will mend on its own," I tried to reach for the drawer that held the herbs. "Move, or get the herbs from the drawer. My body will heal itself as it always does."

Eryx snorted, pulling a tin out of his pocket to produce a joint that he lit, handing it to me. I covered my breasts, accepting the joint. I inhaled the fragrant herb deeply, holding it in my lungs as my head swam with pain and guilt. I didn't blame Lucas for hating me, but I couldn't change what had happened any more than he could.

Saint didn't move to grab a shirt or even bother to take his gaze away from where I covered my naked breasts. Eryx didn't either, choosing to sit in the chair beside my bed, lighting a joint for himself before leaning back to examine me.

"Has this happened before?" Saint asked, nodding at my chest.

"You're going to need to be more specific, but more to the point, I don't need you here. You can return to your girlfriend. Eryx is a sufficient enough babysitter. It's not like I'm in shape to do anything other than sleep. Maybe you can fuck that blonde tonight instead of me since I'm rather—broken. Or, you can do me and ignore the pain you'll be putting me through. Either way, I need to shower and wash the blood from my face and hair."

Saint studied my face, then turned and went to the bathroom. I heard the water turn on as I swallowed the coppery tang of blood that filled my mouth. Saint exited the bathroom with a washcloth in his hand and sat beside me, slowly pushing me back before he carefully washed the blood from my face.

"Alphas scream and rage when their chest cavities are punctured. You barely made a fucking sound, Braelyn," he announced, pushing my hand away from my breasts.

I could feel Saint and Eryx taking in my naked chest with their heated stares, and a blush filled my cheeks. Instead of covering myself as I wanted to do, I looked away from both men, inhaling the weed to calm my inner turmoil.

"What did you tell Lucas to make him think I'm a monster?" I asked, barely hiding the tremor in my voice, threatening to expose my emotions.

"Nothing," Saint lied, his eyes rising to lock with mine. "Finish the joint. Eryx, retrieve the whiskey Sian was preparing for us. My mate needs to take the edge off and let loose a little."

Eryx chuckled as if they were sharing an inside joke as he slipped out of the door to vanish, leaving me alone with Saint. I shivered as he continued washing the blood from my body. He was gentle, studying my face as tears pooled in my eyes. The flesh was tender and burned until it blistered.

"How are you holding it in, Brae?" he whispered, swallowing thickly. "Burns are some of the worst pain we endure, and you're fucking burned badly. You should be screaming right now, but you're holding it all in somehow, aren't you?"

"Would you prefer me to shriek and cry?" I turned

my gaze to him as the tears slipped free, rushing down my face to slip into my ear.

Saint reached up, pushing the hair away from my face as he snorted, "It would make more sense if you did." He leaned over to kiss the tears away but jerked back as the door opened, revealing Sian and Eryx, who entered unannounced.

"Bourbon?" Eryx asked, watching as Saint used the cloth to continue cleaning the blood caked to my ribcage. Eryx sat on the bed, smiling down at me while Sian took the chair, leaning forward to stare at the mottled skin between my breasts.

I started to sit up, but Saint placed a hand on my stomach, shaking his head. My heart hammered against my ribcage, sending more pain into my system. My hands shook as I slowly lifted the joint to my lips, looking anywhere but at the men. It was humiliating to be naked from the chest up, dressed only in panties and nylons.

"I need to shower," I pointed out through trembling lips.

"I don't know, Brae. I'm enjoying the sight of your body covered in blood, trembling in pain. It's turning me the fuck on," Eryx stated, dropping his hooded gaze to my hard nipples. "I think you're enjoying it too, aren't you?"

"Fuck off," I snorted, exhaling smoke with my words.

Saint snorted, helping me sit up as he grabbed the whiskey with his other hand. He bit the cap off, handing it to me, staring at the way my body shook from the pain racking through it. His fingers stroked my spine, and Eryx leaned closer, rubbing his nose over my shoulder.

"Drink," Saint instructed. "Don't stop until I say so, Brat."

"What the hell is this?" I asked, fear spiking through my system.

"You're going to fucking drink, or we're going to force it down that tight throat of yours. Choose which option you prefer," Saint grumbled.

I could barely lift the bottle to my lips, and before I could take a sip, my nose caught the scent of herbs added into the bourbon. Uneasiness entered my mind, but I didn't have many options here. I was wounded, weakened from pain, and exposed to the men within the room.

"Can I put a shirt on or cover myself?" I asked hesitantly.

"How many times were we left exposed so other people could explore us for their entertainment?" Eryx asked, lifting his hand and pushing it against the burn, causing a shaky breath to escape my throat. He didn't relent, pushing his fingers against the scorched flesh while holding my stare. I cried out as he smiled, leaning over to press his lips against my ear. "Drink up, bitch. It will help ease the pain, which is more than you and your sick daddy allowed us."

A shiver snaked down my spine as I held up the bottle, chugging as the men watched. Pulling it away from my mouth, I coughed at the bitter taste of the whiskey. Saint pushed the bottle back toward my mouth, and I drank more of the obnoxious tasting shit until he finally reached up and took it from me. He handed it off to Sian, who tilted the bottle to take a sip.

"Don't drink that shit, asshole," Saint snorted, causing my anxiety to spike and take hold of my mind. What the hell was in the whiskey? I couldn't pinpoint the taste, but even now, my body was relaxing. My skin heated, and Saint released me, allowing me to lay back. Eryx took the joint from my fingers, and I watched the cherry create a trail of light before he took a drag. "Sian, let the others know they can look for that thing we need to find. Eryx, keep my mate here while I deal with the other issue. Do not fucking touch her, asshole."

I watched as the men stood, leaving me at the mercy of Eryx, who I knew had none to offer. He smirked, sensing my fear as the scent escaped the tight hold I'd had on it. When the door closed behind Saint, Eryx sat up, slowly undoing the cuffs to his white shirt, and silently rolled his sleeves up. He produced another joint, lighting it before lying down beside me, studying my face.

"I almost wish you were mine, Brae. I so want to play with that darkness you are hiding from us. We can see it, you know? The need to feel the pain that dances in your pretty eyes," he growled huskily, leaning over to press his mouth against mine, forcing smoke into my lungs. I shuddered at the heat his lips created, which hadn't gone unnoticed.

His fingertips trailed around the burn on my chest. They followed the curve of my breast, though he never allowed his touch to move to my nipple that hardened painfully. Eryx's intense blue gaze watched my face as the smoke billowed out of my lips, curling into the air.

"You're so fucking high right now, aren't you?" he chuckled, leaning over my face to trace his nose over the curve of my jaw. "I used to hate Saint for being the one who got you. I wanted you, Braelyn. I wanted you so fucking bad when we were younger. I always wondered if you'd taste as sweet as you looked or if you'd taste bitter."

"You always scared me," I admitted through chattering teeth.

"I know, but you wondered about me, didn't you?" he laughed coldly, dragging his lips over mine once more before leaning back to inhale the weed. His attention lowered to my hardened peaks, and his fingers drew small, tight circles over my stomach. "If Saint lets me kill you, I fully intend to fuck you first. You won't get out of this life without me knowing what you taste like, Princess. You owe me that much, at least." He took another drag, watching me through heavily hooded eyes.

There were tracers from where the cherry of the joint moved, causing my eyes to close as he lowered his lips against mine, snaking his tongue out to coax me to open to him. Eryx didn't kiss me; he fed me smoke instead. He didn't move away, holding his mouth against mine as his shirt created friction against the sensitive peak of my nipple. I exhaled, and he captured the smoke with his mouth, pushing it back into my lungs. His lips crushed against mine and his teeth tugged at my bottom lip playfully.

"Fuck me if you don't taste like forbidden fruit, Princess," he growled, sitting up quickly as the door to the room opened.

"Get your hands off of her, asshole," Saint growled, stalking into the room.

I followed Saint with my blurred vision as he leaned over the bed, slowly dragging his heated breath over my skin. He dipped his head to kiss along the curve of my breast and growled against the shell of my ear, "Are you ready to play a game, Brat?" Whether it was fear or excitement, I couldn't be sure, but it sent a shudder rushing through me. My mind was foggy, and my entire body felt weighted down as if something held me to the bed with an invisible grip.

"What did you do to me?" I asked, noting that I felt no pain. I felt—free. At the moment, nothing held me prisoner, not even my demons.

"Loosened your tongue," Saint chuckled, holding his hand out for the joint. He inhaled, turning to look at me before blowing the smoke into my face. My eyes grew hooded, watching his tongue sliding over his bottom lip, then sucking it between his teeth.

"How bad do you need to be bent over and fucked right now, Princess?" Eryx asked, his fingers playing with the bow on the stocking of my garter.

My gaze slid from Saint's lips to Eryx's burning stare, then back to Saint as my heart began hammering against my chest. I tried to get up, but they both placed a hand on my shoulders, forcing me back down against the mattress.

"Relax, I don't intend to share you, Brae," Saint scoffed, watching me. "I may want to strangle you, but I sure as shit don't intend to share you. Not unless you're a part of this shit, and if that is the case, you will get what you deserve."

"I'm just playing with you, Princess. For now," Eryx said huskily. He studied my face and slowly slid his gaze down my body before scrubbing his hand over his face and then pushing his fingers through his hair. "You should cover her, asshole. You know how I feel about her. This is fucking torture."

"Grab a nightgown out of her closet, and hand me the bourbon. She's still in possession of her mind if her heart is beating that wildly at the idea of fucking you." Saint sat up to pull his shirt off over his head and dropped it to the mattress. He straddled my body and leaned his mouth against mine. "Can I hurt you, Brat?" His heated stare was burning into mine with a hauntingly familiar expression. "Do you enjoy pain? Is that your fucking kink?"

"I don't understand," I murmured, blinking to dispel whatever the hell was inside the whiskey. He smirked, watching me. "I feel funny."

"It's mugwort and witches thyme. It's an aphrodisiac and hypnotic concoction for our kind, Braelyn," Saint admitted, pressing his mouth into the crook of my neck, kissing my wildly beating pulse. "You'll beg to fuck me, and you'll tell me whatever I want to hear to achieve that end."

Something silky touched my skin, and I looked down at the white nightgown that Eryx tossed to us. Saint crawled over the side of me, leaning against the pillows before reaching for me. He lifted me, slipping the soft fabric over my body, then placing me against his chest. Eryx sat in front of me, the bottle of bourbon held in his lap. I licked my dry lips, shivering against the heat of Saint's hold.

"Open that pretty mouth of yours, Princess," Eryx demanded, holding the bottle up against my mouth.

I opened it, watching as he tipped the bottle up, forcing me to drink or wear the alcohol. Three long pulls from the bottle, and he removed it, lifting his thumb to trace the droplet of whiskey that escaped my lips. My tongue licked it at the same moment his thumb moved to capture it, connecting. Eryx stared at my mouth longingly as I licked his thumb and the corner of my mouth.

"Pretty, isn't she? Like poison ivy, before you know it, you're covered in the shit, and it's too late to back out," Saint growled, causing Eryx to drop his eyes to my mouth, where his thumb remained, even though I'd removed my tongue.

"How are you going to know when this shit kicks in enough to ask her what you want to know?" Eryx asked.

"You're going to kiss her, and if she kisses you back, we'll know. You terrify her, which means if she's kissing you, she's ready to play." Saint laughed darkly as Eryx lowered his heated stare back to my mouth. "It will be the one time you get to kiss her because we both know she wouldn't allow it if her mind were working at full capacity, asshole."

My eyes held Eryx's stare while he studied me, scrubbing his hand over his face before he left the bed to deposit the bottle on the dresser. He pulled his shirt out of his slacks and slowly began to unbutton it while continuing to hold my stare. Eryx moved around the room, pulling off his shirt to reveal intricately inked skulls covering his back. It was hauntingly beautiful and so like him to have something like that on his flesh. Lighting the candles, he moved to the door and flicked off the lights. He leaned casually against the wall, watching as Saint ran his hands over the silk that covered my stomach.

"You always were a lucky bastard," Eryx grunted, smirking with a terrifying look sparkling in his darkened gaze. "I prayed to Fenrir to make her mine once when she had yet to grow those titties you're squeezing. She had a spark in her, one I wanted to snuff out so fucking badly."

"Your prayers fell on deaf ears. Fenrir doesn't give any fucks about us, brother."

"No? Because I'm pretty sure you returned to find your mate untouched and as pure as the snow that falls on the highest mountain peak of Everest. She remained a virgin by some fucking miracle. Deny it, asshole. I fucking dare you. I scented it, and fuck if it didn't make my wolf unhinged."

"Stop being petty as fuck, and come see if my girl responds to you, Eryx," Saint grunted as Eryx pushed off the wall and slowly approached the bed like the monster he was.

Eryx sat in front of me, gradually lowering his mouth to mine as I leaned back into Saint. He pulled back, smiling wolfishly at the way my eyes grew large and rounded at his advance. Instead of forcing it, he lowered his hand to my thighs, holding them while he studied me. No one spoke, and my heart began to calm against the sensation of both of them touching me.

Heat pooled at my apex, and I moaned while trying to remember who I was with and what was happening. Both men continued touching me, but neither of them did anything else.

Time passed, and my head slowly rolled back to rest against Saint's chest, listening to his steady heartbeat. I watched through hooded eyes as Eryx leaned forward, his lips brushing against mine softly. His tongue slipped out, sliding against my lips as he coaxed them apart. The moment I opened them, he devoured me. His kiss was like him, merciless and relentless. My lips moved against his, dueling against him for dominance, and he deepened the kiss until a moan escaped from my chest, filling the silence of the room.

Eryx pulled away, and I chased his mouth as everything inside of me pleaded for him to continue. Saint's arm wrapped around my chest, and I watched Eryx, who stared at me like I was Eve, and he was Adam, and both of us were lost in the taste of forbidden fruit.

"Brae," Saint's voice sounded miles away, even though his heated breath fanned against the sensitive shell of my ear. "Why was Carlson here?"

"To claim me," I admitted, wondering why Eryx wasn't touching me. He was staring at my body, his eyes a mixture of midnight and crimson that called to the monster within me.

"No, he was here for something else. What did he come for?" Saint asked, running his hand down my stomach. "Come on, Brat, focus on me."

"My father called him here," I stated, closing my eyes. I arched into the heat of Saint's touch, needing him to stop the ache growing in my belly.

"To pick up a shipment?" he asked.

"What?"

"Was he here to pick up a shipment?"

I shook my head, trying to dispel the concoction muddling my thoughts. "Maybe, but I don't know. They argued, and Carlson was angry. Harold offered me to Carlton to assuage his pride. He came here to take me and to mend the bridge Harold had tried to burn down."

"Do you know what your father and Carlson did together?" Eryx asked, watching my body move against Saint's touch. "Do you know what they sold, Princess?"

"I wasn't allowed to help them with the business," I admitted.

Eryx's eyes darkened as he lifted his stare to hold mine. "Did you sell us, Braelyn?" He snarled, his face becoming sinister. "Did you help him sell us?"

I blinked, shaking my head as my tongue grew heavy at his words. "I don't understand," I muttered, closing my eyes as Saint's touch promised me release, even though he wasn't touching me where I needed or wanted him.

"Do you know where your father kept his shipment hidden?" Saint asked, his hand lifting my gown while the other slipped beneath it, cupping my sex.

"In the fields, but we're not allowed to go there," I

supplied, gasping loudly as he applied pressure against the pulse between my thighs.

"What fields, Brae?" Eryx asked, his words guttural while he inhaled the scent of the arousal Saint was creating. "Braelyn, I need you to focus on me, Princess. Where are the fields?"

"Behind us, where the meadow is," I uttered, baring my shoulder for Saint to kiss my throat. "You can't go out there. Harold forbids it. It's the killing field," I continued, arching further while Saint pushed his fingers against the panties that were soaked from my need of him to make me come.

"The killing fields?" Eryx continued, his eyes heavily hooded, but there was anger dripping in his tone. "Why do you call them that?"

"Because he did, and he is the alpha. When the wind howls, you can hear the ghosts keening and screaming for help. The soon-to-be damned call to be saved, but no one can save us because the demons are too strong. We're already damned and soon-to-be-dead. No one cares that we cry out for help."

"We're? More like you helped daddy hide the bodies," Eryx growled, his eyes turning cold as the lust left them.

Pounding started at the door, and I turned my body closer to Saint's as it opened. Sian walked in with Phenrys on his heels. Bowen stood in the shadows, meeting Saint's stare. No one spoke, watching as Saint continued running his hand over my belly.

"We found them," Sian stated, shaking his head.

"Where?" Saint asked, his hand pausing as the other slid through my sex, hidden beneath the nightgown I wore.

"Behind the lodge in a wide-open field, buried in storage containers," he announced, and Saint pushed me aside as he grabbed his shirt, glaring down at me.

"And here I was praying you weren't a part of this shit, Braelyn. You were fucking knee-deep in it, weren't you?" he hissed, his eyes filled with hatred as he and the others stared at my limp form. "Bring my mate with us, Eryx. She doesn't get to play dumb anymore. Feed her the tonic that reverses the effects. The rest of you, grab supplies and call in the medivac helicopters. If they've been in the ground for very long, they'll need more medical attention than they can get here. Grab the heating blankets and meet me out there."

Chapter Thirteen

I had shit that tasted like acid forced down my throat, and then I was walking barefooted through the meadow. Eryx didn't stop, not even when pine nettles stuck into my foot. The wind howled, biting into my exposed flesh as we moved further out of the lodge, toward the secondary field behind a small copse of trees.

My hair whipped against my face and a shiver from the cold sent goosebumps over my arms. I could make out voices in the distance, along with the scent of people gathered. Peering up at the waning moon, I exhaled as I pondered where and to what I was being marched.

If I were lucky, maybe they'd finally end it here? It would suck, of course. I hadn't even started living, unable to escape my father's tyranny without hurting the pack. I'd planned it out perfectly, only to have the last person I'd ever expected to see again fuck it all up. Now, I'd probably die without ever experiencing anything other than pain and agony.

We moved past the trees, emerging into the open meadow where people had gathered. My heart stopped, only to restart with a deafening speed that echoed in my ears. I could smell the animosity in the air; hear their hearts thundering with anger as it smothered the oxygen within the meadow.

Eryx walked me closer, snorting as he forced his way through the gathering crowd, dragging me with him. I searched the faces for Saint, sniffing the air to catch his scent, to soothe the fear rushing through me. We stood behind yet another line of people, some turning to look at me with accusing eyes, while others looked like they wanted to dissect me violently.

Shifters and hunters stood around something that was being opened, and the stench that was unleashed caused me to lift my arm over my nose. Soft cries escaped from the ground, making my steps falter.

"Move your ass, Princess. Don't make me snap your fucking neck. Right now, I'd gladly do it," Eryx growled. His hand shot out for my wrist, wrapping his fingers around it bitingly.

We reached where the others stood, and my heart plummeted. Bile burned the back of my throat as a small child was pulled out of the ground. He was filthy, covered in bruises and bloodied clothes. His eyes were darkened with deep bruises and swollen closed. My heart thundered with the reality of what I was seeing.

Fear slithered through me, and guilt washed over me. My entire body shook with horror as more were lifted out of the hole by rope, with someone pulling them up while someone else helped from below. The temperature was already dropping into the low twenties since the sun had set, which meant they'd been out here, underground, freezing and starving.

The alphas stood away from the others, watching me as I noticed them. Lucas was whispering to them, which sent unease rushing through me. I fought back the tears, needing to tell them that this wasn't me, but I'd already been judged and found guilty without a trial. It was in their eyes, the condemnation that burned through each one of them.

"I didn't do this," I whispered, only to hear Eryx snort and turn to face me.

"No? Then why do I smell guilt wafting from you in waves? We can all smell it, Braelyn. You told us where they were hidden. You knew they were here," he accused, his tone damning me to hell.

"I didn't know," I argued through the swelling in my throat.

They pulled child after child from multiple metal storage containers. Eyes watched me, judging me as helicopters began landing at a safe distance from the children. My stomach swirled with bile as the last container was opened, and the stench of death filled the meadow while groups of people whispered angrily, turning to glare at me.

Saint lifted himself out of the last container, heading straight for me as tears swam in my eyes. There was nothing but rage and hatred to be found in him. He grabbed my arm, yanking me with him as he walked me toward the pit. He didn't miss a step as he jumped, pulling me down with him.

My arm rose, covering my mouth as I took in the dead women that were in varying stages of decay. A sob exploded from my throat as I shook my head. Saint watched me, his eyes condemning me until I wanted the ground to swallow me whole, never to see that look burning in his pretty gaze again.

"You fucking murderous bitch. You did this."

"No, I didn't. I didn't do this," I argued. I gagged on the air inside the storage container, shaking my head. "No, Saint. I didn't do this to them."

"You knew they were here. You knew these women and children were out here, suffering. You may not have put them here, but doing nothing to save them is the same thing as being the one to leave them here to fucking die. They're human, Braelyn."

"I didn't know they were here!" I shouted.

"Stop lying!" he snarled, pushing me back until I slipped and landed on a body that squished. "You are a fucking monster. You allowed your father to do this to them. How could you allow him to murder these women and children, trading your own people to be tortured? How the fuck could you do this to them? To me, Braelyn? You allowed your father to sell me, your fucking soul mate, to be tortured!"

"No," I argued as horror filled my expression. "No, you're lying! You left. You were safe from my father hurting you! I sacrificed everything to protect you!"

"You didn't sacrifice shit, Braelyn. I didn't leave

this mountain on my own. I was sold into slavery, to be eviscerated daily for some sick bitch's entertainment," he snorted, shaking his head while I gagged from the putrid air. "You can stay in here with them and apologize for playing a part in their death."

"No, Saint. Please don't leave me here," I whispered through trembling lips. "Don't do this," I pleaded, grabbing his arm only for him to shake me off.

"What's the matter, Princess? Can't stand to see what you and your daddy did to them? Imagine how they felt down here, slowly starving to death with no hope of escaping. Do you know how long it takes to starve to death? Or for hope to slowly fade to nothing but despair? I do. You and your father made damn certain that I knew I wasn't worthy of touching you. I was starved until I ate the poor bastard they'd put into my cell with me, just for fun. Unfortunately, it didn't get enough people willing to pay to watch it unfold, so they got creative with Eryx and me. They learned that people would pay more when alphas are tortured and made to feel powerless as their guts are removed from their bellies. I can tell you how long it takes to die when they removed each organ inside of me, you heartless bitch."

Tears streamed down my cheeks, and I shuddered at the horrors Saint described. I couldn't make myself tell him that I knew that fact as well as he did. I didn't tell him that my father had tried to artificially impregnate me by fucking my uterus after he'd taken it from my body. Saint snorted, shaking his head as he leaped for the open doors of the container. Hefting himself on the ledge, he glared down at me, leaving me alone with the dead.

"Lucas, I want you to return here tomorrow at nightfall and get Braelyn out of here. I am going with the children to ensure each is cataloged and removed from the list of missing and exploited children. When you bring her out, she's to be locked alone in her room until I return. No one is to go in or out of her room, other than guards. Understood?" Saint asked as the container doors were closed, locking me in the darkness with the dead.

"She can fucking rot in there for all I care," Lucas stated, and the others grunted their agreement.

I retched at the smell as I moved toward the light that shone in from small holes, allowing fresh air into the container. The sound of chains scraping on the door echoed, and then something solid slammed against the top of it, blocking the light of the moon from getting to me. I listened as the crowd began moving away, and the blades of the helicopters cutting through the air filled the night.

Panic set in as my foot connected with something cold and soft. I backed up, touching something else as a sob exploded from my chest. My entire body shook with cold and fear as my breathing became labored, and the stench of death filled the enclosed space.

How could Saint think I'd do something like this? I wasn't a monster. Had I ever suspected my father of this? No, but I wouldn't put it past him to be involved with something so horrendous. Harold had always been a monster. He was the monster I'd feared from childhood, the one that tormented and got off on murdering my mother and then took pleasure in torturing his child.

Tears dripped from my cheeks, and pain gripped my chest with the fact that I'd been played. They'd known Cora would turn feral, or Lucas had known. I was the only one who could end her suffering since no other alpha had been present from our pack. They'd all been missing from dinner until Lucas appeared, but only after I had dispatched his sister to the afterlife. Would he have pushed his hand through my chest if Cora had failed? Considering they couldn't have known how it would unfold, I was willing to bet they'd planned on me fighting Lucas after I'd killed his sister.

They'd needed me weakened to use the herbs in the bourbon because mugwort only worked on Fenrir wolves if they were unable to fight off the concoction's effects. It was what made us harder to kill than shifters with potions procured from witches. Saint and Eryx weren't worried about taking away my pain. They just wanted me weakened, asking me shit that hadn't made sense at the time, and now that my mind wasn't addled with pain, or drugs, I could think clearly.

Too little, too late for it to matter. I'm sure Saint had recorded me, us, as they toyed with me and asked their questions about this place. I'd admitted to knowing about the killing fields, but it wasn't because I'd known about the children or women held here. It was because I'd been held and tortured here by my father. I'd listened to the wind howling, and as a child, praying it was the ghost of my mother keeping me safe. I'd called it the killing field because this is where our pack battles had occurred. I'd always known I'd be buried here, and I guess I was right, but I'd gotten my murderer wrong. I'd never expected it to be Saint.

Sitting in the middle of the container, careful of the dead surrounding me, I hugged my knees to my chest. It wasn't the first time I'd been locked inside a container, but if I'm lucky, it would probably be the last time. I listened to the wind howling and wondered once again if it was my mother's ghost, keening with welcome that I'd soon be back in her arms, finally.

Chapter Fourteen

Days went by, and still, no one came to get me out of the dark hole in which they had left me alone. By the seventh day, I'd given up hope of anyone coming to retrieve me. Did the pack not realize that I was gone? Or had Saint made them see what a monster I was? On the eighth day, I was lying on the floor between the bodies when a blinding light disturbed the container.

Lifting my arm, I tried to block out the light as someone jumped down, and then pain ripped through me. I gasped, rolling into a tight ball as a booted foot connected with my stomach. Something metal slammed into my head, and then consciousness faded away.

When I awoke, it was to being propped up on something small. Opening my eyes, I stared at the shadowy figure in front of me. Blood coated my head, and I tasted it inside my mouth. I inhaled, trying to scent who was in the cart with me, but only the stench of blood and death filled my nose.

Turning my head, I screamed as something sliced through my shoulder and throat. Blood ran down my neck, coating my thin silk nightgown. I couldn't see what held me tied, but I knew if I moved, I was dead. I could feel the cold metal embedded in my arms and throat. They'd wrapped more of the same material around my torso and chest.

"It is razor wire," a feminine voice announced. "You move, and you die. Let's see how you enjoy being strung up like a pig at the market. This is what you did to my sister and my daughter. I watched them, you know. When the buyer decided he wasn't interested in raping them anymore, he did this to them. Eventually, your muscles will cramp, and you will fall. I made a promise to myself that if I ever found the bastards who stole them and sold them into torture, I'd make them pay with the same death my family had been forced to face alone."

"I didn't do this," I whispered, blinking as her voice registered.

Carleigh snorted, backing up until the light bathed her golden hair. She peered up, smiling as someone else jumped down into the container, staring at me. I met Lucas's stare as he took in the way she'd strung me up in razor wire, positioned to slice through me when my legs gave out.

"Saint called. He'll be back in a week. He won't be happy that she's dead," he disclosed, staring down at the tattered gown I wore. "I should have seen it earlier. I didn't want to believe them, but you are sick as fuck, Braelyn. You made us all think you were one of us, and this is what you did to our orphans? Did you plan to do this to Cora's son? Sell him off to feed the pack? They'll never trust you again after they watched the new alpha loading children you and your father brought here into those helicopters. You might as well step off that barrel now and do yourself a favor. Saint plans to murder you when he returns, and I'm guessing the razor wire will be an easier death than what he intends to do to you."

"I didn't do this," I repeated, unable to get anything else out. "You know me, Lucas. I didn't do this."

He snorted as Carleigh produced a blade and crept toward me. My breathing hitched as she swung wide, cutting through my thigh. I screamed, crying as pain burned the severed flesh. Lucas swallowed, watching as she continued cutting my thighs, arms, and then my calves open. Sobs ripped from my lungs while blood coated my feet, adding to the cold as the wind entered the shipping container.

"Enough, unless you intend to kill her, Carleigh. That's too easy of a death for the likes of her. Come on, before we miss Saint's call and someone else tells him she isn't inside her bedroom. You want this to work? Then we can't be here when he calls to check in on her."

I sagged against the wires, forcing myself to stand back up as they exited the container, leaving my body riddled with cuts. I slipped in the blood draining to pool at my feet, gasping as the wires sliced deeper into my arms. The sound of the container's doors slamming closed echoed, and I forced my gaze to remain on the front of it. These women and children had been buried with the doors facing the sky, leaving the bottom of it several feet into the earth. Judging by the bone-chilling cold, the container was already frozen in permafrost.

My mind whirled with everything I'd left unfinished. I'd sacrificed my happiness for the packs. I had given up Saint because the idea of my father dissecting and causing him pain had been more than I could stomach, but I'd failed because he'd been tortured, anyway. I hadn't said goodbye to Chaos, and he wouldn't understand any of this. Toralei had to be out there, going crazy without being able to sense my location, or maybe like the others, she was glad I was gone.

Did she believe Saint and his crew? Had she bought their story and hated me as Lucas did now? How had he chosen to do this to me? He had been my friend, and he'd so easily turned on me in his grief. Maybe even before it.

I wouldn't get to be a mother of my own child. I'd given up on it because Saint hadn't been around, but I'd always wanted to have a child of my own. I wanted to feel that blind love that a child bestowed on his mother, knowing she would always do everything to protect them. I wouldn't get that now.

I'd die here in this dark hole of death, and no one would even care. They thought I was a monster, but I'd been the first one to taste my father's madness. I'd been the first to see the sadistic look burning in his eyes as he'd called me into his apartment after the conclusion of my mother's funeral.

And now I was being accused of being like him? This shit fucking sucked, and it was Saint's fault. He wasn't faultless in this. He hadn't noticed the endless pain that I carried. He'd never questioned me going missing for weeks or noticed the dark circles I hid beneath makeup. He'd never seen the bruises that were still present, even after a week of hiding to give them time to heal.

He wanted to say it was all my fault, but I'd protected him and the pack. I'd done what I was supposed to do. My mother raised me always to put the pack before my needs. She had ingrained it into me since birth. She'd told me how to create my mask and hide my fear and pain at all costs because it was a useless emotion that helped no one.

"Look at me, sweet daughter."

"I'm scared, Mommy," I'd whispered, tears rolling down my cheeks onto the paper that had sat in front of me.

"What good does that do? Fear is an emotion. Who controls our emotions?" she'd asked, wiping away my tears.

"We do," I'd muttered, staring into her bright Nordic blue eyes.

"Exactly. It's an emotion that we control. It doesn't get to control us, Braelyn. You cannot show people you're afraid of anything. It gives them power over you. You're the daughter and the granddaughter of the greatest warriors the Fenrir wolves have ever known. You're the granddaughter of queens and kings. Their blood runs in your veins, and without you, our pack will have no heir."

"You carry another heir," I'd informed, dropping my gaze to her swollen belly. "Is she not ours?"

"She will never breathe her first breath. Your father will never allow it to happen. Now focus, Braelyn. Turn off your emotions. Show them who you are and that fear holds nothing for you. Show them that you're stronger than that worthless emotion."

"I don't understand, Mommy."

"I know you don't, and I can't explain it either. I only know that Harold is a monster, and I won't always be here to protect you. I feel it even now. I feel the gods coming for me, and I hate you will be left unprotected. I have pleaded to the gods to give you a strong, invincible alpha as your true soul mate. I have promised them my life and that of your sister so that you may carry on our line, Braelyn. Fenrir protects you, but the other gods protect you as well. You must never fear them. They lead us into the otherworld and welcome us to the afterlife. Promise to remember me. Promise me you always lead the pack and protect them, no matter what the cost. This is your pack now. You lead them, no matter what. Harold is weak, but he is conniving and sinister in his grab for power. You must be weary of him. He craves a son and doesn't understand that women lead our pack. We are of the wolf, and the blood of the Valkyrie runs through our veins. Stand up, Daughter. You are not weak."

I blinked, standing to stare at a ghostly image touching my cheek, creating a wave of warmth that washed through me.

"Stand up, Braelyn. You are stronger than this. I know you are because you are the daughter of Fenrir. His blood courses through you, and your pain is almost over. Be strong as I taught you to be. You are the light in the darkness, and no matter what happens, I am proud of the woman you became. Loki be damned! He cannot have you. You were meant to rule! The gods are meddling to see that of which you're made. So stand up and do not falter. Help is coming."

I heard the scraping of metal as my knees bowed, and I used what little strength I had left to push myself back up. Time held little meaning, and I couldn't tell how many days had passed since Carleigh had carved my flesh, hung me up to die, and the torture I'd endured. Days, maybe weeks? I was at the last of my strength, and even though the cuts had stopped bleeding, new ones from the razor wire continually drained me.

The doors swung open, and my vision swam from the intense light entering the container, blinding me, pushing me toward unconsciousness. Voices echoed, and my body slowly sagged as they cut me free from the wires. Someone grabbed me, screaming at the people behind them, and everything swam around me. Warmth washed through me as if my mother was still here, giving me her strength.

"Mommy," I whispered. "I'm ready to go with you, please."

"Jesus, fuck. Stay with me, Brae. Just fucking stay with me." Saint's angry tone filled the container as blood dripped onto my bare, bloodied feet.

Chapter Fifteen

Saint – A few hours earlier

I stood in the hallway, outside one of the many medical wards that held families uniting with their loved ones. Eryx stood across from me, speaking with a medic that had spent countless hours in the last two weeks tending to the children we'd found on the mountain. I'd spent a week here when we'd caught a lead on another smuggling ring and handled it before preparing to head back up the mountain.

I'd needed the time away from Braelyn to let the anger I'd felt dissipate. I knew what everyone wanted and what was required. Putting Brae down, though, the idea left me cold and dead inside.

She'd known about the killing fields, which meant she'd fucking known it was filled with boxes of victims. Fucking children that were helplessly awaiting torture. It would be endless with their immortality kicking in; even as young as they were, they'd heal if their tormentors didn't take shit too far.

It had knocked me back, knowing she'd been aware of the children buried inside the containers. Seventy-nine children and thirty-one women were recovered, ranging in age from six to thirty-one. That didn't include the ones I'd left her with, unwilling to identify the bodies of the deceased until I could stomach pulling out their remains.

Pulling my phone out, I dialed Lucas to check and make sure Brae wasn't trying to escape again since he'd said she had caused hell by doing so earlier. He'd ensured me he had handled her rebellion easily and that she'd stopped fighting him with no harm to her person.

"Hey, what's up?" Lucas asked, answering the call on the second ring.

"How's Chaos?" I enquired, dancing around what I really wanted to know.

"He's good. He is out with the men, tracking deer as you instructed. He stopped asking where Braelyn was and if he could see her a few days ago. You were right; keeping him busy is helping to keep his mind off of her."

"Good, that's good. Has Braelyn asked to leave the room again?" I watched as Eryx turned, staring me down.

"Nah, we stopped that by threatening to put her back into that storage container," Lucas laughed, but there was something in his tone that made me pause. "All is good here."

"That's good. I'll be home in the next couple of

days or so. Did the pack get enough meat stored away?" I nodded to Eryx, who walked closer, listening to Lucas speak. He swiftly explained total deer caught, salted, and stored before asking about Carleigh, who had shown up here trying to get me back into her bed, to no avail. "She's around here. Has Brae eaten?"

"Yeah, sure. I fed her," Lucas murmured, causing Eryx's eyes to narrow on the phone I held against my ear. "She's been a good prisoner. No problems from her this week."

Eryx frowned, nodding that Lucas spoke the truth. Eryx could read people's tones, minus Brae's, which we'd learned early on as children. She was harder to read, which we chalked up to her lineage, and being the daughter of Brenna Fenrir Haralson. Brae's emotions were the same, meaning she could easily shut everything off.

"How much has she eaten? I don't imagine it's much after being locked inside that car for a full twenty-four hours."

"She was picky at first, but she started eating well enough. You know how women are," he droned on. "Besides, it's not like it matters if she eats, she's a dead-wolf-walking, right, man?"

Eryx shook his head, glaring as I promised to return home shortly to help finalize the winter preparations. Ending the call, I slipped the phone into my pocket, staring at him.

"He's lying about something. His voice didn't hesitate on Braelyn being a dead wolf, though. Something isn't right, Saint."

"Let's go," I growled, heading toward Xavier, who leaned his head against the glass window of the room full of unclaimed children yet to be identified. "We're heading up to the mountain. Lucas is lying about Braelyn, and I need to know why he's lying."

"We'll head back with you. I need to review some of the footage of Jane Doe. Dyson said he found some new videos, some with voices. It might help me figure something out. I need to put her to rest, one way or another. She's out there waiting to be found, or they killed her because her uses ran dry."

"Grab Xari, and we'll head back up. It's an hour-long flight, and we're wasting daylight already. I need to be certain the pack has enough men out hunting before the snow gets too deep," I admitted, scratching my neck as the others gathered around.

"Problem?" Ezekiel and Enzo asked together, which creeped me the fuck out with their twin shit.

"I don't know yet. Something is off, and I've been gone too fucking long. I didn't plan on breaking up another ring while we were away. The asshole I left in charge of Braelyn seems off, and I think he might have helped her escape before the snow hits. He was her friend."

I watched as Carleigh approached. Her eyes were sharply focused on me while I studied the way her hips swayed. She smiled brightly, pushing her hands into her back pockets. "Problem?" she asked, and Eryx started to answer, but I slapped him on the shoulder.

"Nah, we're just going to go chase down a lead. You able to stick around and watch the kids?" I asked, dragging my gaze down her body with a heated look that made her smile turn seductive.

"Sure, but you owe me big time for doing it. You can buy me dinner and a drink when you get back," she announced.

"Sure thing, Car," I murmured, noting the others were watching me with hawk-like gazes. "The rest of you assholes get to the helipad. We don't want to miss this one or mess it up," I announced as Carleigh stared me down.

"Something wrong, Saint?" she asked, her instincts on point. They should fucking be; I'd trained her myself. She stepped back, the smell of fear filling the space around her.

"Grab her," I demanded as Phenrys and Bowen clutched her arms. "Put her in the bird and don't let her out of your fucking sight. I don't know what the fuck you did, hellhound, but it better not be what I think it is."

She smirked, her eyes dancing with laughter as she held my stare. A sick feeling entered my stomach as I turned, heading toward the helipad and the sound of the blades starting up. My mind whirled with what could have happened. Lucas had been a hard sell in turning against Braelyn, but he'd taken it deeper. He'd made it personal, which almost seemed too fucking easy.

Carleigh would probably help him free her so that she could get back into my bed. Hellhounds were territorial, and she'd made no secret about her intention, even after I'd turned her down repeatedly. Hell, I'd even invited Eryx to join me with her, and she still hadn't gotten the message that we weren't exclusive.

It took an hour and a half to reach the lodge, and the moment we landed, Toralei was there screaming at me. I watched her marching up to me, poking her finger into my chest as her rage filled the air between us.

"Where is she?" she demanded, hair wild and messed as if she'd been running her fingers through it in anger. I slid my gaze over her face, noting the way her nostrils flared, and her pupils dilated.

"Where the fuck is who?" I countered, watching her face turn a mottled shade of red.

"Braelyn! What the hell did you do with her, asshole?"

"She's in her fucking room, Toralei. Point that finger at me again, and I'll fucking rip it off."

"Liar! She is not in her fucking room."

"Bullshit! Lucas ensured me she hasn't left it," I argued, watching her chest rise and fall with her anger.

"Lucas left the week after you did, asshole. He left with your bitch, and no one has seen him since! No one has seen Braelyn since Eryx marched her into the woods, and no one will tell me anything! I am her beta. Do you have any idea how fucking insane I feel not being able to feel her? You don't think—where the fuck are you going?"

I was moving toward the lodge, rushing through it as my stomach churned and tightened. I didn't stop running until I was standing above the container, smelling death and blood. A lot of fucking blood. Eryx helped me lift the doors, and I jumped down, staring into the darkness. Others landed around me, lighting flashlights as the blood left my body.

Braelyn was balanced on a barrel precariously. Her body was covered in blood that continually dripped from the razor wire slicing into her body. Her big blue eyes were unfocused, and her lips were moving. Braelyn was filthy, covered in blood, and her hair was matted and caked in something I couldn't identify.

The air left my lungs as she whispered, "Mommy. I'm ready to go with you, please."

"Jesus, fuck. Stay with me, Brae. Just fucking stay with me," I growled, grabbing her as she started to fall forward, causing the razors to slice deeper into her tissue.

"What the actual fuck?" Eryx snarled, helping me push her up. "We need wire cutters, now!" he shouted, holding her upright while staring at the frailness of her body and the blood that covered her from head to toe.

"I want Lucas found, and I want his fucking heart," I snapped. "Carleigh is to be held in a room, and she doesn't leave it until we know what the fuck they did here. They were the only two with keys to the lock I placed on the doors."

"She's bleeding out," Ezekiel announced as if we didn't fucking know it already.

"And she wants to go with her mommy," Enzo stated, flicking a blade open as he cut through the wires that were inside the skin of her thighs. "Someone wanted to kill your mate. This wire is set to cut her to pieces, including her fucking throat the moment she fell."

ALPHA'S CLAIM

I looked at the wire and frowned at the way it was rigged. I'd seen it used many times, where cold-twisted bastards placed bets on how long the victim could remain upright before the wires cut them into pieces, ending the life of even an immortal. Someone had tried to murder Brae while I was away, and I was willing to bet it was Lucas and Carleigh.

Braelyn mumbled more words to her mother, begging her to take her away from the evil, causing nausea to burn the back of my throat. I'd left her here, intending for her to spend one fucking night in the box since the children had been in it for weeks. I'd remained gone to help find their parents. Never had I assumed Lucas and Carleigh would leave her in the container, let alone strung up to die a death like the one the razor wire promised.

"Braelyn, stay with me," I uttered, watching as the last of the wire was cut away from her body, but she remained upright. Eryx helped me bring her down from the barrel, staring at the wounds that hadn't healed due to her body sustaining too much damage. "Her head is split open, and someone cut her up enough that she shouldn't have been able to remain standing, let alone live long enough for us to get back here."

"Judging by the way her wounds look, she's been hung up for days, if not longer." Xavier covered his nose as he pointed to the wounds on her inner thighs in varying healing stages. "That looks like it was done days ago. The edges look more like scars than wounds, but it can't heal with the amount of blood she lost. There are white marks on her calves, which I'm guessing were cuts as well. She's a fighter, Saint. If she weren't, you'd be returning to a corpse."

Braelyn lifted her head, but there was nothing in her gaze. The vacant look she gave me said she didn't even recognize me. Her lips moved, but the sound was so soft that I couldn't make out the words. Leif stepped closer, touching her chin to lift her eyes toward the light.

"It's not Loki, little Princess. He can't have you, and he knows it. It is forbidden for Loki to take one of our kind from this world or the afterlife. Brenna, wake her," he stated, turning his head toward the dark corner of the room. "Either wake her or take her away from the pain, Brenna Haralson. Your daughter suffers because you're holding her to you. She cannot be inside both words."

I peered around at the others, shrugging at their confused expressions. Braelyn gasped in air, her eyes regaining focus before a mask covered her features. Her eyes moved to mine, holding them before she stepped back, faltering, then stood proudly, with no pain visible on her face. If I didn't know better, I'd think she was one of Harold's victims.

"I didn't mean for this to happen." I watched her closely, noting she didn't even look in our direction. She looked through us as if she were alone inside the container. Blood dripped from multiple incisions and tears on her flesh. I moved closer, and she stepped back, uncaring that she stepped into the mushed corpse of a victim. "Let me help you, Brae."

"I do not need your help," she whispered, barely loud enough to be words. Leif looked over her head, catching my attention briefly before turning to the corner, staring at the air.

"Seven days of standing on a barrel, waiting to die," Leif announced, still staring into the shadows. "Your mate, she's an entirely different breed of woman. You got yourself a fucking Valkyrie, lucky prick. Brenna, a pleasure seeing you again. I'm sure you'll be waiting with a blade at the ready when I enter Valhalla. I look forward to it, shield-maiden. You raised a rare one, with silent courage and one hell of a pain tolerance."

"Who the fuck are you talking to, asshole? Brenna Haralson has been dead and gone for fifteen years," I grounded out, watching as Leif pointed his thumb toward the shadows, causing a shiver to rush down my spine.

"Brenna, obviously. I'm guessing she returned to keep her daughter standing until help arrived. Sprits that are in the afterlife can only return when their bloodline is on the brink of extinction. I'm not crazy, Saint. I died, which means I can see beyond the veil that this world can see. We should get Braelyn to the lodge before her mother, who really doesn't like you, accepts her pleas to join her in death." Braelyn moved on her own. I watched her moving toward the light that was fading as day gave in to the moon's demand for dominance over the world.

Fear at how feeble and weak Braelyn appeared, gripped my heart. I hadn't wanted her to suffer any pain. Discomfort, certainly. Those she'd left out in the bone-chilling cold, to starve and sit in their own shit, had suffered more than the twenty-four hours I'd intended for her to spend here. I watched her leap for the ledge, landing hard on the ground while everyone remained away from her.

They knew she wouldn't want help, which burned me inside, watching as she fell to the ground, unable to reach the edge to leave the storage container. It took Braelyn multiple tries before her fingers caught the edge, and we all stared in silence as she hefted her weight up and over the edge. One by one, the others went up until I stood alone, peering into the shadows that Leif had been speaking into, sliding my eyes around it.

"You can't fucking have her yet," I whispered, shaking my head. Something touched my shoulder, forcing my eyes to close as warmth washed over me. "She's my mate, and until I decide otherwise, you don't get her, Brenna. You left her with a monster which turned her into one, too. I have to decide what to do with her, and until I do, she is mine." Pain slid against my forearm, and I looked down at the marks that covered it. Leif wasn't crazy after all. "Thank you for keeping her alive until I got here. Now back off and let me see if I can save her."

Chapter Sixteen

Braelyn

I could hardly walk, but I wouldn't allow anyone to help me. It wasn't pride or something else forcing me forward. It was that I wanted nothing to do with any of them. Saint abandoned me in that container, choosing to give others the responsibility for my care. I thought Lucas was my friend, but I was so very wrong. He watched me being strung up to die, cut multiple times, and returned to continue the torture. The alphas I'd spent my entire life focused on protecting and providing for stood idle while I was left in a dark hole to die.

We passed through the gates, and my gaze slid over the wolves that watched us with curiosity. After a moment, they turned, giving me their backs, albeit hesitantly. My heart clenched, knowing that whatever Saint was selling, they'd bought it. Turn your back on an alpha was a show of disrespect, saved for those who had betrayed the pack.

Fuck them, too, then.

My attention shifted to Toralei, who watched me with horror-filled eyes. I could imagine how I looked. The short, white, silky nightgown was stained brown, with crimson patches from where fresh blood was soaking through. The thin material was ripped in multiple places, revealing the damage to my body. My feet were bare, covered only in the stockings I'd been wearing the day they'd marched me to the storage containers. They were stiff and sticky, covered in blood.

The gash in my head hadn't healed, and my hair was matted from lying beside the dead, using the clothes they wore for warmth. The flesh of my arms was flayed open, revealing the layers of fatty tissue and muscle it had exposed.

Tears swam in Toralei's eyes, yet she didn't move from where she stood. I didn't need to know she would continue standing by me. She was my best friend and my beta. Chaos rushed toward me, his eyes widening with fear as someone caught him. He struggled against their form, but I didn't slow or stop my forward movement.

Saint had taken everything from me. He'd turned the pack against me, accusing me of heinous crimes without proof. He'd claimed me, forcing me to cling to an empty mating that held no meaning. I'd been hung up and left to die, like meat in the freezer. The only thing that remained was my inner strength and my pride. I'd be damned if he took that from me, too.

Inside the lodge, people turned toward me, staring at the dishevelment of my form before slowly turning their backs to me. No emotion escaped the mask I wore.

No sign of pain slipped onto my face as I moved down the hallway, leaving a trail of blood and filth as I headed to my bedroom.

The moment I was inside, I turned, trying to close the door, but Saint shook his head. Both he and Eryx entered my room, watching as I backed away from them. I didn't speak, couldn't manage to get words out past the anger and hurt that hung heavily on my soul. My eyes rolled, and even that hurt to accomplish.

"Start the shower, Eryx," Saint ordered, studying me. "You need to sit down. You're losing too much blood."

I ignored him. Standing tall, I pushed my shoulders back in the stiff position in which I'd grown accustomed since being beaten. My chest rose and fell with short, quick breaths that didn't cause my body to scream in silent agony. I could hear the deep rattle in my chest, knowing I was getting close to the limit of endurance I'd learned to sustain.

"I didn't want you to hurt, Brae. I only intended for you to know what it was like to be locked in a box, waiting for someone to save you. I need you to understand that," Saint urged, searching my face to see if I'd grasped his meaning.

"The water is warm," Eryx stated from the bathroom.

I moved toward the open doorway, entering the room to lean against the counter. Saint came in behind me, watching me struggle to remove the nightgown. Pain tore through my arms as I fought and struggled to remove the garment that reeked of death and decay. My arm went limp, and I closed my eyes as a soft exhale rattled up from my lungs, escaping from my throat.

Saint moved in behind me, flicking a knife open that made the air whoosh from my lungs as my pupils dilated. He swallowed loudly, bringing it up to slice through the spaghetti straps that sat on my shoulders. It didn't drop to the floor, stuck to the wounds that covered my body. He hissed, slowly peeling it off before turning me around, lowering his stare to where the panties had been cut open.

"What the hell?" Saint growled, his eyes flashing with rage before they met mine.

I didn't speak or even acknowledge him. I didn't need to tell him what Lucas had done to me because the cuts still covered my sex from where he'd returned, alone, using a knife on me. He hadn't raped me, but he hadn't left me untouched either.

"Tell me that isn't what I think it is," Eryx growled, his eyes turning dark with rage.

Saint swallowed, shaking visibly with anger. "Who did this, Braelyn?" he demanded, his tone filled thick with emotion.

I leaned over, ripping the garter away as a scream exploded from my lungs. Lucas had bragged about how stupid I was and how naïve I'd been, never actually knowing him. He boasted about how he'd put on the perfect show for everyone, including Carleigh, feigning shock and outrage at the things Saint had accused me of doing. Lucas was proud to have forced my hand to kill his sister, using her and her child as fodder, helping Saint to turn the pack against me. He'd told me all about how he'd helped my father torture me. I'd never been wise to the fact it was Lucas wielding the knife when my father tired of slicing it into my flesh. I'd been foolish to think him a friend, but I'd been starved for companionship when Saint was sent away.

Lucas was the one guy I had counted on for strength, and he had been one of my tormentors all along, hiding his scent with pepper or bleach to keep me from knowing it was him. I'd begged and pleaded for him to stop inside the storage container, but he enjoyed giving pain in the worst imaginable way. Of course, Lucas had bragged about never taking it too far, but Saint had removed Fenrir's protection by mating with me. With the protection gone, Lucas was able to wield other things against me, and my entire nether region was a mass of cuts, proof that he'd enjoyed playing with me.

Eryx lowered to the floor, yanking the stockings down before lifting my foot to remove them. I pushed past Saint when Eryx freed me from the material, trembling violently as the heat from the spray touched my frozen flesh.

A sob exploded from my chest, and I moved to the wall, pressing my forehead against it. I wrapped my arms around my stomach and closed my eyes as I hit the ground, crying out as my strength waned.

Saint entered the shower a few moments later, grabbing the shampoo to lather my hair. Eryx joined us, and they worked together, silently cleaning my battered body. Saint pulled me against him, turning me toward Eryx, who peered down at my body with a murderous look dancing in his gaze.

"We find Lucas, and we return what he did to her tenfold, Saint," he growled, his midnight gaze sliding up to meet mine.

"Agreed," Saint whispered, holding me carefully as Eryx used a soft cloth to wash my body. They worked like they'd done this before, helping one another to ease the pain. My eyes closed against the dark blotches swimming in my vision.

I gasped, screaming as Eryx washed between my thighs. Air refused to reach my lungs as I fought against him cleaning my sex, riddled in shallow cuts. His jaw clenched, and pain filled his eyes.

"She may have internal damage," Eryx admitted.

Saint's hands tightened around my chest, and his lips brushed against my shoulder. He was prepared to subdue me if I fought against Eryx cleaning the wounds. Saint continued, studying my face as I slid the mask back over my emotions. His attention shifted over my shoulder, and he exhaled slowly.

"How do you do that, Princess? How do you just shut it the fuck off?" Eryx asked, finishing with his task.

Saint stood me up with him, stepping into the warm spray before moving us out of the shower. Eryx helped him wrap a towel around me, noticing that blood seeped into the fabric. Before I could protest, he picked me up and walked me into the bedroom where Xari sat on the chair, holding up a bag of blood.

"Vampire blood mixed with healing herbs," she stated, shaking her head. "Ezekiel and Enzo said to make her drink it all and then have her smoke this shit." She tossed a tin onto the bed, lifting her gaze to mine. "My father wants to know if they—if they used a blade?"

"Yes, they did. Have Carleigh placed into a holding cell, and don't let her out of your sight. Have Toralei tell the pack that Lucas is wanted for treason against his alpha. I want that mother fucker hunted down and brought back here alive," Saint whispered, and I shivered at his tone, filled with hatred and rage.

"You won't find him," I stated, trying to get out of his hold.

"Stop fighting me, Brat."

"Don't ever call me that again," I snarled, staring into his rounded gaze with a rage of my own. "Put me down, now."

He didn't argue, placing me on my feet. I moved to my bed, fighting to get the covers off as the towel they'd wrapped around me, dropped to the floor. Sitting carefully on the bed, I lifted one leg onto the mattress and then the other as Xari grimaced, turning white before she hid the horror on her face.

Saint reached over, covering my body with the blankets before he undid the bag of blood and held it out for me to take. I didn't argue, knowing that vampire blood would heal me a lot faster than my body could, given the amount of damage it had sustained this time.

Usually, my father was careful not to inflict too much damage, wanting me to appear whole in front of the pack. After all, he didn't want them knowing he tortured and mutilated his daughter. That would have caused the pack to rise against his rule. He'd been careful and strategic in what he'd done or allowed those to inflict onto my body. And on the occasion that he took things too far, he had told the pack that I was away on pack business.

The one time he'd lost control in a rage, it took me over a month to heal. One thousand shallow cuts, and then they'd flayed the flesh from my body. It had been one of the few times I'd begged for him to end it, to take my life because the pain had been too much to bear. My father was a master of agony, and Lucas, who admitted to cutting the skin from my stomach, thighs, and arms, had been present for that one.

Once I'd finished the blood, Eryx lit a joint from the tin Xariana had tossed onto the bed, handing it to me. My arm wouldn't lift, and my entire body felt as if it were made of solid concrete. He moved closer, taking a drag before pressing his lips against mine, blowing the smoke deep into my lungs.

"Hold it in, Braelyn," he stated, exhaling. "Good girl." He smiled sadly, pushing the wet hair away from my face.

"Move, asshole," Saint grunted, sliding onto the bed beside me, taking the joint from Eryx and holding it against my lips. "Xari, after you've finished disclosing the information to your father, see if the medic can find something to help knock her out."

A knock sounded, and Xariana rose from her chair, opening the door a crack before turning to look at Saint.

"It's your goon squad. They've been outside the door since you two closed it in their faces." Xari stepped back a moment before it swung wide, revealing Saint's crew and a few others that sat in the hallway.

"Brae needs rest," Saint stated, but they ignored him and piled into the room.

"Was she done like the others?" Phenrys asked, his pretty eyes watching mine.

"Yeah, I think we finally found him," Eryx growled, and my stare slid to his, narrowing on him. He noticed my expression and exhaled. "We've been tracking a monster who likes to use knives on females. He flays the flesh from their stomach and then places it onto their vaginas to make them appear…"

"Like dolls," I whispered, holding his stare.

"How did you know that, Brae?" Saint asked.

"An educated guess," I whispered hoarsely, swallowing past the copper taste of blood that remained in my mouth. "Why else would he take flesh from the stomach, placing it over the vagina? Maybe he didn't get enough playtimes with Barbie and was jealous of Ken."

"Sick fucking bastard," Xariana groaned, turning her attention toward the door where the demon twins leaned against it, peering into the room.

"Lucas needs to be put down, and it needs to be done in an excruciatingly painful manner," Enzo stated, dragging his eyes over my face. I shivered at the look of curiosity, as if he knew every dark secret I held without needing to be told. The shadows moved around him, and his lips jerked into a sinister smirk that caused a tremor to rush through me. "Ezekiel, she needs another bag of O positive. See that Ian is thanked, and that he has what we offered him in return. Notify Cole Van Helsing that we need his services to hunt down a Fenrir wolf. One who didn't get enough playtime with Barbie and looks like Ken. Someone should have told that bastard that Barbie gets off with G.I. Joe, and only him."

"Sick, fuck," Ezekiel snorted, his eyes holding mine as he tilted his head. "Don't waste the dragon grass, pretty Princess. It's hard to come by, even for creatures like us. It will free your mind of the pain and allow you to rest without nightmares. Unless, of course, you're into that?" he asked in a hope-filled tone.

"Fuck off, demon. She's not yours to toy with and in no condition to deal with your games," Saint grunted, settling beside me in nothing more than a pair of loose-fitting shorts. "Inhale," he ordered, holding the joint to my lips. I licked my chapped, blood-covered lips, and he sighed, nodding to the men leaning against the wall, silently watching us. "She needs water, more blood, and that fucker's head. In that order, gentlemen."

"I'll grab water," Phenrys announced, pushing off the wall.

"I'll get more blood," Bowen snorted, following him out of the room.

"I'll help Ezekiel convince Cole Van Helsing that we need his assistance to go hunting. Lucas couldn't have made it too far off this mountain," Sian stated, nodding toward Ezekiel, who continued staring at me.

"You're in agony, yet you don't make a sound. You are either very good at hiding the pain, or you've had lots of time to master it, little girl. How much pain have you known in your lifetime to hide that emotion from your pretty eyes?" Enzo asked, creeping closer, inhaling the air as he moved toward me. "You intrigue me."

Worry shone in Xari's eyes before she turned her gaze on me. I was guessing it wasn't a good thing to intrigue a demon. Not that I'd met many of them before, but this one was sex incarnate and leaked lethal vibes from his pores. The other one studied us, his smile lopsided as he slid his gaze over my face, then moved it back to his brother.

"Curiously, she shows no sign of her pain, but her agony hangs in the surrounding air. Her aura is—blue, yet shrouded in darkness."

Leif's snort filled the hallway. "She's Brenna Haralson's daughter. Fenrir wolves mask pain, hiding it from their enemies. They're masters at it and believe that they control their emotions and their fate by doing so. I'd bet my eternal soul that Braelyn's mother showed her how to hide it all. Every emotion she feels is muted, such as fear, pain, and love. Isn't that so, Braelyn?" he asked, leaning into the room to hold my stare.

"Emotions are weapons that can be wielded against you. To allow someone to taste fear is power. To allow them to know your pain is an addiction. Love is a weakness that can destroy you. They're only emotions, and we control them because only we can decide what we feel. My enemies will never see me falter or know that they have given me pain. I have no weakness that can be used against me. Not anymore," I stated, sliding my attention to Saint. "You took it away, and now you have nothing to wield against me. I should probably thank you for that, shouldn't I?"

"And what did I take away from you?"

"My pack, and the only vow I ever pledged to keep. Before my father beat her to death, I promised my mother that I would always put the pack first and protect them. Now they don't respect me, and they're no longer my pack. They're yours."

"What the fuck does that mean, Braelyn?" he demanded.

"It means I am free of my promise," I whispered, licking my lips that continued to crack and bleed from speaking. "No matter what happened or what cost I had to pay to ensure their safety, I paid it without hesitation. But now I am free."

"What she means is, she can leave here free from her obligations to the pack. There's nothing here for her anymore," Leif grunted, shaking his head. "You took away her purpose, and when a wolf is free of her commitments to her pack, she is no longer burdened by them. Isn't that right, little wolf?"

"Exactly right, Leif," I stated, exhaling the pain from my lungs as the weight lifted from my chest. "I am no longer a part of your pack, Saint." I smiled, feeling the burden of holding the pack together, releasing me. "I'm free."

"You're my mate, Braelyn," he pointed out.

"That doesn't mean I give one fuck of an iota about belonging to you anymore. You bit me, and that only means you own my womb. You own nothing else within me. I rejected you to free you from what my father threatened to do to you if I didn't. I tried to protect you, and you returned to destroy me. We're not even on the same level. You want to hurt me, and I wanted to save you from my demons. My only mistake was in thinking my bastard father would uphold his end of the deal, allowing you and your friends to walk away from this place."

"Think we should have mentioned the dragon grass makes the user rather—blunt?" Ezekiel asked, turning to look at Enzo, who snorted.

"I'm enjoying it. She's rather savage, and how often do you see Saint sweating balls?" Leif snorted, causing the others to turn in his direction. "Fuck off! He's been an insufferable prick ever since he announced we were returning here. I intend to enjoy that look of fear in his eyes a moment longer."

I carefully turned onto my side, peering up at Saint, who glared down at me. A soft gasp escaped my lips, barely discernable to even my ear. My lashes fluttered, hearing him snort.

"You even try to escape me, and I will chain your pretty ass to this bed, Brat."

"And do what? Fuck me stupid? I was stupid the moment I rejected you, and every day since I spent watching the horizon, praying to the gods that you would come back to me. How's that shit working out for me? I'd have been better off praying that someone missed a chunk of wood and removed my head with their ax. It would have been kinder. And I told you never to call me that again. I'm not your Brat anymore. I'm your unwanted mate, and you're mine."

"See, savage little thing," Leif snorted, his deep chuckle filling the room as my eyes grew heavy and sleep settled over me.

I felt Saint's finger tracing my cheek, but I couldn't open my eyes. It felt as if someone had glued them closed.

"Get the bag prepped for an IV. She's out." Saint's breath fanned my face as he pressed his forehead against mine. "I want that asshole found and hung up in the courtyard to send a warning to any of Harold's people we've missed. I want those sick bastards to know exactly what happens when you touch my girl."

Chapter Seventeen

It took days to fully heal from my injuries, even with copious amounts of vampire blood that had been fed to me intravenously. During that time, Saint had hovered. He'd been inside the room with me, trying to force conversation, which I'd ignored for the most part. There was a certain freedom in knowing someone else was taking care of the pack and that it wasn't up to me to oversee it all anymore.

On the fifth day of being on bed rest, Saint finally slipped out of the room to deal with a disturbance. It left me alone for the first time since he'd shown up here and ruined my plans. Slipping into the closet, I dressed into a soft pair of jeans and a cashmere top.

I slid my feet into a pair of knee-high leather boots and stepped out of the bedroom, peering up at Xavier, who leaned against the wall with his phone in his hand. He pushed it into his pocket the moment he noticed me.

"How are you feeling?" His kind, blue eyes met

and held my stare.

"Fine," I said sharply as his mouth tipped into a friendly smile.

"Saint didn't want you to leave the room, but a bit of fresh air never hurt anyone. Do you want to go outside for a few? It's not too cold yet, but you might want a jacket."

"Fresh air sounds good," I answered, noting the way his muscles rippled.

Xavier's dark blonde brow rose in silent question, and I shrugged. "I don't get bothered by the cold unless I'm left underground inside a storage container for a few weeks." So, I was being petty and rude, but then he was on Saint's side, and I was done playing nice with all of them.

Not bothering to wait for permission, I started down the long hallway toward the staircase that led down to the main entrance. The cold air blasted against my face as I pushed through the doors. I could smell the promise of snow in the crisp air.

People paused the moment they caught my scent, examining me like I was a threat. A mother grabbed her child, pulling him closer before fleeing with him. It caused an ache in my chest that tightened around my heart.

Men that had been chopping wood paused, staring me down with derision burning in their gazes. I got it; to lie to the pack or place them into a threatening situation was a heinous crime that would sever their trust. It didn't look good, but that they'd assume I was guilty based only on the word of strangers stung.

I'd never given the pack a reason to doubt my loyalty, always placing their needs before my own. Now, they'd chosen to treat me like I wasn't the same girl who had grown up working beside them. They had judged me without a trial or without one person asking if I'd done the crime. Toralei waved, and a soft grin tugged my lips as I turned, peering up at Xavier.

"Am I free to visit, or does my master wish for me to be kept away from everyone?" I asked, and Xavier's eyebrows rose before they creased his forehead.

"You can visit, but don't go too far. Saint is worried you're going to run from him."

"He should be worried because I will eventually," I admitted. "Not today, though. It's cold, and I don't even have a jacket, now do I?" I smiled, batting my eyelashes as he touched his fingers to his forehead, and pointed at a bench.

"I'll be over here if you need me."

I watched him walk to the bench before I turned to join Toralei. When I reached her, she threw herself at me, hugging me tightly.

"Jesus, fuck, Brae. Are you okay?" she asked, turning to hiss at a man who growled at my approach in a warning. "Faithless pricks," she muttered beneath her breath.

"I'm good," I answered, grabbing her hand to pull her with me onto the lookout that peered over the gate of the compound. "I want you to prepare to leave."

"I'm not leaving you," she whispered.

"No, you're not. We're leaving together. I won't

remain here with Saint. He doesn't deserve me. What I did was to protect him, or what I thought would free him of my father's hold. Harold sold them into slavery, and they think I was a part of it."

"That's horse shit." She shook her head, leaning back, resting her elbows on the railing as she looked in one direction while I looked in the other, making sure we wouldn't be overheard. "You wouldn't do what they've accused you of doing. I know you better than they do, but anyone who could think you're a monster can get fucked. That is something I would have noticed. The pack will come around once their brains start functioning again."

"I don't care if they do or not anymore," I admitted. "I have spent my life here in exile from the world because of my father and people like them. Everyone else here has been out into the world and had the opportunity to live off this mountain, Tora. Not me. I've been stuck here as a prisoner to my father, and I need to leave for a while, if not forever."

"Done," she exclaimed. "I'll call Douglas. He will find us a place to stay where we won't be easy to trace. He can get us off the mountain, too, if we can get out from beneath your new jailor's watchful eyes. They're everywhere. I count seven sets of eyes from his team watching you at this moment, not including the hunter he has babysitting you."

"We'll figure it out, and soon. I want to be gone before the snow hits."

"What about Chaos? He misses you, and he isn't buying the shit going around here. That kid has more brains than the entire pack combined right now."

"I'm sure they're shell-shocked. Hell, even I am. My father was a monster, and you and I knew that. We just never considered how black his soul was until Saint exposed it to us. I never even suspected that he was selling people and creatures to other monsters. Lucas—" I swallowed past the bile that burned the back of my throat.

"I know," Tora uttered softly, exhaling. "Saint told me what happened and why he wasn't letting you out of bed yet. He said you were up with the sun, ready to work the next day. I feel like an idiot, Brae. I dated Lucas and never suspected he could do something so heinous. He seemed more beta than alpha, but now we know he wasn't. That asshole fooled both of us."

I smiled tightly, pushing away the images that rushed through my head. Had there been signs we'd missed or overlooked, or was he just good at hiding his true nature? My father had fooled the pack for decades, including my mother. She hadn't realized Harold was a monster until she was pregnant with his second child, and she still hadn't predicted how far the sickness went into his soul.

"Monsters can hide in plain sight, with no one suspecting what lies beneath the surface. The world is filled with them, and most are human. Lucas was always a monster, but he hid it behind kind eyes and smiles. It was my job to find the demons and drive them out, and I failed. Maybe I deserved what I had endured since I'd failed the pack in spotting the monster within our midst. My father never hid the sinister nature he wore like a cloak around him. The pack was always wary of him, but they stayed because of me. Because of my legacy and the bloodline that I hold." Guilt washing over me that I was held in a prison of my own making. Not me, per se, but the blood rushing through my veins drove Fenrir wolves to our gates, where they'd become my responsibility to protect.

"It isn't your fault, Braelyn. What happened to you down there—it shouldn't have happened to anyone. Ever. Saint is coming. I'll call Douglas and secure passage. You figure out how to lose your guards." Tora's eyes followed Saint as he moved across the courtyard. "The pack doesn't want you helping them anymore. They prefer that you keep your distance. The omegas have requested that you be denied access to the children and their quarters."

Saint's footsteps stalled at her words. I caught his scent on the wind, closing my eyes against the pain of her confession. Turning toward her, I nodded.

"You'll need to count the deer in the meat lockers," I instructed. "Also, count the blankets, and if there aren't enough for each person, have the weavers start on more. The roof on the sheds and older houses need shingles replaced." I knew Saint was listening to every word we whispered. As alpha, he could listen in on any conversation within a certain distance from his location. "The berries need picking before the first freeze. Glenda can take some people out to pick them, as she normally handles it. Candy will make jams and freeze the rest of them. I purchased extra jars and wax seals as she'd requested last year after we were short of them. I sold my mother's diamond necklace for lumber that should arrive sometime in the next couple of days; ensure it is weathered and treated before accepting the order."

"You loved that necklace," Tora muttered, scrubbing her hand over her mouth.

"A necklace wouldn't keep the pack warm or the winter air from nipping at them as they sleep at night, but that's no longer my concern as Saint will be handling all these things in the future. Oh, and I almost forgot. I purchased new windows for Lars's pack, as theirs were cracked from the children playing ball too closely to their house. See that he gets them."

"Anything else?" she asked, snorting. "None of them deserve you, Brae. They're all nothing more than faithless assholes."

"Keep Chaos safe from the female alphas. They'll try to hurt him to make me fight. I have no intention of fighting for anything anymore."

"What about the alpha females that will seek out Saint? They're going to try to challenge you for your position," she pointed out angrily.

"I'll concede it," I stated, turning to look at her. "If they want Saint, they can have him and my position. I care not for either of them anymore." I heard Saint grumble under his breath but chose to ignore him.

"Okay, calm your tits. That's crazy talk. If you're not the alpha female…"

"Then I am nothing? No, Toralei. It means I am no longer needed. It means for the first time in my life, I am not beholden to anything or anyone else. As long as I am the alpha female, I am stuck in Saint's shadow. If I concede without allowing the challenge, they take my place with my mate. He does not carry my mark, and we share no eternal bond due to his inability to allow it to happen. Because of his rejection, the bond is only one-sided. I'm perfectly okay having my needs met without a male. Besides, why put up with their shit when you only get a few moments of pleasure from them, anyway? After all, I have successfully achieved many orgasms since I discovered the devil's doorbell and its need to be rung, and didn't need help, right? I am, if nothing else, sufficient at dealing with my needs."

I saw a smirk forming on Saint's lips from the corner of my eye. He sat beside Xavier, watching us from the bench, and Xavier tapped Saint's leg to focus his attention on their conversation about hunter business.

Unlike the others, I knew Saint could hear me. Toralei was aware of it as well, having been at my side since we'd discovered our bond and that even though she was a born alpha, she was my beta. I'd told her secrets no beta had ever been told. Some of what I'd shared were secrets that alphas kept on a tight hold because sometimes betas turned against them, and we were urged never to trust anyone.

"The pack will come around, Braelyn. They just need a moment to get past the shock of it all. Once they do, they'll see you wouldn't do what Saint and his men have accused. You're not the monster they think you are."

"It doesn't matter anymore. The fact that my pack thought I could ever do those things to another is what burns me the most. My father was a monster, and they knew that. I spent my life giving them everything they needed and took no pleasure for myself. I have sacrificed most of my mother's jewels and artifacts from my line to keep them fed and clothed. I wish I had known how easily they would turn with mere words said by strangers. I was taught actions speak louder than accusations, yet they are merely told that I was a part of something horrendous, and they give me their backs, rejecting me without giving me the benefit of the doubt or taking the time to learn the truth."

"Saint told them you knew what was in the killing fields," she pointed out.

"No, I merely said that ghosts could be heard whispering and keening within the killing fields. I also said the damned screamed for help, and yet it fell on deaf ears. I had no idea what was in the ground, only that Harold forbid the pack from entering that section of the mountain, and I enforced his laws. Those fields have been called the killing fields since I was a child, and every child inside the lodge and compound knows it by that name as well. It is where the battles took place when neighboring packs came to challenge us for the mountain. We just stopped calling it by that name openly for fear it would bring new challengers back to our doorstep. There is pepper inside the shipping containers, which prevented us from catching the scents of those victims. I caught a whiff of cayenne and other dried variants of pepper after the smell of the dead dissipated."

"That would make it near impossible for anyone to smell anything from this distance. That's how Harold prevented the pack from scenting others on the mountain. It still doesn't explain how he got them into the containers and buried them without anyone noticing," she mused.

"He could have done that beneath our noses. We were all focused on winterizing, and that kept us busy. There are so many of us and so much to do that everyone is given a job, including the children. It is the perfect way to slip around this place without others noticing. Besides, we were all warned not to go into those fields. We're a pack, and we run as a pack. Harold never did so, and so no one even wondered where he was or what he was doing," I laughed at the fact that I never cared where my father was, so long as he left me alone.

"But not you, Brae," she pointed out, grunting at the smile on my lips. "Stop smiling; you're creeping me out right now. I get the part where no one noticed Harold because he was fucking worthless. But you worked side-by-side with us, never backing down from a challenging job. Shit, there's not a job here that you haven't done at least twice, maybe thrice. So how can they find fault with you?" Tora demanded, her anger brushing over my arm to waft in the air around us.

"It's self-preservation, Tora. The pack is about to be stuck on this mountain with a new alpha they don't know. They know he just proved the last one was a monster, something they already knew. Saint won them over by freeing children, and even I would have accepted that as something deserving of respect. I am just collateral damage at this point because I am part of the old alpha's legacy. He worked beside them, as I have done. Saint isn't a monster like my father was, not to them. He's my monster, and I don't even blame him for hating me for rejecting him. I did that to ensure he had a future. I knew he would hate me for it, but he had to live to hate me, and I was willing to allow it rather than the alternative. They're not wrong to accept him into the pack, or as their alpha, for that matter. The thing is, the packs are black and white. They have laws and rules they swear by. What happened here, and what is happening to me, it's a gray area, and they don't know what to do about it. They're doing what they were taught to do since birth. They are protecting themselves and their families from the storm that is unfolding here."

"By smearing you and your face into the dirt, Braelyn," she grunted, staring at the pack while I did my best to ignore the bustle of people behind us. "It's not right, and you fucking know it. And that smug prick is allowing them to condemn you without any proof that you were involved."

"If he were anyone else, I'd be dead, Toralei. If another alpha had come here and discovered my father's sins, my bloodline would have been eradicated with him. You and I both know that to be true. I'm not dead, not yet, at least. Now, make sure that everyone knows what to do and what to expect for deliveries. I think I've had enough air for today," I stated, leaving her to return to my room.

Saint watched me walk across the courtyard, standing when I got close to his location. His eyes studied my face before slowly sliding back to where Tora remained, leaning against the railing, watching us.

"Where are you off to, Braelyn?" he asked, searching my face carefully.

"To my cell, Saint," I returned icily. "The only

place you've allowed me to be since you returned." I didn't need to look around us to sense the pack watching us. "Do I need permission to return to my cell?"

"I'll escort you, Princess."

Chapter Eighteen

It was a weird feeling not to work with the pack from sunrise to sundown. Instead, I stood on the balcony that looked out over the countryside. My room was one of the few that had a balcony with a view of the sprawling mountain range.

Snow blanketed the peak, indicating that the entire mountain would soon be covered in the soft, icy grip of winter's mercy. Much like Saint, it was without sympathy, making roadways impassable, cutting the pack off from the outside world.

The icy wind bit into my naked arms, sending my hair whipping against my face while I watched the sun setting behind the highest mountain. The thin gown I wore did little to keep the chill from settling in my bones, but I welcomed the cold that burned my face, leaving it red from the freezing air.

Already the pack was behind schedule, running around without no one leading them. The alphas had ignored Toralei's guidance, and even from the front balcony, I could discern that the lumber they'd accepted wasn't weathered or treated. It would rot faster, unprotected from the rain and snow that would rage against it until spring came and thawed out the settlement.

I lifted a joint to my lips, inhaling it as I leaned against the railing. Tears threatened to fall, but they were from the anger and rage churning through me. Saint was sleeping elsewhere, and I'd smelled Carleigh on him more than once when he came to my room. He wanted to fill my womb, telling me it might help smooth things over with the pack, but his offer fell on deaf ears, and I sent him away.

My options were to breed an heir with him or remain locked in my room until I gave him what he wanted from me. Chaos had tried to get in to see me, but Eryx, my babysitter, had turned him away. He'd turned Toralei away as well, which meant I didn't know if she'd set up anything with Douglas yet.

I'd figured out Saint's plan, which was what every other alpha in his place had tried to do to me. My pack was led through the Fenrir bloodlines, which was why my father hadn't murdered me alongside my mother.

Instead, he'd wanted to breed an heir with me to secure his hold on the pack. He'd known I was coming into my strength, and when I did, I would have challenged him for the lead alpha position and won. Now, Saint wanted to breed an heir with me for the same reasons.

Saint was looking out for the pack in that regard, which I should have cared about, but I didn't. They'd turned against me so easily that it left a gaping wound where my heart had been. I'd played victim to my father, enduring countless torture sessions so that they never had to feel his malice or anger.

Sure, they were unaware of what I'd survived because I'd never wanted their pity. I didn't want anyone to know what my father had done to me. It was shameful, and his madness would taint my line if anyone ever learned of his sick, twisted deeds against me. Most of his crimes were out in the open now, except for my torture sessions. What good would it do for me to admit to being his victim? Nothing.

I didn't need their pity or for them to look at me with shame. Bloodlines were everything to a pack, and now, because of Harold, mine was tainted with sickness. It was a disease that would make me a mockery and scorned alpha's mate. It would be whispered about behind hands as they'd condemn me with their eyes. It did no good to dwell on it, and I felt nothing but disgrace because I hadn't been strong enough to fight against him.

Saint's scent filled the air. I inhaled, bringing the joint back up to my lips, knowing he was about to make the same offer to fill my womb, and I would probably take it to escape my room, to escape him. I had no intention of allowing him to breed me and take my child, but I would do whatever it took to flee this place that no longer wanted me.

Saint leaned against the railing, peering out over the mountain range covered in splashes of red, orange, and mauve as the sun set behind it. Exhaling, he turned toward me, and I pretended he hadn't invaded my space, disturbing the calming peace the view offered.

"You're mine, Brat. You've always been mine," his deep voice rumbled, watching the frown that formed on my mouth. "If you ignore it, you chance going feral."

I lifted the joint, inhaling it deeply until my lungs burned. If I were lucky, I'd be able to sleep without nightmares of Lucas haunting me tonight. They'd plagued me every night since he'd taken a blade to my thighs, shredding them until he'd hit bone.

I'd had to remain upright or be cut into pieces by the razor wire holding me up. I hadn't even been able to pass out from the pain or give in to the blanket of unconsciousness where I'd typically gone when Lucas and my father started cutting parts of me open.

The smell of decaying bodies decomposing was forever burned into my memory. I would never forget the scent of them or the way the odor clung to my flesh. I'd scrubbed my body raw every day, trying to remove it, yet I could still smell their rotting corpses—haunting me.

"Are you going to give me the silent treatment for much longer?" Saint pushed his shoulder against mine as he'd often done when flirting before our world had crashed and burned into a fiery death that was beyond salvaging now. "I miss your voice. I missed it every night when I was being ripped apart, Brae. They used to bring me pictures of you and tell me about your life. I heard how you'd been free with your body. Obviously, that had been a ruse to take away what little hope I'd been able to muster up." He reached over, taking the joint from my lips to take a drag.

"The first few months after I was sent away were the hardest for me. I prayed for you, hoping you'd see the error of your ways and rescind the rejection. Eryx said it was false hope and that we'd misjudged you and your intentions. Six months into being tortured, I gave you up. I didn't pray to hear your pretty voice in my dreams because you'd become my nightmare. The one thing that I could never have again," he rumbled, handing me back the joint. "Not because I couldn't come back and take it, but because I no longer thought I was worthy of you," he laughed, moving to cage his body in behind mine.

"I need to know what part Carleigh played in what happened down in that storage container," he growled against my ear. I tried to move away from him, trembling with the memories, but he held me in place. "I know you don't want to talk about it. I get it, trust me. I lived through that shit, too, Braelyn. You didn't even get a taste of what they did to us, but you need to know that I never intended for you to get hurt. I wanted you to know the hopelessness that those taken from their packs felt before being sold off to whatever sick asshole purchased them. You were supposed to be safe and unharmed."

I shuddered violently as angry tears burned my eyes. Saint's scent smothered me in comfort I didn't want or need. His body continued to block mine from escaping. Hands wrapped around my body, and he held me tightly as a sob fought to escape my throat.

"Was she there when…?"

"When he cut me with his blade? Or the time he sliced my thighs open to ensure I couldn't stand anymore? No. She only came in long enough to tie me up, inflict a few cuts of her own, hoping to speed up the process, and left me to die. Don't worry; you don't have to kill your mistress, Saint. The cuts weren't very deep." I whispered, barely audible past the tears that tightened in my throat.

"She was a mother, you know? Carleigh watched traffickers murder her daughter on a live feed. Subscribers paid twenty thousand dollars to watch her daughter and sister tortured. They placed them on a barrel that was tilted, forcing them to balance on it for hours. Her daughter didn't last long. She was severed into pieces because some sick bastard wanted to watch a child die. Her sister lasted until she watched her niece falling to the floor, dead. She stepped off the barrel, willingly."

I closed my eyes against the imagery he painted. Carleigh told me why she put me on the barrel wrapped in razor wire, but I didn't tell that to Saint. It had plagued my dreams, dying similarly because Carleigh wanted me to suffer like her family. Shame burned through me, and Saint growled at what he thought it meant. To him, I was guilty. Every emotion I allowed to slip because of what I had endured, he took to mean that I felt shame at being involved in my father's wickedness.

"I can't fault Carleigh for wanting you dead, Braelyn. From the evidence we've seen, you look guilty," he growled, tightening his arms around me until it became hard to breathe. "Tell me what part you played in this, and I can save you. Or, I can at least figure out what to do with you."

"I didn't play a part in any of this, Saint. You've already condemned me, so what I say doesn't matter. I am guilty just because I share the same blood as my father. You and your people have deemed yourselves my judge, jury, and eventually, you will be my executioner. Carleigh gets a pass because she was forced to endure some sick shit that happened to her, but me? I am found guilty without proof, simply because I failed to notice just how fucked up my father really was."

"There's no way he ran his operation and stored his victims here without your knowledge," he argued. "You are too fucking smart for him to have managed this scale of an operation without you figuring it out."

"See, guilty. Just like I said. Get the fuck off of me," I whispered, fighting to get out of his arms.

"Do you have any idea how many children we pulled out of those fucking containers?"

"They were all covered in cayenne pepper, Saint! You didn't smell them either, did you? Did you hear them screaming? Could you tell they were out there? That field was used for battle, which is why it is called the killing fields. The name had nothing to do with them being out there. Ask anyone what they're called or their previous purpose! I didn't know the containers were even out there. Harold had forbidden anyone from going into those fields. They held no purpose to the pack; none whatsoever, which is why no one questioned his orders."

Saint didn't release me or even acknowledge I'd spoken. He yanked me with him, moving into the bedroom before shoving me down on the bed. His eyes watched as I spun around, standing up to face off against him.

"Go back to your girlfriend. I can smell her all over you. She wants you, and that's more than I can say about me. Besides, why breed a child with someone who would more than likely fucking eat it?" I snarled, watching the way his emotions shut down.

"Because the pack is held through your bloodline," he chuckled coldly. "You and I both know the pack will stay here as long as you or your child remains on this mountain. They're here because they belong here. Without a home, they're in danger of being hunted down and murdered. Fenrir wolves are already on the brink of extinction, which is exactly why they're up here hiding from the world. Would you really be so selfish as to sentence them to death after their daughters, girlfriends, sisters, mothers, and their fucking children were sold by your bloodline? And you wonder why we assume you are part of what happened here? You've given us no other plausible explanation, Braelyn. Everything you've ever done has been to benefit you and your father."

"Get out of my room," I stated angrily.

"Get your pretty ass dressed for dinner, Brae. You're joining me tonight with the pack. We're celebrating our victory and your father's fall from grace."

"They don't want me around anymore, Saint. Go enjoy your dinner with your girlfriend and leave me the fuck out of shit from now on."

"It doesn't work like that," he laughed soundlessly,

stalking me as I stepped back until I hit something solid. His hand landed beside my head, flush against the wall. The other hand lifted, grabbing my hair to rub the silky strand between his fingers. My eyes searched his, noting the way his tongue wetted his lips before he dropped his heated gaze to my mouth. "What's it going to be, Brat?"

"If I agree to what you want, can I be free from your men following me?" I asked, knowing he'd say no.

"Not happening," he snorted, lowering his nose to trail it over the curve of my jawline. "You're too much of a flight risk, and we both know you'd run from me."

"Can I move about freely? I miss the library, Saint. I miss being able to move around the lodge. Your men have prevented me from entering the one place I actually enjoy. I miss reading and lounging by the fireplace with my books."

"I can give you that freedom, but you'd still be watched." His heated breath fanned the flames of need that tightened my belly. He dropped my hair, slowly moving down to the raised peak that pressed against my shirt, rolling my nipple between his fingers, causing a soft gasp to escape my lips. "You make the most delicious noises for me, Brat."

"I need to know the details of how this works before I will consider permitting it to happen." I leaned my head back against the wall as his mouth sucked against the rapidly beating pulse on the soft column of my throat. He chuckled huskily, watching my body succumb to his skillful seduction.

"You'd begin hormone shots tonight. It would increase your libido and your heat cycle to bypass waiting for the moon to assist your womb. Each night you'd allow me to fuck you, maybe even during the day, depending on my schedule. Once you are with child, I'd still fuck you because you're mine."

"And our child? Do I end up removed from their life after I've given birth?" I whispered, whimpering as his hand cupped my sex, holding my stare.

"No, because I intend to breed many from you," he uttered huskily, rubbing his fingers against the clenching pulse he created between my thighs. "Remember when I asked you how many babies you wanted?"

"All the babies," I replied, holding his gaze. "I wanted to be the mother to all of your babies, and you wanted many. I was silly and hadn't been allowed to see how they were brought into the world yet, Saint. I've assisted in births and have changed my mind on how many I want since then."

"You'll give me pretty, powerful alpha babies, Braelyn. I have no intention of staying away from you or your body anymore. I fucked Carleigh before coming back for you on this mountain, and I don't intend to take anyone else now. I have my mate back, and her body is what I crave. This…" he growled, pushing his fingers against my opening. "…is mine to destroy. If you agree to be mine and carry my children for me, I will ensure you and our children are protected."

"And Chaos?" I whispered. My body pushed into his touch, needing to feel him buried in my core. This connection, the one that mates shared, was undeniable.

There was no fighting our chemistry, and I'd allow it to happen because I had no intentions of sticking around here. If fucking Saint meant being free of him, his people, and this mountain, then I'd fuck him like he was my oxygen and the air that filled my lungs.

"If you're a good girl and behave, I will let you around my son again. I won't let you hurt him as you did me, Brat. He doesn't deserve to be in the middle of our fight, and that's where he is. He is devoted to you, blindly so. You're so fucking easy to crave and love that no one can see the evil beneath the surface."

I swallowed, pushing him away from me. "Careful throwing rocks at other people's glass houses, Saint. Once they break the glass, you can never put the demons you unleash back into it. The prettiest cages and palaces hide the ugliest monsters more often than not." I looked away, seeming in thought before turning back to face him. "I'll do it, but only if you allow me to be inside the library without your men hovering. There is only one way in and one way out. I'm just asking to be inside alone and lose myself in fantasies to escape the reality you've created for me here."

His attention slid over my face before he lifted his shirt over his head, tossing it aside. "There are windows you could use to escape the room. You attempted to escape through one of them when I trapped you."

His fingers flicked the button of his jeans open, and he pushed them down as his cock jutted up against his tight, smooth stomach muscles. "I failed because they were too high to reach, easily. Your men would catch me before I could reach them."

"Probably," he admitted, stepping closer to me

to grab the gown I wore, pulling it up over my head. His gaze dropped to my naked breasts, and his hands cupped their heavy weight while he studied me. "I'll agree, but know that my men will be outside the window and stationed at the door. You won't be allowed to be alone with anyone but me inside the library."

Saint slid his hands down my stomach, catching both bows on my hips, untying them to let my panties drop to the ground. He slid a finger against my opening, finding my body ready for his. "That's fine. I've wanted to fuck you inside the library since our link was cemented there, anyway." I lifted my ass, rocking it to show him I was willing. "Show me how willing you are to let me have you, Brat," he rumbled thickly as he took control, smiling devilishly at the scent my body released for him.

"I'm not your Brat any longer, Saint," I reminded.

His deep laughter made my chest tighten as he grabbed my hands, turning me around to face the wall. Saint's feet forced my legs apart, and before I could argue what he was doing, he pushed into my body. I gasped, moaning loudly with how far he stretched my pussy, driving his thick cock into my body slowly.

"Harder," I growled, but he didn't give me what I wanted. Instead, he moved slowly while forcing my body to the edge of the cliff. He rocked his hips, holding mine painfully as he began moving in a torturously slow thrust that seemed—less than what I needed. "Saint, please."

"Please, what? Please fuck you like a whore? You're my mate, Brat. I know what you want and what you need. I sense your need to be used so that you can hate me easier. I feel that desire to have me hurt you as surely as I feel your necessity to run from me. You are mine, and in being mine, I sense everything about you. It's why you'll never finish marking me. I won't allow you to know what I need or want from you. You don't get me, Braelyn. I'll have you, but you will never fully have me. Not after I promised you the world, and it wasn't enough for you."

"I hate you," I whimpered. Leaning my forehead against the wall, I gave in to the emotions he created. Tears slipped free, raining down my cheeks as Saint chuckled behind me. His hand snaked around, rubbing slow, lazy circles against my clit until I shook with the force of the orgasm that rocked through me. I felt him stiffening behind me and knew he was coming from the way he tensed, withdrawing from my body to stare at my arched spine.

"Wash up for dinner and wear something pretty. No panties, though, and make sure your midriff is exposed. The medic I brought with me up the mountain will need easy access to it tonight. You start injections this evening, and I intend to breed you tonight. It might take a while for the injections to work, but there's no reason for me to stay out of your bed or your cunt anymore. You're healed, and I am finding it hard to stay away from you now."

"You'll keep your promise to me?"

"You'll have full access to the library, and privacy to be alone within it, Braelyn. Once you're pregnant with my child, you will be heavily guarded, though. I won't take a chance on someone challenging you while you carry my babe. I've also decided that we will be moving to a larger room, as this one isn't big enough for the two of us. Chaos will join us in your father's old apartments. You and I will live as the alphas to the pack, even if they don't want you here anymore. I still want you, and that is my choice as alpha. They don't have to like it, but they will respect it. I suggest you start packing up your shit so that we can move tomorrow."

Chapter Nineteen

Showered and dressed in a maxi skirt with slits up both hips, I peered at my exhausted reflection. The top I wore was simple and light blue, allowing the outline of my breasts to show through it. My hair hung loose since I was too mentally drained to bother with it or makeup tonight.

Saint hadn't left the room, dressing behind me while studying me through narrowed eyes. If he sensed I was exhausted, he said nothing. Turning to face him, I paused as a knock sounded at the door. I watched him open it while I waited silently behind him.

"I have the shots you ordered, Saint. Is she ready?" Eryx motioned to an older male with soft, brown eyes that peered over to where I stood.

"Hi, Braelyn?" the man said shyly.

"Yes," I answered, staring at the tray he held as he

entered the room.

"I'm Jacob, Jacob Bardwell. I have a few shots that your mate requested. It will help you become more fertile and kick-start your heat cycle. They're safe and relatively painless. He mentioned that you would need some assistance to create a babe." Jacob floundered as I hid the overwhelming need to shove his friendly ass right back out the door.

Did Saint think I couldn't have children? Or was he in a rush to get rid of me? I had no illusion that he wanted a child and planned to rid himself of the burden of me after he succeeded in creating an heir to the pack.

It was what my father had done with my mother, but Saint probably wouldn't wait for me to give him a son as my father had tried to accomplish. Everything Saint had said before was in an attempt to appease me and convince me to do what he wanted.

"Yes, thank you," I replied softly, waiting for instructions as Eryx entered the room, leaning against the wall while Saint settled in beside him.

"If you'd be more comfortable on the bed, you can lay there, and I will administer the shots. I need your stomach exposed, as I will be giving you the injections through your belly," Jacob stated, his arm straightening to encompass that I should relax.

I nodded, slowly walking to the bed and reclining on my back. My hands trembled nervously as I lifted my shirt, exposing my midriff to him. Jacob placed the tray he'd held on my nightstand, pulling a packet from his scrub top before sitting beside me.

"You wanted the full set of shots, correct?" he

asked, as my attention moved to Saint, who nodded. "This will send you into an immediate heat cycle, which should result in conception." I placed my hands behind my head, holding Saint's stare.

Eryx grunted, his eyes sliding over my exposed middle before slowly rolling back to my face with a hungry look. I held his gaze a moment longer before moving my attention to Jacob as something cold touched my belly.

Jacob had put on gloves and was rubbing an alcohol pad over my skin while studying me. His nostrils flared, and I didn't need to know which words he was about to ask because if Saint had paused in his ardor long enough to see beyond the lust, he'd have scented it before his medic had.

"You've never experienced a true heat, have you?" Jacob asked. "You suppress it every month?"

"Yes, without a mate here to assist, there was no reason to endure it. I used herbs to suppress both the alpha tendencies and my cycle. Our medic created a shot that prevented the cycle from becoming a nuisance to the unmated females who had chosen not to breed. A lot of women are choosing to remain childless in this day and age. I supported their decision. I hired a scientist to come up here and help develop an antidote if you would call it that, which prevented needless mating. He engineered a tonic that keeps the frenzied need away, and it also kept the birth rate down."

"Wouldn't you want the opposite of such if you were selling the unwanted offspring?" Jacob asked, and my eyes narrowed on his side profile while he readied the shots.

"I wanted our women to be free to choose rather than to be forced into unwanted offspring or to mate so frequently that it jeopardized the health of the baby. I had to figure out how to feed the children that were planned and born, and since we mate monthly, that also meant more mouths to feed. As you're aware, we only carry our children for five months, and at the end of that time, only fifty percent were born healthy. Our breed is on the brink of extinction, and having children born healthy is more important than breeding just to breed, as some alphas seem to practice and expect. Healthy babes will grow and create more life. Unhealthy infants seldom live long enough to be anything less than fucking tragic."

"That's wise, and I didn't mean to upset you with my question. I just assumed…"

"You assumed I was a murderous bitch that bred children for the enjoyment and entertainment of others," I stated, holding his stare. "You can ask the women here about how hard I pushed for healthy children, rather than the quantity of which they could push out of their cunts, Jacob. If I had been helping my father, I wouldn't have given two shits if they birthed sickly or healthy babes."

"I have asked around, and I'm aware you pushed for them to be selective about breeding. I must say, I am impressed with the overall health of your pack. The women I spoke with did say that you kept them in good health and put their needs before your race's needs. There are less than a thousand Fenrir wolves left, yet you pushed for them to consider the quality of their lives before creating new ones."

"We're immortal. There is time to breed more, and the job of the alpha is to ensure the health of the pack."

Jacob nodded his agreement. "Yet you're pushing yourself to breed?"

"My mate couldn't give two shits if I survived the birth of his child or not." Jacob frowned and glanced at Saint and then Eryx. "Don't worry about me; it's my child you will strive to keep alive. I have agreed to the cycle. You're doing what we both want." Lie. It should have bothered me, but it didn't. I didn't believe his treatment would work, anyway.

"Small pinch," Jacob stated, pushing the needle into my stomach before recapping the tip and doing the next several shots in the same area. He covered the injection sites with a piece of cotton and exhaled. "You'll know if it is working within the next twenty-four hours. Your temperature will rise, which is perfectly normal. You may have some irritation where I injected you, and if it persists, we can add some numbing agent to the spot. You're going to have some mood swings and a craving to reach the end goal. If by the full moon you have not become pregnant, we can try again."

Saint snorted, sliding his attention to where Jacob held the gauze against the spot where he'd injected the hormones into my belly. Jacob slowly backed up, cleaning up his things before he left the room, leaving me with the two alphas studying me like a science project.

Slipping into the bathroom, I ran my fingers over the red, angry skin before I felt Saint's heavy stare on me. Turning, I lifted a brow in silent question.

Exhaling, he rested his head against the doorframe, watching me.

"Anything else you want me to do? Maybe suck you off before we head on down to dinner so that the pack knows you're the all-mighty alpha who conquered the evil bitch?" I moved closer to him as he glared down at me. "Maybe you should beat me. That would show them you're all man and alpha, wouldn't it?"

"You'd probably get off on it since you like it rough. Do you want to suck my dick, Brae? If you do, you need only ask. I won't turn your fucking throat down."

"I'd rather swallow razors and feel them ripping me apart from the inside as they worked their way down through my system. Ahh, but then my father already had me do that once before," I snorted, realizing my mistake as Saint straightened, looking at me.

"What the fuck did you just say?" he demanded.

"Nothing, forget it. I'm tired, and my body aches from not fully healing yet. If you intend to use me again tonight, you should feed me first," I stated, moving past him to grab my shoes.

I walked to the door, leaning against it as my stomach clenched. My hand touched it, turning to look at the men. Saint sat in the chair, pulling out a joint while he examined me carefully.

"Sit down, Brat. Dinner isn't ready, and you're going to need a few moments to make sure you don't have an adverse effect from the shots. Smoke with me," he urged, forcing me to go back to the bed.

My stomach cramped, and I barely contained the groan that slid up to rest at the back of my throat. Saint's eyes narrowed as I settled in front of him. He tapped on the tin, and Eryx lit a joint, handing it to me.

"Here, it will ease those cramps," Eryx announced.

"You've done this to women before?" I asked, snorting while accepting the weed.

"No, but we've seen it used once girls were brought into our facility to be bred," Saint stated, sitting beside me to stretch his legs out. "They tended to suffer cramps and then became crazed with the need to be mounted. Only, their captors didn't touch them. They'd let them suffer for days until they were more animal than a girl. We'd hear them screaming, and then the screams would turn to pleads of mercy. They eventually became pregnant after being trained by those who had come and paid to fuck them. They were often killed when they were done using them."

"Is that your plan for me?" I asked, holding Saint's stare as I exhaled the smoke. "Tie me to a bed and allow others to use me?" His lips jerked up, and he shrugged as my heart clenched. My eyes dropped, unable to stomach the idea of being helplessly bound to a bed, ever again.

"Would you want to be chained up and fucked by anyone that wanted to use you?" he asked with anger burning in his stare. "How dirty are you, Brat?"

"So fucking dirty that I was untouched until you fucked me, asshole," I grunted, watching his forehead shoot up as if he'd momentarily forgotten he'd taken my virginity.

"You've never gone into heat?" he asked, studying my face and the blush that spread over my cheeks as I sucked my lip between my teeth.

"Once, when you were here still," I admitted. "I came to you, remember? You turned me down and told me to go back inside. You said it wasn't time for us to have a babe yet."

He smirked, nodding. "I remember that day. That was the hardest thing I'd ever done in my life. You were too young for that at the time."

"I was ready for you, asshole." I handed the joint to Eryx, who was silently listening to us.

"What did you mean by your father had already made you swallow razor blades?" Eryx asked, forcing me to shut down my emotions and close myself off as those painful memories became visual inside my head.

I shook my head, waiting for Saint to hand me the joint, but he just silently watched me. After a moment had passed, Saint sat forward and offered me the blunt as I looked away from him.

"Did daddy hurt you, Brae?" Saint snorted, standing and heading for the door. "Nah, daddy loved his sweet little girl, didn't he? That's why he got rid of anyone she could have grown attached to," he finished, opening the door. "Dinner is ready. Let's go."

Chapter Twenty

Eryx escorted me into the dining hall as Saint walked ahead of us. I predicted what was coming, preparing myself for the sting against my pride as my pack turned, standing for Saint. The moment I entered, they gave me their backs before sliding into their chairs. This was their response to the fact that they didn't believe Saint had punished me enough.

My attention slid over the pack, knowing that without me informing them of what I'd endured, they wouldn't see it from my side. Showing them my side though, terrified me. What if they thought less of me, knowing I'd been too weak to defend myself against my sick father? Would their pity stares shred me deeper than their sense of betrayal? I hated the idea of them ever looking at me as less than I was. I wanted them to see me as someone who had survived hell and hadn't allowed my tormentor to win.

Starting forward, I groaned, watching the alpha

females form a line on both sides of the walkway between tables. Swallowing down the uneasiness, I smiled at them.

"We challenge you," Katie snarled, her eyes alight with excitement.

"Challenge me for what?" I asked, crossing my arms over my chest to stare her down.

"Your mate," she smirked, flipping her copper-colored hair over her shoulder.

I snorted, staring through the female alphas to where Saint had risen from his chair. He hadn't considered his actions or the ripple-effect they would cause. I was an unwanted mate that hadn't been allowed to seal the connection, leaving me in a precarious position to be challenged for my place at the alpha's side. I was connected to Saint, but he wasn't mine until I rescinded the rejection and marked him.

"Have him," I laughed without emotion. "No challenge needed. You have my blessing," I finished, holding his stare as he returned it with an angry glare.

"No, we're challenging you to the death," Mabel announced, her wide, blue eyes sliding down my thin frame. "You betrayed the pack, and we are here to claim your life for doing what you have to us. You violated our trust and tarnished our pack's image. Your life is the cost for the crimes you committed."

"And you think to be my judge, jury, and executioner? You have proof of my crimes, other than just the words of the new alpha, who also has no proof, correct?" I challenged icily.

Honestly, I was over it already. Saint moved closer, but he knew his mistake and that he couldn't argue their challenge. Toralei settled beside me, her eyes taking in the six alpha females that stood in line, three on either side, leaving Saint the perfect view of where I stood in front of them.

"Do you want to take a moment and think about this? Look, I'm all for battling to the death, but people are eating here. Shall we take it to the killing fields and let the pack eat without the whole blood and gore thing?" I questioned, hoping they saw reasoning.

"Right here is fine," Lucy stated, her obsidian-colored hair running in soft waves to her slender hips. "You are finished here. They won't care how you die, only that you are dead."

"And you're certain you want to fight to the death?" I continued, feeling Tora's uneasiness wafting through me.

"Think this through, guys. You don't have proof yet. You're about to challenge our alpha's mate to the death," Toralei argued.

"Stay out of it, Tora," I ordered, holding Saint's worried gaze.

"This is bullshit, and you know it! It's six alphas against one. Ask me to assist," Tora begged.

"No," I snorted, shaking my head. "This is my fight, Toralei. I don't need help. They want me dead, and Saint gave them the right to ask for it."

"Ladies, there's no reason for this to happen right now," Saint stated, his eyes holding mine.

"By right, we are allowed to challenge her for you. You cannot intervene," Lucy returned, her eyes dragging over Saint with lust burning in her stare.

I snorted, watching her heavy lids taking in my mate, anger pulsing beneath the surface that I refused to acknowledge. We didn't have the numbers to have the pack females challenging me, let alone losing them over baseless claims.

"To the death is so permanent, though. Can we not just fight and call it good?" I asked, hearing Toralei's low growl while she stared the females down crossly.

"To the death, Braelyn," she stated, and the others echoed the finality of her claim. "Your pack's bloodline ends here," Lucy snapped. "We no longer want you or anyone of your ilk within the ranks of this pack. You're a monster."

"This isn't how this is done," Saint snapped, his hackles rising as he counted heads and did the math on my odds of survival. "Braelyn carries the bloodline needed to hold this pack and could already be carrying my heir."

"Which is even more reason to kill her. I would rather take our chances of survival than let her live. The wolf god, Fenrir, would not forsake our pack over this murderous whore," Lucy sneered and then grinned wickedly. "After I'm done with Braelyn, I will deal with the orphaned whelp you left behind. I will not have any potential heir in line ahead of our child."

"Death it is," I stated, and they turned to face me as Saint opened his mouth to speak. My nails descended, and I moved with a violent burst of energy and speed.

Pausing at the end of the line of alpha females who had thought to end my life, I turned, smiling at Lucy. Her eyes had widened with fear, and her mouth opened to speak before her head slid from her body.

Lifting my bloodied fingers to my lips, I licked them while holding Saint's shocked gaze. The other alphas heads dropped to the floor, one-by-one, with a loud thud before their bodies followed. I stepped closer to Saint, dodging the pool of blood forming on the ground at my feet.

"What's for dinner? I'm famished," I declared, slipping my hand through his elbow and turning him toward the table where his people watched the shit show unfold.

"How the fuck did you do that?" Saint demanded, pulling out my chair for me to slide into it.

"Easy, they threatened Chaos, and I decided to end them. I raised him. He may not be my blood, but he's my son in every other sense of the word. Lucy knew that, aiming to raise my anger. So I took her fucking head. The speed, it's a perk of being a Fenrir bloodline wolf, blessed with the power of the god inside my veins. Drink?" I asked, grabbing for the bourbon to pour it into my glass as he stared at me.

Saint reached around, grabbing the bottle from my hand. I narrowed my eyes while he sat beside me silently. I could hear the whispered words of the pack, knowing they were reeling at the fact I'd removed the heads of six female alphas in a matter of seconds. I'd never exposed my speed or my strength to anyone. Not even my beta had been aware of the way I could move. I'd used my speed only a few times, once with Saint recently.

"You... What did you just do?" Xariana's eyes never left the bodies being carted from the dining hall. "I didn't even see you move."

"You wouldn't have since you're human, mostly. Fenrir blessed me. Apparently, the pack needed a reminder of why they have remained on this mountain with us for so long. It wasn't because they cared for my sick, weak-minded father. They stayed because the bloodline protects them. Fenrir descendants, with his power running through their veins, are charged with protecting the pack. Their presence ensures the future of the pack. My child will be born of our god and will also be blessed by him."

"It's been a long time since I've seen a Fenrir wolf with the power of their god driving them. Where was he when you were being tortured? He didn't protect you from Lucas," Leif pointed out.

"He isn't here to protect me in such a manner." I swallowed past the lump forming in my throat. "He protects us from being raped or abused in such a manner until the first time we willingly lay with a man. Once that occurs, Fenrir no longer protects our innocence. He isn't always with me, but when he is, I am stronger, faster, and harder to kill."

"Was he not with your mother when your father murdered her?" Leif asked, tipping his glass up as his eyes slid to the carnage being cleaned up behind us.

"No, he'd abandoned my mother to protect me. I was born, blessed by him with more strength than she had. He favors the stronger wolf, always. My mother said it was because I was born from kings. She said that one day I'd be the queen of our pack and would have to remove the threat that hung over it like a sickness. She didn't survive long after she'd whispered those words so I couldn't ask her what she'd meant by them," I elaborated, turning to look at Saint. "Why did you take my drink away?"

"You've received injections today that don't go with alcohol," he snorted, shifting to look to the right as the door opened.

I watched as Carleigh entered the dining hall, free of chains or restraint. Her green eyes held mine. A twist of her lips formed a victorious smirk before she sat on the other side of Saint, placing her perfectly manicured hand on his forearm.

"I am starving," she exclaimed as my nails dug into my thighs. "I'm so glad you came to your senses and realized that what I did wasn't done in malice but pain."

"If I were you, Car, I'd keep your thoughts to yourself," Eryx snorted, holding my stare.

Carleigh looked behind us, frowning at the blood being mopped from the floor. "Someone stepped out of line against the alpha?" she asked, turning her heavy stare on Saint.

"Someone thought to challenge Braelyn. Six alpha females, to be exact," Saint announced, filling their glasses while a server poured water into mine.

"And you had to step in or lose the bitch?" She made a strangled sound in her throat, looking at me while slowly sizing me up.

"Actually, no. Braelyn murdered them all in seconds, and no one saw her move until they'd been beheaded, still trying to talk." Saint grinned slightly as he took a sip of his drink.

Carleigh blanched, her eyes widening before she concealed the fear. As a hellhound shifter, she wasn't even on par with me. I was a powder keg set to explode, and she was a firecracker that, while able to leave a mark, wouldn't be much of one.

"While I might understand your actions, Carleigh, they were still an act of violence against my mate, and that I cannot excuse. I gave explicit instructions for you to remove Braelyn from the container, and instead of doing so, you thought to inflict your own form of punishment, exposing Braelyn to the monster we've been hunting for many years."

"Don't do this, Saint." Carleigh grabbed Saint's hand in a silent plea, but he pulled his hand from her grip, dismissing her. Xavier stood and placed his hands on the back of Carleigh's chair.

"I've called E.V.I.E. and informed them of your actions. You know what you did was against their rules of conduct and cannot be overlooked. Saint handed your punishment over to your superiors instead of ending your life, which is within his rights to do. A chopper is waiting outside to take you back to Seattle. I'll escort you to your room to gather your things." Xavier pulled Carleigh's chair out, and she rose. Trying but failing to make eye contact with Saint, she strode from the room without a backward glance.

After that, dinner droned on while people talked about missions or what they were working on and doing. I was left out of the conversation, which was for the best. My stomach burned where Jacob had administered the shots. I was experiencing mild cramps causing discomfort, and my heat cycle was beginning to roll through me worse than that.

"Braelyn, are you okay?" Leif asked, his Nordic blue eyes studying my face.

I nodded, lifting the glass of water to my lips to drink. The meal was decent, but then I'd trained the kitchen staff myself. Unlike my father, I'd taken pride in making the most out of what little we had here. Herbs were an essential part of a meal, and from the taste of the potatoes and meat, they'd been scarcely added. It had left the meal bland and tasteless.

"I'm fine," I winced at the pain, pinching my features. "If you'll excuse me. I'm going to retire for the night."

"Sit," Saint growled, turning his attention to where I grabbed my stomach. "Once Eryx has finished eating, you can go to your room and pout."

"Whatever you wish," I answered, leaning back in the chair as heat pulsed in my stomach. I knew Saint scented the state of my body because Leif definitely could. His icy-blue gaze lowered to the way my nipples pebbled against my top, and a quick look of lust entered his stare before he smothered it down. "I think I should go, Saint," I admitted.

"And I want you to stay," he argued, lowering his stare to where I held my side. His attention moved up my face, slowly noting the hair that stuck to the sweat on my neck. My shirt was tacky against my skin, and my hips shifted involuntarily, even though my thighs clenched together, hating that he had forced me into heat. "I'll accompany you."

I swallowed down the urge to tell him to shove it up his ass, but if I intended to leave this mountain before the snow fell, I had to play the part. Saint stood, moving behind me to pull my chair out so that I could easily slide away from the table.

No one stood or tried to stop us as we left the dining hall. It wasn't until we reached the large hallway that led into my room that a sultry moan ripped from my throat. I could feel arousal pooling at my core, and my entire body felt as if it were on fire.

"It's the drugs working, Brat. It won't hurt you. You're just going to be in a state of perpetual need for a few days. Once that is over, you should be with child," he stated clinically and without emotion.

"It isn't natural to force this to happen to someone," I argued, leaning against the wall as I smoothed my hand down my stomach, pressing against the ache pulsing in my cunt.

"Neither is rejecting your mate," he snorted, stepping closer until his body heat wafted over mine. "Don't worry, Brat. I'll make sure you enjoy every moment of this unnatural time we share together."

Chapter Twenty-One

Saint walked me back to the bedroom, leaving me alone inside for hours. While I waited for him, I showered and refused to put my regular clothes back on because the feel of them against my sensitive flesh was too much. I hadn't even been able to wear panties because anything against my sex had created friction, stimulating my need into a painful, heightened state of arousal. I searched my room for my stash of alcohol and herbs, only to find them all gone. Sliding a sheer, baby blue nightgown over my head, I resumed pacing aimlessly.

I felt as if my skin was crawling with tiny bugs. Everything had sharpened; all my senses were fine-tuned and enhanced. My nipples had grown achy, hard tips that pushed against the sheer material of the gown. The friction was causing me to be even more aroused than I already was, if that was even possible.

The door to my room opened, and I turned, staring

at Saint, who entered. I examined him with a predatory gaze, following him as he came further into the room. He stalked inside and sat in the chair before stretching out his legs and lifting his nose to inhale my scent.

"You are very susceptible to the shots we used. I honestly didn't expect it to work this quickly or effectively. Not that I'm complaining," he chuckled, placing his hands on his knees, gazing at the way my chest rose and fell slowly. "Come to me, Brat."

"I ache," I admitted softly, rolling my neck. "You're an asshole for doing this to me."

"Remind me of that when you're riding my dick and screaming my name," he laughed, leaning forward to pull his shirt off from behind his head.

The moment his chest was bare, his scent slammed into me. I closed my eyes, sucking my lip between my teeth to exhale the soft gasp of need that tightened in my chest, rolling up through my throat to escape.

My thighs clenched, and silently stepped closer to him but somehow managed to ignore his order. I sat on the bed, taking in the way his lips jerked into a cocky smile at my subtle act of defiance.

Sitting on the bed, I parted my thighs while holding his stare. Saint's nostrils flared, and I rolled my eyes, pushing my legs together and placing my elbows on my knees. Leaning over, I allowed him to get a bird's-eye view of the ample cleavage my low-cut gown exposed.

"You took my herbs," I growled, and his blue eyes lifted to my face.

"I did," he murmured. "You dressed to seduce

me?"

"No, I dressed in the only thing that didn't make my skin crawl," I snorted, sliding my attention to his pants, which did little to hide his growing erection. I wetted my lips, dragging my gaze over his ripped abs. Heat coursed through me, forcing my entire body to shudder violently. "My herbs won't mess with your fertility crap, jerk."

I smoothed my hands down my stomach, slowly sliding them to where the ache was never-ending. When I reached my sex, I moaned loud and sultry at my touch. Saint's low, building growl sent awareness of his presence into my mind, yet I didn't care if he watched me. I was a fire, one that had been smoldering until flames licked my skin. Lying back on the bed, I parted my thighs while slowly working my sex, the need to end my ache, taking over everything else at the moment.

Saint watched my fingers sliding through the sleek arousal between my thighs, gliding through it as noises slipped from my lips. I was a mess of nerves, all heightened by the drugs he'd had introduced into my system. I shifted one hand to grab the globe of my breast, causing a hiss of need to slide between my clenched teeth. Saint didn't move, and I wasn't sure if I wanted him to or if I wanted to ignore the fact that I needed him buried deep within me.

I wasn't a stranger to getting my own needs to the finish line. Since reaching adulthood, I'd had to do everything myself. I wasn't shy about satisfying myself or owning several toys that stimulated and offered pleasure.

A loud moan escaped the swelling of need in my throat the moment my finger slid into my heated apex. I could feel Saint's stare at my center, watching as I worked my body into a state of painful arousal. The storm growing in my stomach was slowly unfurling, and the moment it released, I jerked my hips faster, riding the wave of pleasure I chased alone.

Hands pushed my legs apart, and before I could argue against it, Saint's mouth was ravishing my pussy. His deep growl vibrated against my arousal-slick core as his dark stare held mine prisoner. I curled my fingers through his hair, holding his mouth against the sensitive flesh of my sex. He devoured it hungrily, daring me with his gaze to challenge his right to feast on my cunt. I gasped, arching into his heated kiss as he chuckled against it.

"Saint," I whimpered, unable to prevent my body from toppling over the edge as he curled his arms around my thighs, holding me against his hungry lips. His tongue slid through the arousal in quick, sharp passes from one end to the other. The moment it circled my clit, I lost the fight as pleasure shot through my center.

"You taste too good to stop eating, Brat," he growled against my cunt, muffled as he continued lapping ravenously against my sex.

"Fucking hell," I cried out, flipping him over with his hold, forcing him onto the bed. I ground against his face, peering down at where he was now pressed into the mattress. Saint chuckled at the eagerness of my clumsy moves while I rocked against his enthusiastic tongue that was spearing into my body. "Don't talk;

you'll ruin it."

Saint sat up, forcing my body to move with his as he lifted me, seating me onto his lap. His mouth opened to speak, but mine crushed against his in a needy kiss. I needed him to shut the fuck up and not ruin this. He growled into my mouth, and I mewled softly. His kiss wasn't violent or angry. Instead, it was soft and pleading as he coaxed me to kiss him back.

I was a fire, and he was the tinder fueling and stoking my flames. I didn't care that he intended to use me or breed me like some bitch that had one purpose. Nothing mattered right now, nothing except ending the pain in my apex that only he could soothe.

I shoved Saint down onto the bed, sliding my hand along his muscular stomach to flick the button of his jeans, freeing his thick cock. Scooting back to escape his touch, I yanked his jeans down, sliding my gaze over the strength of his body. Slowly, I took in every sinewy curve and contour. He kicked his boots off, drawing my stare to where he slowly sat up, slipping the jeans from his legs.

"Come here, Brat," he urged, but I shook my head slowly.

"Lie back and don't talk. You do nothing but shred me to pieces with that tongue of yours. I can't handle you ripping me apart while we try to create life, Saint. Mating should be beautiful, and you'll just turn it into something cheap and abrasive with your words."

He exhaled a deep breath, slowly watching me as I waited for him to do as I'd asked. Once he had lain back, placing his hands behind his head to peer up at me, I swallowed past the lump of desire that formed in my throat. I needed something to take the edge off or to relieve the overwhelming urge to fuck him like he was a war I was waging and couldn't ever win.

"Where are the herbs?" I asked, moving away from the bed to light the sage and lemongrass candles. I grabbed the remote for the stereo, turning it on while leaving the volume low enough that I could hear his heart thundering, almost like he was as nervous as me right now, feeling the deeper call to fulfill our mating. "Fine, then where are yours?" I pried, turning to watch as he moved from the bed, uncaring of his nudity.

Saint opened the door, causing me to yank my nightgown down further. Eryx stepped into the room, his heated gaze sliding to me before he tossed a tin onto the bed and smirked devilishly. He silently handed something else to Saint before turning on his heel and exiting the room.

Remaining against the dresser, I watched as Saint retrieved the tin before stepping to where I stood. He smirked roguishly, setting the tin onto the dresser, then lifting me onto it too. I tensed against the cool wood surface while he settled himself between my thighs. He grabbed and opened the container, and his heat unfurled against my sensitive flesh.

Saint removed and lit a joint, and one smell told me it was my herbal blend, used for lowering my anxiety and making me relax. He flicked the zippo out with ease while inhaling the deliciously strong smoke from the weed. He held it up, offering it to me, and I accepted it, inhaling greedily and gasped as his lips clamped onto my nipple. He chuckled, holding my stare as I choked on the hit I'd taken. Lifting my feet onto the dresser, I leaned back against the wall.

Saint pulled back, sliding his hooded gaze down to my bared sex. Grabbing the joint from my fingers, he placed it between his lips and yanked the nightgown over my head. I allowed it, placing my hands on his broad shoulders for balance. He withdrew the joint from his lips, handing it back to me, and I took a drag, swallowing the smoke to hold it. His hand gripped the back of my neck, pulling my lips against his as I exhaled into his kiss.

I dropped my legs, wrapping around him as he pressed his chest against mine. Turning, I searched for an ashtray to dispose of the joint, and then I slipped my hands through his soft hair. My wolf released her scent to toy with his, and a demonic growl escaped his lips, vibrating against mine as I swallowed it, feeding him back a soft moan.

Saint walked us backward, sitting on the bed before he broke the kiss to lie us back. My hungry mouth dropped, kissing over where my name was tattooed beneath his ribcage. It was the only tattoo beneath his pecks since the other words trailed down his sides, sliding around his back. Kissing my way to his nipple, I teased it with my tongue as his hands slid through my hair.

If I tried to mark him, he'd use my hair to prevent it from happening. I had no intention of marking him because that would seal the connection between us. Once our bond was cemented, it would be impossible to escape him. I lowered my hand, grabbing his thick cock, slowly exploring the silken length with my hand. I moved to the side, sitting up to look him over while he watched me through a hooded gaze.

"You keep playing with it, and I'll make a mess in your tiny hand, Brat," he warned in a tone that was like warm honey.

My stare moved from his arousal back to his face, watching as he peered at me through heavy eyes that sparkled with laughter. I closed the distance between my lips and his stomach, sluggishly exploring his hard muscles with my tongue and mouth. I tasted him, and he hissed with every soft nip of my teeth while I trailed a heated path to his heavy cock.

When I reached his hardened length, I stroked it while tightening my grip. My tongue jutted out, licking around the rounded tip before I slowly opened my mouth to take him into it. He growled, watching me by lifting his head and holding my stare while I pleasured him gently as if we had all the time in the world to learn each other.

Saint lifted, and I pulled back, slamming him down against the bed as I straddled his hips. He grunted, dragging a heated gaze down my body to where my sex was rubbing against his rigid length. I rubbed my scent over him, watching his eyes lose focus as the need to breed took precedence within him as surely as it was with my wolf.

I lifted, slowly pushing against him as he watched our bodies connecting. I slid against his thick tip, moaning as he rocked against my opening. My head dropped forward, and my eyes watched him vanishing into my body as I sat back, crying out while he stretched me full.

"Gods damn," I moaned, rocking my hips to adjust to how much he stretched me out, creating a delicious burning sensation. "Holy shit, Saint," I whimpered, lifting my gaze to find him studying my face.

"You're gorgeous, Brat," he swallowed thickly, sliding his hands to my hips.

He didn't move me, but then he didn't need to. I was slowly rocking my body against his, creating a delicious friction that was building a dangerous storm within me. I could sense his need, his pleasure growing with mine. I could also feel his desire to shove me down, sink his teeth into my shoulder, and unleash hell on my pussy.

Instead, he studied me, discovering my pleasure. This was the first time I'd had any semblance of control during our couplings. I'd never fully participated, and he was learning me as surely as I was learning him. His hands lifted, cupping and squeezing my breasts as his thumb trailed over their hardened, puckered tips. The slight stimulation sent my hips thrusting faster. My need to come took over, and I moaned unabashedly while finding the perfect beat for both of us.

"Oh, God," I moaned, moving faster, the orgasm growing until it pulsed through me. My thighs clenched, and one of his hands lowered, slowly rubbing his fingers against my clit. Everything unfurled, and my noises turned wild and untamed as the wolf within me joined the fray of our bodies.

"Good girl," he urged, rocking up to meet each thrust of my hips, still rolling as I came around him.

He didn't do what he wanted to, which was to roll me beneath him and pound his own need into my core.

Instead, he moved his hips, holding me up while my body grew heavy with the release. Saint continued using my hips to drive the pace I'd held, forcing me toward the edge of the abyss once more. I leaned over him, claiming his mouth in a hungry kiss, filled with urgency. His tongue parted my lips, claiming dominance of my tongue when it found his. Rolling us over, he leaned up, breaking the kiss, driving into my body with slow precision. Each thrust hit the spot within me that had me begging him for more.

"Fuck, that feels good," I moaned, peering up at him. His stare pierced my soul, holding me helpless and prisoner as his pretty gaze swallowed me whole.

"I've dreamed of this a million times, Brat. Never in my wildest dreams did you feel this good beneath me. We fit perfectly together," he whispered huskily, driving into my body slower and deeper than he'd ever gone before.

The muscles in Saint's shoulders bunched tightly, and sweat beaded on his brow. His mouth tightened as he increased his pace, hitting my spot perfectly until I was writhing beneath him. My hands twisted the bedsheets as everything erupted, and he tensed above me, slamming home into my core as he released within me. He lowered his body against mine, and the only sound inside the bedroom was the soft rhythm of our combined heavy breathing.

"Holy shit," he grunted, kissing my throat and the soft hollow column of my neck. He dragged his mouth over it, kissing my shoulder where the faded claiming mark remained. Saint was already growing hard within me, and my hands released the sheet to push through his hair, holding him to me. "It's going to be a long night, Brat. I enjoy your body immensely. You don't appear to be finding it a hardship to be mated, either."

"Not at all," I admitted as he lifted his head, peering down at me. "Fucking you isn't a hardship. It's when you open your mouth that I want to ride it to keep it closed. Maybe I should try it the next time you say something stupid. It's much more pleasant when I'm fucking it."

"Same, I prefer your lips busy on my cock, Brat. Now, shut your pretty mouth, or I'll fuck it until those lips are too swollen to move," he chuckled, thrusting into me hard, causing a gasp of shock to explode from my throat. "Fuck, you make the sexiest noises when you're getting fucked. I might just tie your sexy ass up to this bed and fuck you for days."

"There's that mouth of yours again. Why don't you shut up and do what we both want you to do? Come on, Saint. Fucking wreck me. I want you to fuck me like I'm your dirty little plaything and not your fucking mate," I hissed huskily, wrapping my legs around his waist to force him deeper into my body.

"Gods damn, Brat. You're fucking hot when you get turned on," he murmured, slamming into me as a strangled cry exploded from my throat. "Remember, you fucking asked for it. I'm just asshole enough to give it to you. Now, hold on and close those pretty lips. You only speak if it's to scream my name or cry when this pretty pussy comes for me. Got it, dirty little girl?"

"Saint, move bitch," I demanded, watching his

mouth open with surprise as a heated, wicked look burned in his pretty blue gaze.

Chapter Twenty-Two

Sitting inside the library, I lifted my eyes to find Eryx leaning against the door, facing the hallway. It had been days since the heat cycle had ended, and with every passing day, Saint lowered his guard a little more. We'd spent every night together, but during the day, he slipped away to do whatever it was that he and his men were working on below, in my father's apartment.

I knew that Saint still planned to move us into my father's rooms, but I had no intention of allowing it to ever happen. I'd seen enough of his quarters to last me a lifetime, and the nightmares of them still haunted me. Bad dreams had woken me again last night, drenched in sweat with sobs escaping my throat. Saint had held me through it, which had pissed me off even more than waking up from the hauntingly painful dream.

Turning the page of my book, I read what Toralei had written between the words. We'd started leaving messages inside books, placing them where they wouldn't draw attention. Picking up the pen, I lifted my gaze to make sure that Eryx continued watching the hall as I jotted down my answer to her plan. The moment he looked over his shoulder, I closed the book. Setting it aside on the coffee table, I stretched out on the sofa I'd pushed in front of the fireplace.

When he turned to check on me, I sat up, sipping my tea. Moving my legs over the edge of the couch, I pushed the blanket off before returning to the shelves. Plucking out another book, I replaced the one we had used for today's messages back onto the shelf where it belonged.

Saint's heady scent of bergamot and sage hit me before he entered the library. Ignoring him, I proceeded to pick out a few volumes of random tomes before carrying them back to the fireplace. He lounged in the chair beside the small sofa, watching as I reclined once more, peering over my stack of books.

"You're early for a booty call," I informed, watching his eyes slide from the flames to hold my glare. "Something happen?"

"No, just wanted to see your smiling face," he admitted, standing to move to where I sat. He picked up my legs, sitting beside me. "The infirmary says it is low of supplies. They mentioned you normally handled ordering the needed medicine and herbal combinations for the pack."

"Indeed," I stated, not bothering to elaborate. "I'm sure you'll manage it."

"You'd let your pack suffer because they hurt your pride?" he asked, leaning his head back to close his eyes.

I studied the stubble on his jawline, tightening my grip on the book as my fingers itched to touch him. He looked exhausted, which I knew was from running ragged to secure what the pack of over one hundred and fifty wolves would need to last through the winter.

"They don't deserve my help, and neither do you, Saint," I replied after a moment had passed. His eyes opened, and he turned, staring at me through narrowed slits that both condemned and studied me.

"They hurt your feelings. Get over it. They're your pack, Brat. They're our pack, and they suffer when we fail to provide for them."

"They are your pack now, and they'll suffer when you fail to provide for them," I corrected, opening the book, pulling my legs away from him. Or at least, I tried to. He held them tightly, running his fingertips between my thighs.

"You mixed the herbs, and you are the only person here who knows which of them won't kill people."

"May I suggest you use the assholes in the pack as test subjects when you try your mixture out at first? Trial and error are tricky at best, and more often than not, someone has to be the test-dummy. Best not to put wolfsbane into anything, though, unless you want them to be very sick," I chuckled, knowing I was pissing him off. I was being petty, but neither he nor the pack actually wanted me here anymore.

Saint intended to take my child because I'd heard from enough people in the pack that had started going out of their way to make sure I knew where I stood with them. As far as I was concerned, they could all fuck off and die.

"It snowed outside today," he stated, which made my heart clench.

Rolling my eyes, I wetted my finger to turn the page. He continued staring at me, forcing my gaze to meet his in silent challenge. He reached over, taking the book from me to close it, and set it aside. He lowered his head, kissing the inside of my thigh, and I watched him, closing off my emotions as heat pooled in my center.

"How old were you when you began leading the pack behind your father's back?" He shocked me by asking, causing my eyes to narrow on his dark head. "I have spoken to the alphas, and I admit, I am impressed by you, Brat. You'd stated that you took over, but according to Jim, you began helping with things at the age of eight. You weren't even a teenager, and most eight year olds spend their days chasing butterflies. You provided for an entire pack."

"My father cared little if his people starved or if they got sick through the long winter on the mountain," I admitted, stifling the moan his playful bite forced to my throat. "You could have just asked me, but then you'd have called me a liar, anyway."

"What is in the herbs that you feed the children to stop their aggression?" he continued, pushing his fingers past my panties, sliding one fingertip against my entrance.

"We're in a public place, and Eryx is literally a few feet from us, Saint. Behave and stop trying to use sex to get your answers. You can figure it out yourself and try that mixture on adults first, so it won't harm the children when you fuck it all up," I snapped, pushing his hand away from my sex that clenched with need.

"Have you been to the infirmary for your test?" he changed tactics. "Our children may need that mixture, considering they'll be stuck with us as parents."

I snorted, watching the smirk that tugged at his lips before he blew a heated breath against my sex. "That's a low blow, Saint."

"Chaos has asked to see you," he announced, watching my face. "He misses you, strangely enough. He insists you raised him and that you're the only one who ever cared enough to tend him when he was little. Did you fall in love with my son, Brat?"

My heart thundered against my ribcage as tears burned my eyes. "That's really low, Saint," I snapped, unable to hide the emotion that made my voice sharp.

"He attacked three kids today because they spoke ill of you."

"Is he okay?" I asked, watching his features smooth out, revealing nothing of how he felt. "Saint, is Chaos okay?"

"He kicked all three of their asses, and then Sian broke up the fight when their parents showed up. He got lucky, Braelyn. He informed us that you were his protector and that I'd stolen that away from him right before he attacked me." I laughed, pride blossoming in my chest at the boy I'd raised. "You find it funny that he attacked his friends for speaking ill about you?"

"I find it funny that he attacked you for stealing me from him. Look at it from his point of view, Saint. You came in and took away the only person he trusts. I can understand your need to get to know your son, but I am all he has known since he was a toddler. You are a stranger to him."

"I know that I am, Braelyn. I didn't know he existed, and I know you claim to have tried to find me, but that's hard for me to believe," he snapped.

"Well, I did," I argued. "I searched for an entire year for you. I spent resources that I didn't have to spend, trying to get you back here to take Chaos away from here. I was terrified of what would happen if my father figured out that you were Chaos's father. But my father didn't bother himself with the pack, and your son made it very easy to love him." That was the truth.

"And now he's fighting me to see you," he stated, watching me. "Help me with the medicine, Braelyn."

"The pack doesn't want my help, Saint. They turned against me because of you, and now you're asking me to save them? Think about that. I have spent my entire life sacrificing everything for the pack. I put them above myself and my needs. The first time someone comes in with baseless accusations, without any fucking proof, they turn against me. I know," I exclaimed, sitting up to look him in the eye. "Find a new side-piece. I've already heard from the pack that once you choose one, she will help you raise our child. I'm certain if you two put your heads together, you'll figure it all out without my help." I rose, leaving him and the library as anger pulsed through me.

I had less than twenty-four hours left in this place,

and I didn't intend to spend it dwelling over what the pack needed or didn't need. Chaos didn't need the concoction of herbs. He was a healthy young wolf who would one day be an alpha. He didn't need his nature suppressed because his mother was a shifter, just like his dad. Chaos would be fine now and under the protection of his biological father. On the other hand, I had to escape his father, and I was quickly succumbing to his soft kisses and easy touches meant to seduce me.

Saint was like his son, easy to fall in love with when he turned on the charm. He'd been doing it each night, and every time he tried, I fell a little further into the trap he'd laid. It was time to get away from Saint, and with winter at our doorstep, he wouldn't be able to get to me until spring, even if he tried.

Chapter Twenty-Three

Inside the bedroom, I brushed my hair nervously. I'd packed a bag and tossed it out the window early enough to ensure Tora had been the one to grab it and hide it with hers. Tomorrow, we'd be leaving this place and escaping the mountain before the first heavy snow hit it, which was forecasted for tomorrow night. I intended to leave before nightfall which excited and terrified me.

I'd never been off the mountain. Harold had forbidden it, which was why my mother hadn't fled this place to bring help to free the pack. Maybe if she hadn't been pregnant with my sister or had me, she would have been bold and run from this place.

Fear was daunting, and the idea of leaving the only home I'd ever known was terrifying. Under the guise of being Saint's mate, living my life here with no power or control was one thing. Living here while he and someone else raised our children? Fuck that noise.

I wouldn't be that girl any longer, the one who allowed her life to be controlled by a dictator.

I'd lived that life to protect the pack from Harold's hatred and resentment toward them for not respecting him or his position. The pack had remained here for my mother and then me. Leif had confirmed what I'd suspected. Fenrir would protect the land because my mother's soul had been freed here, and her body placed into the ground. I wasn't the only thing keeping this place blessed by the wolf god.

My father and his devoted followers had lied about it. Little about my father shocked or surprised me. He was a monster, and he'd forced his claim on my mother. He'd seduced her, and then when she refused him, he'd raped her. She had lost the man who had been her soul mate before they'd finished the claiming. Then my dad stepped into the picture.

I wouldn't have been shocked if it had been by Harold's design that the young mate to my mother had met an untimely death before he'd been old enough to finish the claiming ceremony. Our people were often either too early or too late to claim their mate. Being immortal, it happened a lot more than it should have.

Toralei had arranged our escape, but to see it through, we'd have to take down my babysitter, whoever the unlucky prick may be on duty tomorrow. I'd packed clothing and a few other essentials that wouldn't be missed in the morning. I was leaving behind this life, along with everything I had built for myself, to start fresh in a new town, in a new country.

The door to the room opened, and I shifted my attention as Saint entered. His eyes searched me out, his scent reaching me before he did. Standing behind me, he watched me brush through my dark hair. He lowered his lips, placing a soft kiss on the top of my head before he smiled.

"I won't have anyone other than us raise our babies, Brat. I'd never allow that to happen." He moved into the bathroom when I didn't respond. "Come shower with me."

"I'm ready for bed," I returned, slowly walking toward the bathroom.

He stripped out of his clothes, tossing them into the basket that sat beside the shower. My attention roamed over his body, memorizing every sinful curve of it. I latched onto every tattoo and every rippling cord of muscle that covered him. The scent that was uniquely his held me prisoner. My throat tightened, knowing that to escape him, I'd have to ignore the emotion his presence and scent caused within me.

How ironic was it that the one person I'd prayed to return was the one I was now fleeing?

Saint had come home, but it wasn't because he'd wanted me. It was because he'd wanted to remove me from power along with my father. He'd placed me into the same category of a monster as Harold, even though he had no proof.

I'd wanted him to come back and believe that I wasn't involved in what happened to him. How hard was it to look at my deeds and see me for who I was? I got that Saint had been hurt, but I'd suffered longer and harder than any of the others. I'd lived through my father's torture until a year ago when I'd been freed from him. It had been a bloody showdown, and the only reason Harold had stopped was because of who had shown up to defend me.

Since then, I'd been on borrowed time, and every day I waited for my father to murder me or to send me away. I'd planned to take the pack from him, but Saint and his people had shown up, ruining it all. I'd been so close to freedom and bringing down Carlson and my father that I'd tasted it. Carlson wouldn't have left our mating tent alive, and the pack would have backed my plan the moment all hell broke loose.

I didn't even know where half the people had ended up, who were supposed to have helped me by storming the ceremony. I had sent the other half down the mountain to follow the trail of a child who had gone missing. That left the rest of us with our new warlords, hell-bent on saving those we'd already started protecting. Had I known he'd sold them? No, because I'd been too busy trying to survive my father, not knowing that his sickness went beyond what he'd done to me.

Maybe I was guilty of not seeing beyond my pain. I'd done the best I could do, and it hadn't been enough. I understood why the pack turned on me, and I couldn't blame them. Our people had gone missing, and I'd believed they'd run away. I'd made excuses, sending people out to search for them. I hadn't looked deeper because it had been women, and they often couldn't handle living away from people. Teenagers ran away; it happened. I'd always assumed they'd just left, never dreaming they'd been sold into slavery.

"You look lost tonight, Brat," Saint said, running

the towel over his wet body.

"Just tired," I lied, turning to escape his presence.

"Did you stop by the infirmary?" he asked, following me into the room. "Jacob said with the full moon coming, you should be fertile and in heat naturally. I'm game to let nature take its course without the drugs."

"Okay," I said, shuffling out of the lace robe to get into bed.

Saint paused, tilting his head to watch me sliding beneath the covers. "What's wrong with you, Brat? Your scent is off, and you seem—beaten."

"My scent is off because my hormones are screwing with it. The same goes for my mood. You can't mess with a woman's balance and then wonder why she's moody, Saint. That's pretty much common sense."

"Okay." He studied me closely as he shook his wet hair, his attention sliding over the covers and to the wall of pillows I'd placed in the center of the bed. "This shit again?"

"You dictated the rules, and I'm following them. Am I not? You get to use me, and then you can do whatever you want alone, afterward. I prefer the great wall of pillows to waking up tangled in your arms."

Mostly, I hated waking up in his arms because for a moment before my mind had fully processed what was happening, it felt right. The entire world would settle into place, and his scent would soothe me, offering comfort. But the moment we fully woke, it all went to shit.

Saint climbed into bed, naked. He didn't move the pillows, choosing to slide beneath the covers. Before I could guess what Saint intended, he'd yanked on the blanket, lifting it, sending all the pillows shooting into the air, raining down around the bed. He pounced, capturing my wrists above my head, smiling down at me.

"No more walls, woman. You and me, we have to figure out a balance so that we can live together. I know you're struggling because I can feel your turmoil through the link. I can feel your need to run, to escape me, and that isn't happening. I know you, Brae. I know you because you live within in me, inside my fucking soul."

"If you really knew me, Saint, you'd know I would never be involved in anything that would hurt this pack," I whispered, struggling to get out from beneath him.

He allowed me to wiggle from his grip as he settled in beside me. His attention moved over my face before he softly exhaled. "At night, when they'd put us back into our cells. I dreamed of you, about how you would feel pressed against me. I would catch your scent, and for a moment, my world wasn't so dark."

My heart clenched with his words, and my throat tightened with unshed tears. "I would have come for you had I known you were being hurt. I thought you were free and out there in the world, living."

"I never made it off the mountain. Your father had people waiting for us. At first, we assumed they were there to take us away from this place. When it became apparent that something was wrong, we fought, but they were ready for it. We woke up naked, chained to a wall while a woman explained what was happening." He paused, running his fingers over my stomach, causing slight friction as his eyes grew distant. "I promised to escape and slaughter her entire entourage of sick fucks. I killed innocent people to survive captivity. They would put women into a room, feed them drugs to numb the pain, and then force the men to rape them brutally. They murdered those who refused, using them for entertainment in varying ways at first. That's how I met Xavier. He raided the compound and freed us. He gave us a choice: Go back to where we'd been taken, which, for me, wasn't an option. Or, we could join them and help hunt down those who victimized others like us."

"And you couldn't come back here because of me," I stated, holding his gaze. "I'd banished you from the pack which meant you couldn't come back to me. I did that to prevent you from being hurt, and you ended up hurt, anyway. I don't blame you for hating me, Saint."

"I don't hate you, Brat. I hate that even though you rejected me, you were the one thing I couldn't hate. I wanted revenge, and I can't trust you. That doesn't change how much I want you and crave you. You're still the most gorgeous creature I've ever known, but I can't prove you weren't a part of what your father was doing. I can't trust you enough to just take your word for it. Prove it, Braelyn. Prove to me that you weren't involved in the trafficking of your own people."

"I can't," I swallowed thickly. "There lies the

problem, Saint. I can't prove it, and you can't prove that I was. Everyone who could back me up is dead. You killed them when you got here. Those were my father's men you fought."

He snorted, watching me with narrowing eyes. He moved onto his side, yanking me closer. Lifting my leg, he placed a soft kiss on my forehead as his hand shifted my panties aside. His cock slid through the arousal he discovered there, but he didn't push into my body.

"Regardless of the part you played, you will be the mother of my children, Brae. You are protected because of what you are to me. You won't escape me, even though you need and want to run from me. There's nowhere that you can go, that I won't find you. I craved this with you. I considered what it would be like returning here, finding you with someone else. I'd planned to murder them and claim you. I am pleased that you remained untouched and that you burn hot for me." He pushed into my core, which tightened around him as pleasure rushed through me. "We will find a way to make this work because I can't live without you again."

"You'll figure it out," I announced, placing my leg over his hip while rolling him onto his back. I didn't undress or pretend not to enjoy what he made me feel together, like this. "I wish I could make you see I am not a monster. I don't think that would be enough, though, not when you're hurt because I rejected you. I didn't do it because I wanted to hurt you. I did it because my father was a sick, twisted monster who always won. I couldn't imagine a world without you in it and chose to protect you. It was what I had the power to control, Saint." I leaned over, nipping at his bottom lip as he growled.

"I wish I could believe that, Brat. But I went through hell while you remained here pampered in your palace," he flipped me onto my back, grinding against me as my stomach coiled with the pleasure he was driving deep into my body. "Now, I will spend the rest of my life reminding you of what you did to me. You won't escape me, and we will find a way to compromise and live together."

I exploded around him, wrapping my legs around his muscular waist as he went from gentle to hard, fucking me like a possessed man trying to fuck his demons out of his system. I didn't believe him for one moment that he wouldn't lock me away or murder me once I'd given him an heir to my line.

"Saint," I moaned, gasping as he nuzzled my shoulder, reinforcing his claim as I trembled beneath him, coming undone again.

"You're mine now, Brat. Always and forever, which is what you promised me the moment you discovered we were true soul mates."

Chapter Twenty-Four

I'd dressed in a soft pair of jeans and flat, leather, thigh-high boots with multiple buckles covering the top of the leather, curving and hugging my calves. The jacket I'd chosen was army green, with soft fur lining that heated against my arms. Tugging the jacket up tighter, I zipped it while walking the perimeter of the courtyard with Phenrys, my unlucky babysitter for the day.

He was silent and vigilant as we moved through the mostly empty yard. I paused, inhaling the crisp air that threatened snow as it stung against my nose and cheeks.

"It's cold as shit out here," he grumbled, rubbing his hands together while studying the way I moved. "We're going back inside momentarily because I'm over the cold."

"I need to light the candles inside my mother's crypt. They've been neglected, and I'd like to do so before we go back inside."

Phenrys dropped his head, rolling it back to look at me before sliding his gaze to the crypt that sat a few yards away from the newly built ad-on. Nodding, he started toward it as I trailed silently behind him, my heartbeat increasing, which caused him to turn, eyeing me with a suspicious glare.

Stopping at the entrance, he peered inside before stepping back, allowing me to enter as he leaned against the rock doorway. I moved to the large candelabra with multiple candles in an ancient brass holder. Withdrawing the lighter, I lit the candles as they swayed in the wind that drifted through the tomb.

The wind outside was picking up, and I knew that was a sign that time was dwindling from us. Stepping back, I saw something silver moving through the air, and Phenrys turned, intending to shout a warning. It never came. Toralei smiled as he slumped to the floor, unconscious from the blow to his head.

"About time," she stated, stepping to the wall where my mother's memorial was written on the slate surface. She opened the hidden passage, and I followed her inside, grabbing a torch to light our path.

The passageway led to a small tunnel, big enough for one person to move through easily. Douglas leaned against the end of the tunnel where it split into different directions that led out of the mountain. Not wasting time, knowing Phenrys wouldn't stay down for long, we shuffled toward where Douglas waited.

"Hey, beautiful. Finally wanting to escape this place?" Douglas smirked as his eyes slid over my body.

"Yeah, it's time," I answered, watching as his large

form struggled to turn around to lead us out of the smaller section.

It took a while to travel through the narrow tunnel, and when he turned right toward a light source, I frowned. Ducking into the bigger, wider passageway, I sucked my lip between my teeth, peering around.

This tunnel was a lot larger, with small cages that lined the wall. Silently, I examined them, noting that they looked like holding pens. Had they'd been used to hide the people that were sold? It was plausible. The scent of mold and decaying earth smothered the space, along with a light scent of cayenne paper.

"How often have you used these tunnels, Douglas?" Suspicion was coursing through me because these tunnels looked like they had been used for trafficking.

"Not for a long while." Looking around the chamber, Douglas shook his head. "The last time I used these tunnels, it was to smuggle goods in for your mom. After she passed, there wasn't much use for them. Had I known they had used them to hold or harm anyone, I would have gotten word to Tora. I promise you that."

Nodding, we walked forward in silence as I continued to take in more evidence of my father's crimes. My father had spent so much time at my mother's tomb, and part of me had hoped he was sorry for how he had treated her and that his guilt would somehow change him. But all this time, he was using her grave to hide his crimes and as a place of torture.

Clearing his throat, clearly uncomfortable with what we're seeing, Douglas diverted our attention and changed the subject, quickening his pace away from the chamber. "I was surprised when I got the call from Tora that you wanted to leave. You always struck me as someone who would always stay with the pack, no matter what. Glad to see I was wrong about you, Braelyn." Douglas's soft hazel eyes met mine briefly before he undid the straps on his back and pulled out a large container of cayenne pepper, handing one to me before removing two more from his bag. "Start scattering it so no one can track our scent. There's a shitload of tunnels we're about to go through. If we can buy time, it will help. My guys are at the bottom with the four-wheelers waiting for us, but it will be a few hours before reaching them. We'll be backpacking up through the mountains once the trees get too thick to move through with the quads."

"How many days in the woods, do you think?" Tora asked, watching me as I fought past the panic consuming me.

"Three, but I brought an extra tent for you to share. We won't be making fires, but I grabbed extra equipment for you to use. Your bags are already hooked to the quads, and we should make it through the worst patches before the snow hits tonight. My guys are waiting over the border to take you the rest of the way north."

"Thank you," I muttered, fighting the panic attack at the thought of leaving the pack behind.

"Just breathe, Braelyn. You're going to be okay," he said comfortingly, watching the way my features pinched. "You don't deserve what is happening to you. I know that, and you don't have anything to worry

ALPHA'S CLAIM

about from my people. I've known you my entire life, and what they're saying tells me they don't know you at all. They assumed you helped your father, but those close to you know you hated him as much as the pack did."

We walked past a fork in the tunnel, entering another large chamber of dark mouths that led to different exits. Douglas paused, sprinkling the pepper over where we'd walked. He turned once he'd finished, nodding to Tora, who dug out the nightgown I'd worn for the last several nights.

A shadow moved, and my heart sank until I realized it was one of Douglas's men I'd met on one of his trips up the mountain to deliver Canadian whiskey. He nodded at me, his green eyes sliding to Tora with interest burning within them. Holding out his hand, Douglas placed the scented nightgown in his but didn't let go.

"You should run until you reach the furthest exit. It should have anyone trailing Braelyn's scent on your tail while we head in the opposite direction. They aren't expecting her to go through the river, and the rafts will make it near impossible for Saint to catch her scent on the wind. Once you get to the end of the tunnel, Tyler, get on the bike and toss the nightgown over the cliffside. It should have them searching for her until nightfall, leaving us enough time to put some distance between them and us." Douglas dropped the nightgown into Tyler's hand, watching as he took one last long, heated glance at Tora, who smirked wickedly at his interest. "Go, you two can hook up much later once we're off this cursed mountain. The snow is coming, and once it does, we'll be easier to track."

We watched Tyler vanish into one of the many caves. Douglas sprinkled the pepper over the entrance of others, including a light dusting at the one where Tyler had disappeared. Moving to where Tora and I stood, Douglas nodded at us.

"You're going to need to get it into your clothes; that way, your pores suck up your scent that Saint and his people can track and hopefully will prevent more from releasing. It won't feel great, but it's better to play it safe. You happened to mate with one of the meanest trackers and bloodhounds in the north, Braelyn."

"You said we're going to the river? It's dangerous with the rapids at this time of year," I elaborated as he nodded.

"So is leaving your mate for the unknown. That river isn't easy, but it is also why he'll look elsewhere for you. He won't think you were brave enough to chance the rapids to leave him." Douglas watched as I pulled my shirt out, shaking the thick scent of cayenne pepper onto it. His dark brow lifted when I started to put it away, and a mischievous smile played on his full mouth. "In your pants too, sweetheart. He'll be counting on that lady trap to lead him right to you. And, I'm guessing he was trying to plant a pup last night because I can smell him on you."

"Plant a pup?" Tora laughed, causing my fear to ease a little at their banter.

"Hormones too, I'm guessing? He wasn't taking no for an answer," he said, astonished.

"Yeah, basically he wanted to keep my child after

ALPHA'S CLAIM

he'd succeeded in making one." I poured the pepper into my jeans, zipping them up and slapping my hands over my thighs, then smothered a sneeze before it ripped from me. I chuckled, standing as an angry howl echoed through the tunnels, reaching where we stood.

"That's our cue to run, ladies," Douglas starting down the dark tunnel, and we followed in silence.

I listened to the sounds of angry growls and voices rippling through the tunnels. The further we got away from their voices, the easier it became to breathe. Fear of being captured and dragged back up the mountain plagued my mind.

The mountain was the only home I'd ever known, and leaving it hadn't been easy. It was the right choice, though, which I reminded myself on repeat in my head. There was nothing left for me here. Chaos belonged with his father, and while I hated leaving him behind, it was the right thing to do. My chest clenched tightly, but no emotion escaped or was visible on my pinched features. We moved quickly, even as Saint bellowed my name repeatedly, which echoed from all angles as if he was everywhere at once.

Breaking free of the tunnels, we paused to look back at the multiple exits that opened up all over the hillside. Some had nowhere to stand, leading to sheer drops. My chest tightened as I considered Saint or his people falling from the higher openings. Tora grabbed my arm, dispelling the fear as we moved toward the shore of the river.

Douglas's men waited on the bank, handing us life jackets before shuffling us into the thick, black river rafts. Someone handed me an oar, and before I could tell the men that I did not know how to raft, we were shoved off the bank and rushed downstream by the quick-moving rapids.

Water splashed into the boat, soaking us as we continued down the river. The boat jerked, and the water tossed us around as we paddled furiously to stay away from the angrier rapids, trying to avoid any large boulders. The water was deafening, canceling out the words that anyone tried to scream. I peered back in the direction from which we'd escaped, seeing nothing but the bank as we were dragged further down the river.

My heart was stuck in my throat as I watched the mountain growing smaller. The light from the compound was fading, and the sense of dread I'd felt at leaving crept up on me. A hand touched my shoulder, pulling me from my mind, and I turned, finding Toralei watching me with worry burning in her emerald gaze.

She smiled reassuringly as something slammed into the boat, sending us all into the ice-cold water. I gasped, kicking my feet as the water forced me into the rocks. The water hid my screams as I kicked and flailed my arms, peering through the icy depths for Tora. A hand yanked me up, and I was pulled over the edge of a raft.

My entire body trembled, and the coppery tang of blood was thick in the air as I watched Douglas pulling Toralei up from the other side of the raft. Moving into action, I helped him pull her and the two other men out, glancing at the ripped raft we'd been in moments before. It was thrown lifelessly around in the rapids, slamming against a large rock that continually fought to suck the raft below the frozen depths.

It took another hour of battling the raging river before we left the rafts and rushed down the mountainside's rough terrain. At the bottom were more men, all dressed in high-tech gear, seated on four-wheelers. Douglas caught me before I moved toward one of the men, helping me shed my coat, and replacing it with his larger one.

"The raft they were on flipped. We'll need to find a cave to let them get dry and warm. We won't be able to make it far if they end up with hypothermia. Let's move," Douglas ordered, nodding to a man on one of the quads, who scooted back for me to ride in front of him.

It took hours of riding through bone-chilling cold before we found a cave to accommodate our group's size. Douglas had packed thermal clothes, giving us each a set to change. Once we were dry and warmer, we were back on the bikes, riding through the first snow that blanketed the ground.

It took days to reach the Canadian border, and we were given fake passports and identification cards once we arrived. Douglas didn't stop there, handing us cash and giving us an address where we would be staying. He'd even gotten jobs for us, giving us everything we needed to start over from nothing.

I hugged him, crying against his shoulder as he hugged me back. "Thank you. Thank you, Douglas."

"Your mother helped me and mine once upon a time, kid. I never got the chance to repay her for that. Now I have. I have saved her daughter and given her a new chance at a life of her choosing. My debt has been repaid," he announced, standing back as black SUVs pulled up to the side of the road. "You're braver than you think you are, Braelyn Haralson. May the gods protect you and keep you safe."

Chapter Twenty-Five

Saint – Three Months Later

I watched Cole Van Helsing climb out of the Blackhawk helicopter, shielding his eyes as he moved toward me, shaking the snow from his heavy coat. Tattooed fingers righted the collar of his jacket, and he smiled upon seeing me.

"Van Helsing," I announced, running my eyes over the tattoo that covered his brow and his temple to vanish into his hairline.

"Kingsley, pleasure as always," Cole said in a heavily accented tone that most women would fawn over. "You are causing quite the issue for us. I hope your mate is worth it," he concluded, nodding at the other helicopters that were coming in as Cole's took off to refuel.

"She is, and I believe she's pregnant with my child," I announced, watching his face pinch with distaste.

"Seems to be in the water lately," he grumbled. "Someone needs to invent some immortal-proof birth control."

"You too, huh?" I asked.

"No, not me," he said in a tone filled with anger. "Rhys is going to be a daddy, but he's rejected his mate and denounced his child. You could do the same and recall that fucking reward you put on her head."

"Rhys as a father? I didn't see that cankerous ass ever finding someone he trusted enough to have his offspring."

"No one said anything about trust, and she's a Silversmith."

My body jerked to a stop, turning to look at Cole with wide eyes as shock rushed through me. I didn't need to ask to know Rhys wasn't happy with the predicament. I was old enough and had heard of the war between their bloodlines multiple times. It was a tale of legendary enemies that had fought to destroy each other for decades. At one point, the Van Helsing family gathered a group of immortals to murder the Silversmith line.

"Fuck," I exclaimed, unable to get much more past my lips.

"Yeah, fuck. Remington is a newborn and isn't even immortal yet. But she carries Rhys's child, sure as shit. Lucky prick ended up with her on Beltane. Magic, pretty women, and a fertility festival, well, it doesn't end in any other outcome than fucked." I shook my head, thinking Rhys and I had more in common than I thought when it came to the women in our lives.

"Anyway, back to your girl, Kingsley. This million-dollar reward has hunters up in arms. Even the sodden pricks at E.V.I.E. are out hunting for any sign of her. It's caused the sanctuary to be overrun by out-of-towners, and Rhys is in danger of declining sanctuary to them. As you know, Van Helsings aren't allowed to do that." I signaled toward the lodge, and we began to cross the field toward the gates leading up the path. "I should also mention that Carleigh has asked to join the hunt, but she is still awaiting judgment and is not permitted outside of the compound. Given the circumstances, I thought you would want to know."

"Braelyn is carrying my child, and she's never been off this mountain until now. She's alone with her best friend, who we thought was a beta, but we have since learned she is also an alpha. How they ended up paired together, well, who the fuck knows. Our women carry their pregnancies for five to six months, and Braelyn's out there unprotected, Cole. She's my fucking mate."

"So you put a bounty on her head? Why not just track her?" he countered, entering the hall where I'd set up a command room since losing Braelyn's trail inside the tunnels.

"Encouragement, plus it stated she must be alive and unharmed." I turned to one of the monitors as the men infiltrated a trafficking ring. I studied the cells, shivering at the memory of being caged in one for entirely too long.

"How many have you freed?" Cole asked, watching the same monitor that showed Xari and

Xavier entering the screen with their changeling team spread out behind them.

"Too fucking many, and yet never enough. Not until we've freed every one of them from that life," I muttered, nodding at a woman to fill our glasses with whiskey. "I can't stop looking for her, Cole. I have to find her. Braelyn does not know the target that's now painted on her back because of her ties to me. I've more enemies than friends, and while I have very powerful friends, they can't protect her unless we find her. Even if she chose never to come back, I'd feel better with eyes on her."

"You'd let her go?" Cole asked, raising an eyebrow.

"No, I wouldn't. I can't. It's not within me to allow Braelyn to live without being at my side. She rejected me, but I can't stomach living without her near me. She's in my soul. I accused her of being involved in her father's trafficking ring because I couldn't prove she wasn't aware of what had been happening here. We didn't know how Harold could smuggle them in and out without the pack knowing. We found out after she'd left that he'd used the tunnels. Inside her mother's crypt is a mass of tunnels, and one of them leads into his fucking private quarters. Harold didn't even have to enter the lodge with his victims because he'd built a way to bring them in with no one ever knowing he had them."

"So she may not have been aware after all?" Cole steepled his fingers in front of his mouth, and piercing blue eyes studied me, knowing my answer without me saying it. "Did she say she wasn't part of what had been going on here?"

"Of course she did," I scoffed. "I couldn't take her word for it, Cole, especially after she mentioned the killing fields where we found the buried containers. But she had an excuse for that, too." Sighing, I lifted my glass and downed the contents, pushing it forward to be filled again. "Braelyn rejected me as her mate, which she claimed was to protect me. I'd asked her to run away with me multiple times, to escape her father before he discovered we were mates. She declined every time. Then she destroyed me in front of the entire pack. She denounced our match, saying I'd forced her to believe lust was love. Harold banished my entire crew and me. Only they never let us leave, choosing to sell us to the highest bidder to be fucked and tortured by sick assholes passing us around for entertainment. You know the rest since you helped Xavier free us."

Cole blew out a loud breath, grabbing the glass in front of him. I watched him take a long drink of the whiskey before Xavier spoke into the speaker, announcing they were heading back up the mountain. I deflated, peering up at the men and women escorting the children toward the medivac vans that waited.

"If my torturers figure out that Braelyn is mine, they'll go for her. I can't live with that. I can't stomach the idea of Braelyn being held captive by the same sadistic monsters I'm fighting against," I admitted, turning as Eryx entered the room with files in his hands. "More leads?" I asked, watching his dark head nod before he smiled at Cole, grabbing his hand to yank him up, patting him on the back roughly.

"Hey, asshole," Eryx chuckled. "Long time since I saw your ugly face."

"Careful, puppy. If I recall, you called me ugly once before, and I fucked your girlfriend the same night while you fucked her throat."

"She enjoyed it, and it didn't bother me one bit." Eryx shrugged his shoulders before he sat, tapping his fingers on the files. "This shit is driving me insane. One report says someone saw Brae at the circus, riding a donkey."

"I don't foresee her riding a donkey."

"Nah, not riding," Eryx stated, using his fingers to emphasize his meaning. "Riding the donkey, asshole."

"That shit's kinky, even for you, assholes," Cole laughed, running his finger over his bottom lip.

The doors opened, and Xavier and Xari walked through with Enzo and Ezekiel on their heels. They tossed pictures down on the table, and my stomach clenched, hating that we'd be going through them for signs of who they were and from where they'd been taken.

Since the day Braelyn vanished, we'd started bringing the orphans here for rehabilitation. Brae had left the herbal concoction combination and medicine chart with Jacob, surprisingly, and the pack had helped administer the doses. Well, it had surprised the pack, not me. Braelyn may have been hurt by her pack turning against her, but she didn't want them hurt. That simple action spoke more about her character than anything else she'd done since I had returned.

"How many saved?" Eryx asked, his eyes guarded to shield the painful memories those words stirred. Once upon a time, Cole asked the same question as we stood behind him, with the same crew present.

"Twenty-three, one was too far gone to save," Xariana announced.

"Did you find any trace of your Jane Doe there?" I asked, noting Xavier looked paler than usual.

"No, but we found a collection of videos I intend to go through. I can't help but feel like I failed this girl. It's been over a year since there's been any sign of her. I just need to move on and focus on the ones I can save now. The ones that are still alive out there, waiting to be found."

"Speaking of videos," Cole announced. "We raided a compound of shifters a few weeks back. They were heavy into torture and enjoyed watching wolves slaughtered on video. My men came across one that I thought we could watch together. They think this victim was held in the same place you were, Saint, because she called out your name."

"It's possible, but few escaped that bitch's pit when they were placed in there with Eryx or me. Not that I'm bragging, but she pitted us against anyone they put in the pit. They were normally higher on the food chain than we were." I frowned as Cole produced a memory card and slid it to Sian, who had just walked in, his suit on point even though he had no fucking reason to wear one. Zayne smirked, dropping more folders onto the table before I nodded at the card. "Put it in. Let's see if one of us can't identify the girl on the video."

Grabbing the whiskey, I poured everyone a round while Zayne got the feed up on the main screen. Once I'd refilled the glasses, I turned, wincing at the sight that came to life on the monitor. Harold stood beside a victim, his eyes filled with something dark and sinister. The woman was bound, her arms tied above her as he peeled a large piece of skin from her stomach.

Nausea washed through me, knowing exactly how much pain was involved when skinned alive. The entire room watched as Harold tossed the knife aside and spoke to the camera, with no volume, as per his usual shit. It wasn't until someone else entered the room, his face obscured by a mask, that the camera was adjusted, and the volume came to life. I didn't relish the idea of hearing her screams or reliving the tortured memories they'd bring back to life.

"Nothing yet? She's a different breed, Harold," the masked male announced, and even though he was wearing the mask, we all knew it was Lucas.

"There is that sadistic fuck, Lucas. I can't believe he was under our noses all this time, and had been the one to help Harold in his torture session. But why wear the mask?" Eryx gripped his fists and shook in rage.

My eyes slid back to the woman, noting her head was covered, and I was willing to bet she was probably gagged beneath the sack. It helped Harold and Lucas to dehumanize their victims. It took away having to peer into their eyes, knowing that a soul lived beneath it.

"She'll break, eventually. They all do with enough incentive," Harold snorted, dragging the dull edge of the knife over the inside of her thigh. "Isn't that right, little one? Come on. Daddy wants to play with you, sweet girl."

Muffled sounds filled the room. The girl twisted,

ALPHA'S CLAIM

and blood ran down her body, drenching the only clothes she wore, a tiny pair of cotton panties. Every inch of her body was covered in angry bruises, and there was nothing I could see that would identify her.

"Sick bastard," Xariana grunted, drinking from the glass in front of her.

Why Xavier wanted her to learn about monsters like Harold was beyond me. I had to give her credit; she was a fierce little hunter and took no shit. She was young, but her rose-colored glasses had been shattered long ago.

"Tell me you're mine," Harold demanded.

More muffled cries filled the small room where the girl was held. Men entered the frame, freeing her hands, forcing her to stand on legs cut on all sides, showing her thighs' inside sensitive area had been removed. She was a fighter, not that it was doing her any good. She struggled against the men that held her arms, fighting against their hold.

"Give me what I want, and this ends. Tell me you're mine, sweet girl. Come on! Say it, so I don't have to hurt you anymore. You know I don't like to hurt you." Harold leaned closer, tilting his head.

"I thought you said she spoke? She sounds gagged," I asked, not enjoying the show that had my stomach churning with the need to throw up.

"Just wait," Cole snorted, nodding at the monitor. "I was told that she starts talking after Harold removes the hood."

"Great," Eryx muttered, downing his drink before

refilling it to the rim. "Wish we could bring this fuck back to life and murder him again and again…"

"Me too," I agreed, topping off my glass and leaning back to watch as Harold blocked the view of his victim from the camera.

"Say it again, you little bitch!" Harold snarled, ripping the hood off, tossing it behind him. He continued to block the view, struggling to remove the gag in her mouth.

"Saint Kingsley!" The girl's voice filled the room, and my blood turned to ice.

"You fucking little whore! He's gone. He can't ever come back. You will give me what I want from you! I will father a child within your womb, even if I have to fucking cutting it out of you!" Harold snarled, slashing against her chest. He moved, and Braelyn, my Braelyn, lunged, her face coming into the camera's view as everyone around me went dead silent.

Blood drained from my face as the glass in my hand shattered. Braelyn's body was mottled in cuts and bruises, and large pieces of her flesh were missing. Her eyes were wild as she continued screeching my name, maddened by her need to say it. Tears burned my eyes, sliding them over the screen as she fought to attack her father even though her body was broken.

"Jesus fuck," Eryx snapped.

"What the fucking hell," Zayne asked, turning horrified eyes to where I sat, motionless as I watched Braelyn fight a losing battle.

Harold slashed against her stomach, cutting her

open as the men grabbed her from behind, holding her up for his abuse. He punched her, but she refused to stop screaming my name like she was trying to shout it loud enough that I'd hear her and come back. Braelyn's head snapped back as the knife slid through the side of her cheek.

Her tiny hands lifted, holding her face as her father continued slashing through her skin. He dropped the blade, and it crashed to the floor as he slammed his fist into her face. She lurched backward, slipping through her blood, fighting to stay upright.

"Gods damn," Xariana uttered, her tone as horrified as I felt.

"Turn it off," I whispered through the saliva pooling in my mouth, unable to watch anymore. My stomach roiled, threatening to expel the whiskey.

No one moved, disgusted and shocked as the film continued with Braelyn slipping to the floor and alphas attacking her crumpled form. It wasn't until a soft cry erupted behind us that everyone turned to see Chaos, watching the woman he loved and considered his mom, mutilated on the screen.

"Turn it the fuck off," I whispered, unable to make my voice come out higher.

"It's Jane Doe," Xavier stated, forcing my eyes to meet his. "Look at her ankle. Braelyn is Jane Doe."

I turned, staring at where he was pointing, and flinched. On Braelyn's ankle was a small, red mark that was easily missed since it had always been cuffed or bound in the later videos. It had been there when she was younger, which is how Xavier had been identifying her. As she'd grown older, he'd found other ways to try identifying her when they'd used the cuff, such as her non-response to pain, unlike ordinary people. It took immense pain before she would struggle against the people torturing her. I shook my head, unable to process what I was seeing.

Zayne killed the feed as I moved to grab Chaos. I didn't even know what to say to him since I wasn't able to process what I'd seen. I'd accused Braelyn of helping Harold, and she'd been his primary victim. Why hadn't she said anything? Why hadn't she tried to reach me with the truth?

"That's why she was so sad all the time," Chaos whispered, his eyes swimming with unshed tears. "She tried to hide it and pretend not to be sad, but I sensed it. I caught it once when she was trying to pretend she was happy." He sniffled, and I frowned at his words.

I swallowed down the sick feeling as I tried to recall Braelyn ever acting like a victim. "How the fuck did we miss this?" I asked myself, but it was Chaos who answered.

"You had to watch her when she didn't think you were. Fear is an emotion, and so is pain. We control our emotions, and only we allow people to see them." He handed me a phone, and I stared at it. "I saw it because she seemed sad, but she's Braelyn. She is only sad when no one watches her. I put my phone where she didn't know I was watching. It recorded her, but it was fast."

I blinked as Chaos nodded at the phone. Zayne

took it, hooking up the cord to the monitor, and then flipped through the images on the screen. Chaos's phone was filled with photos of him and Brae doing silly things, which tugged at my heart. Then a video began playing.

Chaos was talking to Brae, and a broad smile played on her full mouth. She turned, eyeing the other kids before laughing. Chaos grabbed a radio, watching Brae, who stared after the other kids rushing away to play with the ball they'd been kicking. Train Wreck, by James Arthur, started playing, and she slowly turned to stare at the moon.

I watched the video, aimed at her face, obvious that Chaos had left it sitting somewhere it wouldn't be noticed. Braelyn's eyes swam with silent tears, sliding that Nordic blue gaze to where Chaos had chased after the ball. Her face changed, revealing the pain she never showed.

It wasn't just the pain in her eyes or the way she opened her mouth to scream silently, slapping her hands over her mouth. It was agony, soul-deep suffering she'd let no one know existed. Her chest shook as she continued holding in her scream. It wasn't until someone approached her from behind that she dropped her hands, and her face went neutral, and vacant eyes peered up at the moon. Braelyn controlled her emotions, easily turning off the anguish ripping her apart from within at what she'd endured. Her mask was effortlessly in place, with no tears having escaped.

"Did you see that?" Sian asked. "I've seen that look before on her. The vacant stare that made me assume she was cold."

"I saw it, too," I admitted, swallowing past the lump in my throat. "It's the same way she looked when she rejected me. It was like she had no emotion and had just turned it all off, so she didn't have to feel. If Braelyn is Jane Doe, it means her father tortured her from when she was a child. He tried to break her, and she refused to shatter—and we fucking missed it. We asked her repeatedly, 'What pain would a pampered princess ever know?'"

"And she'd replied carefully, 'Don't throw rocks at glass palaces because they hide the ugliest monsters.' We missed it," Eryx whispered.

"We fucked up," I muttered. "We assumed without evidence that Braelyn was involved with Harold, and the entire time, she was another victim. I painted her into a fucking monster to her pack, and even with everything she'd endured and the way they treated her before she left, she still ensured they would survive. Braelyn has every right to hate us. Fuck, I fucking hate myself now. I'm her mate, and I never even sensed she was hurting. The weeks she went missing, I assumed she was dealing with pack shit, but she had been healing from the sick bastard intending to breed with his daughter."

"We fucked up big time," Eryx agreed, blowing out a deep breath.

Phenrys entered the room, peering around as he placed a thumb drive on the table. I didn't even look down as he searched my face. Sian filled him in on what he'd missed, and I watched him sit, only to miscalculate the chair and land on the floor. Phenrys rose, shaking his head, and nodded at the drive. Zayne grabbed it, searching my face.

"I'm not sure how much more shit I can take tonight," I warned, watching as Zayne stepped to the TV, removing the cord from the phone and pushing the thumb drive into the USB port. The video began, and Brae's image came on the screen. "Where is this?" I asked, watching as she cupped her ear, trying to hear the guy leaning over the bar.

"Calgary, Canada. The video was time-stamped two days ago. The person who tipped us off said it was on them and that they owed you one. They said you'd sent someone back home to them, and they were returning the favor," Phenrys announced. "Her own father? Jesus Christ."

"Get the Blackhawk ready and clear permission to enter Canadian airspace," I swallowed, searching the faces around the table. "Sian, I want you here. I want the pack to know I cleared Braelyn of any wrongdoing. Scratch that; this is my mistake. I'll talk to them. Call in the alphas, and show them the video, but just the part where they can see it's her, not anything else. I turned her people against her, and she didn't deserve that. I need to fix it. Cole, you're coming with me. She hasn't seen you yet, nor will she know who the hell you are. She'll run from us, and I don't fucking blame her. Eryx, Zayne, and Bowen, you're all with me. Everyone else, we will be back."

Chapter Twenty-Six

Braelyn

Stepping out of the shower, I peered around the small cramped room. It was hardly big enough to turn around in, but it was clean. We'd rented a new apartment in a high traffic area, close to work, once we'd noticed the wolves around the one Douglas had chosen for us. It would have been more dangerous to be around wolves, especially considering Saint had left me in a precarious condition.

I dressed in a pair of soft, stretchy jeans and pulled the camisole top over my sensitive breasts. Turning sideways in the cramped room, I looked at the gentle swell of my belly in the mirror. It was noticcable now and hard to hide that I was pregnant. Groaning, I grabbed the sweater and slipped my arms into it, shoving my hair into a messy bun before I left the room.

The stale scent of takeout food made my nose itch,

hating that it wasn't the fresh food we'd had on the mountain. I missed the mountain and the protection it would have offered me in my current condition. I hated waking up every morning and going to bed every night, still worrying about the pack.

"We have twenty minutes to get to the bar, and you already know Jackson is going to be there, pissy as per usual." Toralei came into the front room, the largest in the house since the tiny kitchen with a stove and mini-fridge was only a twinge larger than the bathroom.

"I'm ready to go," I announced.

"Did you take your vitamins? Did you eat?" She mothered me, which was endearing, if not bothersome.

"Yes, mother! I also took the edibles that you left in the cupboard, and we're both pleased with the herbal mixture!" I wiggled my brows, smirking at how her mouth hung open with horror burning in her eyes.

"You did not!" she stated, horrified at my singsong tone before rushing into the tiny alcove to open the one cupboard in the apartment. "That isn't even funny!"

"It was, but then you didn't see the absolute look of horror on your face. I love you, and I love that you worry about the babe and me, but we're fine. I took my vitamins, and I ate two apples and some scrambled eggs. We're good, Tora. Stop mothering me. Everything is okay," I chided, slipping on my thick coat and kissing her cheek. "Now, let's go before Jackson fires us both, and we end up needing a smaller apartment."

"I don't think they get much smaller than this," Tora grumped, hiding her edibles before grabbing her coat.

Outside, I peered up at the bright blue sky, fighting a smile as the air bit at my exposed cheeks. It was freezing, yet still beautiful. The bitter cold in the air reminded me of home, and I missed sitting in front of the fireplace, lost in an amazing story as the snow fell outside the window of the lodge's library.

Passing Mrs. Peterson, I paused, moving to where she was struggling with the heavy snow mucking up the sidewalk. Her husband, Tommy, as he preferred to be called, was disabled, leaving her to do most of the heavy lifting. Grabbing the shovel from her, I smiled against the wind that whipped my hair in my face.

"I'll do it, Angela. Let me help," I offered, watching her soft blue eyes crinkle in the corners.

"You girls, I don't know how I managed before you moved in here," she admonished, curling her arms over her chest to stave off the chilled afternoon air.

"Give me that, Brianna," Tora snapped, grabbing the shovel. I turned, frowning at my new name, still unused to it even after three and a half months of hearing it. "You, go stand by Angela and shoot the shit. You're not supposed to be doing such things in your condition."

"I'm pregnant, not disabled," I argued. I allowed Tora, or Tori as I now called her, to take the shovel from me.

"Back in my day, pregnancy wasn't an excuse not to work. Nowadays, you'd think they believed you were breakable. People act like you will melt and wilt if you do a darn thing by yourself," Angela scoffed, smiling at the way Tora glared at her over her shoulder while making quick work of the sidewalk.

"Tori's a mother bear for certain," I chuckled, watching her finish the sidewalk, handing the shovel back so that we could hurry off to the bar. "Have a nice evening, Mrs. Peterson. Tell Tommy hello for us," I called back, and Toralei grabbed my arm as I moved over a slick part of the sidewalk.

"Watch where you're walking," Toralei groaned.

"You are going to be an amazing daddy, Tora," I laughed, watching her eyes widening at my statement.

We entered the bar with one minute to spare. Both of us quickly clocked in and started taking the chairs down from the tables, setting up for the regulars who lived for the few hours they got between home and the bar after long hours of work.

The Hub was a dive bar that had a lot of regulars. Some people just popped in to see what the atmosphere was like before moving next door to the more boisterous club with loud pop music playing and flashing lights that offered seizures and fun. I preferred this side of the club. The country music reminded me of home, and the regulars were gruff, rough men.

I grabbed glasses from the shelf and placed them into the ice Jackson had poured into a bin for them to chill. He smiled, dropping his soft gray gaze to my belly. Jackson was refreshing but very human and in his early forties. He'd started The Hub with money he'd earned from serving in the armed forces overseas, then opening up his own private security company. The Hub, however, was his dream job.

"How are we feeling, momma?" he asked, causing

a smile to play at the corners of my mouth.

"Great, but ask me again at closing time, and I'm sure the answer will be, exhausted," I laughed, moving around him to chill some of the whiskey I knew would be served tonight.

It wasn't an awful job, and it was off the beaten path, meaning few otherworld beings would come in for a visit. I was doing well at learning to blend in, and we appeared human enough to pass as one of them.

I'd learned early on after arriving here that people didn't care where you came from or your history. No one asked about our past, commented on our height, or that we spoke with a slight accent because everyone else here did too. It was a beautiful, chaotic mixture of varying races.

"If you need a break, Brianna, let me know. We'll cover the slack," Jackson stated, nodding at his girlfriend. "Katie and I don't mind you getting off your feet. You work harder than most of the lazy pricks I've hired over the years, and we don't want you burning out."

"Thanks, but I prefer to stay busy. It keeps my mind off life, and for a dive bar, this place is pretty cozy," I admitted.

Jackson's hands moved over his heart, and a roguish smile covered his lips. "Never call it such, Daisy Dame," he laughed. "I better go fix the jukebox before Floyd gets here and starts beating it again."

"He does love his music," I muttered, turning my attention to the door as it opened.

Royce and Bryce, regulars at the bar, entered, shaking the snow from their jackets as they removed them. Grabbing a pitcher, I tipped it to fill for them and took the $20 bill he placed on the bar, breaking it into change for them to play pool. Once they headed off, I started mixing the drinks we'd serve for the special.

People began filing in as the clock ticked on, and the music got more boisterous. I'd finished mixing the drinks for a group of women who were slumming it, their words, not mine. Jackson worked beside me, moving through the orders for the kitchen while I focused on the drinks.

I was pouring another pitcher of beer when the doors opened, and a man entered. My senses screamed in warning, and I slowly ran my gaze over his form. He didn't smell like a shifter or the undead. In fact, he didn't smell like anything, yet my hackles were up screaming in warning.

The man was tall. He was at least six inches over my height of six feet in the flat boots I wore. A tattoo started above one eyebrow, wrapping around it to vanish into his hairline. It looked sexy on him, where I wouldn't have thought a face tattoo would on anyone. His eyebrow was pierced, along with his lower lip. He wore a suit vest but skipped wearing the jacket.

Sinfully dark blue eyes slid to mine, and I watched in silence as he approached. Placing his coat into the empty chair beside him, he rolled up his white sleeves, revealing tattoos that covered his forearms, all the way down to his knuckles.

"Afternoon, beautiful," he said smoothly, revealing sparkling white teeth. His lip curled up farther on one side than the other, noticing that I was checking him out. "What's good here, other than the company?"

I snorted, rolling my eyes at the cockiness he oozed. "The pale ale or the Cedar Creek Brewery ale that's on tap is good."

"Which one do you prefer?" he asked, searching my face as his tongue played with the ring on his lip. His stare was hypnotizing. I inhaled his scent, stifling a moan as I tried to pinpoint his breed. He smelled intoxicatingly addictive, darkness mixed with masculinity and a hint of citrus.

"I haven't tried either of them," I admitted, watching him closely.

His tongue slid back into his mouth as he frowned, leaning back to tap the bar. "You said they were good, but you don't know if either taste like piss or not?"

"I won't be able to tell you that for a few more months… I didn't catch your name," I stated, tilting my head.

"Cole. Pretty girls get to be on a first-name basis with me. You're not from around here, are you?" he asked, ignoring my comment about not being able to drink.

"Very observant. I'm from a small fishing village in Norway. It's the accent that's throwing you, isn't it?" I asked, pouring him both types of beer and placing them in front of him to decide which he wanted.

"Damn, you're far from home, aren't you? Come here alone, or is the dad here, too? Most men bail the moment they figure out they placed a bun in the oven these days. Assholes don't realize how lucky they are."

I laughed, shaking my head at his bluntness. "He's not in the picture. He wouldn't have run away, though. I just didn't find out before I left, so he's unaware of our bun cooking."

"You intend to tell him?" Cole asked, frowning.

"Eventually," I stated.

"Brianna, when you get a moment, refill?" Floyd asked, holding his empty pitcher up. I nodded, moving toward him to refill it. Marking it down on the paper for the tab, I turned as the door opened and more men entered.

"Something wrong, Brianna?" Jackson asked, and I smiled, covering up the nervousness rushing through me.

"I'm fine, just got flushed for a moment," I answered. Rubbing the back of my neck, I watched the new group make their way to a table. I always got nervous when I caught the scent of wolves entering the bar.

Unclaimed females typically became a target, and though I'd been claimed, Saint's scent had faded. It left me open to becoming a target to young wolves that didn't know any better. One wolf alone wouldn't be an issue, but add a few and my condition, and it could be a huge problem. Toralei slid in beside me, sensing the same thing I had.

"Locals?" she asked, her body shielding mine defensively.

"Probably," I answered, stepping away from her to

return to Cole. "Did you pick one?"

"The Cedar Creek was nice." He turned to watch as the group of men moved toward the bar. "Not friends of yours?" he asked, slowly moving his gaze back to meet mine.

"Not yet," I chuckled as he chewed the piercing, giving me a dazzling smile. "So, Cole," I started pouring his beer while holding his stare. "Are you from around here?"

"No, I'm from the States. I'm up here on business. My friend lost something, and I came up to help him retrieve it."

"Must be important to come all the way up here to get it back," I muttered.

"He thinks so, but then he probably should have figured that out before he lost it. Men, though, right? They tend to realize they fucked up after the fact, more often than not."

"Amen," I snorted, wondering if he was playing for the other team.

He was hot enough to be. The men down the bar shouted at the one at the jukebox, forcing my attention to them. One of the men studied me, his burning gaze sliding over my face before lowering to my midriff. Swallowing down the uneasiness I felt, I saw Jackson move toward them.

"I got this one, Brianna," he muttered, heading for the men. "Gentlemen, what will be your poison tonight?"

Sliding the glass of beer toward Cole, I wiped my

hands on the cloth, turning as Whoever Broke Your Heart, by Murphy Elmore, began to play. Cole tapped the bar with his knuckles, nodding.

I watched as a dark shadow moved beside Cole, my heart leaping into my throat as Eryx sat beside him. My stomach clenched, and my heartbeat thundered in my ears. I turned, staring at the back exit, only to find Bowen leaning against the wall beside it. Fear churned through me as I turned to the main door, watching Saint enter the bar with a smirk on his mouth. Toralei was beside me a moment later, taking in the scene.

They'd blocked the exits, and Saint was moving in with alphas and his crew all flocking around him. Exhaling, I watched as he shuffled out of his jacket and smiled at me. He sat beside Cole, slowly rolling up his shirt sleeves before he rested his elbows on the bar, placing his chin onto his folded hands.

"Hey, gorgeous," he rumbled, lowering his eyes to my pregnant belly. "I think you left with something of mine."

"How did you find me?" I asked, trembling with both anger and fear.

"Problem, Brianna?" Jackson asked, his eyes moving between Saint and me.

"No," I whispered, shaking my head. "No problem, Jackson. Just an old acquaintance from my past," I admitted, watching the sparkle play in Saint's eyes. "There's a one-drink minimum. If you're not ordering, you all need to leave."

I turned on my heel, moving away from the bar to stop the anxiety spiking through me from reaching the shifters at the other end of the bar. Toralei followed me, her panic driving mine as my mind raced with what it meant. There was no way I could fight off Saint and his men. There was also no way they would leave without us, especially now that he knew I carried his child.

"How the hell did they find us?" she whispered, her eyes roving over the men crowding the bar as Jackson took their orders. "He brought his entire crew, and they've blocked all the exits in and out of this place."

"Thanks for pointing out the obvious," I grunted, grabbing a soda to open it, downing it smoothly before wiping off my mouth. "Three and a half months. That's how long we lasted out here." I snorted, shaking my head while she nodded.

"Tell me what to do, and we'll do it, Brae. Say the words, and we will fight our way out of here."

"I love that you think that's an option. We both know it's not," I admitted, sighing heavily, shifting my attention to where Saint sat, watching me. "We'd have more luck escaping from the apartment than here."

"It's a box with no windows," she muttered.

"Exactly my point," I returned, tossing the soda into the trash. "I don't think they're going to leave, either." I smiled tightly at Tora, moving back to where Saint waited with his men and Cole. He'd probably been sent in to survey the bar for any hidden threats before Saint, and his men arrived.

"Did you miss me, Braelyn," Saint asked, and Jackson turned, peering at me with narrowing eyes. "I've missed you. You look good and healthy. Been to see a doctor yet?"

"Your daughter is healthy," I muttered, watching his eyes drop to my stomach. "She's healthy, Saint. Don't pretend you give two shits about me, asshole."

"It's a girl? You're sure?" he asked, his gaze slowly moving back up to mine.

"Disappointed?" I asked, unable to hide the anger that laced my tone.

"Surprised, but not disappointed, Brat," he said softly. "Don't put me into the same category as your father. I am pleased with whatever you carry because it's our child."

"So he's the dad?" Jackson asked, his tone stern. "And you're not Brianna Kingston?"

Saint's lips twitched as I opened my mouth to reply, but he beat me to it. "I'm the daddy and her mate. She's my world, and she damn well knows it."

"I'm not your world, Saint Kingsley."

"You are, and so is that little girl you're carrying. You're coming home where you're safe and protected. Don't make this harder than it has to be. Things have changed since you left, Brae. Shit got twisted, and we need you home." His words echoed through me, forcing questions to run through my head.

"The others?" I demanded as my heart clenched with fear for the pack.

"They're okay. But we need you to come back so that we can fix what we did. I messed up, Brat." His eyes studied my face, but a commotion sounded beside him. I gasped as one of the shifters growled, lunging toward me. Saint didn't let him reach me, slamming him down onto the bar by his throat, still holding my stare. "As I was saying, you're not safe out here. I need to know you and my child are protected. If you can't accept me, I get it. You're above me, Brae. You've always been above me. You, you're a fighter, and you've been fighting your entire life. I didn't see it before, but my eyes are open now."

"Did you do drugs?" I asked, sliding my stare to Eryx, who looked at me with guilt wafting from him. Saint's men moved in, grabbing the shifter and his friends as Jackson, Tora, and I all watched it unfolding.

"No, Brat," he grunted. "You're not hearing me. I fucked up."

"That much was a given, Kingsley. You fucked up by ignoring the fact that she wouldn't ever sell her own people," Tora snarled.

"What the fuck is happening?" Jackson asked, forcing all eyes to swing to him. "Who sold people? I don't have any idea what the fuck is happening, but you all need to leave."

"Jackson, it wasn't like that." I watched as he lifted his hands, staring at me as if he didn't know me at all.

"I don't fucking care, Brianna. You came here for a job, and I asked you to be honest with me. I gave you a chance to get your shit out in the open. I don't employ liars, and I sure as shit don't employ anyone who could be involved in human trafficking. Get out of my bar, now. All of you, get the fuck out before I call the cops."

Tears burned my eyes, but I wouldn't argue that it wasn't what it looked like anymore. Saint had come in once again, ruining the only thing I had for a second time.

"I'm sorry, Jackson. We'll leave," I stated, grabbing for my purse and coat from beneath the bar. I didn't wait to see if the men followed me out, knowing they would. Outside, a long line of black SUVs awaited us. Men stood against the vehicles, watching as we exited the bar. "You just can't let me have anything, can you?" I whispered, watching as Saint turned, peering at me.

"I came to bring you home. If I hadn't been here tonight, those shifters would have attacked you. That man in there, he's human, Brae. He can't protect you, and neither could Tora against six alphas scenting easy pussy. They wouldn't care that you're with child, either. They would have raped you to get what they wanted. I'm a bastard, and I'll be your fucking villain, but I'm not leaving here without you. I suggest you give me directions to your house so we can collect your things. You're coming home with me. It's not up for discussion."

Chapter Twenty-Seven

It took less than ten minutes to pack up our measly belongings. Saint stared at the apartment in horror. His men tried to pile inside, only to figure out it wouldn't allow more than three into the front room. I entered my bedroom with Saint close on my heels. The moment I'd spun around to tell him that there wasn't enough room to pack my bag with him inside the room, he kissed me.

His hand snaked around, grabbing my throat as he crushed his mouth against mine. It was a soul-destroying kiss that left me spinning. He didn't release me, holding me in his embrace even after he'd ended the kiss. There was no burning animosity, and it ached. My emotions were already fucked from the pregnancy, and I hadn't been able to get the herbs to calm the churning anger and pain that drove me.

"What the hell is up with you? Why aren't you gloating or bragging that I didn't escape you?" I demanded, stepping back and almost ending up sprawled on the floor, but he caught me, righting me.

"You did escape me, Brat. You hid for three and a half fucking months. Do you have any idea how worried I was? You've never been off that fucking mountain, and then you were just gone. I found the tunnels and spent days inside of them trying to figure out which direction you'd gone. I discovered the raft, ripped up and torn to shit on the bank of that river, and fuck me if I didn't pray to the gods that you'd escaped it, and me."

"Couldn't lose your heir, right?" I snorted, pushing him away to grab my things, shoving them into the green army bag.

"I couldn't lose you, Braelyn. I never wanted you hurt. I wanted you to know how I felt when you threw me away. Never were my intentions for you to be in physical pain."

"You failed on that accord," I growled, turning to look at him with my bag held in front of me. Saint grabbed the bag, peering down at my baby bump. His forehead furrowed as he tightened his fist, continuing to gaze at it.

Warmth washed over me, and I grabbed his hand as I lifted the shirt, pressing his palm against our daughter. His eyes narrowed until she kicked, forcing them to open wide. I'd be over six months, closer to seven months, and entering the late-term pregnancy if I were human, but shifters have short gestation periods. Saint's lips parted, and he smiled as our daughter continued assaulting me from within.

"Does it hurt you?" he asked, his eyes filled with

wonder as she continually moved within me.

"No, it feels like wings fluttering. She's stronger, though. It's a weird feeling. She is very active, but mostly at night."

"And you're certain it is a girl?" he asked, studying me.

"Yeah, we had an ultrasound done last week. They said she was small for her gestation age, but then I didn't come out and say she was a wolf pup. I think that doctor might have shit herself or had me locked up had I done so."

"Have you named her?" he asked, dropping his hand as I fixed my shirt.

"No, because it felt wrong to pick out a name without you," I admitted, wringing my hands in front of my stomach, feeling her fluttering actively. "I mean, I would have done so obviously. Eventually, because I'd have to call her something," I rambled, my eyes holding his stare prisoner.

"We should go before we end up stuck here. This place is too small to hold us all, and there's a storm coming. I'd prefer to have you two on the mountain and in the safety of the pack before the weather is too bad to fly through."

"Fly?" I asked, swallowing past the lump in my throat. I hadn't even questioned how he'd gotten off the mountain before spring had thawed the roads. Of course, he'd flown because he had an entire arsenal of hunters and people helping him rip apart my world.

"I'll hold your hand if you're a nervous flyer,

Brat."

"I have never flown before," I admitted.

He smiled, grabbing my hand as he started from the room. I looked back over my shoulder, staring at the tiny space. Saint's hand tightened on mine as we stepped out into the front room, overly crowded with his men. Or two of them. Eryx and Bowen looked like giants standing beside the two small chairs we'd bought to lounge in front of the tiny, sixteen-inch TV we'd bought with our first paycheck.

"You couldn't find something better than this shitty place?" Eryx asked, staring pointedly at me.

"Did you think to look for us in this tiny place?" I countered, and his brows creased on his forehead before he nodded in agreement. "It wasn't like we could afford much better, either. It is actually a lot bigger without you ogres in it," I grumbled.

"No, it isn't," he snorted, heading for the door. "It was a strategic move, Princess. I'll give you that, but it's an utter shithole that is unfit for my niece to be born in."

"Who said she would be born here?" I asked, grumbling.

"You'd have had her at the hospital then?" Eryx countered, turning to lift a brow in question as he entered the hallway. "Didn't think so. They'd have freaked out when you had the pup."

"We're close enough to humans that they wouldn't have noticed." I followed behind Saint, who still hadn't released my hand.

"They'd have known," Saint laughed. "She'd have come early, and they'd notice her teeth were already formed, along with other things human babes wouldn't have. Things like claws and glowing pretty blue eyes like her momma's."

I stared at Saint's back, not trusting the fact that he and his men didn't seem upset. They seemed friendly, which made everything within me want to scream with fear. I was already worried about getting onto a plane, let alone flying back to a pack that hated me. Returning home in my condition didn't feel safe. It left me filled with anxiety and worry that the pack would aim their anger and hatred at my child.

"How is Chaos?" I asked, moving down the stairs as the men walked painstakingly slow.

"He misses you. He wanted to come with me to get you back," he admitted, which caused my heart to tighten. "Chaos wants his momma back, and I promised him I'd come to get her."

"I'm not his mother," I argued, hating that I wasn't.

"You raised my son, and you're my mate. You accepted him, and many alpha females wouldn't have done that. When Chaos was sick, you tended to him personally. When he needed comfort, you offered it. You're his mother unless you intend to reject him now?" he asked, pausing his steps to look up at me.

"Of course not!" I growled, glaring at him for even considering it.

"Then as my mate and the woman who raised my son, who now carries my child, you're his mother, Braelyn. We spoke about it, and he agreed that he wants you, too. He's excited at the idea of siblings."

"Siblings?" I asked, faltering at his words. Saint paused and turned to steady me as he peered up at me, eyes sparkling with laughter at my shocked question.

"You once promised me all the babies. I want you to keep that promise," he whispered huskily, his hands coming up to grip my hips. "Once you've healed from this one, of course. You wanted my babies once, Brat. I can admit to using ulterior motives for this one, and I'll allow nature to take its course from here on out. That doesn't change that I want you to be the only mother to my children. You're my mate, and Fenrir, himself, blessed us. So, yes, I want all the babies you promised me."

"I was a child and didn't realize I'd have to be fat and awkward when I made that promise. Look at me, I waddle."

"You're fucking gorgeous, Brae."

"You haven't seen me naked yet, asshole. It's not so cute when I'm naked." His lips jerked into a roguish grin, but my hand covered his mouth, forcing both brows to hike up his forehead. "I am not stripping, so you can make that deduction. I have not forgiven you for turning my pack against me. There are a lot of things I can forgive, but that's not one that is easily going to happen."

Saint's lips tightened before he turned back, releasing me as we moved the rest of the way down the staircase in silence. Outside, men opened the car doors, and we were ushered into the waiting dark SUVs. I gazed over my shoulder, pushing past Saint to get back out of the car.

"Where the hell do you think you're going?" he demanded.

"I need to tell Mrs. Peterson goodbye," I snapped. "They will need to get their own groceries and shovel the walkway without standing outside, expecting us to come do it!"

Saint exhaled a strangled sound. He slipped out of the back seat, watching me walk toward the lower apartment. I knocked on the door, digging out the cash from my pocket. Angela opened the door, staring out at me.

"We're leaving, but I want you to take this," I stated, pushing the wad of hundreds into her hand. "For your kindness and letting us stay in the apartment."

Angela looked over my shoulder, staring down the long line of waiting cars that sat idle. "He finally came to claim you, did he? You're a rare breed of woman, Brianna. You're going to make an amazing mother to that little babe. I can't accept this, though," she said sadly, pushing the money away.

"I won't have any need for it where I am going. Money isn't required in my world, Angela. Take it and hire the boy down the way to shovel this sidewalk. Besides, I owe you rent, and I won't be here to pay it or the utilities. Consider it a thank you for knowing I was hiding and never questioning it."

"Is he good to you?" she asked, sliding her knowing gaze back to Saint, who stood at my back. "You are a gentle, broken soul, girl. It takes one to know one, and that was why I never questioned you or your past. You were running, and I've been there. Don't ever let him hurt you. If he does, you make damn sure you keep him down. It took me severing the ligaments of old Tommy's knees to ensure he would never hurt me again."

"Say what now?" I asked, watching her eyes sparkle. "Damn, that's savage."

"I'm just playing with you, girl. But really, if that man hurts you, go for his balls. It's their weakness. You go, I'll be fine. If you ever need me, you know where I am," she stated, hugging me tightly. "You're going to be fine. The way he looks at you, it is how my Tommy used to look at me before his sight went to shit." She backed up, cupping my face tightly. "Let him love you. Broken things need and deserve to be loved too. In fact, they're often more passionate because they feel as if they don't deserve it. You be happy. If not, give him hell until you are."

I smiled through unshed tears, nodding at her. Backing up, I watched her withdrawing the money I'd slipped into her pocket, and then I turned on my heel to climb back into the car. Saint entered behind me, issuing orders as my attention shifted to Cole, who smirked, holding his hands up.

"I told you my friend lost something important," he exclaimed.

"Are you heading out?" Saint asked, tugging me closer to him while speaking to Cole.

"Yeah, seems Remington just opened a weapons shop with a strip club above it across from the Sanctuary. Rhys is about to have a seizure over it.

He met his match in this one, and she's aware she is untouchable. I'm only a phone call away if you need anything. I have to get back to my own club. One Van Helsing has to control his brain to run the Van Helsing Knights and keep the monsters in check. Xavier being away hasn't gone unnoticed, and Nyota isn't any damn help now since she's made it her personal mission to guard Bullet Van Helsing."

"I still can't believe Rhys is going to be a father," Saint grunted. "Or that his baby is going to be named Bullet just to piss him off. I almost want to meet this girl, to shake her fucking hand for having the balls to take on the Van Helsings."

Cole snorted, hiking his pierced brow as his gaze dropped to my belly. "I got a million on him saying the same fucking thing about you, Kingsley. You two assholes go and get pretty girls, and what's the first thing you do? Fuck it all up the moment you get the world handed to you. That shit isn't happening to me. I've decided to remain a bachelor until I'm ten thousand years old."

Saint grunted, and Cole dug into his pocket, staring at his phone. Answering it, he listened and then snorted loudly.

"Rhys, you can't burn her shop down. She's literally your baby momma." He paused, holding the phone away from his ear as someone screamed on the other end. "Hey, asshole, it doesn't matter if you claim Bullet or not. It's your baby. You fucked Remington and made a Silversmith-Van Helsing milkshake. That's our blood in her womb. You go after her, and Nyota will go after you as Nyx humps your god's damn leg. Leave it alone, and I'll handle it when I get there. Yeah, I'm with Saint Kingsley. Guess who is also going to be a daddy and has women issues up to his dick hole? Yeah, I think he wants his." Cole paused, holding my gaze before he dropped it slowly. "It's his mate, and she's a pretty little thing. Yeah, he doesn't want her handled, other than by him. We're approaching the Blackhawks. Call in the airspace and flight number, and I'll be home to handle Remington soon enough. Unless you can do so without starting a war? Yeah, I didn't think so. I'm heading there now." Cole hung up as the sound of helicopter blades started up.

I peered over my shoulder, staring at the airfield we were approaching as my stomach churned. Saint tightened his grip on my hand, reassuring me as he felt the nervousness rushing through me. His mouth lowered, kissing my forehead, holding me like I was something that mattered now. I didn't understand what had changed, but it terrified me in a way that sent spiders rushing over my flesh, and my stomach turned with nausea.

"It's okay, Brat. It's only scary during takeoff and landing. The rest of the time, you won't even notice we're flying." His words reassured me. Right up until we turned onto the airport's runway and drove toward the Blackhawks, outfitted with military equipment.

Exiting the cars, we were ushered by men in black uniforms adorned with skulls and crosses over the front of them. Saint spoke to one man, and then we were rushed toward a helicopter that had honest to gods guns mounted on the fucker. Men loaded to the teeth helped us into the aircraft, harnessing me into a seat and placing headphones on my head as Eryx and Saint strapped in beside me on either side.

My knees bounced up and down with nervousness, and two hands landed on separate knees. Both men had placed their hands on my legs, and before I could argue it, each of them had taken my hand, holding it silently. I looked between them and then slid my eyes to the male that sat in front of the big-ass gun, who nodded his head, acknowledging me.

"I don't think I like flying." I hadn't even realized I'd said it out loud until masculine laughter filled the headphones. I hoped Tora was doing better than me with Bowen in the other helicopter.

"You'll be okay, Princess. We wouldn't let you fly unless we trusted the pilot enough with our own lives. St. James used to fly these birds inside war zones. He can handle a little snow."

Saint snorted, tightening his grip as the helicopter jerked and tilted. I squeezed my eyes closed, turning to bury my head against Saint's shoulder. His scent filled me with a calmness I knew I didn't feel because he hadn't been lying about takeoff. It was scary, and we were tilting as the wind howled. I shivered, feeling the freezing crisp air as the helicopter continued rising into the sky. Something touched my legs, and I peered down as Eryx covered me up with a thick, wool blanket without a word. He pushed against my side as Saint leaned closer to the other, boxing me in. The fear I'd felt began crawling through me again, and it was probably a good thing they thought it was flying because I'd be hard-pressed to explain what was really causing it unless they knew. That terrified me the most.

Chapter Twenty-Eight

The landing wasn't much better than takeoff, with the Blackhawk swaying before it was firmly on the ground. Apprehension at seeing the pack and feeling the sting of their rejection fluttered through me. As the blades of the helicopter died down, Saint helped free me from the crossed seatbelt while I pulled the headphones off. Saint lowered his lips before I could stand, pressing them against mine softly while cupping my cheek.

"Welcome home, Brat," he said, helping me up while he crouched over to exit. Before I could crawl onto my rear carefully to leave the helicopter, he had reached up and pulled me down, placing me onto my feet.

I watched the heat burning in his stare, but there was worry in his pretty blue eyes. My entire body tensed, turning to stare at the pack that waited for us outside the gates. There was no animosity, and their scents reeked of guilt and shame. My stomach flipped, and everything within me screamed to climb back into the Blackhawk and run from what I knew was coming.

Tears burned in my eyes, yet I wouldn't let them fall. I stood stiffly, staring through the faces of the pack until my attention dropped to the boy walking toward me. Chaos shuffled on his feet, slowly moving away from the others. It took everything I had not to run to him, but I couldn't. I couldn't move.

Chaos wrapped his arms around me, pulling back when his head landed against the small bump of my belly. His eyes widened, peering up at me as the babe within responded to him. My hands balled into tight fists, closing my eyes against the emotion that churned through me.

"You're going to have a baby, Braelyn!" he exclaimed excitedly, his hand lifting to touch my stomach.

"So I am, Chaos," I whispered through trembling lips.

They knew. Everyone knew what had been done to me. It was evident by the show of respect that was being displayed. I wanted to run and hide, shame ripping me apart from the inside out.

I'd never wanted my pack to know what my father had done because it left my demons exposed. It left me looking wounded and not strong enough to lead the pack. Uncurling my fingers, I ruffled Chaos's dark hair while he smiled up at me.

Chaos smiled at Saint, nodding his head before a serious look took control of his face. "You found her and kept your promise. This time, don't lose her. She's a whole person and shouldn't be that easy to lose. Plus, she has another person in her belly."

I laughed, even though it was more of a soft sob than laughter escaping my lips. Leaning down, I cupped Chao's cheeks, placing a soft kiss on the top of his head. His hand pulled away as the babe moved, kicking against where his palm had been.

"Is he trying to escape your belly?" Chaos asked, wonder filling his eyes.

Saint grunted, studying us together. "She. Chaos, you're getting a baby sister."

"But I don't want a sister. I want a brother," he stated, frowning before he leaned closer to my belly, whispering. "I'll still love you, though. I won't let anything happen to you, little baby. I'll protect you always, and always forever, even if you're a girl."

Tears slipped free from my eyes, forcing me to swipe at them to hide my weakness. Saint leaned closer, smiling as he yanked Chaos up, carrying him as we started forward to where the pack waited. Once we reached them, they began lowering their heads in shame.

"What is happening?" Toralei asked, sliding in beside me. "I feel like we stepped into the Twilight Zone."

"We made a mistake," Saint admitted. "We're working to remedy that and earn Brae's respect back."

"I'm tired," I announced, struggling to get my hand out of his.

I didn't give the pack the forgiveness they wanted. Moving past them, I started into the lodge, only for Xavier to step into my path. Lifting my teary gaze, I watched him search my face. He didn't speak, but the way he looked at me made me worry.

"Are you well?" he asked, his voice thick with emotions. "I mean, are you okay?"

"I am okay," I answered, feeling strange with the intensity in which Xavier studied me. "Are you?" I returned cautiously.

He laughed, lifting his hand to press against his heart. My attention moved to his daughter, who studied me with a look that made my emotions churn. She tugged on his arm, and his soft, worry-filled gaze slide to hers.

"Braelyn is exhausted and needs to rest, father. You should let the poor girl get refreshed from her homecoming before you pounce, asking your questions," Xari chided, smiling tightly at me. "Welcome home, Braelyn."

I didn't reply, uncertain why I felt so awkward about her welcoming me back to my home. It surprised me that they were still here since the snow would make it near impossible to escape the mountain. At least, it had been, unless you could afford helicopters, and they apparently could.

Sidestepping past Xavier, we continued into the lodge with Saint's hand against the small of my back, still carrying Chaos. While Chaos was still small enough to carry, it should have been awkward, but it was endearing to see his tiny head on his father's shoulder, walking me to my bedroom. I started toward the hallway, but Saint grabbed my hand, nodding in the opposite direction.

"I moved us," he informed, causing the color to drain from my face.

I shook, physically shook as nausea swirled in my stomach. My head started to shake, and my palms began to sweat. I gagged, ripping my hand away from his to back up. He watched me, running his gaze over my paleness and reaction to his words.

"I can't," I whispered, fighting against the memories that played through my mind. "I can't go down there. I can't fucking go down there!" I screamed. I moved my arms over my belly, protecting my stomach as if I feared my father would appear and ruin my child.

"I know you can't go down there, Braelyn. I had one of the larger apartments redone and made it into a living suite for us. I remember you telling me how you hated it down there. How your father had murdered your mother in the main room, and that you felt sick being in them. I picked one of the rooms that had a view of the mountain you like. Inside the apartment is enough room for our family, Brae. Your room is empty, and I had everything moved so that you could join Chaos and me in our rooms."

I exhaled, fighting against nausea, but I was losing that fight. Toralei stepped between Saint and my body, grabbing a trash bin as my stomach released the water and meal I'd eaten for breakfast. I grabbed it, barfing until I dry heaved. The hallway full of people paused, wincing as I loudly emptied my stomach.

"Is she okay?" Chaos asked.

"Is she?" Saint demanded, trying to get past Toralei's frame, but she kept him away from me, allowing me to finish upheaving.

"Back off," she snarled. "She's had horrible morning sickness, which is a stupid name for something that happens all day long. If she so much as catches a whiff of something, she starts puking! It's horrible," she announced loudly. Turning back to look at me, Tora narrowed her eyes, pointedly glaring at me. "I feel like I am the only one who doesn't know something huge. You and I, we're going to talk when we get to your new room."

"I don't want to talk about it, Toralei," I whispered, fighting the tears while she watched me. "Please, not right now. I need water, food, and then a very warm bath in a tub large enough to sit."

I hadn't been able to even sit in the one inside our apartment. It was a small square tub that wouldn't allow you to do more than stand. It was one of the things I'd missed most about my bedroom, that and my plush bed that hadn't felt like lying on a slab of solid concrete.

"Fine, but I feel like I stepped into an episode of the Twilight Zone, and everyone here knows what's going on except me. I'm your person. I'm your beta and the one who has always had your back. I deserve to know whatever it is, Brae. I'm your gods damn beta!"

"I'll tell you, but get me some water first. And you might want something strong to drink. Saint, I don't want Chaos inside the room when I tell her. Whoever needs to hear it can be there because after I am finished telling my story, it will not ever be told again."

Sweat trickled down my back as I handed the trash bin to Tora, who looked terrified now that I'd offered to tell her what was going on. Saint placed Chaos on his feet, his crew gathering behind him as Xavier stepped into the mix. Eryx handed me a bottle of water, and Saint sidled in beside me, allowing me to follow him silently.

I mentally prepared for what was coming. I'd never spoken about it out loud to another person. There were some things that I wouldn't say out loud still. Images washed through my mind, but Saint grabbed my hand, squeezing it while his crew moved closer around me.

Toralei pushed her way back to my side, peering behind us with worry filling her green gaze. I hated that she would treat me like I was made of glass the moment she knew what I'd endured. The same way they all were now looking at me. As if I was something broken that needed to be handled gently when I wasn't. I'd fought hard to hide my pain and keep the world from ever knowing how really sick my father was.

Chapter Twenty-Nine

The room was filled with people, all waiting for me to speak. I'd locked myself inside the bathroom, fear spiking through me. Splashing cold water over my face, I turned off the faucet and grabbing a towel. A knock sounded, and I turned to glare at the door. Metal scraped against it, and before I could call out, Saint entered.

I backed up, shaking my head as my strength left me. "I can't do this," I whispered thickly, fighting to stay strong when everything was too much. Coming home was too much, and telling them the truth, after I'd fought so hard to hide my demons. "My father was a monster. He was horrible, Saint."

"I know, Brat. I know he was."

"Why would you tell them?" I demanded, tears trailing down my cheeks as Saint stepped closer, pulling me tightly against him. His scent flooded the bathroom, soothing the ache in my chest.

"Cole Van Helsing's men found a video of a girl calling my name. He brought it here to see if we could help identify the victim. Her face was hidden from the camera, and she was gagged to prevent her screams from being heard. When Harold removed the hood and the gag, she screamed my name. Cole assumed I would know who it was. We use the videos to search for marks or tattoos or anything in the room we could use to identify the victims. You screamed my name repeatedly. You screamed for me as he slashed your face open. I heard your voice, and I froze. Everyone inside the room knew it was you, Brae."

"You saw it," I cried, hating that he'd watched my father torture me.

"We all saw it, Brae. We've watched your father do unspeakable things to you on many videos without ever knowing it was you. You're one of the victims we've been searching for."

"I'm not a victim!" I hissed, pushing him away.

"You are a victim. You're also a survivor. Braelyn, you were a child when the sessions began, but you didn't let that monster break you or your spirit even then. You kept this pack alive and placed them in front of your pain. You were fucking eight years old. I failed you, Brat. I didn't see that you were in pain. No one did except Chaos."

"I hid it from him," I whispered.

"You thought you did, but he saw you. Where we all failed to see beyond the mask you wore to hide, Chaos sensed you were sad. A child noticed your pain where everyone else failed you. I failed you, Braelyn.

I can't ever take that back. I don't deserve you, and I know I fucked up."

"So did I, Saint," I whispered thickly, holding his stare. "My world didn't exist without you in it, and I couldn't protect you and the pack. My father promised me you'd be allowed to leave. I thought you were free of him. I wasn't strong enough to protect everyone, not when I was barely able to protect myself."

Saint nodded, pressing his lips against my forehead. "If you can't talk about what happened, you don't have to. I'll clear the room out, and we will just sit in silence if that is what you need." He lowered his hand, brushing it against my belly, and our daughter jerked beneath his touch. His hand flattened on my stomach, holding it against where her foot moved. "I'm going to guess she will be as fierce and strong as her momma."

"As stubborn and bullheaded as her father," I snorted as his lips jerked into a disarming smile.

"Either way, she's ours, Brat. I can't wait to meet her."

A sob ripped from my lungs, and my hand moved to smother it. Saint pulled me against him, kissing the top of my head as our baby continued to kick, sensing the unrest in my emotions. I hadn't expected an unborn child to know her mother's feelings, but she seemed to react to every mood swing or upset I experienced.

"Gods damn, we fucked this up, didn't we?" he asked, rubbing his nose against the shell of my ear as I laughed. "I'll have Jacob bring you some herbs. He assured me that they're not harmful to you or the babe.

I'll try not to smother you, but I'm going to be honest here, Braelyn. I went out of my mind when we found that raft, and the shit that went through my head? I never want to feel that helpless or scared again. I'd rather be back in that cell wondering which brand of torture I was going to endure than to know if you're alive of dead."

"Then I guess you better behave," I replied, as he pulled back, peering down at me.

"I will chain your ass to me, Brat. You hear me? I will handcuff you to me before I ever have to send cadaver dogs down this mountain to find you. You're my fucking world, and that will never change, nor has it," he promised, searching my face. "You and me, we're forever."

"You don't get me back that easily, Saint. You broke me, and all I ever did was try to protect you. You left me in a storage container for Carleigh and Lucas to torture, and then you left with the bitch that strung me up in my home. Now that you know the truth, you know I never did anything out of malice or to hurt you. You can't say the same. You wanted me to feel helpless, but I already knew how those women felt. You wanted me to know what had run through their minds as they sat in the dark, cold pit of despair. My entire life has been a never-ending pit of agony that I couldn't escape. I saved myself, and the one person I wished would come back to me? He did, but he didn't come back to save me. You came back to punish me."

"I did that," he admitted, swallowing hard while holding my gaze. "I also forced you into heat and bred you. I left you unprotected to go with the children to ensure everything possible was done to save them. I assumed Lucas was your friend, and my only fear was that he'd free you so that you could run from me. I left Carleigh here to ensure that didn't happen, and she hurt you. That's on me, and I fully take that blame. I'm not sorry that we're going to have a baby, Brae. I've dreamed of this since the moment I knew you were mine. I can't be sorry for being this happy that you're having my baby."

"Shut up," I groaned, hating that I wanted to hit him and kiss him at the same time.

"You're not happy about the baby," he stated.

"I'm having your baby. I've only ever wanted your baby, Saint. I can't be mad about her. I want her, and I want you. I just don't know how we'll ever get past this or how to move on from here," I admitted. "I don't foresee me forgiving you or the pack for what happened. I turned you down when you asked me to run away because of my obligation to the pack. I couldn't just leave them behind because my father didn't care if they lived or died. He only cared about the power that came with holding the pack and their strength against the outside world. I wanted to run away with you. I wanted to leave this place and be with you more than I wanted air to reach my lungs. I stayed for them, and the first time someone accused me of something, they throw dirt on my face and turn their backs on me."

"Before I came to get you, I made sure the pack knew that I had fucked up. I told them it was on me, not you. That you were the same woman who worked beside them and always made certain they were taken care of and protected. You sacrificed your world for theirs, and that is selfless as fuck, Brae. You're a good person, and I'm not. I am a monster who enjoys dishing out punishment to other monsters. I don't deserve someone like you, and I'm fully aware that when I touch you, I do it with blood on my hands. That doesn't change that you're the one creature in the world that was hand-selected to be mine. I will get you back, and I don't care if it takes an eternity to do so."

I swallowed, slowly shaking my head. Turning away from Saint, I paused. My attention slid back to him, taking in the pain burning in his gaze while he stood waiting for me to acknowledge his words.

"I look forward to it. No matter what happens, Saint, you're my monster. As I said, I don't know where this goes, but I'm done running from it. Now, there's a room filled with people waiting to hear how sick my father really was. Let's not leave them waiting any longer. I'm fucking starving, and I intend to take the longest bath that I've ever taken in my life. After I've eaten something that isn't covered in grease or ordered from a takeout menu," I stated.

"I'll have someone grab you something to eat from the kitchen, and I'll personally run your bath and tend to you myself," he smirked with a sparkle in his eyes.

Entering the bedroom, I paused at the people who leaned against the kitchenette's counter or the other state-of-the-art appliances Saint had installed in our rooms. My eyes landed on Tora, who pushed off the wall and approached me.

"My father tortured me," I told her plainly, not sugar-coating it. "He murdered my mother for carrying another daughter. He saw it as a failure to produce an heir to the pack. He realized his mistake after he'd taken her heart. I became his focus. I am a female descendant of the wolf god Fenrir and would eventually be of an age to breed an heir. It started soon after he'd murdered her. He groomed me, but I had the pack around me. I knew he was evil and that he was a monster. I hadn't known how much of a monster he was, but when I failed to break, he increased his efforts, revealing the depths of his black heart. As a female to the bloodline, I was protected from rape, as are all of our species' females. If I didn't agree to him violating me, then he couldn't. When I reached the age that I could reproduce, he increased his efforts to break me, and that's when Lucas entered the game as another of my torturers." I paused, watching the tears roll down Toralei's cheeks.

"I was set on fire when I refused to let him breed me, but his beta put me out. The second time I had all the flesh of my body removed, except for my face. It took a long time to heal, and the pack noted my absence. Harold got more creative and became crazed with the need to break me. I felt the connection to Saint, and our bond came online. Harold found out, even though we were careful to hide it from him. When he discovered that I was going to mate with Saint, he removed my uterus and proceeded to try to breed it outside of my body."

"Fucking hell," Eryx growled, the men echoing his anger.

His startling blue eyes held mine, and he trembled visibly with rage and pain for what I'd endured. Xavier exhaled and shook his head before dragging his hand over his mouth. Xari stared at me, her eyes holding tears that slowly escaped. She wiped at them, deflating. Leif listened, with pain filling his gaze, but there was a calmness to him, which was terrifying because it told me it wasn't the worst thing he'd ever heard. Enzo watched me, his eyes holding mine briefly before he nodded his head gently as if he'd already known.

I blinked slowly, making a mental note to figure out how Enzo could see into someone's soul and understand their pain. He was incredibly dark, and the shadows around him seemed to drift there, reaching for him as if he owned them.

"How did you stop it?" Xavier asked, filling the silence in the room with his question. His eyes studied my face, and I tilted my head.

"How do you know it stopped?" I returned.

"Because I've spent fifteen years searching for you, Braelyn," he admitted, studying me as my eyes narrowed. "You're Jane Doe in my file. A child I watched set on fire, skinned alive, and received one thousand cuts to your body at what I assumed was age fifteen. I have been searching for you to free you from your tormentor. I came here with Saint because I wanted your father dead, and I needed access to his personal files to locate Jane Doe. I assumed she'd died because there were no new videos. The trail to find you just vanished, and I feared you had been killed in one of his rages. Your story confirms that you are the Jane Doe in which I've been searching. You made him stop. What I need to know is how?"

"I unleashed my rage on him, and he almost murdered me. I revealed that I was an alpha, and I called for my wolf to help me. Unfortunately, we couldn't just murder him. I barely lived through it, and it signed my death warrant. He became aware that I was my mother's daughter, and when she had me, her beast followed me, protecting me. It left her unguarded."

"Fenrir," Leif stated, smirking at me. "You house your god inside of you. You are Fenrir's guard and his keeper. It was never the line that your people followed. They followed the wolf god, who attaches to the soul of the purest of his original bloodline."

"Correct, but Fenrir isn't always with me. He goes to those who need him and those who are lost so that he may lead them here, to his pack. It was at a time when he'd gone that I suffered the worst of my father's abuse. When my daughter is of age, and I have grown too old to protect the pack, he will leave me to go with her. My line is blessed because he is always within it."

"No," Leif chuckled. "Your line is blessed because his blood runs through your veins. Your mother, she was his daughter. Your grandmother laid with Fenrir, in his true form, the kinky bitch." He smiled as if he imagined it inside his head. "He chose your line because you're his granddaughter, Braelyn. He fell in love with Brenhelda, but Fenrir cannot hold a human form. He is a beast, one that loved a princess who was pure and true of heart. She married her king, knowing she carried the child of the wolf god within her womb. It was why I allowed your mother to live when I found her leading her pack to the shores of the Barents Sea. She saw me, and she showed no fear as I walked up to her, fully intending to end her life. The look in her pretty Nordic stare gave me pause. She didn't beg or plead for mercy as the others had done. Your mother looked me dead in the eye and told me to do my worst. She was the only one I couldn't kill because I saw Fenrir within her when she looked into my eyes. I saw him in you, Braelyn. When you took the heads of the alpha females, you held your god in your eyes."

"I didn't know that," I admitted, frowning as Leif smirked.

"I'm not sure your mother even knew she held the god. Brenna lost her mother at the age of sixteen when my pack and I slaughtered most of your bloodline. They'd never needed for Fenrir to defend them, and she found peace when she arrived here before the first settlers. I followed her here, but I never encroached on her territory. Your mother had earned her place and my respect."

"Your father was a monster, and you never told me," Toralei whispered.

Shifting my gaze to hers, I smiled tightly. "What could you have done? My father had over fifty alphas within the pack that were in league with him. If the pack had tried to defend me, they'd have slaughtered them. Telling anyone what was happening to me would have placed everyone in danger." I reached over and squeezed Tora's hand reassuringly. "Harold wasn't stupid. He brought in mercenaries, and people like Carlson backed him up. Nobody could save me from the monster that had sired me. If I had told Saint, he would have tried to save me, and he would have died. If I had told you, you'd have tried to make me leave here. Harold would have slaughtered the pack, and that would have been on me.

"I saved myself because I didn't need anyone else to do it, putting themselves in my father's crossfire. I needed to endure until I was strong enough to take the pack by challenging Harold. He knew I was preparing a coup. That is why he gave me to Carlson. I was becoming too strong, and Carlson promised to send my father our firstborn child. Then, some asshole showed up and led a hostile takeover on the day I'd planned to murder Carlson inside our mating tent, as those outside the gates rushed in to fight anyone who stood with my father." I stared at Saint accusingly, and he frowned.

"The men outside the gates were your father's mercenaries. Your father and Carlson were fully aware of the little coup de grâce you had planned. I know because I spent an hour ripping one's ribcage apart until he told me what to expect inside and what he was doing outside the gates when the celebration was about to begin. Your father prepared to ship the women and children we found in the field and others from the pack, with Carlson, as your dowry. The men you paid were murdered and left in a pile to be burned at the bottom of the mountain," Saint stated, causing my stomach to flip-flop. "Now that everyone knows the story, my mate needs to eat and rest. If you have questions, or anything else, we will deal with it tomorrow."

"Make sure you take your prenatal vitamins and drink some juice. You need juice because you look peckish. Don't forget the vitamin D and B. Oh, and I'll see about getting apples," Toralei stated, rushing her words out as Saint smirked.

"Yes, mother," I said teasingly, placing my hand on my belly. Tora smiled, moving closer to speak low.

"You're right. I would have demanded we left. But we would have returned with a fucking army to murder the prick."

"If I had stepped foot off this mountain while Harold was alive, he'd have started murdering the children. He'd have enjoyed it since they were his preferred victim. It wasn't personal, or because I didn't trust you, because you know I do. I loved you too much to put this burden on you. Knowing what was happening and not being able to stop it would have driven you mad. You'd have slipped up, and you would have paid for it with your life, and I couldn't chance that or live with it. I know you inside and out, Toralei. You're my person. You've been my best friend since we were kids. I couldn't lose you, not when you helped hold me together. I knew I was strong enough and that I would refuse to break. I didn't break, and he's dead."

"Okay, I concede for tonight. Where do you want me?"

"Will you make sure Chaos is okay? Have him bathed and then send him in to see me. I will eat and do the same. I'm sure he wants to be in here, but I really need to soak first because my feet are killing me."

"Phenrys, grab her food from the kitchen we ordered. Eryx, did you get the bath salt from Jacob?" Saint asked, moving toward me, observing me. "You're not kicking me out, Brat. You're wasting time, and our son will be in soon because I already had someone ensure he was bathed. Tora said you were queasy when certain scents were too potent around you. I figured grubby little boys were on that list. Your food has been prepared and is on its way here, so sit down, shut up, and look cute. Any questions, woman?"

I stared at him, opening my mouth to argue as his brow hiked up in warning. "You're fucking bossy, dick."

"And you're not sitting down yet, Brat."

I huffed, doing as he'd said because my feet were killing me, and my ankles would swell if I didn't. Being pregnant wasn't some beautiful thing it was made out to be in the movies. It was miserable, with barfing at the worst imaginable times. Having to pee nonstop made me annoyed more often than not.

It was pathetic to enter a place and mark each bathroom just because you knew you were using it before leaving. My boobs hadn't stopped being sensitive, and my sex drive was overactive. Not to mention, shit swelled that had never swelled before. Sleeping was becoming harder to achieve with the babe playing body slam, wolf edition, in my womb while using my ribs as a jungle gym.

Something grabbed my boot, pulling it off my foot, jarring me from my internal complaint log, and forcing my eyes up. Eryx smiled, baring his teeth as he removed my other boot, tossing them aside as the room emptied. His hands began rubbing my foot, and I moaned, widening my gaze as he massaged my aching feet.

I wasn't sure if I should yank my feet back or let him continue because it was awkward, yet it felt terrific. He chuckled, noticing the indecision playing out on my face. After a moment, he dropped my foot and stood, staring at my round baby bump.

My lips tugged up, and his eyes narrowed as she moved, forcing my stomach to jerk around at her movement. I could sense Saint watching, too, noticing how Eryx was engrossed in our daughter moving within me.

"Give me your hand, Eryx." His eyes lifted to lock with mine.

He hesitated for a moment before stepping closer, holding out his hand. Grabbing it, I pressed it against my belly, and his eyebrows shot up his forehead as the baby turned, making my entire stomach move as a result. Eryx laughed nervously, turning to look at Saint with wonder sparkling in his gaze.

"She's very active," Eryx stated, still holding his hand against my stomach. Saint moved closer, placing his hand on my belly as she wiggled, and a devastating smile spread across his full mouth.

I slid my gaze between the men, noticing that they stared at one another with something silent passing between them. They'd been held together and endured torture by the same tormentor. That kind of shit created a bond, and it went deeper than just friendship. It embedded itself into the soul and forged a bond that couldn't be broken.

"What the hell you put in her? A demon?" Eryx laughed and then laughed harder as Saint growled defensively.

"Our daughter is not a demon!" I growled, offended, and both sets of eyes slid to me as if they just remembered I was in the room. "You two can bugger off. I'm going to bathe before Chaos arrives."

"Guard the door, and make sure Chaos has been fed and is ready for bed before we get out of the bath," Saint stated.

"You're not bathing with me," I grunted, shaking my head while sitting up further.

"I am, and you're not in any position to argue," he laughed, grabbing clothes from the closet while I remained seated, watching him move about our quarters. "Plus, you like me touching you."

"That doesn't mean I want you touching me," I scoffed. Saint's eyes sparkled with joy, and his body rippled with power. He placed one hand behind me to rest on the chair, lowering his lips to my ear.

"Who are you trying to convince here, liar? You or me, because I can smell your need, and it's been three months since I have felt you from the inside," he said in a rough tone that sent a rush of desire through me. "Yeah, I fucking thought so, Brat. I missed you too," he chuckled, pulling back to look at me with hunger burning in his stare. "Now, get up unless you want me to carry you into the bathroom, strip you bare, and kiss every fucking inch of you to show you what belongs to me."

I swallowed past the longing his words created, slowly standing. He didn't back up or give me space. Instead, he slipped his hand around the small of my back, pulling me up against his hard body. Saint tugged me with him, ignoring Eryx, who watched us slowly walk toward the bathroom. Saint's eyes held mine as we entered the room, sending butterflies rushing through me. He was correct in assuming I wanted him, but that didn't mean I'd be easy to convince to just jump into bed with him. Saint had a lot of groveling to do before I would even be close to forgiving him.

Chapter Thirty

Saint ran the bath and dropped heavenly scented bath salts into the water. Silently, I sat on the chair he'd brought in, demanding I sit while he handled running the water. Every once in a while, he would peer up at me, smiling as if he knew something I didn't. I was content just to watch, and the fact that he'd stripped down to only jeans didn't hurt the view.

"You could have told me, Brat."

"Told you what? That my father wanted to breed me? Or that he beat me and enjoyed cutting the flesh from my body in small patches to ensure maximum agony was reached during his 'sessions' as he preferred to call them. You'd have tried to save me because you loved me. You'd have died, and I would have stopped fighting to live if you no longer existed in my world."

"We could have run, Brat. You didn't have to suffer in silence," he returned, sitting on the edge of the tub to stare at me.

"My father would have murdered the children, including Chaos, who neither of us knew existed at the time. We both suffered, but we survived him. The monsters that fought so hard to destroy us are dead and buried. You and I are still here. We won. I wish you'd have known so that when I stood in front of the pack and said I didn't love you, you'd have known what I meant was I would never stop loving you, Saint. I loved you enough to let you go live without me, even though you would have done so hating me. The thing is, you'd have to live to think I hated you."

"I thought you'd realized I was beneath you. That summer with you, it was the best time of my entire life. That time I spent with you, sneaking around and kissing you when no one else was watching us? That kept me fighting to live, Brat. The thought of coming back here, and stealing you, and showing you that you were mine. That is what kept me fighting and alive."

"I loved you, Saint. Making you think otherwise broke me, too. I would rather be set on fire again than ever see the look of betrayal and pain in your eyes on that day. My father was the only person who had ever kept his promises to me, and when he did, people died or suffered. No one ever saw the monster staring out from his eyes. He would have killed you, and I'd have been forced to watch it happen."

Saint nodded, knowing it was the truth. My father had his people here, mixed in among the pack. It was also why I hadn't killed him. I had to know who supported my father and would be against the hostile takeover I had been planning. Saint spun toward the faucet, turning it off.

"Strip, Brat," he demanded, smirking as I stood.

"You're bossy, asshole," I muttered.

He grinned, placing his hands on the tub to lean back. His cyan blue stare slid to my hands as I pulled my shirt off over my head. Nervousness rushed through me the moment his gaze dropped to the perfectly rounded baby bump. My breasts were larger, and my hips had spread, creating a mass of awkward curves. Reaching for the band of my jeans, he smiled at finding them unbuttoned.

"You are absolutely beautiful with my babe growing within you, Brat," he reassured, sensing the uneasiness I felt. "I imagined you like this, us together, and you carrying our child. I never thought it would happen, not even after I'd escaped. You haunted me more than any ghost ever could." He swallowed hard, his throat bobbing at his words. Standing, he watched me slowly walk to him.

"You haunted me too, Saint. I dreamed that you were out there somewhere with someone else. I dreamed that you had a family, and you were happy without me. I wanted that for you, even though it was a nightmare that I dreamed."

He laughed, watching me. "What the hell were the gods thinking putting something as precious as you, with something as rough and abrasive as me?"

"They thought our broken edges might just fit together," I said, allowing the tears to trail down my cheeks. I didn't hide the emotions I'd been trained to conceal since before I could remember. His hands cupped my face, wiping away the tears.

"I think they knew that we would end up together when it was time," he whispered, leaning over to brush his mouth against mine. His kiss was gentle and seeking. I opened to him, allowing him to claim my lips. He wrapped his arms around my lower back, lifting me as he moved us toward the counter.

He stepped back, sliding his eyes over my body slowly with hunger burning in his lucid blue depths. He flicked his thumb against the button of his jeans, letting them drop to the floor, then stepped out of them, shifting closer to settle between my thighs.

"If you don't want this, you better stop me now," he growled huskily.

"Don't stop," I whispered, pulling him closer to feel him against me. "You have no idea how freaking horny I've been without anyone to soothe the ache," I admitted, watching his eyes dancing with laughter.

"You didn't handle that ache?" he asked. "I got off thinking about you playing with your pretty pink pussy," he chuckled.

"I'm going to need you to hurry up," I grunted, rocking my hips to indicate he needed to get his dick buried in my warmth. Waiting to forgive him be damned, I needed this release. "I need you, Saint."

He entered me fast and hard, stealing a shocked cry from my lips. My body moved against his, wrapping my legs around his waist as he held me. Saint released a husky growl, and he walked us from the bathroom, through the apartment, and into a massive bedroom decorated in calming shades of blue and white. Placing me on the bed, he never left my body as he found the perfect beat with his. We made music as my body began to sing for him. A gasp escaped my lips, and I pleaded for him to do whatever he needed.

"Fucking hell, you're on fire," he growled.

"Harder," I demanded, uncaring that my voice came out strangled with need. Saint captured my hands, threading his fingers through mine while he loomed over me. His eyes held me prisoner, watching as they widened against the way he moved. "Fuck, that feels so good. Just like that, please," I moaned, breathless from the storm he was building inside of me.

Saint held the tempo, slowly rocking against my body while managing to ignore the baby bump that I'd feared would make sex awkward. He pretended it wasn't there and instead held my gaze as I came undone for him. I lifted my legs, placing my feet flat against the bed to meet his thrusts, whimpering his name as I fell over the cliff. He didn't stop, not even when the pleasure slowly faded.

He withdrew after a few moments, turning me over to adjust me on my hands and knees before he settled behind me. Saint wasn't gentle when he entered me from behind. His hands gripped my hips, and he moved in and out of me, anger filling the room with each hurried thrust that slammed against me. His hand lifted from my hip, landing hard against my ass cheek, causing a strangled gasp of surprise to escape my throat. It landed again and again before he rubbed the sore cheek.

"If you ever run from me again, Brat, I will tie you up and keep you where I know you're safe. Do you fucking hear me?" he snapped, sliding his fingers up my spine until they threaded through my hair, jerking my body up against his. He didn't stop jackhammering into my body, which had me teetering on the edge of another release. "Answer me, now."

"I understand, Saint," I groaned, leaning my head against his shoulder as his fingers uncurled from my hair, brushing against my throat to hold me up. His other hand slid beneath my belly, finding my clit to rub his fingers in a small circular pattern that had me crying out his name as everything crashed down at once.

"Good girl," he murmured, tensing as a deep growl escaped from his chest, vibrating against my ear. "You feel so fucking good taking me inside your tight cunt, Brat. You like me fucking you and manhandling you, don't you?"

"Yes," I moaned, grunting as he pushed me down onto the bed, slamming into me hard. "Fuck yes, more," I demanded, hearing his wicked laughter as he pushed my thighs apart, lifting them. My head dropped to the bed as he angled my body, driving his cock deep into my core. It clenched hungrily around him, fighting to keep him buried within my channel. Saint growled, thrusting harder until he snarled his release, dropping my hips as he slowly moved behind me.

"I don't even care if the gods knew what the hell they were doing. I'm just glad you're mine because I don't think I could ever get tired of fucking you." He dropped to the bed beside me, pulling me back against his body as his hand settled onto my belly. "You didn't get a bath, Brat."

I chuckled with heavy eyes, turning to look back at him as he grinned roguishly. Chaos's voice echoed through the apartment outside the door, and I smiled. Sitting up, I used a cloth to clean up the mess Saint had created between my thighs and pulling on a pair of panties from my dresser that he'd brought into our room. Once we were dressed, Saint kissed my forehead as we exited the bedroom, staring at the table where Chaos was pigging out on the assortment of fresh fruit that made my stomach growl.

Sitting beside him, I leaned over, kissing his brow before joining him. Saint leaned against the bedroom doorframe, watching us consume the fruit, delicious berries, and melons. Eryx sat in a chair in the front room, his leg slung over the arm of it, also watching us.

"Don't you want any, Saint? It's good, and we never get fresh fruit during wintertime," Chaos exclaimed around a mouthful of watermelon.

"I'm enjoying watching you two eat it," Saint chuckled, sliding his gaze to mine. He smiled and rested his head against the doorframe. "Your momma needs fresh fruit. Jacob said it's good for her and your sister."

I blushed, pushing another chunk of honeydew into my mouth. I smiled around it, sliding my stare to Chaos, who looked down at my belly.

"How do you know she likes it?" Chaos asked curiously. "She can't even talk yet."

"Because I'm not running for the bathroom to empty my stomach," I snorted, laughing as his eyes widened.

"I wish I could do that to the cook when she makes us eat liver," he admitted, causing the room to snort in agreement. "Do you think I made my mom sick? Do you think that is why she didn't want me?"

My heart clenched, and I shook my head. "I think your mom was scared and didn't know how to handle having you. I don't think you were the reason she ran away, Chaos. Sometimes people get scared, and when they're scared, they run away from what spooks them. Having a baby is scary, especially when you're not mated."

"Is that why you ran away?" he asked, holding my stare. "Because of me?"

"No, I didn't run away because of you, Chaos," I said firmly, reaching over to push his dark hair away from his forehead. "I love you; you know that. Leaving you behind was hard, but your father deserves to know what an amazing little monster he created. I left because I was hurt and because I was angry. I wouldn't ever run away because I was scared of something. I felt betrayed by the pack, and the man I loved had come back, but he wanted to punish me because he thought I was like Harold."

"Are you going to stay with us and be a family?" he continued, his eyes swimming with tears.

"Well, I'm entirely too fat to run away right now, right? I don't think I could waddle that fast anymore. You and I could race and see if you can finally beat me," I teased, watching the smile that took control of his face.

"I'd like that," he said, grabbing a handful of fruit to shove into his mouth. "But I'm not going to go easy on you just because you're carrying a baby. You're still a girl, and girls are slower than boys. I proved it by racing Annie and kicking her butt. Then do you know what she tried to do to me? She tried to kiss me, so I pulled her hair and told her she had cooties. Girls are so gross," he announced, annoyance playing on his cherubic face.

"Yeah, remember that," I stated, hearing Saint snorting before my gaze lifted, holding his. "One day, you won't think they're so gross. One day, they'll be your world, and you will want to never go another moment without them."

"Nope, that isn't happening to me. Jimmy kissed Carla, and now they keep staring at each other, and we heard them grunting inside the fort. I went in to see what she was doing to him, and they were naked. It was disgusting!"

My eyes rounded as I swung them back to Chaos as he frowned. "What fort?"

"Some fort up in the woods," he shrugged. "Did you miss the part where they were naked?" Chaos asked, exasperation filling his tone. "It's way up on the hill to the south. There's a big S and B carved on it, but no one knows what it means."

I smiled, turning to watch as Saint's shoulders shake as he silently chuckled. I knew that fort because it was the one Saint built for me, where we'd intended to mate to avoid anyone else catching our scent until we were fully bonded.

I worried my lip with my teeth, holding Saint's heated gaze. It was our place, the one we had escaped to when we'd wanted to be alone. Saint's knowing eyes held mine. Tilting his head, he pushed off the doorframe, moving to sit down with us as we munched on the fruit, of which I couldn't get enough.

Chapter Thirty-One

Days passed, and the nights grew longer and colder. The people who worked with Saint had started rotating, keeping the primary team's higher-ups here while others worked in the cells, disassembling them. I'd kept out of their business or tried to for the most part. Every day around Saint became a little easier to accept him and the changes he'd brought with him.

I hadn't forgiven him or the pack, but I'd settled into a routine and had begun overseeing duties again for the pack on a smaller scale. Today the team was all here, and I'd sent in whiskey and snacks to keep them going throughout the meeting in the main hall.

Settling onto the sofa in the library, I watched Chaos reading one of the comic books, laughing boyishly, and sending warmth rushing through me. The fire had been lit, crackling as the heavy snow fell outside the new picture window that Saint and his crew had framed. Sitting up, I gasped and then cried out as pain ripped through my stomach.

I pushed the rest of the way up, smelling the blood before feeling it on my thighs. Chaos stood in front of me; his eyes widened with worry.

"Chaos, help me up," I whispered thickly, panic pulsing through me.

Chaos shook his head; fear etched on his features before he ran off. It took an effort to get upright, standing as I pushed the pain down and started toward the door of the library. Before I had even reached it, Saint, Eryx, and Leif were there, rushing into the room.

"She's bleeding," Leif stated, his Nordic blue eyes meeting mine with worry.

Saint didn't wait for permission, picking me up to carry me out the door, covering the space between the infirmary and us in moments. Jacob lifted his head when we entered. Sensing the wolves' worry, he rushed, preparing a bed where Saint placed me. Pain sliced through my belly as he settled me on the mattress, peering down at me with fear burning in his stare.

"What happened?" Jacob asked, pushing Saint back to get to me.

"I don't know. I tried to sit up on the couch, and pain shot through my stomach. I smelled blood and tried to get Chaos to help me, but he ran for help."

Jacob nodded, turning to look at the others inside the room. Frowning, his gaze slid back to Saint, who had turned as white as a sheet.

"Do something." Saint's voice quivered, mirroring my fear.

"I'm going to need some privacy to check her out," Jacob stated, stepping to a sink as he removed his lab coat, rolling up his sleeves to reveal a mass of tattoos and scars.

"I'm not moving from her side," Saint snapped.

"I need to check her cervix and make sure she's not dilating. She's at four months, which is too early to go into labor. Your daughter isn't ready to be born. I don't have the equipment that we'd need to sustain her life until we could get her to a hospital that does. If Braelyn is in labor, I need to stop it and get her to a hospital. There are many sets of eyes here, which was what I was pointing out to you, daddy. Unless you wish them all to see her in stirrups, they should step outside for a moment."

The others hesitated until I looked pointedly at them. Eryx didn't budge as everyone else slipped silently out of the room. He moved away from where we were, allowing some resemblance of privacy. His hands balled tightly at his sides, glancing at Saint while pacing, as the scent of his anxiety and fear filled the room, mixing with mine and Saint's.

It took seconds for Jacob to check my cervix and to be cleared and declared healthy. It didn't ease the worry and fear that moved through me. He squeezed a dollop of gel onto my stomach, and then the sweetest sound in the world began thumping through the room. I smiled, meeting Saint's wide-eyed look with tears swimming in mine.

"Is that her?" he asked, settling into the chair Jacob placed beside the bed, grabbing another for Eryx, who continued pacing. "Is that the baby's heartbeat?"

"Yes, and it's strong," Jacob announced.

"Eryx," I called, turning to meet his blue gaze. "Get your ass over here and sit. You're making me nervous."

"I didn't mean to, Princess. I'm freaking the fuck out, and it isn't even my kid."

"Sit," Saint ordered, holding my hand tightly as more cold gel was applied to my belly, and then the wand was pressing against it again as Jacob looked at a monitor.

We all watched in silence as he moved the wand across my belly. The screen was dark, with weird stuff that looked like we'd stepped back in time, peering at a black and white television screen.

"There's her face," he said, pointing out the lines. "She's sucking her fingers."

I laughed nervously and then groaned as pain lanced through me. Exhaling slowly, I peered into Jacob's grey stare as his mouth tightened into a white line. "So, she's okay?"

"She's doing good, momma. Her heartbeat is strong, and she's active. There's fluid leaking though, here," he stated, pointing at bubbles and what looked like a sack. "Oligohydramnios is what it is called, and it is concerning. Your fluid is low, but you're not rupturing. You also have placenta previa, which is probably why there's bleeding. You're going to need to take it easy until she is delivered. I'll get some equipment up here to be more prepared in the event she decides she's impatient to meet her parents."

"So, it is a girl?" Eryx asked, studying the screen beside Saint, who was also watching our child sucking her tiny fingers into her mouth. "Why the hell does she look like an alien?"

"It's an old machine, and most babies look like this on the monitor." Jacob looked up as people came through the door. Chaos stood by the wall, but Saint coaxed him over.

"There's your sister, Chaos."

"Are you okay?" Chaos asked, resting his head against mine. "You have to be okay, Braelyn."

"I'm okay, sweet boy. It just scared me. You were brave," I murmured, kissing his head.

"I wasn't. I was scared," he admitted, placing his hand onto mine and Saint's. "I panicked and ran away."

"You ran for help, which was smart. I panicked and tried to get to the medical ward alone, and I wouldn't have made it. You did what was needed, little monster. You went and got your daddy to help us."

"Lycia," he said, removing his hand from ours to touch my belly. "Lycia Kingsley. I think she'd like that name."

"Don't you think we should let her mother name her, Chaos?"

"Lycia Magena Kingsley," I replied, watching Chaos smirk, scrunching up his nose.

"She will love it," he chuckled, lifting his head to sit in Saint's lap. "Look, she's moving again." We all turned and saw her face pressed against where Jacob held the wand. "Can she see us?" he asked.

"No, buddy," Jacob explained. "She can hear you, though. Say something to her."

Grinning, Chaos leaned close to my belly, "I'm going to be your big brother, Lycia. I'm going to make sure no one ever hurts you. You're going to like our mommy, and our dad is pretty cool so far." Her hand returned to her mouth, and she remained still as if she were listening to him. "We have a big family, and we're learning to be one still. You're going to be ours, and we're going to love you."

"What's her name mean?" Eryx asked, watching the screen intensely.

"Wolf moon," Chaos answered. "It's what Brae would have named me if I'd been a girl, and it's a pretty name if Brae liked it."

"Indeed, it's perfect," Saint stated, wrapping his hand around Chaos. "So, what is your plan, Jacob? Bed rest?"

"That and she'll need to take it easy for a while. If Braelyn can manage to carry her for another two weeks, we'll be able to deliver Lycia without needing machines or an incubator. No vigorous sex and keep an eye on the bleeding. If it gets worse, we can keep Braelyn here to watch her more carefully. Placenta previa can fix itself, but it is troubling with it occurring at this late stage of pregnancy. I think we'll move our visits to every few days until delivery."

"Can we watch Lycia a little longer?" Chaos asked, and Jacob chuckled.

"Sure, for a little while longer, but I think Braelyn needs some rest soon, Champ. In a couple of weeks, you'll be able to see her whenever you want. I'm thinking Lycia has an army of people waiting to meet her." Jacob smiled, peering at the wall of people who'd come to watch.

"I'm the godmother, and I have dibs on being present during the delivery," Toralei grumbled, moving closer. "You're okay?" she asked, and I nodded. "She got big. The last time we saw her, she was tiny."

"They do that," Jacob stated, sliding his gaze over Toralei's face, not even bothering to hide the fact that he was checking her out.

"I think I'm sick," she stated, smiling at him. "I need a doctor."

"I'm a doctor." Jacob crossed his arms over his chest, revealing his heavily tattooed arms. "What ails you, pretty girl?"

"Woman, sir. I'm a woman, which you should know as a doctor," she returned huskily. "And I think my pus…"

"Lalalalalalalalala," I sang, looking pointedly at Tora. "Virgin ears up in here. Two pairs! Take your doctor fetish outside," I groaned.

It took an hour of people coming and going from the room before I was allowed off the monitors and finally back in our apartment. Saint and Eryx fussed over everything. I had random dishes of fruit, meats, and cheeses showing up as I sat in front of the TV with Chaos, watching his mindless cartoons.

Saint's entire crew had crowded into the apartment, and anytime I so much as tried to rearrange myself, they all but shat themselves thinking something was wrong. A knock sounded at the door, and I turned as Enzo entered, carrying bright blue roses. I smiled as he walked toward me. He leaned down and kissed my forehead, which should have been awkward, but he was so smooth I hadn't even processed it before he pushed the roses toward me.

"I heard you had a scare, and all women need a little brightening up after one," he explained, handing me the roses.

"Thank you," I smiled again, lifting them to my nose to smell.

Enzo's hand shot out and stopped me. "They're poisoned. Use them against your enemies, but don't smell them," he stated, forcing me to yank my face back. "More often than not, pretty things are deadly. Such as you, Braelyn. I need to steal your boys for a little while if that is okay?"

"They're not my boys." I stood to put the flowers in water, but Eryx grabbed them, giving Enzo the stink eye before making his way to the small but convenient kitchen area.

"You're certain they're not? They're pacing like caged beasts, worried about their lioness. They're protecting you and worried at the same time," Enzo chuckled, winking at me with his sultry, dark eyes sparkling with laughter. "Saint, a moment, please."

I watched them walk toward the door. Saint paused, turning to look at me with indecision warring in his eyes. I fluffed the pillow beside me, leaning back to smile at him. It was cute that he was worried, and it made me believe that everything would eventually be okay in our world.

"Go, Saint. You have people who need your help. I'm going to take a nap, and I have my most fierce and loyal warrior here with me. Chaos will call you if anything happens. I'll be okay," I reassured him as he strode toward me, kissing me quickly, then dishing out instructions to Chaos before he left.

Chapter Thirty-Two

Peering down at my phone, I studied the text that Saint had sent. He and the others took off yesterday at dawn and had been expected back today by dusk, but a storm had moved in, preventing their return. They were stuck at the mountain base, unable to get to us because of the blizzard and strong winds assaulting the mountain.

I stood outside, watching the trees bow to the strong winds. The sound of the wood cracking and heavy trees uprooting from the ground made worry rush through me. The lights within the lodge had dimmed, lowering the power to ease the strain on the generators. Fires burned throughout the lodge's interior rooms, and those within the thin-walled ad-on were allowed inside to prevent them from becoming chilled.

My gaze followed the men and women outside the gates that struggled to get things down so that they wouldn't become airborne missiles in the wind that howled, forcing me to step back into the alcove of the balcony. Saint had built a patio matching the one in my previous bedroom because he knew how much I loved it. I could have kissed him for the insight and understanding that I loved my room because of the view and access to the fresh air.

Something in the tree line caught my attention, and I paused, searching the woods. Chaos's bright orange coat I'd made for him was barely visible, and every instinct within me screamed. I called his name, but the wind swallowed it, drowning it out.

I entered the apartment, grabbing my coat and phone before heading downstairs. I dialed Saint, explaining what was happening as he listened. He paused, and I heard Eryx talking in a low tone.

"Do not leave the lodge, Braelyn," Saint growled.

"You don't understand how bad it is up here. Trees are uprooting, and Chaos is in the fucking forest. I can't leave him out there."

"Send the alphas. You're not going out in this storm," Saint snapped, worry filling his tone. "Please don't go out there," he growled.

The moment I opened the apartment door, the acrid scent of copper met my nose. My stomach clenched with the need to upheave from the smell filling the hallway. Lifting my hand to my nose, I used the back of it to lessen the scent.

"Saint, something is wrong," I whispered thickly. "I can smell blood," I explained, slipping into the shadows while moving toward the stairs, and silently heading down them. The silence of the lodge was eerie, causing the hair on my nape to rise.

"I need you to get back to the apartment and lock the doors. I'm coming, Brae. Please go back to the apartment. The door is reinforced, and I need to know you're safe. Can you do that for me, Brat?" he asked calmly as I heard the sound of people and weapons being grabbed in the background.

I closed my eyes, leaning my head against the wall until someone rounded the corner. Xariana's gaze met mine, her finger moving to press against her lip for silence. Toralei was close on her heels, both coming from the direction of my room.

"Saint wants me inside the room," I whispered, holding the phone lower on my ear. "Xariana and Toralei are here with me."

"Good, take them with you to the bedroom and wait for us to get there," he ordered, and I heard the sound of snow crunching as blades began to hum to life around him.

"Tell Saint that isn't an option. Vampires are swarming the upstairs hallway. We're heading outside because they're collecting women and children," Xariana stated, her hands reaching for the blades at her hips. She handed me a pair of knives and nodded at Toralei, who had already unsheathed her daggers. "The blades are dipped in deadman's blood. Aim for their heart or head. It won't kill them, but it will slow them down long enough for us to get away."

"How do you even know that?" I asked as Xariana's lips curved into a wicked smirk.

"I was teethed on how to kill Otherworld

creatures and enforce the laws of the fae, humans, and anything else that preys or threatens to expose us," Xariana shrugged, her eyes sparkling at the thought of murdering something or someone. "Someone let these assholes in, so we need to find them and end them for being a traitor."

"I'm coming. Just stay alive for me, Brat. I love you," Saint said thickly.

I paused, staring at the phone before it went dead. "I love you, too, Saint."

I pushed the phone into my jacket, frowning as the sound of feet on the tiled floors echoed around us. Toralei took the lead, moving us silently through the hallway to duck into an alcove that led to an exit inside the omegas' quarters.

The scent of blood grew the closer we got to the exit. My heart clenched, knowing the pack was being hurt, and until reinforcements arrived, we wouldn't be much help. My mind whirled with fear for Chaos, knowing he was out in the storm, alone.

Toralei went through the exit first and snarled as she lifted her blade, running a vampire through with the steel of her dagger. I watched as his crimson eyes widened, grabbing the knife with his hands, causing his skin to sizzle and burn. The vampire hit the ground, jerking up as his spine arched, a strangled scream bubbling from his lips as blood shot into the air.

"Deadman's blood has a nasty effect on vampires, but it's also fun to watch," Xari snorted, nodding her head as if she wanted to pat her own back. I peered at the blades in my hands and grunted, fighting nausea rolling through me at the scent of a burning vampire.

"I'm going to barf," I warned, holding my forearm against my nose and mouth to block out the smell. "That reeks." I gagged, and both women turned, watching me.

Men moved around the corner of the building, rushing at us. I stepped into line between them, lifting the blades, and crisscrossed them down the front of one of the vampires. He hissed, sputtering as he faltered, staring at me before he slammed into me.

I gasped, forcing the blade between our bodies, crying out as it slid through my coat and stomach to pierce his chest. We fell, and the moment I hit the ground, Tora was on him, yanking him off of me to stare down at the front of my coat.

"Gods dammit, Braelyn," she grunted, helping me back to my feet.

No sooner had she got me upright, more vampires swarmed around us. Xariana spun as if dancing. Her legs barely touched the ground as she flipped, turning sideways as vampire parts rained onto the ground at her feet.

My eyes widened as I saw a vampire using speed to try to reach her. He dodged through the pieces of his friends, only for Tora to intercept him, slamming him back with a solid foot against his chest. Her body bent backward, and Xari's sword swung out, barely missing Tora as she cut the vampire into two pieces.

We started forward, sliding between the buildings as we rushed toward the open gate. Once we'd made it outside, I paused and saw Lucas running in our direction with men who held guns aimed at us. He sneered, watching as we backed up.

Lucas's eyes sparkled with rage and triumph. It explained how vampires had reached the lodge, brought into our sanctuary through the tunnels. Lucas knew the tunnels like the back of his hand, and since he'd revealed he was balls-deep in league with my father, it made sense.

"On your knees, now," a vampire demanded, glaring at us through crimson-colored eyes. "This is his whore? You didn't tell me that she was expecting his child, Lucas. I'm pleased that she is. I'll enjoy knowing I cut Saint's bastard out of his mate, right before I skin her down to her bones, and use her insides to paint my walls for his meddling in my business."

"I wasn't aware that he'd knocked the whore up," Lucas sneered, smiling at me with evil in his gaze. "I get the bitch before you finish with her. That was the agreement we made. I kept my end of the bargain. You have enough people to maintain your live shows, and I get to step into Harold's shoes and receive his shares of the monetary gain from our operation. But first, I get to fuck his sweet daughter and hear her sing so prettily when my blade kisses her flesh."

"You will have what you asked for as soon as we're off this godforsaken mountain, wolf. Grab them and do try not to hurt her before she's in chains. I promised my clientele a certain standard of product before airing their torture to the world." The vampire picked invisible lint only he could see from his overcoat, dismissing us.

Men stepped from the shadows behind us, and I

trembled at the freezing wind against the wetness of my stomach. My coat was soaked in blood, the scent mixed with the smell of the undead, making me gag. Unlike most vampires who contained the stench of death and rot, these reeked of it.

Lucas moved closer, his hand snaking up to brush his fingers against my cheek. "Don't look so worried, Braelyn. I have a plan to keep you in place. Your child, though, will bring in more money. They like to watch the tiny ones suffer the most."

"You're sick," I spat, jerking my cheek away from his touch. His hand flew toward my face, knocking me backward as Tora and Xari both lunged at him. They were pushed away by the undead that blocked their path to me.

"Where is your mate, Braelyn?" Lucas asked, kneeling in front of me. His eyes slid over the green army coat I'd grabbed and then moved back to my face.

The scene erupted around us as Saint's voice echoed. "I'm right here, asshole. Get the fuck away from my mate," he warned.

Those around us spun toward the sound of Saint's voice, but he wasn't anywhere I could see him. His scent wafted through the wind, soothing the panic that had held me in thrall. The lead vampire was using it, feeding fear to those close enough to be influenced by his presence.

Lucas stood, searching the tree line around the large parking area. Reaching down, he dug his fingers through my hair, yanking me up to my feet as I cried out in pain. My stomach, where I'd cut it open in my clumsy attempt to take down the vampire, burned, and cramping had started in my lower abdomen. I managed to keep the pain from showing, knowing that Lucas intended to use me to get a response from Saint.

Shadows shifted at the edges of the parking lot. The threat hanging in the air was violence and death, so smothering that I thought I would choke on it. Nausea swam through me as I swayed on my feet. I stepped closer to Toralei and Xariana, ignoring the large vampires that blocked my path.

One turned, studying me as I faced him, smiling cruelly as I approached. If he planned to stop me, he didn't give anything away. I slid between his body and another vampire, settling between the girls. He snorted, turning his focus toward the more threatening problem.

"You won't reach your mate before we end her life, Kingsley," the leader snarled.

"You won't leave this mountain top with her, and if you end the life of my mate and child, yours will follow them into the afterlife, Lestair," Saint's voice boomed, coming from every direction. Those surrounding us paused, sliding their gazes all over in search of Saint. "There's an army standing inside the tunnels, and your people that awaited your return are dead. Let her go, and I will let you walk away from here alive."

Xariana dropped her blades from her sleeves, palming them, and Toralei did the same as I searched the ground for mine. Shivering against the cold, I found them in the snow, where they'd fallen out of reach. Shifting my attention to the edge of the woods, I swallowed down a scream as everything erupted around me.

I didn't pause, didn't think as I rushed toward the woods where Chaos had vanished. Blood pounded in my ears as I entered the forest. I could hear the sound of weapons clashing, and screams filled the night. The wind howled, and the cracking of wood surrounded me.

I caught Chaos's scent in the wind. Turning without stopping, I rushed in the direction from which it came. My blood would lead Saint to me, and he'd find me, hopefully after I'd found Chaos. The wind howled through the trees, whipping my hair against my cheek as I heard the horrifying sound of trees uprooting and ripping free of the ground. Panic flowed through me as I saw a tree coming right for me where I stood. Before it could hit me, something slammed against me, taking me to the ground, hard.

Chapter Thirty-Three

I stared up into Chaos's wide, horrified eyes. He grabbed me, pulling me up with him as shouting started. Swallowing down the scream of pain that rocked through me, I peered around. I understood the reason for Chaos's panic. The men shouting and the power rushing through the woods around us weren't our people.

Standing, I doubled over in pain as Chaos pulled me with him deeper into the woods. I couldn't hear him through wind howling and blood pounding in my ears. My legs were wet, soaked all the way down into my boots. We were fighting to move through the snow, so deep that it was up to our knees. It made it impossible to trudge through, but Chaos didn't give up. He pulled me with him, refusing to leave me behind.

The shouting was getting closer, forcing my head to whip toward it moments before something struck me, sending my body into the snow. I screamed for Chaos, standing as I howled, rage and fear rushing through me as Lestair grabbed him, yanking him off of his feet as Chaos struggled to get free.

My entire body vibrated seconds before I shot toward the vampire, forcing him to drop Chaos. Lestair grabbed me by the throat, shaking me and yanking me off of my feet. Closing my eyes, I swallowed down the pain. Opening them, my wolf peered out, sensing we were in danger. Power rippled through the clearing, and I growled from deep in my chest as Lestair laughed coldly.

I saw a blur from the corner of my eye just as something crashed into us. Lestair snarled, baring his teeth as he grabbed me by my bicep, dragging me with him as his nails tore into my flesh. My eyes slid to where Chaos laid in the snow, blood splatter all around him. I yanked against the vampire's hold, fighting to get back to Chaos.

Men moved in around us, and I watched in horror as Lucas grabbed Chaos by the back of his neck, dragging his limp form with us.

"Protect my children," I whispered the prayer.

"I'm going to fucking eat them while you watch, stupid bitch!" Lestair laughed coldly.

"I choose them, and I free you to protect them," I continued, speaking to Fenrir as the howls of a thousand wolves erupted around us. Power shot through the clearing, pulsing as I released my wolf.

More yelling came from far away as I was dropped to the ground, falling into the frozen snow. Trees snapped and crunched against the wind and vortex of power that rushed around us. The snow increased, making it impossible to see anything beyond my nose. My chest rose and fell as I crawled to where I'd last seen Chaos held.

Shrieks of pain filled the area, my hands numb from the bone-chilling cold I crawled through. I gasped as something brushed against me, and before I could think to attack, warm arms picked me up, moving me away from the fighting.

Sage and bergamot filled my senses, soothing me against the intensity of the pain that consumed my mind. Saint sat me down in Eryx's arms, pushing the hair away from my face. His eyes scanned my body, and then he exhaled.

"Chaos?" I asked, watching him.

His head shook as a loud, blood-curdling howl ripped through the clearing. I sat up as a large, black wolf padded forward, blood-red eyes focusing on me as I lowered mine to see what he carried. Relief washed through me as he opened his jaws, dropping Chaos onto the ground. Sian scooped him up, moving to us as I leaned back, resting against Eryx. Saint grabbed Chaos's limp form, rubbing him as I stared over his head, where thousands of wolves were tearing through the vampires, snarling and ripping them apart.

The men gaped in awe, and no one moved as the souls of Fenrir's wolves protected my children. Leif sat on his knees in the snow beside me, his eyes following Fenrir, who was the size of a large horse. Fenrir watched his wolves work, his head down and ears back, baring his large teeth in warning. No one spoke or made a sound as the scene played out, even as the pain continued pulsing through me, shooting down my spine.

Lucas appeared in the clearing, trying to outrun the wolves, and Fenrir growled, the sound deadly and low. Abandoning his post, Fenrir leaped through the air and caught Lucas by the neck, ripping it open with his teeth as his claws pushed through Lucas's chest, removing his heart before eating it.

It wasn't until Fenrir spun, his eyes going to a deep shade of Nordic blue, that the men tensed. He padded on his feet, covered in the blood of the undead, and leaped toward us, and Saint and his men tensed as they prepared to fight him. Only Fenrir went through them as I opened my mouth, taking the god of my people back into my soul.

Saint's eyes bugged out in wonder, his mouth opening and closing in shock. I screamed, crying out as pain forced my body to tense.

"She's coming," I sobbed, watching the men look at one another in panic and sheer terror. "The baby is coming."

"You can use my fort," Chaos whispered, forcing my eyes to his before Saint grabbed me up and rushed into the forest.

"Hold on, Braelyn," Saint urged, shouting orders to the others as he ran through the snow, taking us to the old fort that had once been our sanctuary. "Don't push."

"No shit," I grunted, holding onto him as he trudged through waist-deep snow before ducking into the fort. "It isn't safe to have the baby here. It's not even sanitary to do this outside!"

"Women have been having babies since the dawn of time, and way before they had hospitals, Braelyn. Your mother had you outside beneath the blood moon," Leif announced, rolling up his sleeves. "Start a fire, and strip out of those coats, gentlemen. We need padding," he ordered, nodding at Chaos. "Get up by your momma's head, boy. You don't want to be at this end of the show."

Panic shot through me, and then pain. Saint removed my pants and then my panties as the men lifted and adjusted me on the coats they had piled onto the fort floor. The wind howled outside, but nothing mattered—nothing except ending the pain and giving in to the need to push.

Saint positioned himself behind me, holding me as Leif forced my knees apart. Chaos held my hand, and I screamed, gritting my teeth as my stomach tensed, and an intense pain radiated around my back, moving to my stomach.

"Breathe, Brat. In through your nose and out through your mouth. You're strong enough to do this," Saint said against my ear, kissing it softly. "You're having our daughter in our sanctuary. How fucking poetic is that?" he continued, nuzzling my ear between contractions. "Remember the day I built this place for us? Nothing can touch us here—nothing can harm us. This fort is our place, where nothing matters except us. This is where I told you I loved you for the very first time. The same place where you kissed me and told me you would give me all your pretty babies. It's only right that you're giving us our daughter inside of it."

"I was stupid back then! They make painkillers for

this shit, ya know? I can't do this. I can't bring her into a world where she could be harmed. She's safe inside of me. I think she should just stay there for a while," I argued, hearing him laugh against my neck.

"I want to meet her, too," he whispered near my ear.

"Me too, so just tell her to get out," Chaos snorted, his hand holding mine tightly, even though I wasn't squeezing his. "Girls are so stubborn."

"That they are," Leif agreed, watching my face. "She's ready to meet her family. You ready to do this, Braelyn?"

I nodded, grabbing my knees and waiting for the next contraction. The moment it hit, I bore down as a scream ripped through me. Saint tightened his hold, whispering against my ear as Chaos cheered me on, oblivious of what he was cheering. The coat over my stomach lifted, and he screamed for an entirely different reason. Saint grabbed him, turning him to face away as Eryx slipped in to take his place, shielding Chaos from seeing what was happening.

"She's crowning, Braelyn. I need you to stop pushing for a moment," Leif stated, peering over my head at Saint.

"What's wrong?" I demanded.

"She's just a little tangled in her cord, and I need to unwrap it from her," he said calmly, making my panic ease a bit. "There you go. Next contraction, you're going to give it everything you have."

On the next contraction, I lifted with how hard my

body pushed to free her. Leif smiled, and then the most beautiful sound I'd ever heard ripped through the fort. An angry cry from being displaced from the warmth of my body tore through the air. Leif handed Lycia to me, removing his shirt to cover her.

"Put her inside your shirt, against your flesh, Braelyn. Help her, Saint. You're going to need to push once more to get everything else out. Once we're done, we'll get you both back to the warmth of the lodge," Leif promised.

I stared at Lycia's red, angry face, watching the fluorescent blue eyes of her wolf peering up at Saint and me as we stared at our daughter in wonder. "Hello, Lycia Magena. We're your parents, sweet girl," I whispered thickly.

"She looks like you," Saint murmured, helping me slip her tiny form into my shirt. "She's perfect, just like you."

"I love you," I whispered through the tears. "I love you, Saint." I wasn't going to wait to tell him, not when our world kept getting turned upside down.

"I've always loved you, Brat. You, you're my moon, and my wolf pines for you. We really need to talk about your wolf, though."

"I freed him to go with her," I admitted. "I permitted him to protect Lycia. I have you now, and she will have all of us," I returned, melting into his heat while Leif cleaned up my lady parts. It was a bit awkward to have him cleaning me, but it was as if he'd done it a million times before.

Jackets were wrapped around us, and before I

could argue against it, Saint picked me up, and we were moving through the snow once more. My arms wrapped around the slight burden, feeling Lycia moving against me as she howled her displeasure to the moon goddess.

We entered the lodge, and everyone was waiting for us. My eyes slid through the people, finding Toralei and Xariana both staring, smiles on their faces. Tora started forward, her eyes leaking waterworks as she stopped in front of me.

"I thought we'd lost…"

Lycia wailed, and Tora's eyes widened as they lowered to my chest. I adjusted the blanket, revealing the top of her black hair, still covered in blood and goo. Tora reached forward and touched Lycia's forehead and gasped, lifting her eyes to hold mine.

"How?" she asked, her mouth dropping wide open. "Please tell me you didn't have our baby in the snow!"

"Ours?" Saint asked, his hold tightening on me.

Jacob pushed through the crowd, his nurse hot on his heels as he stopped in front of us. His grey eyes searched mine, noting the blood covering my shirt and the bruises on my face.

"Bring her to the infirmary, Saint. We should double-check them both and make sure they're healthy. With Braelyn's body healing from childbirth, her wounds will heal slower than usual. I'd like to clean them up and check out Lycia."

"Okay, but we're not letting her out of our sight," Chaos snarled, his arms crossed over his chest as he puffed up.

"That's fine. I see you're already taking on your responsibility of big brother, Chaos. I just want to be certain she's healthy before you spirit her away to your rooms."

"Eryx, have the fire in the apartment burning and ready for when we arrive. Get the bedrooms set up, and bring in the bassinet we built," Saint ordered, even though we were already heading toward the medical ward.

My eyes moved through the pack, watching as they fought to get a peek at the littlest wolf. It made my heart clench, and the familiar family bond we'd shared ache. I missed the closeness we'd once had and the way we'd all worked together, providing and protecting one another from everything else.

"Stop," I said, tugging my shirt down enough that they could see her. "Lycia, this is our family. This is the pack, and they are our people. Welcome to the family, littlest wolf."

Tears swam in my eyes as they slowly stepped closer, smiling as she sucked her hand while taking in their faces. Her eyes were still glowing, which meant a part of Fenrir was still adjusting to its new host. This would cement her bond with the pack and ensure that they felt her as one of their own. More so, it meant they would sense her bond with Fenrir, and they would always need to be near to her and us.

"Our family," Saint murmured, kissing my forehead softly before he started down the hallway that led to the medical ward.

Saint whispering the words sent heat rushing

through me. My heart settled, and there was no fear of the unknown with him holding us. We had a long way to go before everything would be perfect, but this felt right. It felt like I didn't have to continually keep my walls up, guarding my emotions to keep others safe. I wasn't alone anymore. I had a family, and the pack would ensure that our enemies never fucked with us, and if they did, we wouldn't ever be alone in that fight.

Epilogue

Three months later

I studied the men, struggling with their instructions, pointing to things in the heap of metal that sat on the apartment floor. They'd been at it for over three hours, each one growing more frustrated as they took turns reading the manufacturer's instructions. Saint's eyes lifted to mine, holding them, and he smirked while I patted a freshly bathed and fed babe against my shoulder.

Chaos stood a few feet away from me, always close by in case Lycia needed him. He had been true to his word, guarding over her with a protectiveness that just made me love him even more than I already did.

I'd always been terrified of having a child and the love I'd held for Chaos dimming or growing less when my own child arrived. It hadn't. It had intensified and blossomed, knowing he loved her as much as she would one day love him.

"This is bullshit," Eryx snapped, holding up bolts. "Why the hell don't they just come assembled?"

"Because it would be impossible to fit it into the Blackhawk, dumb shit," Zayne stated, holding up a metal bar. "What the hell? It doesn't appear that they sent us the right parts."

"Calm down," Saint demanded, smiling at me as his eyes sparkled.

The other men looked at him with annoyance, but he never acknowledged them. He remained calm, which seemed to be his new thing. Ever since his daughter's birth, Saint had settled into his role a lot easier than I had.

Saint had been calm and collected. I'd asked him how he'd managed it, and he'd replied that with everything we'd been through, raising a daughter would be a cakewalk. However, the moment Lycia fussed, Saint was right there, picking her up. He held her so tenderly that if his enemies ever saw it, they'd think he was growing soft.

A knock sounded at the door, and I moved to open it, revealing Xavier and Xariana. Both hunters were becoming part of the pack based on how often they were here.

There was also the never-ending parade of creatures, hunters, and others who came through with information on more trafficking rings. They also brought the wounded or orphaned and other creatures that needed a safe haven to heal, which our mountain had quickly become.

"She's getting so big," Xariana gushed, her wide

eyes taking in the changes to Lycia with wonder. "What the hell are you feeding her?"

"Titty," Chaos groaned. "I can't even feed her because only Braelyn can," he said with disgruntlement buried in his tone.

"Oh," Xari said, fumbling for something to say to the sullen child.

Xavier let loose a loud bark of laughter before he kissed my forehead and headed toward the boys. "Braelyn, you look happy."

"I am," I admitted, moving with them toward the couch.

I sat beside Chaos, handing him his sister, and his face beamed with pride. He held her tightly, and her pale eyes opened before she leaned closer to his shoulder, closing her eyes to sleep in the protection of his arms.

"What the hell are you assholes doing?" Xavier asked, tilting his head from side to side, angling it to figure out what the mess of metal could be.

"Building Lycia's swing," Saint muttered, dropping the metal he'd held to stand, pulling Xavier in for a quick hug, and then pointed at the paper Bowen held, glaring down at the metal. Bowen had refused even to attempt to build it, but he offered to oversee their efforts. Saint scratched the back of his head, frowning at the mess.

Xavier snorted, rolling up his sleeves as he joined in, making quick work of the swing. The others watched, handing him the part when he pointed at it.

Within five minutes, Xavier had it built and working.

"How the hell did you do that?" Saint asked, folding his arms across his chest and lifting one eyebrow in question.

"Xariana's mom died in childbirth, and I did everything alone. Once you build one of these things, you pretty much get the hang of them all," he shrugged.

"I didn't know she died in childbirth," Saint admitted, his face scrunching up before turning to me as if considering how rough it would be without me.

Xavier shrugged and then exhaled. "I don't talk about it because it still fucking hurts. Death doesn't ever get easier. You just learn to live with that pain as the world moves on without them in it. You get tougher, and you keep moving forward. I started hunting when I lost Xari's mom and began raising Xari the best I could with the shit-hand I'd been dealt. We did pretty well, didn't we, kid?" he asked, turning to look at Xariana.

"Yeah, we did okay, old man," she snorted, but her eyes filled with love when she said it. "Plus, if I'd had a mother, she'd have lost her shit when I started hunting demons down in droves at the age of ten."

Xavier laughed along with the men, and I shook my head. I couldn't imagine doing what she did. Even though I'd held a god within me, I didn't wish to hunt down monsters. Plus, Fenrir had only been allowed to interfere so far, and the rest had been up to me.

"The mountain is thawing, and with it brings new beginnings. I have a few kids who went through hell and need someplace to lie low for a bit. They're good kids, and I intend to train them when they're ready. We have some things happening at the guild, and some old friends have been coming around," Xavier announced.

"They're human, aren't they?" I asked, watching Xavier turn to look at me. "And those old friends, they're not friends at all."

"You're correct, and I can't have these kids around with what those old friends coming around might mean. I'd rather send them here, where they'll be safe. My guild is filled with hunters and those who don't house enough genetics to be considered full-bred, with enough blood to belong to a specific race. We're mutts, with enhanced senses, speed, agility, good for hunting, but not much else since none of us are accepted by our races."

"Have you considered shipping them to E.V.I.E.?" Saint asked, his stare sliding to Chaos, who had fallen asleep with Lycia cradled in his arms. He smirked, sliding his eyes to hold mine with silent laughter.

"Yeah, but Rhys isn't sending more people in while they're shifting alliances. He's got his hands full with his child on the way. He's got a spitfire that wants his nuts mounted above her fireplace. Ian and Hunter offered, but again, they're human. I wouldn't send humans to the King of Vampires, even if he is the head of that house. And Hunter, shit, I wouldn't send my enemies to him. The fae enjoy breaking humans and owning them."

"Send them here," I replied, holding Saint's stare. "We know wounded, and we know how to help them the best so that they can be emotionally and physically healed. We have mixed breeds up here now, and we tend to collect broken things and find a place for them in our pack. Our rate of helping those in need has increased, and they seem to enjoy it here. We have the room and the resources. You helped us when we needed it. We may not have known or assisted my father, but many of the broken people are in that position because of him. We can help them, but we won't keep them here if they decide to leave."

Xavier looked at Saint for the answer, and he smiled tightly at me before nodding. "She's the alpha's mate. Her word is the same as mine here, Xavier. If my mate says yes, then I agree. She's smarter than I am and much wiser than I suspected. However, if they hurt my pack, I will end them. We'll see if they fit in here, and if they do, they can stay. You don't ask for much in return for what you do, so know that if you ever need us, we're here."

"I know that, Saint. I knew what kind of person you were when I saved you and Eryx from that shithole cell where we'd found you. I also knew that you were worth saving, even though you didn't think you were."

Saint hadn't believed he could be saved after he'd been forced to murder others. He'd spent the time with Xavier atoning for his crimes, even though they hadn't been his. He'd told me everything he'd done, explaining shit that made my stomach curl. I hadn't condemned him or judged him because he'd been told to do it or die. I couldn't imagine not having him back with me.

In the little time we'd had together, life had settled into the perfect mess that had been missing from my life. I had people who knew what I'd been through and didn't judge me. They had been through hell too, and somehow, we'd all come out stronger.

Life wasn't what you went through—it was the end result, the happiness you took as the moments came amid the chaos. Our family had a rocky start, but I wouldn't want anyone else at my side. The pack was thriving, and Saint brought a security that I hadn't known was missing. He had been missing from my life when I'd rejected him, but the pack had also suffered without him and his crew.

Saint drew closer, picking me up to sit me on his lap while we watched the men pushing the swing, checking it for safety. They'd turned into protectors and large children around the kids. They were healing, which wasn't something you could force to happen. It had to happen on its own, and time truly did heal wounds when you allowed it.

"You're beautiful and happy," Saint whispered against my ear.

"I am happy. I am so happy that I don't even think it's real half the time," I admitted.

"I love you, Braelyn. This is real. This is our family and us."

"It's perfect," I swallowed thickly as my tone filled with emotions. "I couldn't dream of a better family or ending to a bunch of broken misfits. This is our world, and you are mine. You, Chaos, and Lycia are my reward for enduring all the pain until the world was right. I love you, Saint Kingsley. I can't wait to see what the future holds for us."

"With you at my side? That's a loaded comment," he laughed, kissing my cheeks as he reached over, ensuring his daughter was warm enough in our son's arms.

Phones started chiming, and I adjusted on Saint's lap as he pulled his out of his pocket. He stared at the screen before lifting his eyes to Xavier's, who was peering around the room.

"Enzo hasn't ever asked for help before. This can't be good," Saint stated, even as he tightened his arms around me. "We have to go."

"Yeah, because if the witches are around him, it means his enemies from his past are near. He doesn't ask for help because he and his brother are scary mother fuckers. Whatever it is, it won't be good, and we need to prepare for that. I need to head home and get a team together. I'll meet you guys at Hell's Cauldron. Brae, always a pleasure," Xavier said, leaning over to clasp hands with Saint before placing a chaste kiss on my forehead. "Don't worry. I'll keep him safe. He's got a family now."

"I'm not worried about Saint. I'm worried for whoever is stupid enough to mess with Enzo and Ezekiel. That is probably the biggest mistake someone could make," I admitted.

The men chuckled, but there was worry in it. I stood as Saint rose from the couch before smiling tightly at me. He leaned over to grip my jaw, kissing me hard and fast, then pulled away slowly, studying me.

"I need to go call Enzo and see what we're dealing with and what's happened. Don't worry. Whoever it is, they won't live long enough to be a problem." I smirked at his statement, knowing it wouldn't be as easy as they made it sound. Enzo was powerful, and he was calling in reinforcements. That alone screamed that something big was unfolding. "I'll be back shortly, and when I return, you better be in my bed waiting for me. I'm not leaving here without you being boneless and properly fucked."

"Promise?" I whispered, smiling devilishly.

"I promise you won't be able to speak by the time I'm finished with you," Saint grinned, heading for the door with the others trailing behind him.

Saint had a purpose, and I wouldn't stand in his way. The pack came first, but Saint trusted me to run it while he was out saving lives. I'd accepted who he'd become, and he recognized that I had been running the pack alone and could handle pretty much anything the world threw at me. It was a push-and-pull relationship, but we'd found a balance. I knew that no matter what, Saint would always return to me. At the end of the day, it was the only thing that mattered.

The End

Other Series by Amelia Hutchins

Legacy of the Nine Realms – Epic Fantasy Series

Aria and her sisters return to the human realm of Haven Falls to find one of their own is missing. They soon discover things have changed in the human realm and that nothing is what it seems, including Knox, the egotistical, self-centered, frustratingly gorgeous man who declared himself King during their absence.

Sparks fly when the two enter a fiery battle of wills as Aria learns she is more than just a witch in the Hecate bloodline; she is much, much more.

Will Aria embrace her savage side to find her sister and save her family, or will she burn to ashes from his heated kisses and burning hot embrace?

Knox has ulterior motives for being in Haven Falls and never expected the little witch to show up and brazenly challenge his rule.

It was supposed to be easy; get in and get out. Move pieces into place and set the stage for the war he's been planning for over five hundred years. Aria is his sworn enemy, but something within her calls to him, and he hates himself for craving the fiery kisses that have reignited his cold, dead heart. One taste and he thought he could get her out of his system. He was wrong.

Will Knox let go of the memories of the past,

driving his need for revenge that will destroy the pretty little witch he craves, or will he push the boundaries to fight for and claim what is his by right? Either way, war is inevitable. And nothing will stop him from reaching for what is his.

Begin the journey with book one—Flames of Chaos

The Fae Chronicles – Paranormal Romance Series

Have you ever heard of the old Celtic legends of the Fae, beautiful, magical, deadly, and a love of messing with humans just for kicks and giggles?

Welcome to my world.

What started as a strange assignment leads to one of the most gruesome murder mysteries of our times, and my friends and I are set and resolved to find out who is killing off Fae and witches alike.

There are a couple of problems in the way. I hate the Fae, and the Prince of the Dark Fae is bound and determined that I work for him. He's a rude, overbearing, egotistical ass with a compulsive need to possess, dominate, and control me. Oh, did I mention that he is absolutely sex-on-a-stick gorgeous, and he makes me feel things that I never ever wanted to feel for a Fae?

Every time he touches me or looks at me with those golden eyes, he seems to pull me further under his spell, despite my better judgment.

My friends and I can't trust anyone and nothing is as it seems on the surface. Not even me.

My story begins with me—Fighting Destiny

Monsters – Dark Fantasy Romance Series

My coven has remained hidden in the shadows for centuries. We've avoided the 'real world' altogether, hiding from monsters and other creatures sharing this planet.

We found refuge in the Colville National Forest, nestled in a town protected

by magical barriers. But our powers are locked by an ancient curse; one meant to protect us from being found.

Until now.

The past has a way of repeating itself. A new game is beginning, and no one is safe.

He's coming for me.

He's hunting.

The monster we've run from for centuries has found us.

How far will this deadly game go?

How far will I be able to take it, or will he destroy me and everything I care about?

Will the one thing I can't live without be the key to destroying and undoing the past?

Or will the past destroy me before I can save the people I love from what I've done?

Begin the ride—Playing with Monsters

Bulletproof Damsel – Urban Fantasy Series

One sassy female weapons master who doesn't get out much.

One alpha-hole who lays claim to her the moment he sets eyes on her.

Remington is a weapon in the hands of her enemies, and Rhys intends to use her.

An ancient family feud between the infamous Van Helsings and Silversmiths who once made their weapons legendary...

What could possibly go wrong?

For Remington Silversmith? Apparently everything.

When Remi comes face-to-face with Rhys Van Helsing, the world will never be the same again.

One little Bullet incites war—Bulletproof Damsel

Moon-Kissed – High Fantasy

Alexandria Helios is on a mission to find her brother. Landon disappeared on his quest to find the Sacred Library that holds the cure to the moon sickness affecting their people. There is one problem. Alexandria's journey will take her through the Kingdom of Night and directly into Torrin's path as the head of the Night King's army. He's egotistical, sexy, sin incarnate, and everything she knows she shouldn't want, but his whispered promise of dark desires awakens something deep within her that makes him hard to resist.

Torrin didn't expect the lead assassins of the Moon Clan to walk into his trap. Alexandria has ignited something within him he thought was gone, and he knows he shouldn't crave her, but he does. She's a fire in a world of ice, bathed in blood and moonlight that calls to the darkness within him.

Secrets are unraveling as both are tossed into a ploy that neither is destined to survive. Can they find common ground and work together to defeat the darkness? Or will the world come crashing down around them as they tear each other apart?

Anything can happen once you're—Moon-Kissed

About the Author

Amelia Hutchins is the number one national bestselling author of the Monsters, The Fae Chronicles, and Nine Realm series. She is an admitted coffee addict, who drinks magical potions of caffeine and turns them into magical worlds. She writes alpha-hole males and the alpha women who knock them on their arses, hard. She doesn't write romance. She writes fast-paced books that go hard against traditional standards. Sometimes a story isn't about the romance; it's about rising to a challenge, breaking through them like wrecking balls, and shaking up entire worlds to discover who they really are. If you'd like to check out more of her work, or just hang out in an amazing tribe of people who enjoy rough men, and sharp women, join her at Author Amelia Hutchins Group on Facebook.

Printed in Great Britain
by Amazon